THE
CAMBRIDGE EDITION OF
THE LETTERS AND WORKS OF
D. H. LAWRENCE

THE WORKS OF D. H. LAWRENCE

THE TRESPASSER

D. H. LAWRENCE

EDITED BY
ELIZABETH MANSFIELD

CAMBRIDGE UNIVERSITY PRESS
CAMBRIDGE
LONDON NEW YORK NEW ROCHELLE
MELBOURNE SYDNEY

Published by the Press Syndicate of the University of Cambridge
The Pitt Building, Trumpington Street, Cambridge CB2 1RP
32 East 57th Street, New York, NY 10022, USA
296 Beaconsfield Parade, Middle Park, Melbourne 3206, Australia

 Acknowledgement is made to William Heinemann Ltd who hold the exclusive book publication rights in the UK for the work as originally published (copyright 1912), for the authorisation granted to Cambridge University Press through the Frieda Lawrence Ravagli Estate for use of the work as originally published in preparing the new scholarly text. The manuscript of *The Trespasser* has been made available, and chapter 12 of 'The Saga of Siegmund' is published, by permission of the Bancroft Library, University of California at Berkeley. The three diaries by Helen Corke, © the Estate of Helen Corke 1981, are published by permission of the Estate and The Humanities Research Center, The University of Texas at Austin, which holds the original manuscripts.

Printed in the United States of America

British Library Cataloguing in Publication Data

Lawrence, David Herbert
The trespasser. – (Cambridge edition of the letters and works of D. H. Lawrence).
I. Title II. Mansfield, Elizabeth
III. Series
823'.9'1F 80-41663

ISBN 0 521 22264 8 hard covers
ISBN 0 521 29424 X paperback

CONTENTS

GENERAL EDITORS' PREFACE

D. H. Lawrence is one of the great writers of the twentieth century – yet the texts of his writings, whether published during his lifetime or since, are, for the most part, textually corrupt. The extent of the corruption is remarkable; it can derive from every stage of composition and publication. We know from study of his MSS that Lawrence was a careful writer, though not rigidly consistent in matters of minor convention. We know also that he revised at every possible stage. Yet he rarely if ever compared one stage with the previous one, and overlooked the errors of typists or copyists. He was forced to accept, as most authors are, the often stringent house-styling of his printers, which overrode his punctuation and even his sentence-structure and paragraphing. He sometimes overlooked plausible printing errors. More important, as a professional author living by his pen, he had to accept, with more or less good will, stringent editing by a publisher's reader in his early days, and at all times the results of his publishers' timidity. So the fear of Grundyish disapproval, or actual legal action, led to bowdlerisation or censorship from the very beginning of his career. Threats of libel suits produced other changes. Sometimes a publisher made more changes than he admitted to Lawrence. On a number of occasions in dealing with American and British publishers Lawrence produced texts for both which were not identical. Then there were extraordinary lapses like the occasion when a compositor turned over two pages of MS at once, and the result happened to make sense. This whole story can be reconstructed from the introductions to the volumes in this edition; cumulatively they will form a history of Lawrence's writing career.

The Cambridge edition aims to provide texts which are as close as can now be determined to those he would have wished to see printed. They have been established by a rigorous collation of extant manuscripts and typescripts, proofs and early printed versions; they restore the words, sentences, even whole pages omitted or falsified by editors or compositors; they are freed from printing-house conventions which were imposed on Lawrence's style; and interference on the part of frightened publishers has been eliminated. Far from doing violence to the texts Lawrence would have wished to see published, editorial intervention is essential to recover them. Though we have to accept that some cannot now be recovered in their entirety because early states have not survived, we must be glad that so much evidence remains. Paradoxical as it may seem, the outcome of this recension will be texts which differ, often radically and certainly frequently, from those seen by the author himself.

Editors have adopted the principle that the most authoritative form of the text is to be followed, even if this leads sometimes to a 'spoken' or a 'manuscript' rather than a 'printed' style. We have not wanted to strip off one house-styling in order to impose another. Editorial discretion has been allowed in order to regularise Lawrence's sometimes wayward spelling and punctuation in accordance with his most frequent practice in a particular text. A detailed record of these and other decisions on textual matters, together with the evidence on which they are based, will be found in the textual apparatus. This gives significant deleted readings in manuscripts, typescripts and proofs; and printed variants in forms of the text published in Lawrence's lifetime. We do not record posthumous corruptions, except where first publication was posthumous.

In each volume, the editor's introduction relates the contents to Lawrence's life and to his other writings; it gives the history of composition of the text in some detail, for its intrinsic interest, and because this history is essential to the statement of editorial principles followed. It provides an account of publication and reception which will be found to contain a good deal of hitherto unknown information. Where appropriate, appendixes make available extended draft manuscript readings of significance, or important material, sometimes unpublished, associated with a particular work.

Though Lawrence is a twentieth-century writer and in many respects remains our contemporary, the idiom of his day is not invariably intelligible now, especially to the many readers who are not native speakers of British English. His use of dialect is another difficulty, and further barriers to full understanding are created by now obscure literary, historical, political or other references and allusions. On these occasions explanatory notes are supplied by the editor; it is assumed that the reader has access to a good general dictionary and that the editor need not gloss words or expressions that may be found in it. Where Lawrence's letters are quoted in editorial matter, the reader should assume that his manuscript is alone the source of eccentricities of phrase or spelling. An edition of the letters is still in course of publication: for this reason only the date and recipient of a letter will be given if it has not so far been printed in the Cambridge edition.

ACKNOWLEDGEMENTS

I wish to express gratitude for the cooperation of the many individuals and institutions that assisted in the preparation of this edition. In particular, the Bancroft Library, University of California at Berkeley, has loaned a photocopy of *The Trespasser* manuscripts to make the project possible. David Farmer, Director of Special Collections at McFarlin Library, University of Tulsa, allowed me to use an uncatalogued Helen Corke collection so that the edition would not be delayed. Without the late Helen Corke's willingness to release very personal information, the introduction to this volume would have been seriously restricted. Special appreciation is extended to George Lazarus for his generous invitation to view his private collection of D. H. Lawrence manuscripts. Dr Lola Szladits of the Berg Collection was unfailingly resourceful. The following people provided seemingly tireless editorial assistance: Michael Black, Andrew Brown and Lindeth Vasey of the Cambridge University Press; and Carl Baron, James T. Boulton and Warren Roberts of the editorial board.

Colleagues from other institutions who assisted continuously were Professors Phillip L. Marcus, William M. Murphy and Bruce Steele.

I also wish to thank the residents of Eastwood, Nottinghamshire, who generously shared their knowledge of Lawrence's past: Garry Akers, Michael Bennett, Mrs Lanna Coak, Laurence and Jessie Flint, Jesse and Enid Goodband, Thomas and Margaret Needham and Owen V. Watson.

Appreciation is extended to the following individuals: Marshall Best, W. H. Clarke, Keith Cushman, Emile Delavenay, Ellen Dunlap, Donald Eddy, W. Forster, the late David Garnett, D. R. Hale, Mitchell Kennerley Jr, Gerald M. Lacy, Kenneth Lohf, Arthur Mizener, Andrew Robertson, Anthony Rota, Mrs Hilda Mary Snoswell, Kimberly Sparks, John Worthen, Walter Wriggins and the staff of Viking Press.

Appreciation is extended as well to the following institutions: Beinecke Library (Yale University), Ellen Clarke Bertrand Library (Bucknell University), Eastwood Public Library, Humanities Research Center (University of Texas at Austin), Lilly Library (University of Indiana), Nottinghamshire County Libraries, Olin Library (Cornell University), Skidmore College Library, University of Nottingham Library, University Research

Library (University of California at Los Angeles) and Vassar College Library.

Finally, I wish to express appreciation for the technical assistance of Cynthia W. Ketchum, Jean MacFadden and Racemark International.

CHRONOLOGY

11 September 1885	Born in Eastwood, Nottinghamshire
September 1898–July 1901	Pupil at Nottingham High School
1902–1908	Pupil teacher; student at University College, Nottingham
7 December 1907	First publication: 'A Prelude', in *Nottinghamshire Guardian*
11 October 1908	To Croydon: teacher at Davidson Road School
Late autumn or winter 1908	Meets Helen Corke
24? April 1909	Walk with Helen Corke on Wimbledon Common
31 July–14 August 1909	Lawrence family holiday at Shanklin, Isle of Wight
31 July 1909	Helen Corke goes to Freshwater, Isle of Wight
1 August 1909	Herbert Baldwin Macartney joins her
7 August 1909	Macartney says goodbye to Helen Corke and commits suicide
6 September 1909	Helen Corke begins diary 'The Letter'
Autumn 1909	Becomes acquainted with Helen Corke's story
c. 11 September 1909	In London to meet Ford Madox Hueffer
November 1909	Sequence of poems, 'A Still Afternoon', in *English Review*
23 December 1909–9 January 1910	Eastwood for Christmas
February 1910	'Goose Fair' in *English Review*
11 April 1910	Sends Sydney Pawling 'Nethermere' MS
c. 11 April 1910	Begins 'The Saga of Siegmund'
13–22 May 1910	Whitsuntide holiday
End of July 1910	Jessie Chambers in Croydon, meets Helen Corke
August 1910	Breaks 'betrothal of six years standing' to Jessie Chambers
4 August 1910	Finishes 'The Saga of Siegmund'
22–28 August 1910	At Leicester. Mrs Lawrence seriously ill
October 1910	'Three Poems' in *English Review*
3 December 1910	To Leicester: becomes engaged to Louie Burrows

9 December 1910	Mrs Lawrence dies
19 January 1911	*The White Peacock* published in New York (20 January in London)
13 March 1911	Has begun 'Paul Morel' again
26 April 1911	Decides to suppress 'The Saga'
June 1911	'Odour of Chrysanthemums', in *English Review*
September 1911	'A Fragment of Stained Glass', in *English Review*
4 October 1911	Meets Edward Garnett
13–15 October 1911	First visit to Edward Garnett at The Cearne, Edenbridge, Kent
4 November 1911	Two poems in *Nation*
19 November 1911–4 January 1912	Ill with pneumonia in Croydon
4 December 1911	Has sent Garnett 'The Saga' manuscript
30 December 1911	Tells Garnett he will begin rewriting 'The Saga'
3 January 1912	Finished first chapter of revision
6 January 1912	Arrives in Bournemouth
10 January 1912	Revision going slowly
19 January 1912	Has 'rewritten' first 135 pages
21 January 1912	180 or 190 pages of revision done
29 January 1912	300 pages of revision done
February 1912	'Second Best' in *English Review*
3 February 1912	Last meeting with Helen Corke
3–9 February 1912	The Cearne
4 February 1912	Breaks engagement to Louie Burrows
28 February 1912	Resignation from teaching post
8 March 1912	Receives offer from Duckworth to publish *The Trespasser*
16 March 1912	'The Miner at Home' in *Nation*
17? March 1912	Meets Frieda Weekley
4 April 1912	First batch of proofs arrives
27–28 April 1912	The Cearne with Frieda
3 May 1912	Leaves England with Frieda
11 May 1912	First three of eight 'Schoolmaster' poems in *Saturday Westminster Gazette*, 11 May – 1 June
23 May 1912	*The Trespasser*
September 1912–March 1913	At Gargnano, Lago di Garda, Italy
February 1913	*Love Poems and Others*
29 May 1913	*Sons and Lovers*
June–August 1913	In England
August 1913–June 1914	In Germany, Switzerland and Italy
13 July 1914	Marries Frieda Weekley in London

July 1914–December 1915	In London, Buckinghamshire and Sussex
26 November 1914	*The Prussian Officer*
30 September 1915	*The Rainbow*; suppressed by court order on 13 November
June 1916	*Twilight in Italy*
July 1916	*Amores*
15 October 1917	After twenty-one months' residence in Cornwall, ordered to leave by military authorities
October 1917–November 1919	In London, Berkshire and Derbyshire
December 1917	*Look! We Have Come Through!*
October 1918	*New Poems*
November 1919–February 1922	To Italy, then Capri and Sicily
20 November 1919	*Bay*
November 1920	Private publication of *Women in Love* (New York), *The Lost Girl*
10 May 1921	*Psychoanalysis and the Unconscious* (New York)
12 December 1921	*Sea and Sardinia* (New York)
March–August 1922	In Ceylon and Australia
14 April 1922	*Aaron's Rod* (New York)
September 1922–March 1923	In New Mexico
23 October 1922	*Fantasia of the Unconscious* (New York)
24 October 1922	*England, My England* (New York)
March 1923	*The Ladybird*, *The Fox*, *The Captain's Doll*
March–November 1923	In Mexico and U.S.A.
27 August 1923	*Studies in Classic American Literature* (New York)
September 1923	*Kangaroo*
9 October 1923	*Birds, Beasts and Flowers* (New York)
December 1923–March 1924	In England, France and Germany
March 1924–September 1925	In New Mexico and Mexico
August 1924	*The Boy in the Bush* (with Mollie Skinner)
10 September 1924	Death of his father, John Arthur Lawrence
14 May 1925	*St Mawr together with The Princess*
September 1925–June 1928	In England and mainly Italy
7 December 1925	*Reflections on the Death of a Porcupine* (Philadelphia)
January 1926	*The Plumed Serpent*
June 1927	*Mornings in Mexico*
24 May 1928	*The Woman Who Rode Away and Other Stories*
June 1928–March 1930	In Switzerland and, principally, in France
July 1928	*Lady Chatterley's Lover* privately published (Florence)

September 1928	*Collected Poems*
July 1929	Exhibition of paintings in London raided by police. *Pansies* (manuscript earlier seized in the mail)
September 1929	*The Escaped Cock* (Paris)
2 March 1930	Dies at Vence, Alpes Maritimes, France

CUE-TITLES

(The place of publication is London unless otherwise stated.)

BBC interview	'D. H. Lawrence and the Dreaming Woman', transcript of BBC television interview of Helen Corke by Malcolm Muggeridge (July 1967) (summary published in *The Listener*, 25 July 1968).
Complete Poems	Vivian de Sola Pinto and Warren Roberts, eds. *The Complete Poems of D. H. Lawrence.* 2 volumes. Heinemann, 1964.
Corke, *As I Saw Him*	Helen Corke, 'D. H. Lawrence As I Saw Him', *Renaissance and Modern Studies*, iv (1960), 5–13.
Corke, *Portrait*	Helen Corke, 'Portrait of D. H. Lawrence, 1909–10', *The Texas Quarterly*, v (Spring 1962), 168–77.
Corke, *Early Stage*	Helen Corke, 'D. H. Lawrence: the Early Stage', *D. H. Lawrence Review*, iv (Summer 1971), 111–21.
Corke, *Trespasser*	Helen Corke, 'The Writing of *The Trespasser*', *D. H. Lawrence Review*, vii (Fall 1974), 227–39.
Corke, *Infancy*	Helen Corke. *In Our Infancy*. Cambridge: Cambridge University Press, 1975.
Draper	R. P. Draper, ed. *D. H. Lawrence: The Critical Heritage*. Routledge and Kegan Paul, 1970.
E.T. [Jessie Wood].	*D.H. Lawrence: A Personal Record.* Jonathan Cape, 1935; reprinted Cambridge University Press, 1980.
Letters	James T. Boulton, ed. *The Letters of D. H. Lawrence.* Volume 1. Cambridge: Cambridge University Press, 1979.
Phoenix II	Warren Roberts and Harry T. Moore, eds. *Phoenix II: Uncollected, Unpublished and other Prose Works by D. H. Lawrence.* Heinemann, 1968.

INTRODUCTION

INTRODUCTION

'Here am I a stranger in a strange land', wrote D. H. Lawrence on 15 October 1908, soon after he left his home in Eastwood to become a teacher at the Davidson Road Elementary School in Croydon.[1] That winter he met the woman whose story provides the basis of *The Trespasser*: Helen Corke.

It is difficult to trace Lawrence's experiences in Croydon through his testimony alone, but the various accounts by Helen Corke provide a detailed, if sometimes confusing, record. Four of her extant accounts appear to have been contemporary records of the events that inspired the novel: 'The Letter', a retrospective diary of August 1909 started in September of that year; 'The Freshwater Diary', a diary of 1909–10; 'The Way of Silence', a play dated winter 1909–10; and 'The Cornwall Writing' of 1911–12, another retrospective diary.[2] Her later accounts include a novel, *Neutral Ground* (dated 1918 but not published until 1933); interviews, lectures, articles and correspondence from 1950 to 1978; and *In Our Infancy*, part of an autobiography, written in the 1930s but not published until 1975.[3] Because of the painful involvement of the narrator in the story she relates, her

1 *Letters*, i. 82.

2 For 'The Letter', 'The Freshwater Diary', and 'The Cornwall Writing' see pp. 281, 293, 302, 318, below.

3 The following list of accounts is not complete, since Helen Corke also gave unrecorded lectures on the subject. *Neutral Ground* (1933); *D. H. Lawrence and 'Apocalypse'* (1933); *D. H. Lawrence's 'Princess': A Memory of Jessie Chambers* (1951); 'Concerning *The White Peacock*', *The Texas Quarterly*, ii (Winter 1959), 186–90; 'D. H. Lawrence As I Saw Him', *Renaissance and Modern Studies*, iv (1960), 5–13; *Songs of Autumn and Other Poems* (Austin, 1960); 'Portrait of D. H. Lawrence, 1909–10', *The Texas Quarterly*, v (Spring 1962), 168–77; 'D. H. Lawrence and the Dreaming Woman', transcript of BBC television interview of Helen Corke by Malcolm Muggeridge (July 1967) (summary published in *The Listener*, 25 July 1968); 'D. H. Lawrence: the Early Stage', *D. H. Lawrence Review*, iv (Summer 1971), 111–21; 'The Writing of *The Trespasser*', *D. H. Lawrence Review*, vii (Fall 1974), 227–39; *In Our Infancy: an Autobiography, Part I: 1882–1912* (Cambridge, 1975); 'D. H. Lawrence – the young schoolmaster, as I knew him', lecture to the DHL Society, Eastwood, 14 July 1976.

Edward Nehls, ed. *D. H. Lawrence: A Composite Biography*, i (Madison, Wisconsin, 1957) draws upon conversations and correspondence with Helen Corke in 1952 and 1954. He quotes excerpts from 'Lawrence As I Knew Him', a lecture given to the Colchester Literary Society (18 September 1950), and from the BBC radio Third Programme's 'Son and Lover' (8 May 1955).

accounts are a questionable source of information. They display the intentions of a patient undergoing self-therapy, rather than those of an objective chronicler; Helen Corke had reasons for concealing some things and placing others in a particular light. In her middle age she interpreted the actions of her youth in a way that was impossible when they occurred; and though in her old age her memory became unreliable, she continued to place confidence in it. Nonetheless, it seems essential to summarise the impressions of the person who was most closely connected with Lawrence at the time he began to write *The Trespasser*, and to add evidence from other sources – particularly his own writings – whenever possible.

Helen Corke met David Lawrence (as he was known to his Croydon friends)[4] for the first time during the winter of 1908–9.[5] She was a teacher at another school in Croydon, but Agnes Mason, her intimate friend who taught at the Davidson Road School, perceived the difficulties Lawrence was encountering in the classroom, as well as his loneliness, and she befriended him.[6] She invited Lawrence to her home one evening. Helen Corke, who was also invited, arrived late and stayed very briefly, but long enough for Agnes Mason's new friend to make a strong impression on her.[7] After this first meeting, however, Helen Corke saw Lawrence rarely until the autumn of 1909.

One occasion that she recalled was a Saturday in April, probably 24 April, when she joined Lawrence and Agnes Mason for a walk on Wimbledon Common.[8] Helen Corke had a particular reason for remembering that day. She had been involved for some time in a passionate relationship with her music master, Herbert Baldwin Macartney. 'H.B.M.' (as she always referred to him in her non-fictional accounts) was a married man whose warm feelings for his student had grown to love, and to a need for physical fulfilment. On

4 At home, in Eastwood, DHL was called 'Bert'. Although Jessie Chambers, his childhood sweetheart, would have used that name originally, when she met Helen Corke she began to refer to him as 'David', as shown in her letters to Helen Corke and Helen Corke's testimony. The letters have been published in 'The Collected Letters of Jessie Chambers' edited and with an introduction by George J. Zytaruk in a special issue of *D. H. Lawrence Review*, xii (Spring and Summer 1979), vii–238.

5 Corke, *As I Saw Him* 5. In no account is Helen Corke more specific about this date.

6 See the letters and poems DHL wrote at this time, especially *Letters*, i. 82, 85, 97 and 'The Schoolmaster' poems in *Complete Poems* 897–903.

7 See Nehls, *D. H. Lawrence: A Composite Biography*, i. 95. This account concurs with the others, except for Corke, *Trespasser*, where Helen Corke describes their first meeting 'at a Mason musical evening, when she had played violin solos to Agnes's accompaniment' (227).

8 In her 1976 talk to the Eastwood DHL Society, Helen Corke noted that Swinburne had died 'about a fortnight before' this meeting. He died on 10 April 1909, and since Lawrence was in Eastwood for the Easter holidays from 8 to 18 April, 24 April is the most likely date.

the morning of this walk Macartney had asked her to spend a few days' holiday with him in August.

He asks with a kind of desperation which makes me afraid for him – I feel that I cannot, and dare not at the moment, refuse. When I assent he tells me that he has not seen the sea since the days of his boyhood, when the whole family used to migrate each summer to Freshwater, in the Isle of Wight. He would like to visit the old place again.[9]

Coincidentally, Lawrence went to the Isle of Wight – for a fortnight's holiday with his mother and sister Ada – leaving on the very same day, 31 July 1909. Meeting Helen Corke by chance a few days earlier, he had suggested that they travel together; but she, 'in no mood to meet strangers', deliberately caught the first train to Portsmouth.[10]

After her five-day holiday with Macartney, Helen Corke went to Cornwall with Agnes Mason and another woman friend. She became alarmed after several days at having no letter from Macartney; in desperation she took the train home; and there, in a local paper, was confronted by the report of his suicide on 7 August.[11] In her extreme grief, she withdrew into herself, despite the efforts of her parents and Agnes Mason. Three months later she still claimed: 'Two real things I have found: the joy of our five days and the pain which has succeeded them, and which stretches before me indefinitely.'[12] Her parents feared that she might take her own life, but Helen Corke abided by her lover's last words to her: 'I want you to promise that, whatever happens to me, you will go on.'[13]

Gradually in the autumn of 1909, Helen Corke and Lawrence became closer. Probably just after the school term began on 30 August, Lawrence learned from Agnes Mason of the tragedy.

She was suffering, Agnes said, from extreme mental and emotional shock, and now, a month after the event, was acting like a sleepwalker, hardly aware of her environment. Lawrence was intrigued and asked questions; he learned that the dead man had been a member of the Covent Garden Opera orchestra, one of its first violins. 'Nell' [Helen] had been his pupil for several years. Although interested, Lawrence did not brood upon the story, his mind being more happily occupied with consideration of a welcome change in his own future prospects.[14]

9 Corke, *Infancy* 166.

10 Ibid. 169.

11 Reports of the inquest appeared in *The Surbiton Times* (13 August 1909) and *The Surrey Comet* (14 August 1909). The latter is reproduced below, p. 324. (I am indebted to Professor Bruce Steele for this information.) See also Corke, *Infancy* 170, and pp. 307–8, below.

12 See below, pp. 287–8.

13 See below, p. 281. Quoted by Helen Corke with slightly different wording in other accounts. In *The Trespasser* (p. 194, below), DHL uses the same wording as 'The Letter'.

14 Corke, *Trespasser* 229.

The suggestion here that Lawrence did not become immediately involved with Helen Corke's emotional breakdown fits in with the events as we know them from other sources of that early autumn and his slight acquaintance with her.

He was beginning to enter into the literary world. Ford Madox Hueffer (Ford) had accepted some poems for publication in the *English Review*. Some time before 11 September Lawrence visited Hueffer for, on that day, he told a friend:

> The truth is, I am very much occupied with some work of my own. It is supposed to be a secret, but I guess I shall have to tell you. The editor of the *English Review* has accepted some of my Verses, and wants to put them into the *English Review*, the November issue. But you see they are all in the rough, and want revising, so this week and so on I am very hard at work, slogging verse into form.[15]

Lawrence was excited that Hueffer also liked his first novel, *The White Peacock* (known at this stage as 'Nethermere'), and recommended it to William Heinemann's partner Sydney Pawling for publication. Hueffer introduced Lawrence to 'various literary and artistic people', among them William Butler Yeats and Ezra Pound.[16]

With all this literary activity as well as his teaching duties, it is remarkable that Lawrence still found time, during the late autumn and winter of 1909–10, to give Helen Corke his friendship and support, walking a considerable distance to her home two or three evenings a week.[17] According to her accounts, Lawrence accepted the task of drawing her out of her 'living-death'.[18] He read to her from Goethe and Heine, Blake and Yeats, and from Gilbert Murray's translations of the Greek dramatists. 'Sometimes', Helen Corke relates, 'he would ask me to read a poem of his own, written in the college notebook he kept always in his pocket.'[19] Lawrence may also have shown her his play, *A Collier's Friday Night*, and suggested that she try to dramatise her own experiences, using it as a model.[20] The resemblances between the first acts of her 'The Way of Silence' and his play are too close to be coincidental.

[15] *Letters*, i. 137.

[16] E.T. 163.

[17] The opening chapter of *The Trespasser* presents DHL's record of his first visit and of many similar ones, Corke, *As I Saw Him* 8. In her BBC interview, Miss Corke stated that they met 'twice a week' at this time (reel 3A, page 1). (Hereafter references to the interview will be given in the form 3A/1.) In her play, 'The Way of Silence', she dramatised one of these visits, noting on the manuscript that the scene was 'reporting'.

[18] Corke, *As I Saw Him* 8.

[19] Ibid. It is likely that this was the Botany Notebook, which contains poems from the Croydon period (privately owned; a photocopy is deposited in the University of Nottingham).

[20] DHL apparently showed an early draft of the play to Jessie Chambers in November 1909 (E.T. 166).

During the Christmas holidays and for a short time afterwards Lawrence's relationships with women underwent several changes. These are most cogently reflected in a letter of 28 January 1910. The first woman he mentions is Agnes Holt, a fellow teacher in Croydon, with whom for a time he contemplated marriage. The second is Jessie Chambers (the prototype for Miriam in *Sons and Lovers*) to whom he had been unofficially engaged for six years.

What do you want me to tell you about – my latest love? Well – she's off again – I don't like her...She still judges by mid-Victorian standards, and covers herself with a woolly fluff of romance that the years will wear sickly. She refuses to see that a man is a male, that kisses are the merest preludes and anticipations, that love is largely a physical sympathy that is soon satisfied and satiated...

I have been sick of her some little time. At Christmas an old fire burned up afresh, like an alcohol flame, faint and invisible, that sets fire to a tar barrel. It is the old girl, who has been attached to me so long...She is coming to me for a week-end soon; we shall not stay here in Croydon, but in London. The world is for us, and we are for each other – even if only for one spring – so what does it matter! What would my people and hers say? – but what do I care – not a damn! – they will not know.

I wonder why I tell you all these things, that I would not breathe to another soul! Because you ask me, I suppose. But put my letter in the fire, will you please! And tell me – do *you* think I am wrong?[21]

The letter (which fortunately the recipient, Blanche Jennings, did not burn) makes clear both the need that Lawrence felt for a sexual relationship and the guilt which accompanied it. These feelings bear on the way he would soon address the whole question of Helen Corke's relationship with Macartney.

'The Saga of Siegmund' (the first version of *The Trespasser*)

In beginning his second novel Lawrence had as written sources Helen Corke's records of her experience and response to it. Soon after her lover's death, she had begun to write down her memories of him. She appears to have started 'The Letter' on 5 September, but pre-dated the first entry 'Aug 6th' – the day before his suicide. The entry for 26 November refers to her other diary 'The Freshwater Diary': 'I am writing the story of our five days. It is good to live it all over again in the writing of it. At present every detail is clear – I write but enough to suggest the whole – '.[22] Some time between 9 January and 25 March (Good Friday) 1910,

[21] *Letters*, i. 153–4.

[22] See below, p. 288.

Lawrence read 'The Freshwater Diary'.[23] Helen Corke described his response.

There is a new urgency in his voice when he returns it. 'What are you going to *do* with these prose poems?' he asks. I reply, nothing. They are written; it is enough. He declares, and insists, that the act of expression in writing preassumes a reader, and also that human experience is the common property of humanity...

He returns to the subject later – comes with a request that he take the diary and expand its theme – use the poems as basis for a more comprehensive rendering of the story. He will bring me his work as it grows; nothing shall stand with which I am not in agreement.[24]

How much time elapsed between his reading the diary and conceiving the idea of expansion into a novel is also uncertain. By 8 May, Helen Corke had written in the last entry in 'The Letter': 'I have drawn another life into mine – to hold as I hold you [Macartney] dear. What can I do?'[25] The suggestion is that she has drawn Lawrence's life into her own, through his involvement in the writing of her story.

In one account, Helen Corke claimed that 'The Saga of Siegmund', the first version of *The Trespasser*, was begun 'during the fortnight succeeding the Easter holidays'.[26] According to Jessie Chambers, towards the end of that holiday Lawrence had been planning to use one of her brothers as hero in his next novel, but 'Almost immediately on returning to Croydon he wrote, apparently very much disturbed, saying that he found he had to write the story of Siegmund... It was in front of him and he had got to do it. He begged me to go to Croydon and make the acquaintance of "Helen".'[27] Jessie Chambers then makes the statement often quoted: 'His second novel, *The Trespasser*, was written in feverish haste between the Whitsuntide and

[23] To establish a date for the first time that DHL read 'The Freshwater Diary' is one of the most difficult problems in the chronology of the composition of *The Trespasser*. See the entries in 'The Letter' for 9 January – 'The story of our last week is not yet finished' p. 290 – and 25 March, where the implication is that he has seen the diary, p. 292. In Corke, *Trespasser* and *Portrait* the accounts of DHL's reading the diary follow directly that of his February illness (at which time Helen Corke first saw the 'Nethermere' manuscript). In Corke, *Infancy* the two events are placed in reverse order. In Corke, *Early Stage* (often the most specific piece), the order is implied: 'With *Nethermere*, now *The White Peacock*, accepted by Heinemann [mid-December 1909] and on its way into print [revision complete 11 April 1910], Lawrence began to seek material for a second novel. His mind ranging the Midlands, was suddenly diverted to the tragic story told him during the autumn by Agnes Mason' (117).

[24] Corke, *Portrait* 171–2. This account is repeated in Corke, *Early Stage*; Corke, *Infancy* 176–7 follows this wording fairly closely.

[25] See below, p. 292.

[26] Corke, *Trespasser* 233. But in the BBC interview, she commented parenthetically: 'I suppose he might have begun it about the Easter of 1910...' (BBC interview 5/6).

[27] E.T. 181.

Midsummer of 1910'.[28] She is mistaken. We can be certain that Lawrence began the first version of *The Trespasser* before Whitsuntide (15 May) because on 27 April he had already told Sydney Pawling: 'I have written about half of another novel.'[29] Although Lawrence may have exaggerated the number of pages he had written, it is highly improbable that he would have made such a claim before he had even begun writing. Also the sense of urgency mentioned by both Helen Corke and Jessie Chambers, as well as their independent references to the Easter holidays, suggests that Lawrence began 'The Saga of Siegmund' soon after his return to Croydon on 3 April. It is likely that Lawrence did not begin to write his second novel until the 'Nethermere' manuscript (*The White Peacock*) was completed and mailed to Pawling on 11 April.[30] As he told his publisher in July, he would like to finish the proofs of this first book in order to be 'quite free to take up the second again. I like to have clear breathing room.'[31]

Before beginning 'The Saga' – and not long after learning the story from Helen Corke – Lawrence probably read George Moore's *Evelyn Innes* and *Sister Teresa* as well as H. G. Wells's *Ann Veronica*.[32] This confluence of fictional works on the subject of sexual emancipation and its effect on women may have been coincidental, or Lawrence may have been exploring approaches to a theme that he was considering for his new novel. While writing the first draft, he borrowed a copy of Gerhart Hauptmann's play, *Einsame Menschen*, the story of a man's choice between his wife and another woman, culminating in his apparent suicide.[33] He also borrowed Hauptmann's *Elga*, yet another treatment of infidelity, and read it with Helen Corke.[34] And, finally, a more general background of tragedy was present in the Greek drama they had been reading together.

Some additional direction came from their study of Wagner, although the extent of that study is uncertain. In October 1909, they had arranged to read German, so that Helen Corke might have 'more insight into Wagner's philosophy'.[35] Certainly the Wagnerian allusions in 'The Saga' contribute

[28] E.T. 181.

[29] *Letters*, i. 159.

[30] Ibid. 158.

[31] Ibid. 170. DHL's accidental inclusion of the name 'Siegmund' in the 'Nethermere' manuscript might suggest an earlier date of composition; but it can be accounted for by his familiarity with Helen Corke's story since the autumn of 1909, and their using that name for Macartney in their discussions. DHL could easily have had 'Siegmund' on his mind before he began 'The Saga'. (I am indebted to Mr Andrew Robertson for pointing out three appearances of the name 'Siegmund' in the 'Nethermere' manuscript, and to Mr George Lazarus for allowing me to examine it.)

[32] He lent *Evelyn Innes* to Helen Corke in December 1909, see below p. 289.

[33] *Letters*, i. 171.

[34] Ibid. 164.

[35] See below, p. 287. For the lessons, DHL used a 'little ragged copy of German lyric verse, bought for two-pence from a secondhand bookstall' (Corke, *Portrait* 170). All the quotations

to the atmosphere of tragic love, although the random nature of these references and their occasional inaccuracy suggest that Lawrence had only a passing acquaintance with Wagner's operas, probably gleaned from Helen Corke herself. He had seen, and was disappointed by, *Tristan und Isolde*.[36] It is not known whether he had attended any of the four operas in the *Ring* before he completed 'The Saga'. About the original title 'The Saga of Siegmund', Miss Corke stated: 'One evening this spring [1910] D.H.L. brings me the first chapters of *The Saga of Siegmund*, saying that here is the beginning of a work of art that must be a saga since it cannot be a symphony.'[37] His choice of the word 'saga' suggests the associations of such well-known legends as *Volsunga Saga* and the *Nibelungenlied*, with particular emphasis on the themes of heroic achievement and death. The name 'Siegmund' was a sobriquet Helen Corke had chosen for Macartney during a performance of *Die Walküre*, and he reciprocated by calling her 'Sieglinde'.[38] The names for the hero and heroine of Lawrence's modern saga were, then, biographically derivative and indicate a stronger initial commitment to Wagnerian parallels than his more detached artistic perspective allowed in revision nearly two years later. A general allusiveness, appropriate to main characters who are ardent Wagnerians, remains in the completed work.[39]

The biographical material in 'The Saga' came largely from detailed discussions of Helen Corke's experiences with Macartney on long walks that she and Lawrence took over the Surrey downs during the spring weekends of 1910.[40] In addition to these reminiscences and 'The Freshwater Diary', Lawrence's other source was 'The Cornwall Writing', since, according to Helen Corke, by 1912 he had read 'some of it'.[41]

In the process of delving into the personalities of Helen Corke and her dead lover, it seems that Lawrence himself began to have feelings for her

of German poetry in *The Trespasser* are to be found in this volume, *German Poetry for Schools*, ed. C. H. Parry and G. Gidley Robinson (1889). This book is now in the possession of Dr Warren Roberts.

36 *Letters*, i. 140.

37 Corke, *Portrait* 172.

38 Helen Corke to the editor in conversation, 28 April 1977. See also Corke, *Infancy* 158.

39 Before the final draft DHL had at least seen *Siegfried* (*Letters*, i. 327). For a summary of the Wagnerian allusions in *The Trespasser*, see pp. 325–7, below.

40 Helen Corke said in the BBC interview (5/5): 'He [Lawrence] knew everything that another person could know in relation to the story that he was making of it, you see, the actual facts. And rather more than that because we used to wander over the Surrey Hills, I feeling that Siegmund was almost a third person.' Specific mention of the context of these discussions does not occur until this interview.

41 See *Letters*, i. 373 n. (Nowhere has Helen Corke suggested that he read 'The Letter'.)

stronger than friendship, as suggested in the last chapter of *The Trespasser*. Describing him in 'The Letter' as 'young and lusty', she confessed rather cryptically: 'I am afraid of leaning upon him – afraid of discovering yet more unworthiness in my own nature.'[42] In a later account, she identified her awareness of the change, but without giving any date.

At the top of a green hill which falls away to meadow, David challenges me to race down the slope, passes me, and turns in my path, catching me as I try to check. Recovering balance, we laugh, but David clasps me longer than is necessary; when we move he holds my hand fast, protectively and possessively; we are silent. I try to face the position objectively. It may be that David's feeling for me is quite other than the deep affection I have for him. The thought is disquieting, but I argue that his present reaction is induced by the writing of the Saga. He is putting himself, imaginatively, in H.B.M.'s place; the conditions are both abnormal and temporary. I must not confuse the man with the artist. When this work is finished he will see me from another angle and in other lights.[43]

In the BBC interview, she qualified the cause-and-effect relationship: 'whether he did it instinctively and out of a sort of primal feeling for me, or whether he was actually more interested in realising the character of Siegmund, I'm not quite sure'.[44] This identification is also present in Lawrence's 'Siegmund' poems – sympathetic studies of the ill-fated love affair – which appear in the 'college notebook' mentioned above.[45]

Jessie Chambers testified that during the writing of 'The Saga' Lawrence 'implored' her not to attempt to hold him: '"For this I need Helen, but I must *always* return to you," he said earnestly, "only you must always leave me free."'[46] The conflicting feelings expressed to Jessie Chambers were relayed to Helen Corke as well, in a letter of mid-May that documents the uncertain ground of his relationship with these two women and, further, the emotional strain under which he was writing.

I had a letter from Muriel [Jessie Chambers] yesterday morning. She knew she had won. She wrote very lovingly, and full of triumphant faith. Since when, I have just lain inert...Yet I have a second consciousness somewhere actively alive. I write 'Siegmund' – I keep on writing, almost mechanically: very slowly, and mechanically. Yet I don't think I do Siegmund injustice...

[42] See below, p. 292.

[43] Corke, *Portrait* 173.

[44] BBC interview 2/2.

[45] These seemingly early versions are included in the 'Juvenilia' section of *Complete Poems*, 'A Love Passage' and 'Red' in particular. The early version of 'Red' is underlined and preceded by roman numeral II, and is perhaps a sequel to the poem 'Blue', which appears on the previous page of the college notebook. In this version of 'Red' the man addresses the speaker as 'Helen'. Other versions of these poems are in the Berg Collection, the New York Public Library.

[46] E.T. 181, 182.

> [You] are part of his immortality. That is what would make me go wild, if I woke up. You see, I know Siegmund is there all the time. I know you would go back to him, after me, and disclaim me. I know it very deeply. I know I could not bear it. I feel often inclined, when I think of you, to put my thumbs on your throat.
>
> Muriel will take me.[47]

The nature of Lawrence's relationship with Helen Corke by the late summer is suggested by the extent to which he discussed his feelings for Jessie Chambers with her. He had arranged a meeting between the two women in July. Helen Corke liked Jessie: 'I was very much impressed by the beauty and personality of his friend. She gave me a feeling of satisfaction and security...I watched the grace of her movements, and the dignity of her service [of tea].'[48] Lawrence talked with her about Jessie Chambers after this meeting and wrote: 'She is very pretty and very wistful...She kisses me. It makes my heart feel like ashes. But then she kisses me more and moves my sex fire. Mein Gott, it is hideous...I must tell her...that we ought finally and definitely to part.'[49]

During this summer holiday, Lawrence did break off his unofficial engagement to Jessie Chambers 'completely'.[50]

His perplexity about Helen Corke is indicated as well in the postcard he sent to her on 15 August: 'Why did you not go to Plymouth? What in the world are you doing? I give it up. It is true, I don't know what to say.'[51] In late August, however, he began revising *The White Peacock* proofs, with which Helen Corke helped him.[52] Despite this cooperation, a degree of uneasiness remained, which she described:

> Some change in my relationship with David is inevitable...The grace and tenderness of his former bearing towards me show rarely; he is sullen, or irritation flares suddenly into fierce irony and pitiless criticism. ...the depression [is] caused by his indecision over future relations with Muriel and myself...
>
> My sense of responsibility is awakened. It was so easy to admit David into the zone of intimacy between H.B.M. and myself – David the sensitive, impersonal artist. I should have foreseen that he might endanger his impersonality – but grief is stupid, and his nearness, his comprehending sympathy, were healing. The onus of the position is with me – I am senior by more than three years.

47 *Letters*, i. 159–60. Before writing this letter, DHL had shown Helen Corke 'A Fly in the Ointment', which is based on his relationship with Jessie Chambers and begins 'Muriel had sent me some mauve primroses' (*Phoenix II* 13). From then on they referred to Jessie Chambers as 'Muriel'.

48 Corke, *As I Saw Him* 10. Helen Corke remembered this visit as taking place at the end of July in Corke, *As I Saw Him*, but Professor Boulton believes it was 3 July (*Letters*, i. 158 n. 3).

49 *Letters*, i. 173.

50 E.T. 182.

51 *Letters*, i. 175.

52 See below, p. 292.

> If it were merely a sex debt I have incurred, it might be paid. Then, eventually, David and Muriel could marry. *Would* they complement one another – would they be happy?[53]

The difficulties were to continue for the remainder of Lawrence's stay in Croydon, and even after.

These questions of relationship yielded precedence to an event that overshadowed all else. Mrs Lawrence became gravely ill, and on 22 August Lawrence went to Leicester to be with her. He stayed until the 28th, when he had to return to Croydon for the new term. She died on 9 December 1910. Just six days earlier, he had proposed to a close friend of his youth, Louie Burrows, and they became officially engaged. Their engagement did little to assuage the grief he felt at the loss of the person he loved most. In the college notebook are early drafts of poems about Mrs Lawrence's death. As he wrote in 1928: 'The death of his mother wiped out everything else – books published, or stories in magazines. It was the great crash, and the end of his youth';[54] and, 'Then, in that year, for [him] everything collapsed, save the mystery of death, and the haunting of death in life.'[55]

When Lawrence returned to school after the Whitsuntide holidays in 1910, he told Helen Corke that he had promised Heinemann 'the next novel', i.e. 'The Saga'. 'Will he want it? This transacting of literary business makes me sick...Will you tell me whether the Saga is good? I am rapidly losing faith in it...I assure you, I am not weeping into my register. It is only that the literary world seems a particularly hateful yet powerful one.'[56] His entry into the literary world brought with it a sense of insecurity, because he was aware that he had outgrown what he had just written, but could not disavow it completely because he recognised that it had merits. This insecurity continued to appear in his letters about his first two novels, the second in particular.

On 24 June, he wrote about 'the Saga' to Frederick Atkinson, Heinemann's general editor:

> The other book goes pretty well. A month will see it cast. Then I shall leave it a month or two, after which I will chisel it and shape it as best I can. It is horribly poetic: Covent Garden market, floral hall. I shall never do anything decent till I can grow up and cut my beastly long curls of poetry...When I have *finished* a writing, I hate it. In it, I am vulnerable, naked in a thickly clothed crowd.[57]

[53] Corke, *Portrait* 176.
[54] 'Autobiographical Sketch', *Phoenix II* 301.
[55] 'Preface', *Complete Poems* 851.
[56] *Letters*, i. 161–2.
[57] Ibid. i. 167.

'A month' from 24 June 'will see it cast': yet according to Helen Corke's accounts, 'The Saga' was finished by the end of June or beginning of July.[58] Her dating is not accurate: through July and into August Lawrence was writing letters about his progress with the novel. He told Grace Crawford, an acquaintance whom he had met through Ezra Pound, on 9 July: 'I have just hanged my latest hero: after which I feel queer.'[59] On 15 July, he wrote to Atkinson: 'Tonight I shall write my last half dozen pages of the new work...During the next six or seven weeks I will lend the book to one or two of my people: then I will overhaul it rigorously: then I will send it to you.'[60] He wrote to Grace Crawford on 4 August: 'I have just finished my second novel.'[61]

Lawrence sent the manuscript to Hueffer and promised to let Sydney Pawling see it by the end of August. It was not until 9 September that Lawrence received Hueffer's comments: 'Hueffer wrote me this morning concerning the second novel. He says it's a rotten work of genius, one fourth of which is the stuff of masterpiece. He belongs to the opposite school of novelists to me: he says prose *must* be impersonal, like Turguenev or Flaubert. I say no.'[62] Hueffer's criticism as later reported by Lawrence to Garnett included another charge: 'Also it is erotic – not that I, personally, mind that, but an erotic work *must* be good art, which this is not.'[63]

On 18 October, when Pawling had acknowledged receiving the manuscript, Lawrence replied:

> I am glad, and much relieved, to hear that you have the MSS. of the S[aga] of S[iegmund] in your hands...I shall wait with some curiosity to hear your opinion of the work. It contains, I know, some rattling good stuff. But if the whole is not to your taste, I shall not mind...Of course, you have only got the rapid work of three months. I should want, I do want, to overhaul the book considerably...I am not anxious to publish it, and if you are of like mind, we can let the thing stay, and I

58 In the earliest accounts, she implies a date by indirect references. In Corke, *As I Saw Him*, for example, she states 'In July, 1910, Lawrence was feeling in full the reaction that comes after a period of strenuous inspirational work' (9). In Corke, *Portrait*, she explains that Jessie had read 'The Saga' before visiting Croydon in July. In Corke, *As I Saw Him* and the BBC interview, Helen Corke said that 'The Saga' was finished in about three months: 'That would have been in the June 1910, the end of June, 1910' (BBC interview 5/5).

59 *Letters*, i. 168.

60 Ibid. 169–70. DHL wrote to Helen Corke from Eastwood on 31 July without mentioning 'The Saga' (173).

61 Ibid. 175.

62 Ibid. 178. DHL wrote in December 1911: '"The book" he [Hueffer] said "is a rotten work of genius. It has no construction or form – it is execrably bad art, being all variations on a theme"', and he believed that Hueffer 'was prejudiced against the inconsequential style' (339, 330).

63 Ibid. 339. See also pp. 317, 330. For Edward Garnett, see p. 19 below.

will give you – with no intermediary this time – my third novel, Paul Morel [the early title for *Sons and Lovers*], which is plotted out very interestingly (to me), and about one-eighth of which is written.[64]

Lawrence may have exaggerated the speed of composition, expecting a negative response from Pawling, and so representing 'The Saga' as a very rough draft. The promise, which Helen Corke claimed he made to her, to wait five years before publishing 'The Saga' perhaps also continued to trouble him.[65] Moreover, he may have been concerned that others – the public as well as the publishers – might be critical of the novel, as Hueffer had been, and that this would hurt his reputation.

Lawrence then waited for Heinemann to return 'The Saga' manuscript. He later recalled that it had been in the publisher's hands for three months when Atkinson wrote, after reading part of the novel: 'I don't care for it, but we will publish it.'[66] Lawrence had probably received this letter when he wrote to Atkinson on 11 February 1911 outlining his own criticisms:

You are going to tell me some nasty things about ['The Saga']. I guess I have told them, most of them, to myself – amid acute inner blushes. The book is execrable bad art: it has no idea of progressive action, but arranges gorgeous tableaux-vivants which have not any connection one with the other: it is 'chargé' as a Prince Rupert's drop (if you know that curiosity): its purple patches glisten sicklily: it is, finally, pornographic. And for this last reason, I would wish to suppress the book, and beg you to return the MSS to me, with any additional comments. I shall not publish it ever in its present state; and in any state, not for some years.[67]

The decision not to publish may have been the result of a 'great long' but 'very friendly' letter that Lawrence had recently received from Hueffer.[68] Atkinson did not reply and on 15 March Lawrence wrote once more requesting the manuscript and adding that he was working on 'Paul Morel' again.[69] The implication may have been that, since a more acceptable novel was in progress, Heinemann need not be anxious about 'The Saga'.

Lawrence was still concerned that 'The Saga' might damage his reputation. In June 1911 he informed Martin Secker the publisher, who had recently sought material from him, that he did not want to publish it 'because it is erotic...I am afraid for my tender reputation'.[70] The 'erotic' reference may have been prompted by another letter from Hueffer.[71] The coincidence of correspondence from Hueffer and Lawrence's use of words like 'porno-

64 Ibid. 184.
65 Corke, *As I Saw Him* 9.
66 *Letters*, i. 339.
67 Ibid. 229–30. A Prince Rupert's drop is molten glass dropped into cold water, when it takes the shape of a tadpole; it disintegrates with a loud bang if its tail is broken.
68 Ibid. 228.
69 Ibid. 240.
70 Ibid. 276.
71 Ibid.

graphic' and 'erotic' is noticeable. Some months later Lawrence recalled that he had informed Hueffer of his decision not to publish 'The Saga', and Hueffer had replied: 'You are quite right not to publish that book – it would damage your reputation, perhaps permanently.'[72] In December 1911, more than a year after receiving Hueffer's original comments, Lawrence still seemed anxious about them: 'Is Hueffer's opinion worth anything, do you think? Is the book *so* erotic?'[73] Nevertheless at the end of the same month Lawrence, having finally received the manuscript from Heinemann, started to revise 'The Saga'.

The Trespasser (the second version)

Helen Corke saw the Lawrence of 1911 as 'a changed man, whose prevailing mood was ironic and bitter'.[74] Despite his engagement to Louie Burrows, he continued to make sexual demands on her. In a letter of 12 July 1911, the state of their relationship is clear.

> Surely, surely it is *my* tenet, that an emotion is genuine even though next day an antagonistic feeling supplants it. What we are to each other, we are. Some of you I should always love. Then again, I must break free. And I *cannot* marry save where I am not held...
>
> What is between you and me is sex. I was good on Saturday so long as I remained just sufficiently dimmed by alcohol. But in the end comes the irony that you know is stultified passion...
>
> But I will never ask for sex relationship again, never, unless I can give the dirty coin of marriage: unless it be a prostitute, whom I can love because I'm sorry for her. I cannot stand the sex strain between us – that's all my judgment – And I'll never ask you again, nor anybody. It is a weakness of mine – I can't stand the sex strain. Of course, with a girl like Gussy, it doesn't act – it merely runs by titillation into harmless flirting. But there has been more between you and me.[75]

The struggle between Helen's nature and Lawrence's can be seen in the 'Helen' poems; in 'Intimacy', the first draft of the story 'The Witch à la Mode'; and in *The Trespasser*. Only in 'Intimacy' (which he had completed by 10 September 1911)[76] does he imagine Helen Corke yielding willingly to him; and there it is the man who ends the embrace, in the knowledge that he is betraying his fiancée. Unlike the version published in 1934 as 'The

[72] Ibid. 339.

[73] Ibid.

[74] Corke, *As I saw Him* 11.

[75] *Letters*, i. 285–6. 'Gussy' may be Gussie Cooper, Rooks Nest, Whytecliffe Road, Purley, entered under G, at first without her surname, in an address book of Lawrence's now owned by the Bancroft Library, University of California at Berkeley.

[76] Ibid. 299–300, 301, 307. See below, n. 170, for discussion of paper.

Witch à la Mode', 'Intimacy' gives conscious motivation to the act of upsetting the lamp and starting a fire. Lawrence inserted in an intermediate version, 'The White Woman': 'He saw her thus, knew she wanted no more of him than that kiss.'[77] The description of the passionate embrace in 'Intimacy' suggests a date of composition before Lawrence's conviction that Helen Corke would never be physically responsive to him. The original description of the embrace agrees with the conception of the Helena of 'The Saga', written when Lawrence could imagine Helen Corke yielding to a lover. When he ceased to believe in that possibility, perhaps because of his own failure to arouse her, he altered the characterisation – at each later stage of composition – of both the woman in 'Intimacy' and the heroine of *The Trespasser* – towards a final portrait of something close to frigidity.

The issues here are delicate, and the answers can only be inferences; but the questions arise naturally, and they affect our understanding of *The Trespasser* and the relationships behind it. It is suggested in chapter VIII that the two lovers consummate their love. The narrative implies that a certain type of woman satisfies the desires of a 'physical' man out of affection:

> That night she met his passion with love. It was not his passion she wanted, actually. But she desired that he should want *her* madly, and that he should have all – everything. It was a wonderful night to him. It restored in him the full 'will to live.' But she felt it destroyed her. Her soul seemed blasted.[78]

So Siegmund is given his own fulfilment, even if it is not mutual; in the earlier version of this passage, the fulfilment was shared: 'That night, she met his love with love as blazing as his own.'[79] But Helen Corke did not see the final version before publication, and this may be the passage which she referred to as the 'one imaginary scene' where Lawrence had 'heightened' the 'eroticism'.[80]

77 All three MSS are in the possession of the Ellen Clarke Bertrand Library, Bucknell University (Lindeth Vasey, ed. 'A Checklist of the Manuscripts of D. H. Lawrence', in Keith Sagar's *D. H. Lawrence: A Calendar of his Works*, Manchester, 1979, E438a–c).

A later portrayal of Helen Corke appears in *Lady Chatterley's Lover*, where Mellors recalls the women with whom he has been involved. 'Then I took on with another girl, a teacher, who had made a scandal by carrying on with a married man and driving him nearly out of his mind. She was a soft, white-skinned, soft sort of a woman, older than me, and played the fiddle. And she was a demon. She loved everything about love, except sex. Clinging, caressing, creeping into you in every way: but if you forced her to the sex itself, she just ground her teeth and sent out hate. I forced her to it, and she could simply numb me with hate because of it' *Lady Chatterley's Lover*, chap. XIV.

78 See below, p. 87.

79 MSII 14. For the complete passage, see below, pp. 34–5.

80 Corke, *Infancy* 216.

It is clear from Lawrence's letters that he sought a sexual relationship with her, was repulsed (however kindly) and was bitter. He came to think of Helen Corke as one of the 'Dreaming Women' whose 'passion exhausts itself at the mouth'. The allusion is to Rachel Annand Taylor's poem 'The Epilogue of the Dreaming Women' which he had read in October 1909;[81] this is also a point made in chapter XIII by the 'stranger', Hampson, whose harsh comments about these women Siegmund does not dispute.[82]

In the contemporary diary accounts, there is evidence both of Helen Corke's reluctance to have a sexual relationship with Macartney, and of her eventual acquiescence. In 'The Letter', she refers to times when 'the passion that touched [her] only racked and seared [him]' and she 'added fuel to flame' and told herself that she was helping him to 'cultivate self control'.[83] In *Neutral Ground*, she describes the continual struggle with the 'beast' in Macartney that preceded their days on the Isle of Wight. At the same time, she is able to conclude that he was 'an ordinary male type' and to ask 'what strange development of humanity' expressed itself in her.[84] The title, *Neutral Ground*, which seems strangely inappropriate at first, was intended to indicate a point in sexuality between committed homosexuality and committed heterosexuality.[85] In a letter to Harry T. Moore, Helen Corke defined *Neutral Ground* as 'an honest attempt to deal with the problem of a Lesbian temperament'.[86] The unpublished half of her autobiography makes even clearer what she makes fairly plain in *In Our Infancy*: that she was from childhood more drawn to her own sex than to men, though men were drawn to her.[87] She offered Macartney and Lawrence a spiritual relationship when they wanted a physical one, but in the case of Lawrence she came to believe that he, also, occupied the same 'neutral ground' and that this explained both the affinity and the conflict between them.[88] George Neville, a childhood friend to whom Lawrence related Helen Corke's story, concluded: 'She apparently misunderstood her feelings for him [Macartney], for she failed him at the crucial moment: failed him and drove him to utter despair.'[89] Neville implies that Lawrence's relationship with her did not

81 See p. 64 below and *Letters*, i. 141. Awaiting the return of 'The Saga', DHL had embarked on a project: the Croydon 'English Association' asked him to give a talk on a living poet, and he chose Rachel Annand Taylor (1876–1960), Ada Lawrence and G. Stuart Gelder, *Young Lorenzo: Early Life of D. H. Lawrence* (Florence, 1932), pp. 233–43. DHL's suggested title 'The Man and the Dreaming Woman' for *The Trespasser* may also derive from this poem (see below p. 22).

82 *Trespasser*, p. 112.

83 See below, p. 282.

84 *Neutral Ground* 179–82.

85 BBC interview 6/3.

86 20 May 1951, University of Tulsa.

87 University of Tulsa.

88 BBC interview 6/3.

89 I am grateful to Mr James Neville for permission to quote from this memoir. A new edition of the memoirs of George Neville edited by Carl Baron is a forthcoming publication from Cambridge University Press.

parallel her earlier love affair, but his memory was not always reliable nor supported by other accounts. A case can be made for the reverse conclusion: that Helen Corke's relationship with Macartney was consummated, if unhappily (as *The Trespasser* suggests) and she chose not to repeat the experience with Lawrence. In the 'Cornwall Writing', Helen Corke implies that she had had to wait to learn whether she was pregnant. 'I know that if I have Siegmund's child – when it wakes – nay, before it wakes – I shall take it back to him.'[90] That seems to be an acknowledgement of a physical relationship. But it is evasively literary, and one asks what the last three clauses mean: a threat of suicide presumably. Or is it just an opportune allusion to the story in Wagner (at the end of *Die Walküre*, Sieglinde is indeed carrying Siegmund's child)?

The bitterness that Helen Corke observed in the Lawrence of 1911 was due in part to his conflicting feelings about her and his fiancée and the loss of his mother, but probably also to his lack of progress in the literary world. He was soon to have new encouragement. By 25 August, he was corresponding with Edward Garnett, who became his adviser; they met at Duckworth's, where Garnett worked as reader, on 4 October. The relationship became friendly, and on the week-end of 13–15 October Lawrence paid the first of many visits to The Cearne, Garnett's home near Edenbridge. By 20 October, Garnett had expressed interest in seeing the manuscript of 'The Saga', which Heinemann had still not returned.[91]

In the meantime, Lawrence had become critically ill with pneumonia on Sunday 19 November, the result of a chill caught during a week-end visit to The Cearne.[92] It was not until 2 December that his sister Ada, who had come to Croydon to nurse him, was able to inform Garnett that her brother was over the worst,[93] and two days later Lawrence himself wrote: 'I have sent to The Cearne, the MSS of the erotic novel which I have at last extorted from William Heinemann...I shall like to hear your opinion of the work.'[94] His uneasiness continued while Garnett was reading 'The Saga':

> I shall look for you on Wednesday. Don't bring back that novel MSS. unless you have read all you want to read. I don't want it a bit. It is a work too chargé, too emotional. It's a sponge dipped too full of vinegar, or wine, or whatever – it wants squeezing out. I shrink from it rather.[95]

The next day, he received Garnett's 'very exciting' letter, apparently

[90] See below, p. 315. See also her recollection of the statement: 'I will never have an illegitimate child', p. 304.
[91] *Letters*, i. 317.
[92] Ibid. 328 n 1.
[93] Ibid. 329 n 1.
[94] Ibid. 330.
[95] Ibid. 337.

expressing approval of the manuscript. Replying, Lawrence described his experience with Hueffer and the publishers, and revealed his fear of being 'talked about in an *Anne Veronica* fashion'.[96] The clear parallel between H. G. Wells's novel and 'The Saga' is that each is about a single woman who runs away with a married man, though the endings are quite different. Lawrence used the notes that Garnett made for their discussion of the manuscript (which probably occurred on Wednesday, 20 December) when he revised the book.

Helen Corke recalled that, before Lawrence went to Bournemouth for convalescence in early 1912, 'he asked me to sanction the publication of the *Saga*. His doctors had warned him against returning to the school, and he would try to make a living by writing.'[97] The income that another book would bring, together with the prospect of improving it through revision, apparently overcame his previous reluctance, once he had her consent.

On 30 December, Lawrence told Garnett: 'I shall begin re-writing the first part today', and suggested possible titles: 'For a title to that MS. called at present The Saga, will "Trespassers in Cythera" or The Trespasser or something like that, do? Or for "Cythera" what can one put – what are the Isles of the Happy – ? Evin, Evna? – Help me out.'[98] Garnett must have approved *The Trespasser*, for it was that title which Lawrence normally used from 7 January 1912 on.[99] The sequence of proposed titles suggests the primary sense Lawrence intended by the word 'trespasser' – one who enters illegally the property of others, and especially the territory of love, implied by the reference to Cythera, birthplace of Aphrodite. Other implications may have occurred to him, such as the French word *trépasser* (to die) or the position of Cecil Byrne, the Lawrence figure, as trespasser in the private memories of Helena.

By 3 January 1912, he had begun the novel again: 'done the first chapter – heaps, heaps better. There was room for improvement, by Jove! – I

[96] Ibid. 339. One reviewer saw *Ann Veronica* as a dangerous model which others might follow. (See *H. G. Wells, The Critical Heritage*, ed. Patrick Parrinder, 1972, p. 162.) Wells's lovers marry and live happily ever after, very successfully in fact – with fame, fortune, an expected baby, and even acceptance by the woman's family. If retribution for wrongdoing made a novel acceptable, then Siegmund's suicide and Helena's grief should have been considered less controversial than this affair which is approved and rewarded.

[97] Corke, *As I Saw Him* 13. This request may have been made by letter, as Helen Corke specifies in Corke, *Infancy* 214.

[98] *Letters*, i. 343. His dissatisfaction with the title of the first version had been expressed in October 1910: 'By the way, don't you think the title idiotic? I am a failure there. How would The Livanters do?' (184).

[99] Ibid. 345.

was so young – almost pathetically young – two years ago.'[100] After two days in Bournemouth, on 8 January, he informed Louie Burrows: 'I do about 2 hrs work a day, and get on', and on the 10th he told Garnett: 'I get on very slowly with the "Saga".'[101] On 7 January, he had written to Garnett: 'I will try and get the *Trespasser* done in a month or so. I should like him published this spring. Must I tell Wm Heinemann about him?'[102] Whether or not Lawrence informed that publisher that he was revising 'The Saga' to submit to Duckworth, on 19 January he sent Garnett a letter from Heinemann which apparently exerted pressure on him not to give the book to another firm. He commented to a Croydon colleague: 'I wrote Heinemann – William is away – they are indefinite concerning the poems – and tried to soft-sawder me into not giving the second, love-novel which they practically refused, to Duckworth.'[103]

In writing to Garnett, Lawrence revealed some of the insecurities which Heinemann's treatment of 'The Saga' must have aggravated.

> I really don't think the Saga was ever read at Wm Heinemann's – not by anyone. But they make me feel so uncertain and down about the wretched thing...
>
> I have done the first 135 pages of the *Trespasser* – rewritten them. Shall I send them on? At the bottom of my heart I don't like the work, though I'm sure it has points, and I don't think it retrograde from the *White Peacock*. It surprises me by its steady progressiveness – I hate it for its fluid, luscious quality.[104]

By this time, he had started incorporating some of the pages from 'The Saga' manuscript into this new version, which increasingly became his way of working. (See below, p. 32.) By 21 January, he had completed 180 or 190 pages, and his uncertainty about their value expanded into another fear. 'I hope the thing is knitted firm – I hate those pieces where the stitch is slack and loose. The "Stranger" piece is probably still too literary – I don't feel at all satisfied.'[105] On 29 January, he wrote to Garnett that the revision was going well; he had completed 300 pages. His uncertainty remained – accompanied, however, by the conviction that he must let the work stand

100 Ibid. 344. Since the first twelve pages of chapter I are missing from 'The Saga' MS, it is difficult to assess, from the five pages remaining, the 'improvement' DHL saw room for. His sense of having been 'pathetically young' when he wrote the early draft may reflect a new perspective on his relationship with Helen Corke, which is the autobiographical theme of chapter I of *The Trespasser* and appears to have been that of chapter I of 'The Saga' as well.

101 Ibid. 347, 349.

102 Ibid. 345.

103 Ibid. 355–6. DHL had written to Garnett: 'What do you think of the enclosed? Is it merely soft sawder?' (351).

104 Ibid. 351.

105 Ibid. 353. 'The "Stranger" piece' became chapter XIII of the published text. See below, pp. 109–13.

as it was. He added that he would finish revising by the end of his visit to The Cearne in early February. When Garnett had read it, they could decide about publication, but Lawrence liked Garnett's suggestion of April or May.[106]

On 1 February Lawrence soothed Helen Corke's uneasiness about the revision: 'I tell you again I am not altering the substance of the Saga, so that, in spite of my present tone, you will not find it perverted from what of original truth it had. I re-cast the paragraphs, and attend to the style.' He expressed his conception of *The Trespasser* as 'a work of fiction on a frame of actual experience', and as *his* presentation of that experience: 'The necessity is not that our two views should coincide, but that the work should be a work of art.'[107] Although Lawrence said he would send her the manuscript, he did not – possibly because the decision to publish *The Trespasser* in May did not allow time, or perhaps because he feared that his revised treatment of the character Helena would offend her, and he wanted to avoid an unpleasant confrontation.[108]

While Lawrence awaited Duckworth's decision on *The Trespasser*, he again 'tackled' his third novel, 'Paul Morel' (*Sons and Lovers*), which was 'going pretty well'.[109] Having submitted his resignation from his teaching post at the end of February and being committed to earning his living as a writer, Lawrence not surprisingly was uneasy during the waiting period. To contribute to his anxiety he learned that Heinemann did not want to publish his *Love Poems*.[110] He was concerned that his novel might be rejected also, but heard by 8 March that Duckworth had accepted it.[111]

While he awaited proofs, the title was again debated: Lawrence found that *The Trespasser* had been used before, and suggested 'A Game of Forfeits or The Forfeit or The Man and the Dreaming Woman'.[112] The first batch of proofs arrived on 4 April, and Lawrence wrote to Garnett the next day: 'I will wage war on my adjectives. Culpa mea!'[113]

During his correction of the proofs, Lawrence was probably distracted by his growing involvement with Frieda Weekley. He had broken his engagement

[106] Ibid. 358.

[107] Ibid. 359. See Corke, *Infancy* 214 for her concern.

[108] DHL probably had part of the revised manuscript with him when he met Helen Corke on the train on his way to The Cearne, but according to her account of the pre-arranged meeting they avoided controversial subjects (Corke, *As I Saw Him* 3).

[109] *Letters*, i. 367.

[110] Ibid. 368.

[111] Ibid. 373.

[112] Ibid. 378. Duckworth apparently decided on 'A Game of Forfeits', but neglected to alter the title on the proofs. For the possible source of the title 'The Man and the Dreaming Woman', see above, note 81.

[113] Ibid. 381.

to Louie Burrows in early February, explaining that the doctors felt he ought not to marry for a long time.[114] But in mid-March he met Mrs Weekley, and they soon decided to elope.[115] In spite of the uncertainty of the future and the need to make arrangements for leaving, it appears from the correspondence that he had enough time in Eastwood to correct the proofs, and was able to concentrate his attention on them. Although he was leaving for Germany on 3 May, Lawrence was sufficiently concerned about his second novel to ask Garnett in two consecutive letters of 29 April and 1 May when Duckworth would publish it;[116] *The Trespasser* was published on 23 May 1912.

Reception

In her autobiography, Helen Corke recalled her first impression of *The Trespasser*:

> When the book arrives I open it with mingled exaltation and dread. Why, if there has been no sacrifice of its essential truth to his Moloch of technique and form, did he not send me the revised manuscript as promised? But indeed the work remains substantially the same – the eroticism of one imaginary scene has been heightened; there are several interpolations of imaginary dialogue – and I miss a fine piece of symbolism – yet it is still the record, faithful enough, of Lawrence's exploration into the territory of H.B.M.'s experience.[117]

Lawrence described the letter she wrote to thank him for the copy as 'fearfully affected' and 'fishing for me back'; how much of this perception was influenced by Frieda can only be surmised from his tone. Her letter ended: 'We are such stuff as dreams are made on – but aye we make fair dreams, what matter!'[118] These were the last words Lawrence would ever hear from the woman whose story became *The Trespasser*.

Helen Corke wrote in her copy: 'I claim clothing for the soul of Siegmund and voice for his silence.'[119] In the BBC interview she said that the changes made after she saw the manuscript were 'very slight ones'.[120] On the question of the characterisation of Siegmund: 'It is as true a conception as one mind could possibly make of another.'[121] On the characterisation of Helena – and the woman in the 'Helen' poems – she commented: 'I'm only there in those works in the sense that David's image of me is presented there.

114 Ibid. 361.
115 Ibid. 374 n. 4.
116 Ibid. 388, 389.
117 Corke, *Infancy* 216.
118 *Letters*, i. 419.
119 Helen Corke's copy is now at Nottinghamshire County Libraries. These words appear also in 'The Cornwall Writing', p. 318.
120 BBC interview 2/6.
121 Ibid. 3A/2.

And the image which he had of me is not necessarily and in this case certainly was not the image of the actual individual.'[122] Speaking of the accuracy of *The Trespasser* as a chronicle of her experience, Miss Corke said: 'Part of it was fiction, very definitely fiction. The end of *The Trespasser* is Lawrence, complete Lawrence.'[123] Although generally satisfied with the book, she felt the need to clarify certain points, so she wrote *Neutral Ground* in 'an attempt to show the situation from the woman's point of view'.[124] She also included events that had been left out of Lawrence's version: 'For instance, there's no indication in *The Trespasser* of the leading up to the whole incident. In actual life, you see, there was five years of leading up.'[125]

The critics judged *The Trespasser* by much less personal criteria, and Lawrence was eager to know what they thought. On 2 June he asked Garnett for reviews, and on 10 June he asked Walter de la Mare for his opinion of the novel.[126] At the end of June Lawrence thanked Garnett for the *Westminster* review, which was the only one he had seen so far: 'quite good, wasn't it – who was it?' he asked.[127] The unidentified reviewer classified *The Trespasser* among the novels 'written by inspiration, and generally without much self-criticism on the author's part' and such books were 'seldom without faults'. The latter were summarised as 'over-emphasis and unreserve', 'peculiarities of vocabulary' and passages 'which might be pruned to half their present length and lose nothing in clarity or force'. Perhaps what struck Lawrence as 'quite good' was the review's conclusion.

But when all this has been admitted, 'The Trespassers' remains a book of extraordinary beauty and power, one not to be put into the hands of the timid or the frivolous, but one which, rightly understood, leads the mind to a deeper recognition of the inexorable physical and moral laws which, holding humanity in bondage, work out for every trespasser a certain doom.[128]

Lawrence had also heard that the *Daily News* said he must 'cultivate an intenser vision'.[129] The review is entitled 'Possibilities', but dwells more on the defects than on Lawrence's 'great gifts of fancy and sensibility'. The reviewer betrays a moral bias: 'He wastes his energies chiefly in recording the sensibilities of the flesh...Unhappily, we learn a great deal more about the sensations of the chief characters than about their souls.' The phrase which was passed on to Lawrence appears in the conclusion. 'We look

122 Ibid. 10/6.

123 Ibid. 2/6.

124 Ibid. 3A/2. For further explanation of the intentions behind her novel, see above, p. 18.

125 BBC interview 2/7.

126 *Letters*, i. 415, 417.

127 Ibid. 419.

128 *Westminster Gazette*, 8 June 1912, p. 18. The *Westminster Gazette* was just then publishing DHL's 'Schoolmaster' poems.

129 *Letters*, i. 419.

forward to the day when Mr Lawrence will burn with an intenser vision than anything he communicates here. If only he can get below surfaces, he has in him the makings of an artist in literature.'[130]

The *Outlook*'s brief notice carried moral indignation further: Mr Lawrence did not know 'the value of the decent fig-leaf... Still, his book may have its uses if only as an object-lesson, that these things must not be written after these ways if readers are not to be sickened and – bored.'[131] Still another moral evaluation was to come, from Lawrence's own Nottinghamshire. The *Nottinghamshire Guardian Literary Supplement* reminded the reader that Lawrence had attended Nottingham University College; after an unsympathetically slanted plot-summary, the reviewer presented his fundamental objection: 'The philosophy is neither paganism nor sensualism, but what we call animalism, which is human animalism. It is part of the pose that a monumental ignorance of the Bible is assumed.'[132] Lawrence received this criticism with equanimity, for he wrote to Garnett soon after: 'Nothing pleases me like the "Reprehensible Jaunt" of the *Nottingham Guardian*. My beautiful *Trespasser* called a Reprehensible Jaunt.'[133] If he had seen the notice in the *Nation*, he might have had cause for alarm. Titled '"Marriage" and Another', this joint review of H. G. Wells's *Marriage* and *The Trespasser* opens with the warning: 'There is a good deal in Mr Lawrence's new novel that reminds one of the exotic writers of the nineties', which the reader must approach in the appropriate state of mind, or he 'will be left unsatisfied, if not repelled'. The reviewer complains specifically of descriptions 'too full of anatomy'.[134]

The *Eye-witness*'s reviewer also placed Lawrence in the larger literary tradition. *The Trespasser* was an example of the modern novel that ought not to be asked to pass 'a test of centuries'; and it was judged 'a novel that stands out from the ruck'.[135] Although the *Eye-witness*'s reviewer had reservations concerning 'the overwhelming importance of sex-relations' and excessive seriousness and refinement of the characters, he acknowledged 'flashes in the book that illuminate and passages of beauty almost as intense as in a book by Keats'.[136]

The Trespasser was reviewed jointly with a translation of Dostoevsky's *Brothers Karamazov* by Edward Garnett's wife, Constance Garnett, in the

130 *Daily News and Leader*, 21 June 1912, p. 8.
131 *Outlook*, 29 June 1912, p. 950.
132 *Nottingham Guardian Literary Supplement*, 2 July 1912. The reviewer cites '"And there shall be no more sea," she quoted to herself, she knew not wherefrom' (p. 119, below).
133 *Letters*, i. 425.
134 *Nation*, 19 October 1912, pp. 152–4.
135 *Eye-witness*, 11 July 1912, p. 123.
136 *The Standard*'s reviewer (21 June 1912, p. 5) adopted a very similar line.

Athenæum. The title 'Two Realists: Russian and English' put the young Lawrence in very august company, and the reviewer continued the parallel: Siegmund's homecoming and mental deterioration 'are clear and strong in their psychological intensity, reminding us of the best Russian school' and the discovery of his body is 'poetic realism of a Dostöevskian order'. Lawrence is praised for his 'skill in catching shades of social atmosphere' and his 'unobtrusive art'; he is criticised for one small blemish – 'that Siegmund, at the age of thirty-eight, is credited with feeling the ecstatic passions of youth'.[137]

The most extensive review so far discovered was written by Rebecca West in the *Freewoman* of 11 July. After dismissing two books, she turned to *The Trespasser*: '[a book] on a different plane, a book that was worth the writing'. With characteristic directness, she stated: 'Mr Lawrence has conquered. This book is magic.' The title of the review expresses its focus – 'Spinsters and Art' – from which develops a powerful censure of the heroine. 'That was her sin. She despised Life. Even her love was a cold-blooded theft...So she steals his [Siegmund's] passion to build herself more feeble, romantic dreams, and gives him nothing in return.' The perception of Helena as 'drunk with the spinster's ethereal conception of man' is accompanied by a deep appreciation of what Lawrence was trying to accomplish. 'The description of the ecstasy of love has been done before...But Mr Lawrence not only treats it with reality, but he attains past it to the most godlike point of discontent; he perceives the failure of love.'[138]

Other reviewers, in considering *The Trespasser* as a second novel saw promise of a developing talent. The *English Review*, which had 'discovered' Lawrence, assessed the book in these terms.

> *The Trespasser* is his second novel, and if as a story it is somewhat disappointing, as a piece of writing it is unquestionably an achievement. In D. H. Lawrence we have a new power, still immature, perhaps one who will never be a great story-teller, possibly not even a creative artist, yet for all that an artist of a most exquisite delicacy and of a sure and penetrating observation... As an observer and portrayer of nature, D. H. Lawrence has no peer... Here is a writer with style. We have yet to wait for the author's message.[139]

The *Morning Post* classified Lawrence's second novel as 'another interesting and ugly piece of work', which dealt with 'abnormal people...in an extremely sincere and interesting way'. What this reviewer felt lacking was 'a complete human harmony...our sympathy is only partially evoked'.

137 *Athenæum*, 1 June 1912, pp. 613–14 (Draper 44–5).
138 *Freewoman* (Rebecca West), 11 July 1912, pp. 147–9.
139 *English Review*, vol. xi, no. 4, July 1912, p. 661.

Lawrence's descriptive talent and the structure of the book were applauded: 'The story itself has an unusual artistic unity, aided by the effective epic construction which begins it in the middle and keeps the sense of tragedy hovering, as it were, over love scenes and purging them of earthly grossness.' The reviewer ends with a warning common to several notices that *The Trespasser* was 'a remarkable book, but it needs to be read by the discriminating and the experienced, who will not take its blemishes for its attractions'.[140]

The *Saturday Review* made a different point about Lawrence's second novel: 'Had it been the work of almost any other man it would have satisfied, for it is no common novel but for some months we have been waiting for this book with the highest hopes.' The reviewer criticised Lawrence's failure to relate the episodes to the central theme.[141] Basil de Selincourt in the *Manchester Guardian* pointed to a particular type of failure: 'a remarkable study of a tragic theme, enveloping it, however, in an ironical rather than in a tragical atmosphere', with the result that the characters do not affect us as deeply as they ought.[142] The reviewer for *Rhythm* (probably Frederick Goodyear) expressed a strong dislike for what he called 'a study in morbid psychology' and blamed the author for not viewing his characters with sufficient objectivity.[143]

In the United States the *New York Times Book Review* received the book with virtually unqualified admiration.

From the beginning of time...we have been made wearily familiar with a certain type of wicked and ruinous lady who has set, more or less successfully, snares for men's feet. She has been a robust sort of animal, varying with much or little subtlety her natural instinct and her physical pursuit; she has been over-sexed, and she has been entirely bad. But that she was not the only, not perhaps the most, dangerous sort of enchantress we have most of us vaguely guessed. It has remained for an almost unknown author to put the other kind of woman into a book. And *The Trespasser* is not only the frankest of serious contemporary novels; it comes near to being the best...

The Trespasser combines some of the most exquisite imaginative writing in modern fiction with a nakedness of physical detail that is almost morbid in its ugliness. Helena and Siegmund spend their holiday by the sea; and we have little today to equal the author's descriptions of wind and wave and far sea-mist, of shore and moor. The story itself – the narrative of a passion that took a man away from a wretched home, and of his miserable return when holiday time was over – is a revolting tragedy.[144]

140 *Morning Post*, 17 June 1912, p. 2 (Draper 48–9).
141 *Saturday Review*, 22 June 1912, pp. 785–6.
142 *Manchester Guardian* (B[asil de] S[elincourt]), 5 June 1912, p. 5 (Draper 46–7).
143 *Rhythm* (F[rederick] G[oodyear]), ii (November 1912), 278. See *Letters*, i. 507.
144 *New York Times Book Review*, 17 November 1912, p. 677 (Draper 50).

Like several of the English reviews, this notice closes with a warning – in this case a further tribute – as to the type of reader who will not appreciate the book: the commonplace reader will find it only a commonplace book.

On 20 July, the *New York Herald* quoted an excerpt from the *Westminster Gazette*'s review and commented that the book 'appears to be something out of the ordinary'.[145] Except for a neutral two-sentence description in the *New York Tribune*, no other reviews in American periodicals have been located.[146] That there were others seems evident from a letter which Mitchell Kennerley, the American publisher of *The Trespasser*, sent to Edward Garnett; he enclosed copies of the American reviews and continued: 'The reception of *The Trespasser* has been such that I should like the opportunity of copyrighting the new book.'[147] It seems that Kennerley's initial interest in the new novel, *Sons and Lovers*, derived from the favourable reception of *The Trespasser* in America – in terms of reviews or sales, or both. Kennerley's optimism about Lawrence and sales in March 1913 is indicated in his offer to Garnett that despite the 200 unsold copies he would send 'a check in settlement of royalties on the entire edition'.[148]

Lawrence responded to Hueffer's criticism of the final published version of 'The Saga' with equanimity. On 10 December, he replied to a letter from Hueffer:

> Thanks for your full opinions on the *Trespasser*. I agree with you heartily. I rather hate the book. It seems a bit messy to me. But whether it injures my reputation or not, it has brought me enough money to carry me – so modestly, as you may guess – through a winter here on the Lake Garda. One must publish to live.[149]

This novel was Lawrence's first attempt to support himself exclusively by his own writing. He hoped that a favourable reception would enable him to sell stories and articles: 'Won't somebody in America have my stories now the *Trespasser* is out there?'[150] The reception of his second novel had important material implications for Lawrence, as well as the usual effect on a writer's pride in his work.

[145] *New York Herald*, 20 July 1912, p. 6.

[146] *New York Tribune*, 21 December 1912, p. 10. Other English reviews located are *Evening Standard* (12 June 1912), *Sheffield Daily Telegraph* by 'A.N.C.L.' (4 July 1912), *Birmingham Daily Post* (12 July 1912) and *Academy* (5 October 1912).

[147] *Letters*, i. 522 n. 4. I am indebted to Mr Mitchell Kennerley Jr for permission to quote his father's letters.

[148] Ibid. 542, n. 2.

[149] Ibid. 485.

[150] Ibid. 430.

Publication

Lawrence's arrangements for publishing *The Trespasser* seem extremely casual, especially when one remembers that he had to 'publish to live'.[151] It is almost certain that he never had a contract for his second novel. In 1912, he had not signed one, and the following February, still did not have one.[152] The advance for the *Trespasser* seems likely to have been £50, since in February 1913 Lawrence was asking Garnett: 'Will the *Trespasser* bring any more than the £50 I have had, or not?'[153] It may be that Lawrence's sensitivity on the subject of his personal financial difficulties accounted for his failure to insist upon a formal contract initially – and perhaps ever.[154]

The 'first batch of proofs' reached Lawrence on 4 April 1912.[155] The extant uncorrected set of page proofs bears notations indicating the date when a section was proofread by a printer's reader,[156] and the earliest date, 28 March, suggests that these were the proofs to which Lawrence referred as the 'first batch'. It was not uncommon even at that time for an author to receive page proofs without first having received galley proofs, especially for an uncomplicated book such as a novel.

Duckworth published *The Trespasser* on 23 May.[157] There is no record of the size of the first impression; it may have included sheets for a Colonial edition.[158] At least part of the first impression, and most likely the whole, was printed directly from standing type, plates being made at a later stage.[159]

151 Ibid. 485.

152 The Duckworth contracts for DHL's books eventually reached Heinemann's files, Messrs Heinemann having acquired the English rights for the whole DHL property in January 1935, but there is no contract for *The Trespasser* among this material. (I am indebted to Mr Andrew Robertson for this information.)

153 *Letters*, i. 511.

154 Ibid. 339, 408–9, 415.

155 Ibid. 381.

156 The nineteen signatures were dated 28 March (1), 2 April (2), 3 April (2), 4 April (4), 9 April (2) and 10 April (8) in seven hands.

157 Review copies of *The Trespasser* at the University of Nottingham and in the collection of Professor Keith Cushman are stamped: 'To Be Published on 23 May 1912'; the price of 6/- (six shillings) is written underneath on a dotted line.

158 Neither the printers, Billing and Sons Ltd of Guildford, nor Messrs Duckworth have any material relating to *The Trespasser* in their files. Sheets were printed for a Colonial edition, but the dates are not known.

159 The initial letter in 'Curtiss' on p. 37 has dropped below the line of type in nearly all known copies of the first impression, although Cornell University and University of California at Los Angeles have copies with the 'C' correctly aligned. On the page proofs, the name was 'Brinton', so the 'C' must have dropped after DHL revised the proofs, and while sheets were being printed from type. The plates were made after the 'C' dropped, and this feature is reproduced in all reprintings.

Copies exist in blue and green bindings; the green was for the Colonial issue and is stamped 'Australasian Edition' on the spine.[160] Duckworth issued a second impression early in July 1912.[161]

Later in 1912, the first American edition was published by Mitchell Kennerley, using sheets supplied by Duckworth.[162] The arrangement was probably similar to that which Kennerley suggested for *Love Poems and Others* in 1913, when he agreed to 'take a small edition of Mr Lawrence's book of poems'.[163] The number of copies he purchased of *The Trespasser* is not known. The American copies were bound in a light pea-green cloth (which tended to fade to tan), with a brown line border on the front cover and brown lettering. Lawrence's comment in January 1913 was: 'It is ugly.'[164]

No contract for the American edition nor correspondence from Garnett or Duckworth with Kennerley is included in the collection of Kennerley's papers at Vassar College,[165] but the date 27 May 1912 on the reader's report in this collection indicates that Kennerley's negotiations for *The Trespasser* probably began after Duckworth had issued his first impression, and that the sheets bound with the American title-page were of a later impression.

The final format had one peculiarity: up to and including p. 69 the number of lines per page was thirty-four; from p. 70 the number became thirty-three. The immediate cause of this line reduction on p. 70 appears to be the removal of 'two moths' (see below, 87: 39) – although why the reduced number became the norm is not clear. This feature is reproduced in subsequent reprintings. Pages 276–9 only have thirty-two lines of type.

160 Edward D. McDonald examined one copy in green binding, unstamped (now at the Humanities Research Center, University of Texas at Austin) and concluded that the green cloth was a trial binding. See McDonald, *The Writings of D. H. Lawrence, 1925–1930: A Bibliographical Supplement* (Philadelphia, 1931), p. 128. Closer examination reveals that the stamp was at one time blocked on the spine. I am grateful to Dr Warren Roberts for assistance in solving this mystery.

161 Duckworth reprinted it again in 1924; in 1927 and 1929 Secker reprinted the novel from the Duckworth plates, as part of their cheap thin-paper series.

There were new settings for the *c.* 1934 Albatross Modern Continental Library (volume 98) and Heinemann's 1955 Phoenix edition. For a more complete list see Warren Roberts, *A Bibliography of D. H. Lawrence* (Rupert Hart-Davis, 1963; second edition forthcoming from Cambridge University Press).

162 Even the title-page was probably printed in Great Britain, because the publisher's device used by Kennerley is missing.

163 *Letters*, i. 542 n. A letter from DHL to Amy Lowell, dated 18 December 1914, suggests that the publishing arrangements for *The Trespasser* were conducted by Duckworth, although DHL may be referring only to *Sons and Lovers*: 'I haven't kept proper accounts with him [Kennerley], because Duckworths made the agreement and all that.'

164 *Letters*, i. 502. Whether he meant the binding or a dust jacket, no copy of which has been found, is not known.

165 In an unpublished letter at Vassar College Library (Kennerley correspondence file no. 1, Village Press Collection) of 8 October 1934, Mitchell Kennerley claimed that he destroyed 'thousands' of letters when he moved his office in 1916.

The dates of known reviews in America also suggest that Kennerley's publication was later in the year, possibly as late as November.[166] Kennerley did not register *The Trespasser* for an ad interim copyright, very likely because he did not anticipate sufficient sales to warrant the expense of printing the book to meet United States copyright regulations.[167]

Manuscripts and selection of base-text

The pre-publication material known to exist consists of a partial and a complete autograph manuscript, and a set of uncorrected page proofs. The two manuscripts are in the Bancroft Library, University of California at Berkeley. The proof copy is in the Hopkin Collection of the Eastwood Public Library, and may be the one that on 19 August 1912, Lawrence asked Mrs Sallie Hopkin, an Eastwood friend, to give to his sister Ada.[168] Since he left England before the publication date, the corrected proofs were probably not returned to him by the publishers.

The partial manuscript is designated 'MSI' and the complete one 'MSII'. The relationship of these two manuscripts has been ascertained by matching cancelled (but still visible) page numbers in MSII to the remaining pages in MSI. The history of composition reveals two drafts: 'The Saga of Siegmund' (*c.* 11 April to 4 August 1910) and *The Trespasser* (*c.* 30 December 1911 to 2 February 1912). MSII is clearly the latter and the final revised manuscript submitted to Duckworth: spike holes and printer's notations indicate that the edition was set directly from it. MSI then is the draft which immediately preceded II, and there is no evidence of an intermediate version, so it is very probable that MSI was the first version, 'The Saga of Siegmund'.[169]

Both manuscripts are written on one side of what Lawrence called 'sermon paper',[170] and are in Lawrence's hand, in ink, with a few of his revisions

166 On 20 July 1912, the *New York Herald* quoted the review in the London *Westminster Gazette*, with no mention of an American edition ('What English Critics Say of Recent Books', p. 6). The earliest known date for a review of the Kennerley edition is 17 November 1912.

167 United States copyright regulations did not at that time give protection to a book printed outside the United States or even to one printed from plates made outside the United States.

168 *Letters*, i. 442.

169 For a description of 'The Saga' manuscript, see Bruce Steele, 'The Manuscript of D. H. Lawrence's *Saga of Siegmund*', *Studies in Bibliography*, xxxiii (1980), 193–205.

170 The paper is ruled, unstitched and folded in gatherings of six leaves, bearing the watermark 'Boots/Cash Stationers'. Only one fold in MSII remains intact, the bolts having apparently been cut to make loose leaves for ease in typesetting. The top page of each original gathering was numbered consecutively by DHL in roman numerals. The horizontal dimension – approximate since the leaves have been cut – is about 16·3 cm; the vertical dimension varies

in pencil on MSII. Many pages contain extensive interlinear revision in each manuscript, but all the revisions and most of the deleted passages are legible.

The most significant fact is the considerable number of pages transferred from MSI, and the type of revision involved in this process. Out of the total of 485 pages in the final manuscript, 296 come from the earlier manuscript, and have been renumbered.[171] The transferred pages are often in long sequences: the last 190 pages of MSII were borrowed entire from MSI.[172] Lawrence followed several procedures when he borrowed pages: he crossed out one word or several lines to make a transition, or he added lines in the top margin of a borrowed page, or in the bottom margin of the preceding page in MSII. The amount of material crossed out or rewritten on the remaining pages of MSI may explain why he did not salvage them; sometimes, the text is sufficiently different from the matching page in MSII to suggest that Lawrence may have attempted to revise and then decided to rewrite them. Frequently, the pages he transferred contained few revisions originally, and received little further revision.

When Lawrence began MSII, he had received critical responses to 'The Saga' from Ford Madox Hueffer and Edward Garnett. After discussing 'The Saga' with the latter during December 1911, Lawrence used Garnett's notes, written to serve as reminders, on the backs of the pages of MSI.[173] The brief notes, mostly in pencil, are signalled by pencil lines in the margin of the corresponding page. As a result, the notes can be studied to see how much attention Lawrence paid to them in his revision.

For example, on the back of p. 276/260 (MSI and MSII numbers respectively) is a note referring to a passage, which Lawrence simplified when he rewrote the page: 'p. 272 ?Bromios/ ?too recondite'. The allusion to

slightly, but is just over 20 cm. *White Peacock*, 'Saga', 'Intimacy' and *A Collier's Friday Night* were written on 'sermon' paper; see Harry T. Moore, *The Priest of Love* (1974), p. 90.

171 MSII is numbered 1–487 with a few errors: five pages bear two numbers, three with a repeated number (two of which have an 'a' added).

172 The borrowed pages from MSI correspond to the following passages in this edition (page and line numbers given in parentheses):

49	(59: 13–30)	198–201	(118: 23–119: 34)
89–90	(78: 21–79: 13)	203–7	(120: 11–122: 17)
116–26	(88: 20–93: 4)	245–64	(134: 9–142: 26)
130–1	(93: 33–94: 19)	275–6	(145: 24–146: 12)
140–6	(97: 16–99: 36)	279–309	(146: 39–159: 13)
148–53	(100: 12–102: 26)	314–503	(160: 27–230: 9)
155–69	(103: 6–108: 30)		

173 That all the notes were written on pages of MSI is clear when the page numbers are studied, and this correspondence is another means of identifying MSI as the first draft, 'The Saga', and the one Garnett read in December 1911.

Bromios (Dionysus) was familiar to Lawrence, who had been reading Gilbert Murray's translations of Euripides, including *The Bacchae*. Lawrence had written in MSI: 'Her life of life she gave to Bromios in mystical ritual. She had confused, for long enough, Siegmund with Bromios, her man with her God, as women will, until she cried aloud to Bromios and Siegmund had failed to answer, when she repulsed him.' When he rewrote the passage on a new page in MSII, Lawrence at first retained the allusion. 'She gave herself to Bromios. For some time she had confused Siegmund with her God. Yesterday, she had cried to Bromios and found only Siegmund.' In further revision of this page – perhaps after Garnett had reread it – Lawrence omitted 'Bromios', changing the first mention to 'her fancies only' and the second to 'her ideal lover'.[174] Lawrence may have accepted Garnett's opinion that the reference was 'too recondite', or (as in other revisions of MSII) he may have felt that it conflicted with the altered characterisation of his heroine.

A note in MSI to p. 367 reads: 'not so good[?], this imagery'. Lawrence responded by crossing out nearly a page and a half of extended images, replacing them with a few lines which appeared in the first edition, and thus eliminating approximately 135 words.[175] The most extensive note pertains to 'the "Stranger" piece'; both Garnett's note and the MSI version of this chapter (XIII) are given in an appendix.[176]

Generally, the pages that Lawrence did not re-use display a more extensive rewriting. Through the revision, changes both in style and in Lawrence's conception of the characters can be observed. Stylistic revisions were nearly always a matter of condensing description: many adjectives were removed. Collation of the uncorrected proofs and the text of the first edition reveals that this process continued: 121 adjectives were removed, and many adjectival phrases were eliminated as well. Although one cannot be completely certain, in the absence of corrected proofs, that Lawrence was entirely responsible for revisions appearing in the published text, the process of condensation in MSI and MSII strongly suggests that the final, more concise, form was his own.

The development of characterisation, which can be observed at all stages of revision, is most obvious in the heroine, whose name Lawrence changed in the second chapter of MSI from 'Helena' to 'Sieglinde' but then restored to 'Helena' in MSII. This may be indicative of his uncertainty about the heroine at the time he was writing 'The Saga'. Lawrence's original choice

[174] See below, pp. 144–5.
[175] See below, pp. 179: 40–180: 3.
[176] See below, pp. 319–23.

of 'Helena' was an obvious reference to Helen Corke.[177] When he introduced the name 'Sieglinde' in chapter II, he must have realised the confusion it might cause, and so in one one place he corrected 'Sieglinde' to read 'Helena-Sieglinde'.[178] This is the only appearance of the two names together; after this, with only a few exceptions, the heroine is referred to as 'Sieglinde'.[179] Perhaps Lawrence first intended that Siegmund should call the heroine 'Sieglinde', even though her name was 'Helena', just as Macartney occasionally used that nickname. Lawrence may have perceived that using two names for one character was an awkward device, and decided to use only 'Sieglinde'. But when he began MSII, he chose the name 'Helena' and used it consistently.[180] Lawrence when writing 'The Saga' may have liked the idea of his two main characters bearing the Wagnerian names but later when rewriting decided that the parallel was too mechanical, and conflicted with his view of the heroine. Helen Corke believed that the change back to 'Helena' reflected a decision to make the character 'more like the actual person' – that is, more like herself.[181]

Besides the change of name, there are revisions which, though not extensive, are significant for the characterisation of Helena. A study of MSII shows that Lawrence added the reference to Helena belonging to 'that class of "Dreaming Women", with whom passion exhausts itself at the mouth'.[182] This idea appeared in his 'Helen' poems, including 'Repulsed', and his letters. The main conscious focus of this interest is the 'Stranger' episode, especially as reworked in MSII.

There is also an important change between MSII and the first edition in a crucial passage. MSII reads

That night, she met his love with love as blazing as his own. They were not themselves, but transfigured ⟨into⟩ ⌜in⌝ pure, fiery ⟨love,⟩ ⌜passion⌝ ⟨for⟩ which

177 According to Helen Corke, DHL pronounced the name 'He-*lay*-na' (BBC interview 8/3). In earlier drafts of the poems 'Release' and 'Under The Oak', the name 'Helena' appears; it was replaced by 'Helen' in 'Release'. (The manuscripts of these poems are at the University of Nottingham.)

178 Since DHL made his dashes the same length as his hyphens and often placed them the same distance from the adjoining words, it is impossible to tell whether he intended to write a hyphenated name or to suggest indecision – his own or Siegmund's – by a pause-indicating dash.

179 She is addressed as 'Nellie', a nickname for Helen Corke which her family and friends used; 'Nell'; 'Nelly' (twice); and 'Helena' (thrice).

180 Pages transferred to MSII from MSI contain many examples where 'Sieglinde' remains uncorrected. The revision has been made in some places by an unidentified hand in MSII and in the rest by the printers (with one exception, see p. 56: 17). DHL's uncertainty about his heroine's name (apparent in both manuscripts) is accompanied by fairly frequent alteration of names among the minor characters, e.g. see note on 42: 28.

181 Helen Corke to the editor in conversation, 28 April 1977.

182 MSII, p. 60; see also note 81 above.

they themselves merely held located, like the burning bush. They far transcended their own beings. It was a wonderful night to achieve.[183]

This is a much more positive statement than the published version, which begins 'That night she met his passion with love.'[184] The revision was made in the proofs; so that the first edition text is consistent with the ultimate characterisation of Helena, where MSII is not. It is possible that Lawrence did not notice the inconsistency until he read the proofs, and he then made these very necessary changes. The distinction between Helena's reaction and Siegmund's is essential. Lawrence's perception of the character Helena as a sexually unresponsive woman was prompted by his personal experience, which gave him a new understanding of what the fictional Siegmund would have suffered.

Lawrence's revision produced, rather than eliminated, one instance in *The Trespasser* of what Hueffer might have called an 'erotic' passage. In MSI the wording was vague:

He covered her with his coats, and crushed her into his breast. He had borne for many months a dull, empty feeling on his chest; this had sometimes concentrated into a deep, almost unbearable pain, which he knew would never be healed till he pressed the bosom of Sieglinde into his. Now he strained her savagely to his breast, and she lay there hurt and stifled, but very willing ⟨that⟩ death should come that way, if it came at all. Siegmund remained perfectly still, his muscles set hard, holding Sieglinde. He was conscious of nothing, not even of Sieglinde. Siegmund did not exist, nor Sieglinde. It was just a burning bush, ⟨flaming⟩ ⌜passionate⌝ relief and joy flaming through their tissues.

Revising this passage in MSII, Lawrence began to use language more familiar to readers of his later works: 'his blood flushed up, and up again, with fire, till all Siegmund was hot blood, and his breast was one great ache', and 'at that moment, he was a tense, vivid body of flesh, without a mind; his blood, alive and conscious, running towards her'.[185] He made this revision despite his earlier concern over Hueffer's charge that the novel was 'erotic'; his new confidence may be the result of Garnett's encouragement. It seems that, with Garnett's support, Lawrence's sense of artistic integrity overcame his vulnerability to criticism; he wrote what he now believed had to be said, using the words that conveyed it most effectively. Already in his

183 The following transcription practices have been used in the introduction and in the explanatory notes: a first deleted reading is in single pointed brackets; a second deleted reading is given in double pointed brackets; and an addition is shown in half brackets thus: ⌜ ⌝. MSII, p. 115.

184 See above, p. 17, and below, p. 87.

185 MSI, p. 57; MSII, pp. 58–9, and below, p. 63.

second novel, Lawrence was moving towards language which would eventually become his hallmark.

Despite the extensive revision of detail, the manuscripts of *The Trespasser* show no substantial change in the structure of the novel. The text of MSI is similar in outline to that of MSII, and the chapter divisions come at approximately the same places in the action.

Selection of base-text

The absence of corrected proofs is the most significant factor in determining the selection of a base-text for *The Trespasser*. Without them, it is impossible to prove final authority of the first edition readings. A study of manuscripts is essential to the selection of the base-text and decisions about emendation. Any judgement about variant readings introduced between the final MSII and the first edition must take into account the directions in which Lawrence was moving during composition and revisions previous to proof-stage. There is external evidence that Lawrence corrected the proofs, and internal evidence (such as examples cited earlier) which strongly suggests that he revised phrases and passages at proof-stage. The considerable number of substantive errors in the proofs which reappear in the first edition suggest that, as was his usual practice, he did not check the proofs against his manuscript (MSII).[186]

The careful reader may be quite naturally concerned, however, at Lawrence's initial willingness to allow others to change what he had written, for instance Walter de la Mare in 1912 with the 'Schoolmaster' poems, and, notoriously, Edward Garnett with *Sons and Lovers*.[187] So we must consider the possibility that Garnett was responsible, at proof-stage, for changes in the published text of *The Trespasser*. Had he been given permission (as De la Mare was) to improve the text, or had he been permitted to cut it as he later did *Sons and Lovers*? There is no evidence that Lawrence gave Garnett blanket approval to alter proofs of *The Trespasser*.

A complete collation of MSII, the uncorrected proofs and the first edition reveals that nearly all accidental variants were introduced during typesetting. The standard followed for punctuation and spelling was a consistent house-style, which disregarded Lawrence's intention as expressed in the final revised manuscript. It is probable that Lawrence accepted these changes of necessity, and that any attempt he made to restore an original reading was

186 Among the more obvious errors were 101: 16, 113: 4; 146: 7; 163: 9; 210: 24; 215: 15.

187 *Letters*, i. 385, 481–2, 517.

overruled by Duckworth's proofreaders or even by Garnett himself, because there are very few instances of changes in punctuation between the proofs and the first edition.[188] The final manuscript (MSII) has therefore been chosen as base-text for accidentals, except for punctuation within emended wording, punctuation which has been affected by emended wording, and clearly inadvertent spelling errors by Lawrence. While using the final revised manuscript as base-text eliminates any punctuation changes Lawrence may have made on the proofs, more importantly it avoids reproducing the imposed house-styling.

The final revised MSII, however, should not be considered in every detail to represent Lawrence's final intention for substantives. To do so would be to proceed as if Lawrence had not corrected the proofs. To supply the first edition wording only as variant readings would eliminate revisions that he almost certainly made, ignoring his promise to 'wage war' on his adjectives; and it would restore errors in the manuscript, such as his failure to change the name 'Sieglinde' to 'Helena' at least thirty-five times. MSII is, therefore, emended to accord with the first edition in all substantive variants except where a compositor's error is apparent.[189] The intention of this edition is to reproduce the novel as Lawrence finally revised it for publication.

> But this is a work one can't regard easily – I mean, at one's ease. It is so much oneself, one's naked self. I give myself away so much, and write what is my most palpitant, sensitive self, that I loathe the book, because it will betray me to a parcel of fools...I wish the *Trespasser* were to be issued privately, to a few folk who had understanding. But I suppose, by all the rules of life, it must take open chance, if it's good enough.[190]

188 In the case of *The White Peacock*, where a corrected set of proofs survives, there is evidence of DHL's unwillingness to accept house-styling. He restored divisions within chapters, and rejected the house-style where it interfered too much, e.g. deleting a hyphen in the word 'tomorrow', altering double to single quotation marks around place names. (I am grateful to Mr Andrew Robertson for this information.)

189 E.g., the first edition reading at 41 : 31 corrects an obvious error in MSII, while the reading at 101 : 1 is clearly a misprint.

190 *Letters*, i. 353.

THE TRESPASSER

Note on the text

The base-text for this edition is the manuscript (MSII) from which the first edition was set, and which is now in the possession of the Bancroft Library, University of California at Berkeley. It has been emended to agree with the first edition text in all cases of variant wording except where noted otherwise in the textual apparatus.

The apparatus records all textual variants, except the following silent emendations:

1 Accidental omissions – such as incomplete quotation marks or a missing full stop – have been supplied.

2 DHL sometimes presented colloquial contractions without joining them up, e.g., 'would n't' and 'I' ve'; the compositors normally set these as 'wouldn't' and 'I've'. In all cases, this normalisation has been accepted or adopted.

3 Sometimes in MSII, a question mark or exclamation mark within a speech is followed by a comma, which DHL may have neglected to remove when adding the stronger mark of punctuation. His general practice was to supply a comma only where the speech did not have another end mark of punctuation. The excess commas in such cases have been deleted.

4 Where DHL neglected to change the name 'Sieglinde', the name 'Helena' has been supplied, as it was consistently in the proofs.

5 The first edition consistently printed: 'to-day', to-morrow', 'to-night' and 'good-bye', 'good-morning', 'good-night' (DHL wrote these as one unhyphenated word); 'apologize', 'economize', 'fertilize', 'realize', 'recognize', 'sympathize' and 'tyrannize' (DHL spelled these and their derivative forms with an 's'); hyphenated numbers (DHL wrote them as two words); 'Mr.' and 'Mrs.' (DHL wrote them without the full stop.) In all these instances, DHL's practice has been preserved.

6 Clearly inadvertent errors, made by DHL, e.g. 'expression of of fear' (216: 3) and obvious typesetter's errors, e.g. 'Seigmund' (103: 20) have not been recorded.

7 Omitted and misplaced apostrophes have been corrected. The apostrophe in 'o'clock' has been supplied.

8 DHL did not indicate the continuation of Siegmund's narratives (122: 29–124: 1 and 162: 16–37) by placing opening quotation marks before each paragraph, nor did he use single quotation marks to indicate other speakers within the first narrative. These conventions, supplied by the compositor, have been retained.

THE TRESPASSER

I

"Take off that mute, do!" cried Louisa,* snatching her fingers from the piano keys, and turning abruptly to the violinist. Helena* looked slowly from her music.

"My dear Louisa," she replied, "it would be simply unendurable." She stood tapping her white skirt with her bow in a kind of apathetic forbearance.

"But I can't understand it," cried Louisa, bouncing on her chair with the exaggeration of one who is indignant with a beloved. "It is only lately you would even submit to muting your violin. At one time you would have refused flatly, and no doubt about it."

"I have only lately submitted to many things," replied Helena, who seemed weary and stupefied, but still sententious. Louisa drooped from her bristling defiance.

"At any rate," she said, scolding in tones too naked with love, "I don't like it."

"Go on from 'Allegro'," said Helena, pointing with her bow to the place on Louisa's score of the Mozart sonata. Louisa obediently took the chords, and the music continued.

A young man, reclining in one of the wicker arm-chairs by the fire, turned luxuriously from the girls to watch the flames poise and dance with the music. He was evidently at his ease, yet he seemed a stranger in the room.

It was the sitting room of a mean house standing in line with hundreds of others of the same kind, along a wide road in South London. Now and again the trams hummed by, but the room was foreign to the trams, and to the sound of the London traffic. It was Helena's room, for which she was responsible. The walls were of the dead green colour of August foliage, the green carpet with its border of polished floor lay like a square of grass in a setting of black loam. Ceiling and frieze and fireplace were smooth white. There was no other colouring.

The furniture, excepting the piano, had a transitory look: two light wicker arm-chairs by the fire, the two frail stands of dark, polished wood, the couple of flimsy chairs, and the case of books in the recess, all seemed uneasy, as if they might be tossed out to leave the room clear, with its green floor and walls, and its white rim of skirting-board, serene.

On the mantel-piece were white lustres, and a small soap-stone Buddha from China, grey, impassive, locked in his renunciation. Besides these, two tablets of translucent stone, beautifully clouded with rose and blood, and carved with Chinese symbols; then a litter of mementoes, rock crystals and shells and scraps of sea-weed.*

A stranger, entering, felt at a loss. He looked at the bare wall-spaces of dark green, at the scanty furniture, and was assured of his unwelcome. The only objects of sympathy in the room were the white lamp that glowed on a stand near the wall, and the large, beautiful fern with narrow fronds, which ruffled its cloud of green within the gloom of the window bay. These only, with the fire, seemed friendly.

The three candles on the dark piano burned softly, the music fluttered on, but like numbed butterflies, stupidly. Helena played mechanically. She broke the music beneath her bow, so that it came lifeless, very hurting to hear. The young man frowned, and pondered. Uneasily, he turned again to the players.

The violinist was a girl of twenty eight. Her white dress, high-waisted, swung as she forced the rhythm, determinedly swaying to the time as if her body were the white stroke of a metronome. It made the young man frown as he watched. Yet he continued to watch. She had a very strong, vigorous body. Her neck, pure white, arched in strength from the fine hollow between her shoulders, as she held the violin. The long white lace of her sleeve swung, floated after the bow.

Byrne* could not see her face, more than the full curve of her cheek. He watched her hair, which at the back was almost of the colour of the soap-stone idol, take the candle light into its vigorous freedom in front, and glisten over her forehead.

Suddenly Helena broke off the music, and dropped her arm in irritable resignation. Louisa looked round from the piano, surprised.

"Why," she cried, "wasn't it all right?" Helena laughed wearily.

"It was all wrong," she answered, as she put her violin tenderly to rest.

"Oh, I'm sorry I did so badly," said Louisa in a huff. She loved Helena passionately.

"You didn't do badly at all," replied her friend, in the same tired, apathetic tone. "It was I."

When she had closed the black lid of her violin-case, Helena stood a moment as if at a loss. Louisa looked up with eyes full of affection, like a dog that did not dare to move to her beloved. Getting no response, she drooped over the piano. At length Helena looked at her friend, then slowly closed her eyes. The burden of this excessive affection was too much for her. Smiling faintly, she said, as if she were coaxing a child:

"Play some Chopin, Louisa."

"I shall only do that all wrong, like everything else," said the elder plaintively. Louisa was thirty five. She had been Helena's friend for years.

"Play the mazurkas," repeated Helena calmly.

Louisa rummaged among the music, Helena blew out her violin candle, and came to sit down on the side of the fire opposite to Byrne. The music began. Helena pressed her arms with her hands, musing.

"They are inflamed still!" said the young man.

She glanced up suddenly, her blue eyes, usually so heavy and tired, lighting up with a small smile.

"Yes," she answered, and she pushed back her sleeve, revealing a fine, strong arm which was scarlet on the outer side from shoulder to wrist, like some long red-burned fruit. The girl laid her cheek on the smarting, soft flesh, caressively.

"It is quite hot," she smiled, again caressing her sun-scalded arm, with peculiar joy.

"Funny to see a sunburn like that in mid-winter," he replied, frowning. "I can't think why it should last all these months. Don't you ever put anything on to heal it?"

She smiled at him again, almost pitying, then put her mouth lovingly on the burn.

"It comes out every evening like this," she said, softly, with curious joy.

"And that was August, and now it's February!" he exclaimed. "It must be psychological, you know. You make it come, the smart; you invoke it."

She looked up at him, suddenly cold.

"I! I never think of it," she answered, briefly, with a kind of sneer.

The young man's blood ran back from her at her acid tone. But the mortification was physical only. Smiling quickly, gently,

"Never?" he re-echoed.

There was silence between them for some moments, whilst Louisa continued to play the piano for their benefit. At last:

"Drat it!" she exclaimed, flouncing round on the piano-stool.

The two looked up at her.

"'Ye did run well—what hath hindered you?'"* laughed Byrne.

"You!" cried Louisa. "Oh I can't play any more," she added, dropping her arms along her skirt pathetically. Helena laughed quickly.

"Oh I can't, Helen!" pleaded Louisa.

"My dear," said Helena, laughing brief, "You are really under *no* obligation *whatever*."

With the little groan of one who yields to a desire contrary to her self-respect, Louisa dropped at the feet of Helena, laid her arm and her head languishingly on the knee of her friend. The latter gave no sign; but continued to gaze in the fire. Byrne, on the other side of the hearth, sprawled in his chair, smoking a reflective cigarette.

The room was very quiet, silent even of the tick of a clock. Outside, the traffic swept by, and feet pattered along the pavement. But this vulgar storm of life seemed shut out of Helena's room, that remained indifferent, like a church. Two candles burned dimly as on an altar, glistening yellow on the dark piano. The lamp was blown out, and the flameless fire, a red rubble, dwindled in the grate, so that the yellow glow of the candles seemed to shine even on the embers. Still no one spoke.

At last Helena shivered slightly in her chair, though did not change her position. She sat motionless.

"Will you make coffee, Louisa?" she asked. Louisa lifted herself, looked at her friend, and stretched slightly.

"Oh!" she groaned voluptuously. "This is so comfortable!"

"Don't trouble then, I'll go. No, don't get up," said Helena, trying to disengage herself. Louisa reached and put her hands on Helena's wrists.

"I will go," she drawled, almost groaning with voluptuousness and appealing love.

Then, as Helena still made movements to rise, the elder woman got up slowly, leaning as she did so all her weight on her friend.

"Where is the coffee?" she asked, affecting the dullness of lethargy. She was full of small affectations, being consumed with uneasy love.

"I think, my dear," replied Helena, "it is in its usual place."

"Oh—OO—Oh!" yawned Louisa, and she dragged herself out.

The two had been intimate friends for years, had slept together and played together and lived together. Now the friendship was coming to an end.

"After all," said Byrne, when the door was closed. "If you're alive you've got to live."

Helena burst into a titter of amusement at this sudden remark.

"Wherefore?" she asked indulgently.

"Because there's no such thing as passive existence," he replied, grinning.

She curled her lip in amused indulgence of this very young man.

"I don't see it at all," she said.

"You can't," he protested, "any more than a tree can help budding in April—it can't help itself, if it's alive; same with you."

"Well, then"—and again there was the touch of a sneer—"if I can't help myself, why trouble, my friend."

"Because—because I suppose *I* can't help myself—if it bothers me, it does. You see I"—he smiled brilliantly—"am April."

She paid very little attention to him, but began, in a peculiar reedy, metallic tone, that set his nerves quivering:

"But I am not a bare tree. All my dead leaves, they hang to me—and—and go through a kind of 'danse macabre'— —."

"But you bud underneath—like beech," he said quickly.

"Really, my friend," she said coldly. "I am too tired to bud."

"No," he pleaded. "No!" With his thick brows knitted, he surveyed her anxiously. She had received a great blow, in August, and she still was stunned. Her face, white and heavy, was like a mask, almost sullen. She looked in the fire, forgetting him.

"You want March," he said—he worried endlessly over her—"to rip off your old leaves. I s'll have to be March," he laughed.

She ignored him again, because of his presumption. He waited awhile, then broke out once more.

"You must start again—you must. Always you rustle your red leaves of a blasted summer. You are not dead. Even if you want to be, you're not. Even if it's a bitter thing to say, you have to say it: you are not dead..."

Smiling a peculiar, painful smile, as if he hurt her, she turned to gaze at a photograph that hung over the piano. It was the profile of a handsome man in the prime of life. He was leaning slightly forward, as if yielding beneath a burden of life, or to the pull of fate. He looked out musingly, and there was no hint of rebellion in the contours of the regular features. The hair was brushed back, soft and thick, straight from his fine brow. His nose was small and shapely, his chin rounded, cleft, rather beautifully moulded. Byrne gazed also at the photo. His look became distressed and helpless.

"You cannot say you are dead with Siegmund,"* he cried brutally. She shuddered, clasped her burning arms on her breast, and looked into the fire.

"You are not dead with Siegmund," he persisted, "so you can't say you live with him. You may live with his memory. But Siegmund is dead, and his memory is not he—himself." He made a fierce gesture of impatience. "Siegmund now—he is not a memory—he is not your dead red leaves—he is Siegmund Dead. And you do not know him, because you are alive, like me, so Siegmund Dead is a stranger to you."

With her head bowed down, cowering like a sulky animal, she looked at him under her brows. He stared fiercely back at her; but beneath her steady, glowering gaze, he shrank, then turned aside.

"You stretch your hands blindly to the dead; you look backwards. No, you never touch the living," he cried.

"I have the arms of Louisa always round my neck," came her voice, like the cry of a cat. She put her hands on her throat as if she must relieve an ache. He saw her lip raised in a kind of disgust, a revulsion from life. She was very sick, after the tragedy.

He frowned, and his eyes dilated.

"Folk are good, they are good for one. You never have looked at them. You would linger hours over a blue weed, and let all the people down the road go by. Folks are better than a garden in full blossom— —"

She watched him again. A certain beauty in his speech, and his passionate way, roused her when she did not want to be roused, when moving from her torpor was painful. At last

"You are merciless, you know, Cecil," she said.

"And I will be," protested Byrne, flinging his hand at her. She laughed softly, wearily.

For some time they were silent. She gazed once more at the photograph over the piano, and forgot all the present. Byrne, spent for the time being, was busy hunting for some life-interest to give her. He ignored the simplest, that of love, because he was even more faithful than she to the memory of Siegmund, and blinder than most, to his own heart.

"I do wish I had Siegmund's violin," she said, quietly, but with great intensity. Byrne glanced at her, then away. His heart beat sulkily. His sanguine, passionate spirit dropped and slouched under her contempt. He, also, felt the jar, heard the discord.* She made him, sometimes, pant with her own horror. He waited, full of hate and tasting of ashes, for the arrival of Louisa with the coffee.

II

Siegmund's violin, desired of Helena, lay in its case beside Siegmund's lean portmanteau, in the white dust of the lumber room, in Highgate. It was worth £20, but Beatrice* had not yet roused herself to sell it; she kept the black case out of sight.

Siegmund's violin lay in the dark, folded up as he had placed it for the last time, with hasty familiar hands, in its red silk shroud. After two dead months, the first string had snapped, sharply striking the sensitive body of the instrument. The second string had broken near Christmas, but no one had heard the faint moan of its going. The violin lay mute in the dark, a faint odour of must creeping over the smooth, soft wood. Its twisted, withered strings lay crisped from the anguish of breaking, smothered under the silk folds. The fragrance of Siegmund himself, with which the violin was steeped, slowly changed into an odour of must.

Siegmund died out even from his violin. He had infused it with his life, till its fibres had been as the tissue of his own flesh. Grasping his violin, he seemed to have his fingers on the strings of his heart, and of the heart of Helena. It was his little beloved, that drank his being, and turned it into music. And now Siegmund was dead, only an odour of must remained of him, in his violin.

It lay folded in silk in the dark, waiting. Six months before, it had longed for rest; during the last nights of the season,* when Siegmund's fingers had pressed too hard, when Siegmund's passion, and joy, and fear had hurt too the soft body of his little beloved, the violin had sickened for rest. On that last night of opera, without pity, Siegmund had struck the closing phrases from the fiddle, harsh in his impatience, wild in anticipation.

The curtain came down, the great singers bowed, and Siegmund felt the spattering roar of applause quicken his pulse. It was hoarse, and savage, and startling on his inflamed soul, making him shiver with anticipation, as if something had brushed his hot nakedness. Quickly, with hands of habitual tenderness, he put his violin away.

The theatre-goers were tired, and life drained rapidly out of the opera house. The members of the orchestra rose, laughing, mingling their weariness with good wishes for the holiday, with sly warning and suggestive advice, pressing hands warmly ere they disbanded. Other years, Siegmund had lingered, unwilling to take the long farewell of his associates of the orchestra. Other years, he had left the opera house with a little pain of regret. Now he laughed, and took his comrades' hands, and bade farewells, all distractedly, and with impatience. The theatre, awesome now in its emptiness, he left gladly, hastening like a flame stretched level on the wind.

With his black violin-case, he hurried down the street, then halted to pity the flowers massed pallid under the gas-light of the market-hall.* For himself, the sea and the sunlight opened great spaces, tomorrow. The moon was full above the river. He looked at it as a man in abstraction watches some clear thing, then he came to a standstill. It was useless to hurry to his train. The traffic swung past, the lamplight shone warm on all the golden faces, but Siegmund had already left the city. His face was silver and shadows to the moon; the river, in its soft grey, shaking golden sequins among the folds of its shadows, fell open like a garment before him, to reveal the white moonglitter brilliant as living flesh. Mechanically, overcast with the reality of the moonlight, he took his seat in the train and watched the moving of things. He was in a kind of trance, his consciousness seeming suspended. The train slid out amongst lights and dark places. Siegmund watched the endless movement, fascinated.

This was one of the crises of his life. For years, he had suppressed his soul, in a kind of mechanical despair doing his duty and enduring the rest. Then his soul had been softly enticed from its bondage. Now he was going to break free altogether, to have at least a few days purely for his own joy. This, to a man of his integrity, meant a breaking of bonds, a severing of blood ties, a sort of new birth. In the excitement of this last night his life passed out of his control, and he sat at the carriage window, motionless, watching things move.

He felt busy within him a strong activity which he could not help. Slowly, the body of his past, the womb which had nourished him in one fashion for so many years, was casting him forth.* He was trembling in all his being, though he knew not with what. All he could do now, was to watch the lights go by, and to let the translation of himself continue.

When at last the train ran out into the full, luminous night, and Siegmund saw the meadows deep in moonlight, he quivered with a low anticipation. The elms, great grey shadows, seemed to loiter in their cloaks across the pale fields. He had not seen them so before. The world was changing.

The train stopped, and with a little effort, he rose to go home. The night air was cool and sweet. He drank it thirstily. In the road, again he lifted his face to the moon. It seemed to help him; in its brilliance amid the blonde heavens, it seemed to transcend fretfulness. It would front the waves with silver as they slid to the shore, and Helena, looking along the coast, waiting, would lift her white hands with sudden joy. He laughed, and the moon hurried laughing alongside, through the black masses of the trees.

He had forgotten he was going home for this night. The chill wetness of his little white garden gate reminded him, and a frown came on his face. As he closed the door, and found himself in the darkness of the hall, the sense of his fatigue came fully upon him. It was an effort to go to bed. Nevertheless, he went very quietly into the drawing room. There the moonlight entered, and he thought the whiteness was Helena. He held his breath and stiffened, then breathed again. "Tomorrow," he thought, as he laid his violin-case across the arms of a wicker chair. But he had a physical feeling of the presence of Helena: in his shoulders he seemed to be aware of her. Quickly, half lifting his arms, he turned to the moonshine.—"Tomorrow!" he exclaimed quietly, and he left the room, stealthily, for fear of disturbing the children.

In the darkness of the kitchen burned a blue bud of light. He quickly turned up the gas to a broad, yellow flame, and sat down at table. He was tired, excited, and vexed with misgiving. As he lay in his arm-chair he looked round with disgust.

The table was spread with a dirty cloth, that had great brown stains betokening children. In front of him was a cup and saucer, and a small plate with a knife laid across it. The cheese, on another plate, was wrapped in a red-bordered fringed cloth, to keep off the flies, which even then were crawling round, on the sugar, on the loaf, on the cocoa tin. Siegmund looked at his cup. It was chipped, and a stain had gone under the glaze, so that it looked like the mark of a dirty mouth. He fetched a glass of water.

The room was drab and dreary. The oilcloth was worn into a hole near the door. Boots and shoes of various sizes were scattered over the floor, while the sofa was littered with children's clothing. In the black stove the ash lay dead; on the range were chips of wood, and newspapers, and rubbish of paper, and crusts of bread, and crusts of bread-and-jam. As Siegmund walked across the floor, he crushed two sweets underfoot. He had to grope under sofa and dresser, to find his slippers: and he was in evening dress.

It would be the same, while ever Beatrice was Beatrice, and Siegmund her husband. He ate his bread and cheese mechanically, wondering why he was miserable, why he was not looking forward with joy, to the morrow. As he ate, he closed his eyes, half wishing he had not promised Helena, half wishing he had no tomorrow.

Leaning back in his chair, he felt something in the way. It was a small teddy-bear, and half of a strong white comb. He grinned to himself. This was the summary of his domestic life: a broken, coarse comb, a child crying because her hair was tugged, a wife who had let the hair go till now, when she had got into a temper to see the job through; and then the teddy-bear, pathetically cocking a black worsted nose, and lifting absurd arms to him.

He wondered why Gwen had gone to bed without her pet. She would want the silly thing. The strong feeling of affection for his children came over him, battling with something else. He sank in his chair, and gradually his baffled mind went dark. He sat, overcome with weariness and trouble, staring blankly into the space. His own stifling roused him. Straightening his shoulders, he took a deep breath, then relaxed again. After a while he rose, took the teddy-bear, and went slowly to bed.

Gwen and Marjory, aged nine and twelve,* slept together in a small room. It was fairly light. He saw his favorite daughter lying quite uncovered, her wilful head thrown back, her mouth half open. Her black hair was tossed across the pillow: he could see the action. Marjory snuggled under the sheet. He placed the teddy-bear between the two girls.

As he watched them, he hated the children, for being so dear to him. Either he himself must go under, and drag on an existence he hated, or they must suffer. But he had agreed to spend this holiday with Helena, and meant to do so. As he turned, he saw himself like a ghost cross the mirror. He looked back; he peered at himself. His hair still grew thick and dark from his brow: he could not see the grey at the temples. His eyes were dark and tender, and his mouth, under the black moustache, was full with youth.

He rose, looked at the children, frowned, and went to his own small room. He was glad to be shut alone in the little cubicle of darkness.

Outside the world lay in a glamourous pallor, casting shadows that made the farm, the trees, the bulks of villas, look like live creatures. The same pallor went through all the night, glistening on Helena as she lay curled up asleep at the core of the glamour, like the moon; on the sea rocking backwards and forwards till it rocked her island as she slept. She was so calm, and full of her own assurance. It was a great rest to be with her. With her, nothing mattered but love, and the beauty of things. He felt parched and starving. She had rest and love, like water and manna for him. She was so strong in her self-possession, in her love of beautiful things, and of dreams.

The clock downstairs struck two.

"I must get to sleep," he said.

He dragged his portmanteau from beneath the bed, and began to pack it. When at last it was finished, he shut it with a snap. The click sounded final. He stood up, stretched himself, and sighed.

"I am fearfully tired," he said.

But that was persuasive. When he was undressed, he sat in his pyjamas for some time, rapidly beating his fingers on his knee.

"Thirty eight years old," he said to himself. "And disconsolate as a child!" He began to muse of the morrow.

When he seemed to be going to sleep, he woke up to find thoughts labouring over his brain like bees on a hive. Recollections, swift thoughts flew in and alighted upon him as wild geese swing down and take possession of a pond. Phrases from the opera tyrannised over him, he played the rhythm with all his blood. As he turned over this torture, he sighed, and recognised a movement of the de Beriot concerto* which Helena had played for her last lesson. He found himself watching her as he had watched then, felt again the wild impatience when she was wrong, started again as, amid the dipping and sliding of her bow, he realised where his thoughts were going. She was wrong, he was hasty, and he felt her blue eyes looking intently at him.

Both started as his daughter Vera entered suddenly. She was a handsome girl of nineteen. Crossing the room, brushing Helena as if she were a piece of furniture in the way, Vera had asked her father a question, in a hard, insulting tone, then had gone out again, just as if Helena had not been in the room.

Helena stood fingering the score of "Pelléas."* When Vera had gone, she asked, in the peculiar tone that made Siegmund shiver:

"Why do you consider the music of 'Pelléas' cold?"

Siegmund had struggled to answer. So they passed everything off, without mention, after Helena's fashion ignoring all that might be humiliating—and to her, much was humiliating.

For years she had come as pupil to Siegmund, first as a friend of the household. Then, she and Louisa went occasionally to whatever hall or theatre had Siegmund in the orchestra, so that shortly the three formed the habit of coming home together. Then Helena had invited Siegmund to her home: then the three friends went walks together: then the two went walks together, whilst Louisa sheltered them.

Helena had come to read his loneliness and the humiliation of his lot. He had felt her blue eyes, heavily, steadily gazing into his soul, and he had lost himself to her.

That day, three weeks before the end of the season, when Vera had so insulted Helena, the latter had said, as she put on her coat, looking at him all the while with heavy blue eyes, "I think, Siegmund, I cannot come here any more. Your home is not open to me any longer." He had writhed in confusion and humiliation. As she pressed his hand, closely and for a long time, she said: "I will write to you." Then she left him.

Siegmund had hated his life that day. Soon she wrote. A week later, when he lay resting his head on her lap, in Richmond Park, she said:

"You are so tired, Siegmund." She stroked his face, and kissed him softly. Siegmund lay in the molten daze of love. But Helena was, if it is not to debase the word, virtuous: an inconsistent virtue, cruel and ugly for Siegmund.

"You are so tired, dear. You must come away with me and rest, the first week in August."

His blood had leapt, and whatever objections he raised, such as having no money, he allowed to be overridden. He was going to Helena, to the Isle of Wight,* tomorrow.

Helena, with her blue eyes so full of storm, like the sea, but, also like the sea, so eternally self-sufficient, solitary; with her thick white throat, the strongest and most wonderful thing on earth, and her small hands, silken and light as wind-flowers, would be his tomorrow, along with the sea and the downs. He clung to the exquisite flame which flooded him....

But it died out, and he thought of the return to London, to Beatrice, and the children. How would it be? Beatrice, with her furious dark eyes, and her black hair loosely knotted back, came to his mind as she had been the previous day, flaring with temper when he said to her:

"I shall be going away tomorrow for a few days' holiday."

She asked for detail, some of which he gave. Then, dissatisfied and inflamed, she broke forth in her suspicion and her abuse, and her contempt, while two large-eyed children stood listening by. Siegmund hated his wife, for drawing on him the grave, cold looks of condemnation from his children.

Something he had said touched Beatrice. She came of good family, had been brought up like a lady, educated in a convent school in France. He evoked her old pride. She drew herself up with dignity, and called the children away. He wondered if he could bear a repetition of that degradation. It bled him of his courage and self-respect.

In the morning Beatrice was disturbed by the sharp sneck* of the hall door. Immediately awake, she heard his quick, firm step hastening down the gravel path. In her impotence, discarded like a worn-out object, she lay for the moment stiff with bitterness.

"I am nothing, I am nothing," she said to herself. She lay quite rigid for a time.

There was no sound anywhere. The morning sunlight pierced vividly through the slits of the blind. Beatrice lay rocking herself, breathing hard, her finger nails pressing into her palm. Then came the sound of a train slowing down in the station, and directly the quick chuff-chuff-chuff of its drawing out. Beatrice imagined the sunlight on the puffs of steam, and the two lovers, her husband and Helena, rushing through the miles of morning sunshine.

"God strike her dead—Mother of God, strike her down," she said aloud, in a low tone. She hated Helena.

Irene, who lay with her mother, woke up and began to question her.

III

In the miles of morning sunshine, Siegmund's shadows, his children, Beatrice, his sorrow, dissipated like mist, and he was elated as a young man setting forth to travel. When he had passed Portsmouth Town, everything had vanished but the old gay world of romance. He laughed as he looked out the carriage window.

Below, in the street, a military band passed glittering. A brave sound floated up, and again he laughed, loving the tune, the clash and glitter of the band, the movement of scarlet, blithe soldiers beyond the park. People were drifting brightly from church. How could it be Sunday! It was no time, it was Romance, going back to Tristan.*

Women, like crocus flowers in white and blue and lavender, moved gaily. Everywhere fluttered the small flags of holiday. Every form danced lightly in the sunshine.

And beyond it all, were the silent hillsides of the island, with Helena. It was so wonderful, he could bear to be patient. She would be all in white, with her cool, thick throat left bare to the breeze, her face shining, smiling as she dipped her head because of the sun, which glistened on her uncovered hair.

He breathed deeply, stirring at the thought. But he would not grow impatient. The train had halted over the town, where scarlet soldiers, and ludicrous blue sailors, and all the brilliant women from church shook like a kaleidoscope down the street. The train crawled on, drawing near to the sea, for which Siegmund waited breathless. It was so like Helena, blue, beautiful, strong in its reserve.

Another moment, they were in the dirty station. Then the day flashed out, and Siegmund mated with joy. He felt the sea heaving below him. He looked round, and the sea was blue as a periwinkle flower, while gold and white and blood-red sails lit here and there upon its blueness. Standing on the deck, he gave himself to the breeze and to the sea, feeling like one of the ruddy sails, as if he were part of it all. All his body radiated amid the large, magnificent sea noon like a piece of colour.

The little ship began to pulse, to tremble. White, with the softness of a bosom, the water rose up frothing and swaying gently. Ships drew near like inquisitive birds: the old "Victory" shook her myriad pointed flags of yellow and scarlet:* the straight old houses of the quay passed by.

Outside the harbour, like fierce creatures of the sea come wildly up to look, the battle-ships* laid their black snouts on the water. Siegmund laughed at them. He felt the foam on his face like a sparkling, felt the blue sea gathering round.

On the left stood the round fortress,* quaintly chequered, and solidly alone in the walk of water, amid the silent flight of the golden and crimson winged boats.

Siegmund watched the bluish bulk of the island. Like the beautiful women in the myths, his love hid in its blue haze. It seemed impossible. Behind him, the white wake trailed myriads of daisies. On either hand the grim and wicked battle-ships watched along their sharp noses. Beneath him the clear green water swung and puckered as if it were laughing. In front, Sieglinde's island* drew near, and nearer, creeping towards him, bringing him Helena.

Meadows and woods appeared, houses crowded down to the shore to meet him, he was in the quay, and the ride was over. Siegmund regretted it. But Helena was on the island, which rode like an anchored ship under the fleets of cloud that had launched whilst Siegmund was on water. As he watched the end of the pier loom higher, large ponderous trains of cloud cast over him the shadows of their bulk, and he shivered in the chill wind.

His travelling was very slow. The sky's dark shipping pressed closer and closer, as if all the clouds had come to harbour. Over the flat lands near Newport, the wind moaned like the calling of many violoncellos. All the sky was grey. Siegmund waited drearily on Newport station, where the wind swept coldly. It was Sunday, and the station and the Island were desolate, having lost their purposes.

Siegmund put on his overcoat and sat down. All his morning's blaze of elation was gone, though there still glowed a great hope. He had slept only two hours of the night. An empty man, he had drunk joy, and now the intoxication was dying out.

At three o'clock of the afternoon, he sat alone in the second-class carriage, looking out. A few raindrops struck the pane, then the blurred dazzle of a shower came in a burst of wind, and hid the downs and the reeds that shivered in the marshy places. Siegmund sat in a chilly torpor. He counted the stations. Beneath his stupor his heart was thudding heavily with excitement, surprising him, for his brain felt dead.

The train slowed down: Yarmouth! One more station then! Siegmund watched the platform, shiny with rain, slide past. On the dry grey under the shelter, one white passenger was waiting. Suddenly Siegmund's heart leaped up, wrenching wildly. He burst open the door, and caught hold of Helena. She dilated, gave a palpitating cry as he dragged her into the carriage.

"You *here*!" he exclaimed, in a strange tone. She was shivering with cold. Her almost naked arms were blue. She could not answer Siegmund's question, but lay clasped against him, shivering away her last chill as his warmth invaded her. He laughed in his heart as she nestled in to him.

"Is it a dream now, dear?" he whispered. Helena clasped him tightly, shuddering because of the delicious suffusing of his warmth through her.

Almost immediately they heard the grinding of the brakes.

"Here we are then!" exclaimed Helena, dropping into her conventional, cheerful manner at once. She put straight her hat while he gathered his luggage.

Until teatime, there was a pause in their progress. Siegmund was tingling with an exquisite vividness, as if he had taken some rare stimulant. He wondered at himself. It seemed that every fibre in his body was surprised with joy, as each tree in a forest at dawn utters astonished cries of delight.

When Helena came back, she sat opposite to him, to see him. His naïve look of joy was very sweet to her. His eyes were dark blue, showing the fibrils, like a purple veined flower at twilight, and somehow, mysteriously, joy seemed to quiver in the iris. Helena appreciated him, feature by feature. She liked his clear forehead with its thick, black hair, and his full mouth, and his chin. She loved his hands, that were small, but strong and nervous, and very white. She liked his breast, that breathed so strong and quietly, and his arms, and his thighs, and his knees.

For him, Helena was a presence. She was ambushed, fused in an aura of his love. He only saw she was white and strong and full fruited, he only knew her blue eyes were rather awful to him.

Outside, the sea-mist was travelling thicker and thicker inland. Their lodging was not far from the bay. As they sat together at tea, Siegmund's eyes dilated, and he looked frowning at Helena.

"What is it?" he asked, listening uneasily.

Helena looked up at him, from pouring out the tea. His little anxious look of distress amused her.

"The noise, you mean?—Merely the fog horn, dear,—not Wotan's wrath, nor Siegfried's dragon..."*

The fog was white at the window. They sat waiting. After a few seconds the sound came low, swelling, like the mooing of some great sea-animal, alone, the last of the monsters. The whole fog gave off the sound for a second or two, then it died down into an intense silence. Siegmund and Helena looked at each other. His eyes were full of trouble. To see a big, strong man anxious-eyed as a child because of a strange sound, amused her. But he was tired.

"I assure you, it *is* only a fog horn," she laughed.

"Of course. But it is a depressing sort of sound."

"Is it?" she said curiously. "Why? Well—yes—I think I can understand it's being so to some people. It's something like the call of the horn across the sea to Tristan."*

She hummed softly—then three times she sang the horn call. Siegmund, with his face expressionless as a mask, sat staring out at the mist. The boom of the siren broke in upon them. To him, the sound was full of fatality. Helena waited till the noise died down, then she repeated her horn call.

"Yet, it is very much like the fog horn," she said, curiously interested.

"This time next week, Helena!" he said.

She suddenly went heavy, and stretched across to clasp his hand as it lay upon the table.

"I shall be calling to you from Cornwall," she said.

He did not reply. So often, she did not take his meaning, but left him alone with his sense of tragedy. She had no idea how his life was wrenched from its roots, and when he tried to tell her, she balked him, leaving him inwardly, quite lonely.

"There is *no* next week," she declared, with great cheerfulness. "There is only the present." At the same moment, she rose, and slipped across to him. Putting her arms round his neck, she stood holding his head to her bosom, pressing it close, with her hand among his hair. His nostrils and mouth were crushed against her breast. He smelled the silk of her dress, and the faint, intoxicating odour of her person. With shut eyes, he owned heavily to himself again that she was blind to him. But some other self urged with gladness, no matter how blind she was, so that she pressed his face upon her.

She stroked and caressed his hair, tremblingly clasped his head against her breast as if she would never release him; then she bent to kiss his forehead. He took her in his arms, and they were still for awhile.

Now he wanted to blind himself with her, to blaze up all his past and future in a passion worth years of living.

After tea, they rested by the fire, while she told him all the delightful things she had found. She had a woman's curious passion for details, a woman's peculiar attachment to certain dear trifles. He listened, smiling, revived by her delight, and forgetful of himself. She soothed him like sunshine, and filled him with pleasure; but he hardly attended to her words.

"Shall we go out, or are you too tired?—No, you are tired, you are very tired," said Helena.

She stood by his chair, looking down on him tenderly.

"No," he replied, smiling brilliantly at her, and stretching his handsome limbs in relief. "No, not at all tired now."

Helena continued to look down on him in quiet, covering tenderness. But she quailed before the brilliant, questioning gaze of his eyes.

"You must go to bed early tonight," she said, turning aside her face, ruffling his soft, black hair. He stretched slightly, stiffening his arms, and smiled without answering. It was a very keen pleasure to be thus alone with her, and in her charge. He rose, bidding her wrap herself up against the fog.

"You are sure you're not too tired?" she reiterated.

He laughed.

Outside, the sea-mist was white and woolly. They went hand in hand. It was cold, so she thrust her hand with his into the pocket of his overcoat, while they walked together.

"I like the mist," he said, pressing her hand in his pocket.

"I don't dislike it," she replied, shrinking nearer to him.

"It puts us together, by ourselves," he said. She plodded alongside, bowing her head, not replying. He did not mind her silence.

"It couldn't have happened better for us, than this mist," he said.

She laughed curiously, almost with a sound of tears.

"Why?" She asked, half tenderly, half bitterly.

"There is nothing else but you, and for you there is nothing else but me—look!" He stood still. They were on the downs,* so that

Helena found herself quite alone with the man, in a world of mist. Suddenly, she flung herself sobbing against his breast. He held her closely, tenderly, not knowing what it was all about, but happy and unafraid.

In one hollow place, the siren from the Needles* seemed to bellow full in their ears. Both Siegmund and Helena felt their emotion too intense. They turned from it.

"What is the pitch?" asked Helena.

"Where it is horizontal?—It slides up a chromatic scale—" said Siegmund.

"Yes, but the settled pitch—is it about E?"

"E!" exclaimed Siegmund. "More like F."

"Nay, listen!" said Helena.

They stood still and waited till there came the long booing of the fog horn.

"There!" exclaimed Siegmund, imitating the sound. "That is not E." He repeated the sound. "It is F."

"Surely it is E," persisted Helena.

"Even F♯," he rejoined, humming the note.

She laughed, and told him to climb the chromatic scale.

"But you agree?" he said.

"I do not," she replied.

The fog was cold. It seemed to rob them of their courage to talk.

"What is the note in 'Tristan'?"* Helena made an effort to ask.

"That is not the same," he replied.

"No, dear, that is not the same," she said, in low, comforting tones. He quivered at the caress. She put her arms round him, reached up her face yearningly for a kiss. He forgot they were standing in the public footpath, in daylight, till she drew hastily away. She heard footsteps down the fog.

As they climbed the path the mist grew thinner, till it was only a grey haze at the top. There they were on the turfy lip of the land. The sky was fairly clear overhead. Below them the sea was singing hoarsely to itself.

Helena drew him to the edge of the cliff. He crushed her hand, drawing slightly back. But it pleased her to feel the grip on her hand becoming unbearable. They stood right on the edge, to see the smooth cliff slope into the mist, under which the sea stirred noisily.

"Shall we walk over, then?" said Siegmund, glancing downwards. Helena's heart stood still a moment at the idea, then beat heavily. How could he play with the idea of death, and the five great days in front! She was afraid of him just then.

"Come away, dear," she pleaded.

He would, then, forego the few consummate days! It was bitterness to her to think so.

"Come away, dear!" she repeated, drawing him slowly to the path.

"You are not afraid?" he asked.

"Not afraid, no..." Her voice had that peculiar, reedy, harsh quality that made him shiver.

"It is too easy a way," he said, satirically. She did not take in his meaning.

"And five days of our own before us, Siegmund!" she scolded. "The mist is Lethe. It is enough for us if its spell lasts five days."

He laughed, and took her in his arms, kissing her very closely.

They walked on joyfully, locking behind them the doors of forgetfulness.

As the sun set, the fog dispersed a little. Breaking masses of mist went flying from cliff to cliff, and far away beyond the cliffs the western sky stood dimmed with gold. The lovers wandered aimlessly over the golflinks to where green mounds and turfed banks suggested to Helena that she was tired and would sit down. They faced the lighted chamber of the west, whence, behind the torn, dull-gold curtains of fog, the sun was departing with pomp.

Siegmund sat very still, watching the sunset. It was a splendid, flaming bridal chamber where he had come to Helena.* He wondered how to express it; how other men had borne this same glory.

"What is the music of it?" he asked. She glanced at him. His eyelids were half lowered, his mouth slightly open, as if in ironic rhapsody.

"Of what, dear?"

"What music do you think holds the best interpretation of sunset?"

His skin was gold, his real mood was intense. She revered him for a moment.

"I do not know," she said quietly; and she rested her head against his shoulder, looking out west.

There was a space of silence, while Siegmund dreamed on.

"A Beethoven symphony—the one— —" and he explained to her.

She was not satisfied, but leaned against him, making her choice. The sunset hung steady—she could scarcely perceive a change.

"The Grail music, in 'Lohengrin'—"* she decided.

"Yes," said Siegmund. He found it quite otherwise, but did not trouble to dispute. He dreamed by himself. This displeased her. She wanted him for herself. How could he leave her alone while he watched the sky! She almost put her two hands over his eyes.

IV

The gold march of sunset passed quickly, the ragged curtains of mist closed to. Soon Siegmund and Helena were shut alone within the dense, wide fog. She shivered with the cold and the damp. Startled, he took her in his arms, where she lay and clung to him. Holding her closely, he bent forward, straight to her lips. His moustache was drenched cold with fog, so that she shuddered slightly after his kiss, and shuddered again. He did not know why the strong tremor passed though her. Thinking it was with fear and with cold, he undid his overcoat, put her close on his breast, and covered her as best he could. That she feared him at that moment was half pleasure, half shame to him. Pleadingly, he hid his face on her shoulder, held her very tightly, till his face grew hot, buried against her soft, strong throat.

"You are so big, I can't hold you," she whispered, plaintively, catching her breath with fear. Her small hands grasped at the breadth of his shoulders ineffectually.

"You will be cold. Put your hands under my coat," he whispered.

He put her inside his overcoat and his coat. She came to his warm breast with a sharp intaking of delight and fear; she tried to make her hands meet in the warmth of his shoulders, tried to clasp him.

"See, I can't," she whispered.

He laughed short, and pressed her closer.

Then, tucking her head in his breast, hiding her face, she timidly slid her hands along his sides, pressing softly, to find the contours of his figure. Softly her hands crept over the silky back of his waistcoat, under his coats, and as they stirred, his blood flushed up, and up again, with fire, till all Siegmund was hot blood, and his breast was one great ache.

He crushed her to him, crushed her in upon the ache of his chest. His muscles set hard and unyielding; at that moment he was a tense, vivid body of flesh, without a mind; his blood, alive and conscious, running towards her. He remained perfectly still, locked about Helena, conscious of nothing.

She was hurt and crushed, but it was pain delicious to her. It was marvellous to her, how strong he was, to keep up that grip of her like steel. She swooned in a kind of intense bliss. At length she found herself released, taking a great breath, while Siegmund was moving his mouth over her throat, something like a dog snuffing her, but with his lips. Her heart leaped away in revulsion. His moustache thrilled her strangely. His lips, brushing and pressing her throat beneath the ear, and his warm breath flying rhythmically upon her, made her vibrate through all her body. Like a violin under the bow, she thrilled beneath his mouth, and shuddered from his moustache. Her heart was like fire in her breast.

Suddenly she strained madly to him, and, drawing back her head, placed her lips on his, close, till at the mouth they seemed to melt and fuse together. It was the long, supreme kiss, in which man and woman have one being, Two-in-one, the only Hermaphrodite.*

When Helena drew away her lips, she was exhausted. She belonged to that class of 'Dreaming Women',* with whom passion exhausts itself at the mouth. Her desire was accomplished in a real kiss. The fire, in heavy flames, had poured through her to Siegmund, from Siegmund to her. It sank, and she felt herself flagging. She had not the man's brightness and vividness of blood. She lay upon his breast dreaming how beautiful it would be to go to sleep, to swoon unconscious there, on that rare bed. She lay still on Siegmund's breast, listening to his heavily-beating heart.

With her, the dream was always more than the actuality. Her dream of Siegmund was more to her than Siegmund himself. He might be less than her dream—which is as it may be. However, to the real man she was very cruel.

He held her close. His dream was melted in his blood, and his blood ran bright for her. His dreams were the flowers of his blood. Hers were more detached and inhuman. For centuries, a certain type of woman has been rejecting the 'animal' in humanity, till now her dreams are abstract, and full of fantasy, and her blood runs in bondage, and her kindness is full of cruelty.

Helena lay flagging upon the breast of Siegmund. He folded her closely, and his mouth and his breath were warm on her neck. She sank away from his caresses, passively, subtly drew back from him. He was far too sensitive not to be aware of this, and far too much of a man not to yield to the woman. His heart sank, his blood grew sullen at her withdrawal. Still he held her; the two were motionless and silent for some time.

She became distressedly conscious that her feet, which lay on the wet grass, were aching with cold. She said softly, gently, as if he was her child whom she must correct and lead:

"I think we ought to go home, Siegmund." He made a small sound, that might mean anything, but did not stir or release her. His mouth, however, remained motionless on her throat, and the caress went out of it.

"It is cold and wet, dear, we ought to go," she coaxed, determinedly.

"Soon," he said thickly.

She sighed, waited a moment, then said very gently, as if she were loth to take him from his pleasure:

"Siegmund, I am cold."

There was a reproach in this which angered him.

"Cold!" he exclaimed. "But you are warm with me— —"

"But my feet are out on the grass, dear, and they are like wet pebbles."

"Oh dear!" he said. "Why didn't you give them me to warm?" He leaned forward and put his hand on her shoes.

"They are very cold," he said. "We must hurry and make them warm."

When they rose, her feet were so numbed she could hardly stand. She clung to Siegmund laughing.

"I wish you had told me before," he said, "I ought to have known..."

Vexed with himself, he put his arm round her and they set off home.

V

They found the fire burning brightly in their room. The only other person in the pretty, stiffly-furnished cottage, was their landlady, a charming old lady who let this sitting room more for the change, for the sake of having visitors, than for gain.

Helena introduced Siegmund as "My friend." The old lady smiled upon him. He was big, and good looking, and embarrassed. She had had a son years back...And the two were lovers. She hoped they would come to her house for their honeymoon.

Siegmund sat in his great horse-hair chair by the fire, while Helena attended to the lamp. Glancing at him over the glowing globe, she found him watching her with a small, peculiar smile, of irony, and anger, and bewilderment. He was not quite himself. Her hand trembled so, she could scarcely adjust the wicks.

Helena left the room to change her dress. "I shall be back before Mrs Curtiss brings in the tray. There is the Nietzsche* I brought— —."

He did not answer, as he watched her go. Left alone, he sat with his arms along his knees, perfectly still. His heart beat heavily, and all his being felt sullen, watchful, aloof, like a balked animal. Thoughts came up in his brain like bubbles, random, hissing out aimlessly. Once, in the startling inflammability of his blood, his veins ran hot, and he smiled.

When Helena entered the room his eyes sought hers swiftly, as sparks lighting on the tinder. But her eyes were only moist with tenderness. His look instantly changed. She wondered at his being so silent, so strange.

Coming to him in her unhesitating, womanly way—she was only twenty six to his thirty eight—she stood before him holding both his hands and looking down on him with almost gloomy tenderness. She wore a white dress that showed her throat gathering like a fountain-jet of solid foam to balance her head. He could see the full white arms passing clear through the dripping spume of lace, towards the rise of her breasts. But her eyes bent down upon him with such gloom of tenderness, that he dared not reveal the passion burning in him. He could not look at her. He strove almost pitifully to be with her sad, tender, but he could not put out his fire. She held both his hands firm, pressing them in appeal for her dream love. He glanced at her wistfully, then turned away. She waited for him. She wanted his caresses and tenderness. He would not look at her.

"You would like supper now, dear?" she asked, looking where the dark hair ended, and his neck ran smooth, under his collar, to the strong setting of his shoulders.

"Just as you will," he replied.

Still she waited, and still he would not look at her. Something troubled him, she thought. He was foreign to her.

"I will spread the cloth then," she said, in deep tones of resignation. She pressed his hands closely, and let them drop. He took no notice, but, still with his arms on his knees, he stared into the fire.

In the golden glow of lamp-light she set small bowls of white and lavender sweet peas, and mignonette, upon the round table. He watched her moving, saw the stir of her white, sloping shoulders, under the lace, and the hollow of her shoulders firm as marble, and the slight rise and fall of her loins as she walked. He felt as if his breast were scalded. It was a physical pain to him.

Supper was very quiet. Helena was sad and gentle, he had a peculiar, enigmatic look in his eyes, between suffering and mockery and love. He was quite intractable; he would not soften to her, but remained there aloof. He was tired, and the look of weariness and suffering was evident to her through his strangeness. In her heart she wept.

At last she tinkled the bell for supper to be cleared. Meanwhile, restlessly, she played fragments of Wagner on the piano.

"Will you want anything else?" asked the smiling old landlady.

"Nothing at all, thanks," said Helena, with decision.

"Oh! Then I think I will go to bed when I've washed the dishes. You will put the lamp out dear?"

"I am well used to a lamp," smiled Helena. "We use them always at home."

She had had a day before Siegmund's coming in which to win Mrs Curtiss' heart, and she had been successful. The old lady took the tray.

"Goodnight dear—Goodnight Sir. I will leave you. You will not be long, dear?"

"No, we shall not be long. Mr MacNair* is very evidently tired out."

"Yes—yes. It is very tiring, London."

When the door was closed, Helena stood a moment undecided, looking at Siegmund. He was lying in his arm-chair in a dispirited way, and looking in the fire. As she gazed at him with troubled eyes, he happened to glance to her, with the same dark, curiously searching, disappointed eyes.

"Shall I read to you?" she asked, bitterly.

"If you will," he replied.

He sounded so indifferent, she could scarcely refrain from crying. She went and stood in front of him, looking down on him heavily.

"What is it, dear?" she said.

"You," he replied, smiling with a little grimace.

"Why me?"

He smiled at her ironically, then closed his eyes. She slid into his arms with a little moan. He took her on his knee, where she curled up like a heavy white cat. She let him caress her with his mouth, and did not move, but lay there curled up and quiet and luxuriously warm.

He kissed her hair, which was beautifully fragrant of itself, and time after time, drew between his lips one long, keen thread, as if he would ravel out with his mouth her vigorous confusion of hair. His tenderness of love was like a soft flame lapping her voluptuously.

After a while they heard the old lady go upstairs. Helena went very still, and seemed to contract. Siegmund himself hesitated in his love-making. All was very quiet. They could hear a faint breathing of the sea. Presently the cat, which had been sleeping in a chair, rose and went to the door.

"Shall I let her out?" said Siegmund.

"Do!" said Helena, slipping from his knee. "She goes out when the nights are fine."

Siegmund rose to set free the tabby. Hearing the front door open, Mrs Curtiss called from upstairs: "Is that you, dear?"

"I have just let Kitty out," said Siegmund.

"Ah thank you—Goodnight!"—they heard the old lady lock her bedroom door.

Helena was kneeling on the hearth. Siegmund softly closed the door, then waited a moment. His heart was beating fast.

"Shall we sit by firelight?" he asked tentatively.

"Yes—if you wish," she replied, very slowly, as if against her will. He carefully turned down the lamp, then blew out the light. His whole body was burning and surging with desire.

The room was black and red with firelight. Helena shone ruddily as she knelt, a bright, bowed figure, full in the glow. Now and then red stripes of firelight leapt across the walls. Siegmund, his face ruddy, advanced out of the shadows.

He sat in the chair beside her, leaning forward, his hands hanging like two scarlet flowers listless in the fire glow, near to her, as she knelt on the hearth, with head bowed down. One of the flowers awoke and spread towards her. It asked for her mutely. She was fascinated, scarcely able to move.

"Come," he pleaded softly.

She turned, lifted her hands to him. The lace fell back, and her arms, bare to the shoulder, shone rosily. He saw her breasts raised towards him. Her face was bent between her arms as she looked up at him afraid. Lit up by the firelight, in her white, clinging dress, cowering between her uplifted arms, she seemed to be offering him herself to sacrifice.

In an instant he was kneeling, and she was lying on his shoulder, abandoned to him. There was a good deal of sorrow in his joy.

* * * * *

It was eleven o'clock when Helena at last loosened Siegmund's arms and rose from the arm-chair where she lay beside him. She was very hot, feverish and restless. For the last half hour he had lain absolutely still, with his heavy arms about her, making her hot. If she had not seen his eyes blue and dark, she would have thought him asleep. She tossed in restlessness on his breast.

"Am I not uneasy?" she had said, to make him speak. He had smiled gently.

"It is wonderful to be as still as this," he said.

She had lain tranquil with him then, for a few moments. To her, there was something sacred in his stillness and peace. She wondered at him, he was so different from an hour ago. How could he be the same! Now he was like the sea, blue and hazy in the morning, musing by itself. Before, he was burning, volcanic, as if he would destroy her.

She had given him this new, soft beauty. She was the earth in which his strange flowers grew. But she herself wondered at the flowers produced of her. He was so strange to her, so different from herself. What next would he ask of her, what new blossom would she rear in him then. He seemed to grow and flower involuntarily. She merely helped to produce him.

Helena could not keep still: her body was full of strange sensations, of involuntary recoil from shock. She was tired, but restless. All the time Siegmund lay with his hot arms over her, himself so incomprehensible in his haze of blue, open-eyed slumber, she grew more breathless and unbearable to herself.

At last she lifted his arm and drew herself out of the chair. Siegmund looked at her from his tranquillity. She put the damp hair from her forehead, breathed deep, almost panting. Then she glanced hauntingly at her flushed face in the mirror. With the same restlessness, she turned to look at the night. The cool, dark, watery sea called to her. She pushed back the curtain.

The moon was wading deliciously through shallows of white cloud. Beyond the trees and the few houses was the great concave of darkness, the sea, and the moonlight. The moon was there to put a cool hand of absolution on her brow.

"Shall we go out a moment, Siegmund," she asked fretfully.

"Ay, if you wish to," he answered, altogether willing. He was filled with an easiness that would comply with her every wish.

They went out softly, walked in silence to the bay. There they stood at the head of the white, living moon-path, where the water whispered at the casement of the land, seductively.

"It's the finest night I have seen," said Siegmund. Helena's eyes suddenly filled with tears, at his simplicity of happiness.

"I like the moon on the water," she said.

"I can hardly tell the one from the other," he replied, simply. "The sea seems to be poured out of the moon, and rocking in the hands of the coast. They are all one, just as your eyes and hands and what you say, are all you."

"Yes," she answered, thrilled. This was the Siegmund of her dream, and she had created him. Yet there was a quiver of pain. He was beyond her now and did not need her.

"I feel at home here," he said; "as if I had come home, where I was bred."

She pressed his hand hard, clinging to him.

"We go an awful long way round, Helena," he said, "just to find we're all right." He laughed pleasantly. "I have thought myself such an outcast! How can one be outcast in one's own night—and the moon always naked to us—and the sky half her time in rags. What do we want!"

Helena did not know. Nor did she know what he meant. But she felt something of the harmony.

"Whatever I have or haven't from now," he continued, "the

darkness is a sort of mother, and the moon a sister, and the stars children, and sometimes the sea is a brother: and there's a family in one house, you see."

"And I, Siegmund?" she said softly, taking him in all seriousness. She looked up at him piteously. He saw the silver of tears among the moonlit ivory of her face. His heart tightened with tenderness, and he laughed, then bent to kiss her.

"The key of the castle," he said. He put his face against hers, and felt on his cheek the smart of her tears.

"It's all very grandiose," he said comfortably, "but it does for tonight, all this that I say."

"It is true for ever," she declared.

"In so far as tonight is eternal," he said.

He remained with the wetness of her cheek smarting on his, looking from under his brows at the white transport of the water beneath the moon. They stood folded together, gazing into the white heart of the night.

VI

Siegmund woke with wonder in the morning. "It is like the magic tales," he thought, as he realised where he was, "and I am transported to a new life, to realise my dream. Fairy tales are true after all."

He had slept very deeply, so that he felt strangely new. He issued with delight from the dark of sleep into the sunshine. Reaching out his hand, he felt for his watch. It was seven o'clock. The dew of a sleep drenched night glittered before his eyes. Then he laughed and forgot the night.

The creeper was tapping at the window, as a little wind blew up the sunshine. Siegmund put out his hands for the unfolding happiness of the morning. Helena was in the next room, which she kept inviolate. Sparrows in the creeper were shaking shadows of leaves among the sunshine; a milk-white shallop of cloud stemmed bravely across the bright sky; the sea would be blossoming with a dewy shimmer of sunshine.

Siegmund rose to look, and it was so. Also the houses, like white, and red, and black cattle were wandering down the bay, with a mist of sunshine between him and them. He leaned with his hands on the window ledge looking out of the casement. The breeze ruffled his hair, blew down the neck of his sleeping jacket upon his chest. He laughed, hastily threw on his clothes, and went out.

There was no sign of Helena. He strode along, singing to himself, and spinning his towel rhythmically. A small path led him across a field and down a zig-zag in front of the cliffs. Some nooks, sheltered from the wind, were warm with sunshine scented of honeysuckle and of thyme. He took a sprig of woodbine, that was coloured of cream and butter. The grass wetted his brown shoes and his flannel trousers. Again, a fresh breeze put the scent of the sea in his uncovered hair. The cliff was a tangle of flowers above and below, with poppies at the lip being blown out like red flame, and scabious leaning inquisitively to look down, and pink and white rest-harrow everywhere, very pretty.

Siegmund stood at a bend where heath blossomed in shaggy lilac, where the sunshine but no wind came. He saw the blue bay curl away to the far-off headland. A few birds, white and small, circled, dipped by the thin foam-edge of the water; a few ships dimmed the sea with silent travelling; a few small people, dark or naked white, moved below the swinging birds.

He chose his bathing place where the incoming tide had half covered a stretch of fair, bright sand that was studded with rocks resembling square altars, hollowed on top. He threw his clothes on a high rock. It delighted him to feel the fresh, soft fingers of the wind touching him and wandering timidly over his nakedness. He ran laughing over the sand to the sea, where he waded in, thrusting his legs noisily through the heavy green water.

It was cold, and he shrank. For a moment he found himself thigh-deep, watching the horizontal stealing of a ship through the intolerable glitter, afraid to plunge. Laughing, he went under the clear green water.

He was a poor swimmer. Sometimes a choppy wave swamped him, and he rose gasping, wringing the water from his eyes and nostrils, while he heaved and sank with the rocking of the waves that clasped his breast. Then he stooped again to resume his game with the sea. It is splendid to play, even at middle age, and the sea is a fine partner.

With his eyes at the shining level of the water, he liked to peer across, taking a seal's view of the cliffs as they confronted the morning; he liked to see the ships standing up on a bright floor; he liked to see the birds come down.

But in his playing he drifted towards the spur of rock, where as he swam, he caught his thigh on a sharp, submerged point. He frowned at the pain, at the sudden cruelty of the sea; then he thought no more of it, but ruffled his way back to the clear water, busily continuing his play.

When he ran out onto the fair sand, his heart and brain and body were in a turmoil. He panted, filling his breast with the air that was sparkled and tasted of the sea. As he shuddered a little, the wilful palpitation of his flesh pleased him, as if birds had fluttered against him. He offered his body to the morning, glowing with the sea's passion. The wind nestled in to him, the sunshine came on his shoulders like warm breath. He delighted in himself.

The rock before him was white and wet like himself; it had a pool of clear water, with shells and one rose anemone.

"She would make so much of this little pool," he thought. And as he smiled, he saw, very faintly, his own shadow in the water. It made him conscious of himself, seeming to look at him. He glanced at himself, at his handsome, white maturity. As he looked he felt the insidious creeping of blood down his thigh, which was marked with a long red slash. Siegmund watched the blood travel over the bright skin. It wound itself redly round the rise of his knee.

"That is I, that creeping red, and this whiteness I pride myself on is I, and my black hair, and my blue eyes are I. It is a weird thing to be a person. What makes me myself, among all these?"

Feeling chill, he wiped himself quickly.

"I am at my best, at my strongest," he said proudly to himself. "She ought to be rejoiced at me, but she is not, she rejects me as if I were a baboon, under my clothing."

He glanced at his whole handsome maturity, the firm plating of his breasts, the full thighs, creatures proud in themselves. Only he was marred by the long, raw scratch, which he regretted deeply.

"If I was giving her myself, I wouldn't want that blemish on me," he thought.

He wiped the blood from the wound. It was nothing.

"She thinks ten thousand times more of that little pool, with a bit of a pink anemone and some yellow weed, than of me. But by Jove, I'd rather see her shoulders and breast than all heaven and earth put together could show...Why doesn't she like me—?" he thought as he dressed. It was his physical self thinking.

After dabbling his feet in a warm pool, he returned home. Helena was in the dining room arranging a bowl of purple pansies. She looked up at him rather heavily as he stood radiant on the threshold. He put her at her ease. It was a gay, handsome boy she had to meet, not a man, strange and insistent. She smiled on him with tender dignity.

"You have bathed—?" she said, smiling, and looking at his damp, ruffled black hair. She shrank from his eyes, but he was quite unconscious.

"You have not bathed!" he said, then bent to kiss her. She smelled the brine in his hair.

"No—I bathe later," she replied. "But what—?"

Hesitating, she touched the towel, then looked up at him anxiously.

"It *is* blood?" she said.

"I grazed my thigh—nothing at all," he replied.

"Are you sure?"

He laughed.

"The towel looks bad enough," she said.

"It's an alarmist," he laughed.

She looked in concern at him, then turned aside.

"Breakfast is quite ready," she said.

"And I for breakfast—but shall I do?"

She glanced at him. He was without a collar, so his throat was bare above the neck band of his flannel shirt. Altogether she disapproved of his slovenly appearance. He was usually so smart in his dress.

"I would not trouble," she said, almost sarcastically. Whistling, he threw the towel on a chair.

"How did you sleep?" she asked, gravely, as she watched him beginning to eat.

"Like the dead—solid," he replied. "And you?"

"Oh pretty well, thanks," she said, rather piqued that he had slept so deeply, whilst she had tossed, and had called his name in a torture of sleeplessness.

"I haven't slept like that for years," he said, enthusiastically. Helena smiled gently on him. The charm of his handsome, healthy zest came over her. She liked his naked throat, and his shirt-breast, which suggested the breast of the man beneath it. She was extraordinarily happy, with him so bright. The dark-faced pansies, in a little crowd, seemed gaily winking a golden eye at her.

After breakfast, while Siegmund dressed, she went down to the sea. She dwelled, as she passed, on all tiny, pretty things: on the barbaric, yellow ragwort, and pink convolvuli, on all the twinkling of flowers and dew and snail-tracks drying in the sun. Her walk was one long lingering. More than the spaces, she loved the nooks, and fancy more than imagination.*

She wanted to see just as she pleased, without any of humanity's previous vision for spectacles. So she knew hardly any flower's name, nor perceived any of the relationships, nor cared a jot about an adaptation or a modification. It pleased her that the lowest, browny florets of the clover hung down: she cared no more. She clothed everything in fancy.

"That yellow flower hadn't time to be brushed and combed by the fairies, before dawn came. It is towzled...," so she thought to herself. The pink convolvuli were fairy horns, or telephones from the day fairies to the night fairies. The rippling sunlight on the sea was the Rhine Maidens spreading their bright hair to sun.* That was her favourite form of thinking. The value of all things was in the fancy they evoked. She did not care for people; they were vulgar, ugly, and stupid as a rule.

Her sense of satisfaction was complete as she leaned on the low sea-wall, spreading her fingers to warm on the stones, concocting magic out of the simple morning. She watched the indolent chasing of wavelets round the small rocks, the curling of the deep blue water round the water-shadowed reefs.

"This is very good," she said to herself. "This is eternally cool and clean and fresh. It could never be spoiled by satiety."

She tried to wash herself with the white and blue morning, to clear away the soiling of the last night's passion.

The sea played by itself, intent on its own game. Its aloofness, its self-sufficiency, are its great charm. The sea does not give and take, like the land and the sky. It has no traffic with the world. It spends its passions upon itself. Helena was something like the sea, self-sufficient and careless of the rest.

Siegmund came bare-headed, his black hair ruffling to the wind, his eyes shining warmer than the sea—like cornflowers, rather; his limbs swinging backward and forward like the water. Together they leaned on the wall, warming the four white hands upon the grey, bleached stone, as they watched the water playing.

When Siegmund had Helena near, he lost the ache, the yearning towards something, which he always felt otherwise. She seemed to connect him with the beauty of things, as if she were the nerve through which he received intelligence of the sun and wind and sea, and of the moon and the darkness. Beauty she never felt herself, came to him through her. It is that, makes love. He could always sympathise with the wistful little flowers, and trees lonely in their crowds, and wild, sad sea-birds. In these things he recognised the great yearning, the ache outwards towards something, with which he was ordinarily burdened. But with Helena, in this large sea-morning, he was whole and perfect as the day.

"Will it be fine all day?" he asked, when a cloud came over.

"I don't know," she replied, in her gentle, inattentive manner, as if she did not care at all. "I think it will be a mixed day—cloud and sun—more sun than cloud."

She looked up gravely to see if he agreed. He turned from frowning at the cloud to smile at her. He seemed so bright, teeming with life.

"I like a bare blue sky," he said, "sunshine that you seem to stir about as you walk."

"It is warm enough here, even for you," she smiled.

"Ah here!" he answered, putting his face down to receive the radiation from the stone, letting his fingers creep towards Helena's. She laughed, and captured his fingers, pressing them into her hand. For nearly an hour they remained thus in the still sunshine by the sea-wall, till Helena began to sigh, and to lift her face to the little breeze that wandered down from the west. She fled as soon from warmth as from cold. Physically, she was always so;—she shrank from anything extreme. But psychically, she was an extremist, and a dangerous one.

They climbed the hill to the fresh-breathing west. On the highest point of land stood a tall cross, railed in by a red iron fence.* They read the inscription.

"That's all right—but a vilely ugly railing!" exclaimed Siegmund.

"Oh, they'd have to fence-in Lord Tennyson's white marble," said Helena, rather indefinitely. He interpreted her according to his own idea.

"Yes—he did belittle great things, didn't he?" said Siegmund.

"Tennyson!" she exclaimed.

"Not peacocks and princesses*—but the bigger things—"

"I shouldn't say so," she declared.

"Ha-a!"

He sounded indeterminate, but was not really so.

They wandered over the downs westward, among the wind. As they followed the headland to the Needles, they felt the breeze from the wings of the sea brushing them, and heard restless, poignant voices screaming below the cliffs. Now and again, a gull, like a piece of spume flung up, rose over the cliff's edge and sank again. Now and again, as the path dipped in a hollow, they could see the low, suspended intertwining of the birds passing in and out of the cliff shelter.

These savage birds appealed to all the poetry, and yearning in Helena. They fascinated her, they almost voiced her. She crept nearer and nearer the edge, feeling she must watch the gulls thread out in flakes of white above the weed-black rocks. Siegmund stood away back, anxiously. He would not dare to tempt fate now, having too strong a sense of death to risk it.

"Come back, dear. Don't go so near," he pleaded, following as close as he might. She heard the pain and appeal in his voice. It thrilled her, and she went a little nearer. What was Death to her, but one of her symbols, the death of which the Sagas* talk—something grand and sweeping and dark.

Leaning forward, she could see the line of grey sand, and the line of foam broken by black rocks, and over all, the gulls, stirring round like froth on a pot, screaming in chorus.

She watched the beautiful birds, heard the pleading of Siegmund, and she thrilled with pleasure, toying with his keen anguish.

Helena came smiling to Siegmund, saying:

"They look so fine down there."

He fastened his hands upon her, as a relief from his pain. He was filled with a keen, strong anguish of dread, like a presentiment. She laughed as he gripped her.

They went searching for a way of descent. At last Siegmund inquired of the coastguard the nearest way down the cliff. He was pointed to the "Path of the Hundred Steps."

"When is a hundred not a hundred?" he said sceptically, as they descended the dazzling white chalk. There were sixty eight steps. Helena laughed at his exactitude.

"It must be a love of round numbers," he said.

"No doubt," she laughed. He took the thing so seriously.

"Or of exaggeration," he added.

There was a shelving beach of warm white sand, bleached soft as velvet. A sounding of gulls filled the dark recesses of the headland, a low chatter of shingle came from where the easy water was breaking; a confused, shell-like murmur of the sea between the folded cliffs. Siegmund and Helena lay side by side upon the dry sand, small as two resting birds, while thousands of gulls whirled in a white-flaked storm above them, and the great cliffs towered beyond, and high up over the cliffs the multitudinous clouds were travelling, a vast caravan en route. Amidst the journeying of oceans and clouds and the circling flight of heavy spheres lost to sight in the sky, Siegmund and Helena, two grains of life in the vast movement, were travelling a moment side by side.

They lay on the beach like a grey and white sea-bird together. The lazy ships that were idling down the Solent observed the cliffs and the boulders, but Siegmund and Helena were too little. They lay ignored and insignificant, watching through half-closed fingers the diverse caravan of Day go past. They lay with their latticed fingers over their eyes, looking out at the sailing of ships across their vision of blue water.

"Now, that one with the greyish sails—" Siegmund was saying.

"Like a housewife of forty going placidly round with the duster—yes—" interrupted Helena.

"—That is a schooner—you see her four sails, and— —."

He continued to classify the shipping, until he was interrupted by the wicked laughter of Helena.

"That is right, I am sure," he protested.

"I won't contradict you," she laughed, in a tone which showed him he knew even less of the classifying of ships than she did.

"So you have lain there amusing yourself at my expense all the time—?" he said, not knowing in the least why she laughed. They turned and looked at one another, blue eyes smiling and wavering as the beach wavers in the heat. Then they closed their eyes with sunshine.

Drowsed by the sun and the white sand and the foam, their thoughts slept like butterflies on the flowers of delight. But cold shadows startled them up.

"The clouds are coming," he said regretfully.

"Yes—but the wind is quite strong enough for them," she answered.

"Look at the shadows—like blots floating away. Don't they devour the sunshine?"

"It is quite warm enough here," she said, nestling in to him.

"Yes, but the sting is missing. I like to feel the warmth biting in."

"No, I do not. To be cosy is enough."

"I like the sunshine on me, real and manifest and tangible. I feel like a seed that has been frozen for ages. I want to be bitten by the sunshine."

She leaned over and kissed him. The sun came bright-footed over the water, leaving a shining print on Siegmund's face. He lay with half-closed eyes, sprawled loosely on the sand. Looking at his limbs, she imagined he must be heavy, like the boulders. She sat over him, with her finger stroking his eyebrows, that were broad and rather arched. He lay perfectly still, in a half-dream.

Presently she laid her head on his breast, and remained so, watching the sea and listening to his heart-beats. The throb was strong and deep. It seemed to go through the whole island, and the whole afternoon, and it fascinated her: so deep, unheard, with its great expulsions of life. Had the world a heart?—Was there also deep in the world a great God thudding out waves of life, like a great Heart, unconscious? It frightened her. This was the God she knew not: as she knew not this Siegmund. It was so different from the half-shut eyes with black lashes, and the winsome, shapely nose. And the heart of the world, as she heard it, could not be the same as the curling splash and retreat of the little sleepy waves. She listened for Siegmund's soul, but his heart overbeat all other sound, thudding powerfully.

VII

Siegmund woke to the muffled firing of guns on the sea. He looked across at the shaggy, grey water in wonder. Then he turned to Helena.

"I suppose," he said, "they are saluting the Czar.* Poor beggar!"

"I was afraid they would wake you," she smiled.

They listened again to the hollow, dull sound of salutes from across the water and the downs.

The day had gone grey. They decided to walk, down below, to the next bay.

"The tide is coming in," said Helena.

"But this broad strip of sand hasn't been wet for months. It's as soft as pepper," he replied.

They laboured along the shore, beside the black, sinuous line of shrivelled fucus. The base of the cliff was piled with chalk débris. On the other side, was the level plain of the sea. Hand in hand, alone and overshadowed by huge cliffs, they toiled on. The waves staggered in, and fell, overcome at the end of the race.

Siegmund and Helena neared a headland, sheer as the side of a house, its base weighted with a tremendous white mass of boulders, that the green sea broke amongst with a hollow sound, followed by a sharp hiss of withdrawal. The lovers had to cross this desert of white boulders, that glistened in smooth skins, uncannily. But Siegmund saw the waves were almost at the wall of the headland. Glancing back, he saw the other headland white-dashed at the base with foam. He and Helena must hurry, or they would be prisoned on the thin crescent of strand still remaining between the great wall and the water.

The cliffs over head oppressed him, made him feel trapped and helpless. He was caught by them in a net of great boulders, while the sea fumbled for him. But he had Helena. She laboured strenuously beside him, blinded by the skin-like glisten of the white rock.

"I think I will rest awhile," she said.

"No, come along," he begged.

"My dear," she laughed, "there is tons of this shingle to buttress us from the sea."

He looked at the waves curving and driving maliciously at the boulders. It would be ridiculous to be trapped.

"Look at this black wood," she said. "Does the sea really char it?"

"Let us get round the corner," he begged.

"Really Siegmund, the sea is not so anxious to take us," she said ironically.

When they rounded the first point, they found themselves in a small bay jutted out to sea: the front of the headland was, as usual, grooved. This bay was pure white at the base, from its great, heaped mass of shingle. With the huge concave of the cliff behind, the foothold of massed, white boulders, and the immense arc of the sea in front, Helena was delighted.

"This is fine, Siegmund!" she said, halting and facing west. Smiling ironically, he sat down on a boulder. They were quite alone, in this great white niche thrust out to sea. Here, he could see, the tide would beat the base of the wall. It came plunging not far from their feet.

"Would you really like to travel beyond the end?" he asked.

She looked round quickly, thrilled, then answered as if in rebuke:

"This is a fine place. I should like to stay here an hour."

"And then where?"

"Then—? Oh, then I suppose it would be teatime."

"Tea on brine and pink anemones, with Daddy Neptune."

She looked sharply at the outjutting capes. The sea did foam perilously near their bases.

"I suppose it *is* rather risky," she said, and she turned, began silently to clamber forwards.

He followed: she should set the pace.

"I have no doubt there's plenty of room, really," he said. "The sea only looks near."

But she toiled on intently. Now it was a question of danger, not of inconvenience, Siegmund felt elated. The waves foamed up, as it seemed, against the exposed headland, from which the massive shingle had been swept back. Supposing they could not get by. He began to smile curiously. He became aware of the tremendous noise of waters, of the slight shudder of the shingle when a wave struck it, and he [almost] laughed to himself.* Helena laboured on in silence, he kept just behind her. The point seemed near, but it took longer than they thought. They had against them the tremendous cliff, the enormous weight of shingle, and the swinging sea. The waves struck louder, booming fearfully; wind, sweeping round the corner, wet their faces. Siegmund hoped they were cut off, and hoped anxiously the way was clear. The smile became set on his face.

Then he saw there was a ledge or platform at the base of the cliff, and it was against this the waves broke. They climbed the side of this ledge, hurried round to the front. There the wind caught them wet and furious, the water raged below. Between the two, Helena shrank, wilted. She took hold of Siegmund. The great, brutal water flung itself at the rock, then drew back for another heavy spring. Fume and spray were spun on the wind like smoke. The roaring thud of the waves reminded Helena of a beating heart. She clung closer to him, as her hair was blown out damp, and her white dress flapped in the wet wind. Always, against the rock, came the slow thud of the waves, like a great heart beating under the breast. There was something brutal about it that she could not bear. She had no weapon against brute force.

She glanced up at Siegmund. Tiny drops of mist greyed his eyebrows. He was looking out to sea, screwing up his eyes, and smiling brutally. Her face became heavy and sullen. He was like the heart, and the brute sea, just here; he was not her Siegmund. She hated the brute in him.

Turning suddenly, she plunged over the shingle towards the wide, populous bay. He remained alone, grinning at the smashing turmoil, careless of her departure. He would easily catch her.

When at last he turned from the wrestling water, he had spent his savagery, and was sad. He could never take part in the great battle of action. It was beyond him. Many things he had let slip by. His life was whittled down to only a few interests, only a few necessities. Even here, he had but Helena, and through her the rest. After this week—well, that was vague. He left it in the dark, dreading it.

And Helena was toiling over the rough beach, alone. He saw her small figure bowed as she plunged forward. It smote his heart with the keenest tenderness. She was so winsome, a playmate with beauty and fancy. Why was he cruel to her, because she had not his own bitter wisdom of experience? She was young, and naïve, and should he be angry with her for that? His heart was tight at the thought of her. She would have to suffer also, because of him.

He hurried after her. Not till they had nearly come to a little green mound, where the downs sloped and the cliffs were gone, did he catch her up. Then he took her hand as they walked.

They halted on the green hillock, beyond the sand, and, without a word, he folded her in his arms. Both were out of breath. He clasped her close, seeming to rock her with his strong panting. She felt his body lifting into her, and sinking away. It seemed to force a rhythm, a new pulse, in her. Gradually, with a fine, keen thrilling, she melted down on him, like metal sinking on a mould. He was sea and sunlight mixed, heaving, warm, deliciously strong.

Siegmund exulted. At last she was moulded to him in pure passion.

They stood folded thus for some time. Then Helena raised her burning face, and relaxed. She was throbbing with strange elation and satisfaction.

"It might as well have been the sea as any other way, dear," she said, startling both of them. The speech went across their thoughtlessness like a star flying into the night, from nowhere. She had no idea why she said it. He pressed his mouth on hers. "Not for you," he thought, by reflex. "You can't go that way yet." But he said nothing, strained her very tightly, and kept her lips.

They were roused by the sound of voices. Unclasping, they went to walk at the fringe of the water. The tide was creeping back. Siegmund stooped, and from among the water's combings, picked up an electric-light bulb. It lay in some weed at the base of a rock. He held it in his hand to Helena. Her face lighted with a curious pleasure. She took the thing delicately from his hand, fingered it with her exquisite softness.

"Isn't it remarkable!" she exclaimed joyously. "The sea must be very, very gentle—and very kind."

"Sometimes," smiled Siegmund.

"But I did not think it could be so fine fingered," she said. She breathed on the glass bulb till it looked like a dim magnolia bud; she inhaled its fine savour.

"It would not have treated *you* so well," he said. She looked at him with heavy eyes. Then she returned to her bulb. Her fingers were very small and very pink. She had the most delicate touch in the world, like a faint feel of silk. As he watched her lifting her fingers from off the glass, then gently stroking it, his blood ran hot. He watched her, waited upon her words and movements attentively.

"It is a graceful act on the sea's part," she said—"Wotan is so clumsy*—he knocks over the bowl, and flap-flap flap go the gasping fishes, pizzicato!—but the sea—!"

Helena's speech was often difficult to render into plain terms. She was not lucid.

"But life's so full of anti-climax," she concluded. Siegmund smiled softly at her. She had him too much in love to disagree, or to examine her words.

"There's no reckoning with life, and no reckoning with the sea. The only way to get on with both is to be as near a vacuum as possible, and float," he jested. It hurt her that he was flippant. She proceeded to forget he had spoken.

There were three children on the beach. Helena had handed him back the senseless bauble, not able to throw it away. Being a father:

"I will give it to the children," he said.

She looked up at him, loved him for the thought.

Wandering hand in hand, for it pleased them both to own each other publicly, after years of conventional distance, they came to a little girl who was bending over a pool. Her black hair hung in long snakes to the water. She stood up, flung back her locks to see them as they approached. In one hand she clasped some pebbles.

"Would you like this?—I found it down there," said Siegmund, offering her the bulb.

She looked at him with grave blue eyes, and accepted his gift. Evidently she was not going to say anything.

"The sea brought it all the way from the mainland without breaking it," said Helena, with the interesting intonation some folk use to children.

The girl looked at her.

"The waves put it out of their lap on to some sea-weed with such careful fingers—!"

The child's eyes brightened.

"The tide-line is full of treasures," said Helena, smiling.

The child answered her smile a little.

Siegmund had walked away.

"What beautiful eyes she had," said Helena.

"Yes," he replied.

She looked up at him. He felt her searching him tenderly with her eyes. But he could not look back at her. She took his hand and kissed it, knowing he was thinking of his own youngest child.

VIII

The way home lay across country, through deep little lanes where the late foxgloves sat seriously, like sad hounds; over open downlands rough with gorse and ling, and through pocketed hollows of bracken and trees.

They came to a small Roman Catholic church in the fields. There the carved Christ looked down on the dead whose sleeping forms made mounds under the coverlet. Helena's heart was swelling with emotion. All the yearning and pathos of Christianity filled her again.

The path skirted the churchyard wall, so that she had on the one hand the sleeping dead, and on the other, Siegmund, strong and vigorous, but walking in the old, dejected fashion. She felt a rare tenderness and admiration for him. It was unusual for her to be so humble-minded; but this evening she felt she must minister to him, and be submissive.

She made him stop to look at the graves. Suddenly, as they stood, she kissed him, clasped him fervently, roused him till his passion burned away his heaviness, and he seemed tipped with life, his face glowing as if soon he would burst alight. Then she was satisfied, and could laugh.

As they went through the fir corpse, listening to the birds like a family assembled and chattering at home in the evening, listening to the light swish of the wind, she let Siegmund predominate; he set the swing of their motion, she rested on him like a bird on a swaying bough.

They argued concerning the way. Siegmund, as usual, submitted to her. They went quite wrong. As they retraced their steps, stealthily, through a poultry farm whose fowls were standing in forlorn groups, once more dismayed by evening, Helena's pride battled with her new subjugation to Siegmund. She walked head down, saying nothing. He also was silent, but his heart was strong in him. Somewhere in the distance a band was playing "The Watch on the Rhine."*

As they passed the beeches and were near home, Helena said, to try him, and to strike a last blow for her pride:

"I wonder what next Monday will bring us."

"Quick curtain," he answered joyously. He was looking down and smiling at her with such careless happiness, that she loved him. He was wonderful to her. She loved him, was jealous of every particle of him that evaded her. She wanted to sacrifice to him, make herself a burning altar to him: and she wanted to possess him.

The hours that would be purely their own came too slowly for her.

That night she met his passion with love. It was not his passion she wanted, actually. But she desired that he should want *her* madly, and that he should have all—everything. It was a wonderful night to him. It restored in him the full "will to live." But she felt it destroyed her. Her soul seemed blasted.

At seven o'clock in the morning Helena lay in the deliciously cool water, while small waves ran up the beach full and clear and foamless, continuing perfectly in their flicker the rhythm of the night's passion. Nothing, she felt, had ever been so delightful as this cool water running over her. She lay and looked out on the shining sea. All, it seemed, was made of sunshine more or less soiled. The cliffs rose out of the shining waves like clouds of strong, fine texture; and rocks along the shore were the dapplings of a bright dawn. The coarseness was fused out of the world, so that sunlight showed in the veins of the morning cliffs and the rocks. Yea, everything ran with sunshine, as we are full of blood, and plants are tissued from green-gold, glistening sap. Substance and solidity were shadows that the morning cast round itself to make itself tangible: as she herself was a shadow cast by that fragment of sunshine, her soul, over its inefficiency.

She remembered to have seen the bats flying low over a burnished pool at sunset, and the web of their wings had burned in scarlet flickers, as they stretched across the light. Winged momentarily on bits of tissued flame, threaded with blood, the bats had flickered a secret to her.

Now the cliffs were like wings uplifted, and the morning was coming dimly through them. She felt the wings of all the world upraised against the morning in a flashing, multitudinous flight. The world itself was flying. Sunlight poured on the large round world till she fancied it a heavy bee humming on its iridescent atmosphere across a vast air of sunshine.

She lay and rode the fine journey. Sunlight liquid in the water made the waves heavy, golden, and rich with a velvety coolness like cowslips. Her feet fluttered in the shadowy underwater. Her breast came out bright as the breast of a white bird.

Where was Siegmund, she wondered. He also was somewhere among the sea and the sunshine, white and playing like a bird, shining like a vivid, restless speck of sunlight. She struck the water, smiling, feeling alone with him. They two were the owners of this morning, as a pair of wild, large birds inhabiting an empty sea.

Siegmund had found a white cave welling with green water brilliant and full of life as mounting sap. The white rock glimmered through the water, and soon Siegmund shimmered also in the living green of the sea, like pale flowers trembling upward.

"The water," said Siegmund, "is as full of life as I am," and he pressed forward his breast against it. He swam very well that morning; he had more wilful life than the sea, so he mastered it laughingly with his arms, feeling a delight in his triumph over the waves. Venturing recklessly in his new pride, he swam round the corner of the rock, through an archway, lofty and spacious, into a passage where the water ran like a flood of green light over the skin-white bottom. Suddenly he emerged in the brilliant daylight of the next tiny scoop of a bay.

There he arrived like a pioneer, for the bay was inaccessible from the land. He waded out of the green, cold water on to sand that was pure as the shoulders of Helena, out of the shadow of the archway, into the sunlight, on to the glistening petal of this blossom of a sea-bay.

He did not know till he felt the sunlight how the sea had drunk with its cold lips deeply of his warmth. Throwing himself down on the sand that was soft and warm as white fur, he lay glistening wet, panting, swelling with glad pride at having conquered also this small, inaccessible sea-cave, creeping into it like a white bee into a white, virgin blossom that had waited, how long, for its bee.

The sand was warm to his breast and his belly and his arms. It was like a great body he cleaved to. Almost, he fancied, he felt it heaving under him in its breathing. Then he turned his face to the sun, and laughed. All the while, he hugged the warm body of the sea-bay beneath him. He spread his hands upon the sand: he took it in handfuls, and let it run smooth, warm, delightful, through his fingers.

"Surely," he said to himself, "it is like Helena," and he laid his hands again on the warm body of the shore, let them wander, discovering, gathering all the warmth, the softness, the strange wonder of smooth, warm pebbles, then shrinking from the deep weight of cold his hand encountered as he burrowed under the surface, wrist-deep. In the end, he found the cold mystery of the deep sand also thrilling. He pushed in his hands again and deeper, enjoying the almost hurt of the dark, heavy coldness. For the sun and the white flower of the bay were breathing and kissing him dry, were holding him in their warm concave, like a bee in a flower, like himself on the bosom of Helena, and flowing like the warmth of her breath in his hair came the sunshine, breathing near and lovingly: yet, under all, was this deep mass of cold, that the softness and warmth merely floated upon.

Siegmund lay and clasped the sand and tossed it in handfuls till over him he was all hot and cloyed. Then he rose and looked at himself and laughed. The water was swaying reproachfully against the steep pebbles below, murmuring like a child, that it was not fair, it was not fair he should abandon his playmate. Siegmund laughed, and began to rub himself free of the clogging sand. He found himself strangely dry and smooth. He tossed more dry sand, and more, over himself, busy and intent like a child playing some absorbing game with itself. Soon his body was dry and warm and smooth as a camomile flower. He was, however, greyed and smeared with sand-dust. Siegmund looked at himself with disapproval, though his body was full of delight and his hands glad with the touch of himself. He wanted himself clean. He felt the sand thick in his hair, even in his moustache. He went painfully over the pebbles till he found himself on the smooth rock bottom. Then he soused himself, and shook his head in the water, and washed and splashed and rubbed himself with his hands assiduously. He must feel perfectly clean and free, fresh, as if he had washed away all the years of soilure in this morning's sea and sun and sand. It was the purification. Siegmund became again a happy priest of the sun. He felt as if all the dirt of misery were soaked out of him, as he might soak clean a soiled garment in the sea, and bleach it white on the sunny shore. So white and sweet and tissue-clean he felt, full of lightness and grace.

The garden in front of their house, where Helena was waiting for him, was long and crooked, with a sunken flagstone pavement running up to the door by the side of the lawn. On either hand the high fence of the garden was heavy with wild clematis and honeysuckle. Helena sat sideways with a map spread out on her bench under the bushy little laburnum tree, tracing the course of their wanderings. It was very still. There was just a murmur of bees going in and out the brilliant little porches of nasturtium flowers. The nasturtium leaf-coins stood cool and grey: in their delicate shade, underneath in the green twilight, a few flowers shone their submerged gold and scarlet. There was a faint scent of mignonette. Helena, like a white butterfly in the shade, her two white arms for antennae stretching firmly to the bench, leaned over her map. She was busy, very busy, out of sheer happiness. She traced word after word, and evoked scene after scene. As she discovered a name, she conjured up the place. As she moved to the next mark she imagined the long path lifting and falling happily.

She was waiting for Siegmund, yet his hand upon the latch startled her. She rose suddenly, in agitation. Siegmund was standing in the sunshine at the gate. They greeted each other across the tall roses.

When Siegmund was holding her hand, he said, softly laughing:

"You have come out of the water very beautiful this morning."

She laughed. She was not beautiful, but she felt so at that moment. She glanced up at him, full of love and gratefulness.

"And you," she murmured, in a still tone, as if it were almost sacrilegiously unnecessary to say it.

Siegmund was glad. He rejoiced to be told he was beautiful. After a few moments of listening to the bees and breathing the mignonette, he said:

"I found a little white bay—just like you—a virgin bay—I had to swim there."

"Oh!" she said, very interested in him, not in the fact.

"It seemed just like you. Many things seem like you," he said.

She laughed again in her joyous fashion, and the reed-like vibration came into her voice.

"I saw the sun through the cliffs and the sea, and you," she said.

He did not understand. He looked at her searchingly. She was white and still and inscrutable. Then she looked up at him: her earnest eyes, that would not flinch, gazed straight into him. He trembled, and things all swept into a blur. After she had taken away her eyes he found himself saying:

"You know, I felt as if I were the first man to discover things: like Adam when he opened the first eyes in the world."

"I saw the sunshine in you," repeated Helena quietly, looking at him with her eyes heavy with meaning.

He laughed again, not understanding, but feeling she meant love.

"No, but you have altered everything," he said.

The note of wonder, of joy in his voice touched her almost beyond self-control. She caught his hand and pressed it, then quickly kissed it. He became suddenly grave.

"I feel as if it were right—you and me, Helena—so, even righteous. It is so, isn't it? And the sea and everything, they all seem with us. Do you think so?"

Looking at her, he found her eyes full of tears. He bent and kissed her, and she pressed his head to her bosom. He was very glad.

IX

The day waxed hot. A few little silver tortoises of cloud had crawled across the desert of sky, and hidden themselves. The chalk-roads were white, quivering with heat. Helena and Siegmund walked eastward bare-headed under the sunshine. They felt like two insects in the niche of a hot hearth, as they toiled along the deep road. A few poppies here and there among the wild rye floated scarlet, in sunshine like blood-drops on green water. Helena recalled Francis Thompson's poems,* which Siegmund had never read. She repeated what she knew, and laughed, thinking what an ineffectual pale shadow of a person Thompson must have been. She looked at Siegmund walking in large easiness beside her.

"Artists are supremely unfortunate persons," she announced.

"Think of Wagner,"* said Siegmund, lifting his face to the hot bright heaven and drinking the heat with his blinded face. All states seemed meagre, save his own. He recalled people who had loved, and he pitied them: dimly, drowsily, without pain.

They came to a place where they might gain access to the shore by a path down a landslip. As they descended through the rockery yellow with ragwort they felt themselves dip into the inert, hot air of the bay. The living atmosphere of the uplands was left overhead; among the rocks of the sand, white as if smelted, the heat glowed and quivered. Helena sat down and took off her shoes. She walked on the hot, glistening sand till her feet were delightfully, almost intoxicatingly scorched. Then she ran into the water to cool them. Siegmund and she paddled in the light water, pensively watching the haste of the ripples like crystal beetles running over the white outline of their feet; looking out on the sea that rose so near to them, dwarfing them by its far reach.

For a short time they flitted silently in the water's edge. Then there settled down on them a twilight of sleep, the little hush that closes the doors and draws the blinds of the house after a festival. They wandered out across the beach above high-water mark, where they sat down together on the sand, leaning back against a flat brown stone,

Siegmund with the sunshine on his forehead, Helena drooping close to him, in his shadow. Then the hours ride by unnoticed, making no sound as they go. The sea creeps nearer, nearer, like a snake which watches two birds asleep. It may not disturb them, but sinks back, ceasing to look at them with its bright eye.

Meanwhile the flowers of their passion were softly shed, as poppies fall at noon, and the seed of beauty ripened rapidly within them. Dreams came like a wind through their souls, drifting off with the seed-dust of beautiful experience which they had ripened, to fertilise the souls of others withal. In them, the sea and the sky and ships had mingled and bred new blossoms of the torrid heat of their love. And the seed of such blossoms was shaken as they slept, into the hand of God, who held it in his palm preciously, then scattered it again, to produce new splendid blooms of beauty.

A little breeze came down the cliffs. Sleep lightened the lovers of their experience, new buds were urged in their souls as they lay in a shadowed twilight, at the porch of death. The breeze fanned the face of Helena, a coolness wafted on her throat. As the afternoon wore on, she revived. Quick to flag, she was easy to revive, like a white pansy flung into water. She shivered lightly, and rose.

Strange, it seemed to her, to rise from the brown stone into life again. She felt beautifully refreshed. All around was quick as a garden wet in the early morning of June. She took her hair and loosened it, shook it free from sand, spread and laughed like a fringed poppy that opens itself to the sun. She let the wind comb through its soft fingers the tangles of her hair. Helena loved the wind. She turned to it, and took its kisses on her face and throat.

Siegmund lay still, looking up at her. The changes in him were deeper, like alteration in his tissue. His new buds came slowly, and were of a fresh type. He lay smiling at her. At last he said:

"You look now as if you belonged to the sea."

"I do. And some day I shall go back to it," she replied.

For to her at that moment the sea was a great lover, like Siegmund, but more impersonal, who would receive her when Siegmund could not. She rejoiced momentarily in the fact. Siegmund looked at her and continued smiling. His happiness was budded firm and secure.

"Come!" said Helena, holding out her hand. He rose somewhat reluctantly from his large, fruitful inertia.

X

Siegmund carried the boots and the shoes while they wandered over the sand to the rocks. There was a delightful sense of risk in scrambling with bare feet over the smooth irregular jumble of rocks. Helena laughed suddenly from fear as she felt herself slipping. Siegmund's heart was leaping like a child's with excitement as he stretched forward, himself very insecure, to succour her. Thus they travelled slowly. Often she called to him to come and look in the lovely little rock-pools, dusky with blossoms of red anemones and brown anemones that seemed nothing but shadows, and curtained with green of finest sea-silk. Siegmund loved to poke the white pebbles and startle the little ghosts of crabs in a shadowy scuttle through the weed. He would tease the expectant anemones, causing them to close suddenly over his finger. But Helena liked to watch without touching things. Meanwhile the sun was slanting behind the cross far away to the west, and the light was swimming in silver and gold upon the lacquered water. At last Siegmund looked doubtfully at two miles more of glistening, gilded boulders. Helena was seated on a stone dabbling her feet in a warm pool, delicately feeling the wet sea-velvet of the weeds.

"Don't you think we had better be mounting the cliffs?" he said.

She glanced up at him, smiling with irresponsible eyes. Then she lapped the water with her feet, and surveyed her pink toes. She was absurdly, childishly happy.

"Why should we?" she asked lightly.

He watched her. Her child-like indifference to consequences touched him with a sense of the distance between them. He himself might play with the delicious warm surface of life, but always he recked of the relentless mass of cold beneath, the mass of life which has no sympathy with the individual, no cognisance of him.

She loved the trifles and the toys, the mystery and the magic of things. She would not own life to be relentless. It was either beautiful, fantastic, or weird, or inscrutable; or else mean and vulgar, below consideration. He had to get a sense of the anemone and a sympathetic knowledge of its experience, into his blood, before he was satisfied.

To Helena, an anemone was one more fantastic pretty figure in her kaleidoscope.

So she sat dabbling her pink feet in the water, quite unconscious of his gravity. He waited on her, since he never could capture her.

"Come," he said, very gently. "You are only six years old today."

She laughed as she let him take her. Then she nestled up to him, smiling in a brilliant, child-like fashion. He kissed her with all the father in him sadly alive.

"Now put your stockings on," he said.

"But my feet are wet," she laughed.

He kneeled down and dried her feet on his handkerchief, while she sat tossing his hair with her finger-tips. The sunlight grew more and more golden.

"I envy the savages their free feet," she said.

"There is no broken glass in the wilderness—or there used not to be," he replied.

As they were crossing the sands, a whole family entered by the cliff track. They descended in single file, unequally, like the theatre: two boys, then a little girl, the father, another girl, then the mother. Last of all trotted the dog, warily, suspicious of the descent. The boys emerged into the bay with a shout, the dog rushed barking after them. The little one waited for her father, calling shrilly:

"Tiss can't fall now, can she, Dadda? Shall I put her down?"

"Ay, let her have a run," said the father.

Very carefully she lowered the kitten, which she had carried clasped to her bosom. The mite was bewildered and scared. It turned round pathetically.

"Go on, Tissie, you're all right," said the child. "Go on, have a run on the sand."

The kitten stood dubious and unhappy. Then, perceiving the dog some distance ahead, it scampered after him, a fluffy, scurrying mite. But the dog had already raced into the water. The kitten walked a few steps, turning its small face this way and that, and mewing piteously. It looked extraordinarily tiny as it stood, a fluffy handful, staring away from the noisy water, its thin cry floating over the plash of waves.

Helena glanced at Siegmund, and her eyes were shining with pity. He was watching the kitten and smiling.

"Crying because things are too big, and it can't take them in," he said.

"But look how frightened it is," she said.

"So am I," he laughed. "And if there are any gods looking on and laughing at me, at least they won't be kind enough to put me in their pinafores..."

She laughed very quickly.

"But why!" she exclaimed. "Why should you want putting in a pinafore?"

"I don't," he laughed.

On the top of the cliff they were between two bays, with darkening blue water on the left, and on the right, gold water smoothing to the sun. Siegmund seemed to stand waist deep in shadow, with his face bright and glowing. He was watching earnestly.

"I want to absorb it all," he said.

When at last they turned away:

"Yes," said Helena slowly, "one can recall the details, but never the atmosphere."

He pondered a moment.

"How strange!" he said. "I can recall the atmosphere, but not the detail. It is a moment to me, not a piece of scenery. I should say the picture was in me, not out there."

Without troubling to understand—she was inclined to think it verbiage—she made a small sound of assent.

"That is why you want to go again to a place, and I don't care so much, because I have it with me," he concluded.

XI

They decided to find their way through the lanes to Alum Bay, and then, keeping the cross in sight, to return over the downs with the moon-path broad on the water before them. For the moon was rising late. Twilight, however, rose more rapidly than they had anticipated. The lane twisted among meadows and wild lands and copses, a wilful little lane, quite incomprehensible. So they lost their distant landmark, the white cross.

Darkness filtered through the daylight. When at last they came to a sign-post, it was almost too dark to read it. The fingers seemed to withdraw into the dusk, the more they looked.

"We must go to the left," said Helena.

To the left rose the downs, smooth and grey near at hand, but higher, black with gorse, like a giant lying asleep with a bearskin over his shoulders.

Several pale chalk-tracks ran side by side through the turf. Climbing, they came to a disused chalk pit, which they circumvented. Having passed a lonely farm-house, they mounted the side of the open down, where was a sense of space and freedom.

"We can steer by the night," said Siegmund, as they trod upwards pathlessly. Helena did not mind whither they steered. All places in that large fair night were home and welcome to her. They drew nearer to the shaggy cloak of furze.

"There will be a path through it," said Siegmund.

But when they arrived there was no path. They were confronted by a tall, impenetrable growth of gorse, taller than Siegmund.

"Stay here," said he, "while I look for a way through. I am afraid you will be tired."

She stood alone by the walls of gorse. The lights that had flickered into being during the dusk grew stronger, so that a little farm-house down the hill glowed with great importance on the night, while the far-off invisible sea became like a road-way, large and mysterious, its specks of light moving slowly, and its bigger lamps stationed out amid the darkness. Helena wanted the day-wanness to be quite wiped off the west. She asked for the full black night, that would obliterate everything save Siegmund. Siegmund it was that the whole world meant. The darkness, the gorse, the downs, the specks of light, seemed only to bespeak him. She waited for him to come back. She could hardly endure the condition of intense waiting.

He came, in his grey clothes almost invisible. But she felt him coming.

"No good," he said, "no vestige of a path. Not a rabbit run."

"Then we will sit down awhile," said she calmly.

"'Here on this mole-hill— —'"* he quoted mockingly.

They sat down in a small gap in the gorse, where the turf was very soft, and where the darkness seemed deeper. The night was all fragrance, cool odour of darkness, keen, savoury scent of the downs, touched with honeysuckle and gorse and bracken-scent.

Helena turned to him, leaning her hand on his thigh.

"What day is it, Siegmund?" she asked, in joyous, wondering tone. He laughed, understanding, and kissed her.

"But really," she insisted, "I would not have believed the labels could have fallen off everything like this."

He laughed again. She still leaned towards him, her weight on her hand stopping the flow in the artery down his thigh.

"The days used to walk in procession like seven marionettes, each in order and costume, going endlessly round— —" She laughed, amused at the idea.

"It is very strange," she continued, "to have the days and nights smeared into one piece, as if the clock-hand only went round once in a lifetime."

"That is how it is," he admitted, touched by her eloquence. "You have torn the labels off things, and they all are so different. This morning! It does seem absurd to talk about this morning. Why should I be parcelled up into mornings and evenings and nights? *I* am not made up of sections of time. Now, nights and days go racing over us like cloud-shadows and sunshine over the sea, and all the time we take no notice."

She put her arms round his neck. He was reminded by a sudden pain in his leg how much her hand had been pressing on him. He held his breath from pain. She was kissing him softly over his eyes. They lay cheek to cheek, looking at the stars. He felt a peculiar tingling sense of joy, a keenness of perception, a fine, delicate tingling as of music.

"You know," he said, repeating himself, "it is true. You seem to have knit all things in a piece for me. Things are not separate: they are all in a symphony. They go moving on and on. You are the motive, in everything."

Helena lay beside him, half upon him, sad with bliss.

"You must write a symphony of this, of us," she said, prompted by a disciple's vanity.

"Some time," he answered. "Later, when I have time."

"Later," she murmured, "later than what?"

"I don't know," he replied. "This is so bright—we can't see beyond!" He turned his face to hers and through the darkness smiled into her eyes that were so close to his. Then he kissed her long and lovingly. He lay, with her head on his shoulder, looking through her hair at the stars.

"I wonder how it is you have such a fine natural perfume," he said, always in the same abstract, inquiring tone of happiness.

"Haven't all women?" she replied, and the peculiar penetrating twang of a brass reed was again in her voice.

"I don't know," he said, quite untouched. "But you are scented like nuts, new kernels of hazel-nuts, and a touch of opium— —." He remained abstractedly breathing her with his open mouth, quite absorbed in her.

"You are so strange," she murmured, tenderly, hardly able to control her voice to speak.

"I believe," he said slowly, "I can see the stars moving through your hair. No, keep still, *you* can't see them." —Helena lay obediently very still—"I thought I could watch them travelling, crawling like gold flies on the ceiling," he continued in a slow sing-song. "But now you make your hair tremble, and the stars rush about—," —then, as a new thought struck him—"Have you noticed that you can't recognise the constellations lying back like this. I can't see one. Where is the north, even?"

She laughed at the idea of his questioning her, concerning these things. She refused to learn the names of the stars, or of the constellations; as of the wayside plants: "Why should I want to label them?" she would say. "I prefer to look at them, not to hide them under a name." So she laughed when he asked her to find Vega or Arcturus.

"How full the sky is!" Siegmund dreamed on, "like a crowded street. Down here, it is vastly lonely in comparison. We've found a place far quieter and more private than the stars, Helena. Isn't it fine to be up here, with the sky for nearest neighbour?"

"I did well to ask you to come?" she inquired wistfully. He turned to her.

"As wise as God for the minute," he replied softly. "I think a few furtive angels brought us here—smuggled us in."

"And you are glad?" she asked. He laughed.

"'Carpe diem'," * he said. "We have plucked a beauty, my dear. With this rose in my coat I dare go to Hell or anywhere."

"Why Hell, Siegmund?" she asked in displeasure.

"I suppose it is the 'postero'. In everything else I'm a failure, Helena. But," he laughed, "this Day of ours is a Rose not many men have plucked."*

She kissed him passionately, beginning to cry in quick, noiseless fashion.

"What does it matter, Helena?" he murmured. "What does it matter!—We are here yet."

The quiet tone of Siegmund moved her with a vivid passion of grief. She felt she should lose him. Clasping him very closely, she burst into uncontrollable sobbing. He did not understand, but he did not interrupt her. He merely held her very close, while he looked through her shaking hair at the motionless stars. He bent* his head to hers, he sought her face with his lips, heavy with pity. She grew a little quieter. He felt his cheek all wet with her tears, and, between his cheek and hers, the ravelled roughness of her wet hair, that chafed and made his face burn.

"What is it, Helena?" he asked, at last, "why should you cry?"

She pressed her face in his breast, and said in a muffled, unrecognisable voice:

"You won't leave me, will you Siegmund?"

"How could I? How should I!" he murmured soothingly. She lifted her face suddenly and pressed on him a fierce kiss.

"How could I leave you?" he repeated, and she heard his voice waking, felt the grip coming into his arms, and she was glad.

An intense silence came over everything. Helena almost expected to hear the stars moving, everything below was so still. She had no idea what Siegmund was thinking. He lay with his arms strong around her. Then she heard the beating of his heart, like the muffled sound of salutes, she thought. It gave her the same thrill of dread and excitement, mingled with a sense of triumph. Siegmund had changed again, his mood was gone, so that he was no longer wandering in a night of thoughts, but had become different, incomprehensible to her.

She had no idea what he thought or felt. All she knew was that he was strong, and was knocking urgently with his heart on her breast, like a man who wanted something, and who dreaded to be sent away. How he came to be so concentratedly urgent she could not understand. It seemed an unreasonable, an incomprehensible obsession, to her. Yet she was glad, and she smiled in her heart, feeling triumphant and restored. Yet again, dimly, she wondered where was the Siegmund of ten minutes ago, and her heart lifted slightly with yearning, to sink with a dismay. This Siegmund was so incomprehensible. Then again, when he raised his head and found her mouth, his lips filled her with a hot flush like wine, a sweet, flaming flush of her whole body, most exquisite, as if she were nothing but a soft rosy flame of fire against him for a moment or two. That, she decided, was supreme, transcendental.

The lights of the little farm-house below had vanished, the yellow specks of ships were gone. Only the pier-light, far away, shone on the black sea like the broken piece of a star. Overhead was a silver-greyness of stars: below was the velvet blackness of the night and the sea. Helena found herself glimmering with fragments of poetry, as she saw the sea, when she looked very closely, glimmered dustily with a reflection of stars.

"Tiefe Stille herrscht im Wasser
Ohne Regung ruht das Meer— —."*

She was very fond of what scraps of German verse she knew. With French verse she had no sympathy; but Goethe and Heine and Uhland* seemed to speak her language.

"Die Luft ist kühl, und es dunkelt,
Und ruhig fliesst der Rhein."*

She liked Heine best of all:

"Wie Träume der Kindheit seh'ich es flimmern
Auf deinen wogenden Wellengebiet,
Und alte Errinnrung erzählt mir auf's Neue
Von all dem lieben herrlichen Spielzeug,
Von all den blinkenden Weihnachtsgaben— —."*

As she lay in Siegmund's arms again, and he was very still, dreaming she knew not what, fragments such as these flickered and were gone, like the gleam of a falling star over water. The night moved on imperceptibly across the sky. Unlike the day, it made no sound and gave no sign, but passed unseen, unfelt over them. Till the moon was ready to step forth. Then the eastern sky blenched, and there was a small gathering of clouds round the opening gates.

"Aus alten Märchen winkt es
Hervor mit weisser Hand,
Da singt es und da klingt es
Von einem Zauberland."*

Helena sang this to herself as the moon lifted slowly among the clouds. She found herself repeating them aloud, in a forgetful sing-song, as children do.

"What is it?" said Siegmund. They were both of them sunk in their own stillness, therefore it was a moment or two before she repeated her sing-song, in a little louder tone; he did not listen to her, having forgotten that he had asked her a question.

"Turn your head," she told him, when she had finished the verse, "and look at the moon."

He pressed back his head, so that there was a gleaming pallor on his chin and his forehead, and a deep black shadow over his eyes and his nostrils. This thrilled Helena with a sense of mystery, and magic.

"'Die grosse Blumen schmachten,'"* she said to herself, curiously awake and joyous: "The big flowers open with black petals and silvery ones, Siegmund. You are the big flowers, Siegmund; yours is the bridegroom face, Siegmund, like a black and glistening flesh-petalled flower, Siegmund, and it blooms in the Zauberland, Siegmund; this is the magic-land."

Between the phrases of this whispered ecstasy, she kissed him swiftly on the throat, in the shadow, and on his faintly gleaming cheeks. He lay still, his heart beating heavily: he was almost afraid of the strange ecstasy she concentrated on him. Meanwhile she whispered over him sharp, breathless phrases in German and English, touching him with her mouth and her cheeks and her forehead.

"'Und Liebesweisen tönen'*—not tonight, Siegmund. They are all still—gorse and the stars and the sea and the trees, are all kissing, Siegmund. The sea has its mouth on the earth, and the gorse and the trees press together, and they all look up at the moon, they put up their faces in a kiss, my darling. But they haven't you—and it all centres in you—my dear—all the wonderlove is in you, more than in them all, Siegmund—Siegmund—"

He felt the tears falling on him as he lay with heart beating in slow, heavy drops, under the ecstasy of her love. Then she sank down and lay prone on him, spent, clinging to him, lifted up and down by the beautiful strong motion of his breathing. Rocked thus on his strength, she swooned lightly into unconsciousness.

When she came to herself she sighed deeply. She woke to the exquisite heaving of his life beneath her.

"I have been beyond life. I have been a little way into death," she said to her soul, with wide-eyed delight. She lay dazed, wondering upon it. That she should come back into a marvellous, peaceful happiness astonished her.

Suddenly she became aware that she must be slowly weighing down the life of Siegmund. There was a long space between the lift of one breath, and the next. Her heart melted with sorrowful pity. Resting herself on her hands, she kissed him, a long, anguished kiss, as if she would fuse her soul into his for ever. Then she rose, sighing, sighing again deeply. She put up her hands to her head and looked at the moon. "No more," said her heart, almost as if it sighed too: "No more!"

She looked down at Siegmund. He was drawing in great heavy breaths. He lay still on his back, gazing up at her, and she stood motionless at his side, looking down at him. He felt stunned, half-conscious. Yet as he lay helplessly looking up at her, some other consciousness inside him murmured "Hawwa,—Eve—Mother!"* She stood compassionate over him. Without touching him, she seemed to be yearning over him like a mother. Her compassion, her benignity, seemed so different from his little Helena. This woman tall and pale, drooping with the strength of her compassion, seemed stable, immortal, not a fragile human being, but a personification of the great motherhood of woman.

"I am her child, too," he dreamed, as a child murmurs unconscious in sleep. He had never felt her eyes so much as now, in the darkness, when he looked only into deep shadow. She had never before so entered and gathered his plaintive masculine soul to the bosom of her nurture.

"Come," she said gently, when she knew he was restored. "Shall we go?"

He rose, with difficulty gathering his strength.

XII

Siegmund made a great effort to keep the control of his body. The hillside, the gorse, when he stood up, seemed to have fallen back into shadowed vagueness about him. They were meaningless dark heaps at some distance, very great, it seemed.

"I can't get hold of them," he said distractedly to himself. He felt detached from the earth, from all the near, concrete, beloved things; as if these had melted away from him, and left him, sick and unsupported, somewhere alone on the edge of an enormous space. He wanted to lie down again, to relieve himself of the sickening effort of supporting and controlling his body. If he could lie down again perfectly still, he need not struggle to animate the cumbersome matter of his body, and then he would not feel thus sick and outside himself.

But Helena was speaking to him, telling him they would see the moon-path. They must set off down hill. He felt her arm clasped firmly, joyously round his waist. Therein was his stability and warm support. Siegmund felt a keen flush of pitiful tenderness for her as she walked with buoyant feet beside him, clasping him so happily, all unconscious. This pity for her drew him nearer to life.

He shuddered lightly, now and again, as they stepped lurching down the hill. He set his jaws hard to suppress this shuddering. It was not in his limbs, or even on the surface of his body, for Helena did not notice it. Yet he shuddered almost in anguish, internally.

"What is it?" he asked himself in wonder.

His thought consisted of these detached phrases which he spoke verbally to himself. Betweenwhiles, he was conscious only of an almost insupportable feeling of sickness, as a man feels who is being brought from under an anaesthetic; also, he was vaguely aware of a teeming stir of activity, such as one may hear from a closed hive, within him.

They swung rapidly down hill. Siegmund still shuddered, but not so uncontrollably. They came to a stile which they must climb. As he stepped over, it needed a concentrated effort of will to place his foot securely on the step. The effort was so great that he became conscious of it.

"Good Lord!" he said to himself. "I wonder what it is."

He tried to examine himself. He thought of all the organs of his body, his brain, his heart, his liver. There was no pain, and nothing wrong with any of them, he was sure. His dim searching resolved itself into another detached phrase. "There is nothing the matter with me," he said.

Then he continued vaguely wondering, recalling the sensation of wretched sickness which sometimes follows drunkenness, thinking of the times when he had fallen ill.

"But I am not like that," he said, "because I don't feel tremulous. I am sure my hand is steady."

Helena stood still to consider the road. He held out his hand before him. It was as motionless as a dead flower on this silent night.

"Yes, I think this is the right way," said Helena, and they set off again, as if gaily.

"It certainly feels rather deathly," said Siegmund to himself. He remembered distinctly, when he was a child and had diphtheria, he had stretched himself in the horrible sickness which he felt was,—and here he chose the French word—"l'agonie."* But his mother had seen and had cried aloud, which suddenly caused him to struggle with all his soul to spare her her suffering.

"Certainly it is like that," he said. "Certainly it is rather deathly. I wonder how it is."

Then he reviewed the last hour.

"I believe we are lost," Helena interrupted him.

"Lost! What matter!" he answered indifferently, and Helena pressed him tighter, nearer to her, in a kind of triumph. "But did we not come this way?" he added.

"No, see"—her voice was reeded with restrained emotion,—"we have certainly not been along this bare path which dips up and down."

"Well then, we must merely keep due eastward, towards the moon pretty well, as much as we can," said Siegmund, looking forward over the down where the moon was wrestling heroically to win free of the pack of clouds, which hung on her like wolves on a white deer. As he looked at the moon he felt a sense of companionship. Helena, not understanding, left him so much alone: the moon was nearer.

Siegmund continued to review the last hours. He had been so wondrously happy. The world had been filled with a new magic, a wonderful, stately beauty which he had perceived for the first time.

For long hours he had been wandering in another, a glamourous primordial world.

"I suppose," he said to himself, "I have lived too intensely. I seem to have had the stars and moon and everything else for guests, and now they've gone my house is weak."

So he struggled to diagnose his case of splendour and sickness. He reviewed his hour of passion with Helena.

"Surely," he told himself, "I have drunk life too hot, and it has hurt my cup. My soul seems to leak out—I am half here—half gone away. That's why I understand the trees and the night so painfully."

Then he came to the hour of Helena's strange ecstasy over him. That, somehow, had filled him with passionate grief. It was happiness concentrated one drop too keen, so that what should have been vivid wine, was like a pure poison scathing him. But his consciousness, which had been unnaturally active, now was dulling. He felt the blood flowing vigorously along his limbs again, and stilling his brain, sweeping away his sickness, soothing him.

"I suppose," he said to himself for the last time, "I suppose living too intensely kills you, more or less."

Then Siegmund forgot. He opened his eyes and saw the night about him. The moon had escaped from the cloud-pack, and was radiant behind a fine veil which glistened to her rays, and which was broidered with a lustrous halo, very large indeed, the largest halo Siegmund had ever seen. When the little lane turned full towards the moon, it seemed as if Siegmund and Helena would walk through a large Moorish arch of horse-shoe shape, the enormous white halo opening in front of them. They walked on, keeping their faces to the moon, smiling with wonder and a little rapture, until once more the little lane curved wilfully, and they were walking north. Helena observed three cottages crouching under the hill and under trees to cover themselves from the magic of the moonlight.

"We certainly did not come this way before," she said, triumphantly. The idea of being lost delighted her.

Siegmund looked round at the grey hills smeared over with a low, dim glisten of moon-mist. He could not yet fully realise that he was walking along a lane in the Isle of Wight. His surroundings seemed to belong to some state beyond ordinary experience: some place in romance, perhaps, or among the hills where Brünnhilde lay sleeping in her large bright halo of fire.* How could it be that he and Helena were two children of London wandering to find their lodging in Freshwater

He sighed, and looked again over the hills where the moonlight was condensing in mist ethereal, frail, and yet substantial, reminding him of the way the manna must have condensed out of the white moon-lit mists of Arabian deserts.*

"We may be on the road to Newport," said Helena presently, "and the distance is ten miles." She laughed, not caring in the least whither they wandered; exulting in this wonderful excursion. She and Siegmund alone in a glistening wilderness of night, at the back of habited days and nights! Siegmund looked at her. He by no means shared her exultation, though he sympathised with it. He walked on alone in his deep seriousness, of which she was not aware. Yet when he noticed her abandon, he drew her nearer, and his heart softened with protecting tenderness towards her, and grew heavy with responsibility.

The fields breathed off a scent as if they were come to life with the night, and were talking with fragrant eagerness. The farms huddled together in sleep, and pulled the dark shadow over them to hide from the supernatural white night: the cottages were locked and darkened. Helena walked on in triumph through this wondrous hinterlandt of night, actively searching for the spirits, watching the cottages they approached, listening, looking for the dreams of those sleeping inside, in the darkened rooms. She imagined she could see the frail dream-faces at the windows: she fancied they stole out timidly into the gardens, and went running away among the rabbits on the gleamy hillside. Helena laughed to herself, pleased with her fancy of wayward little dreams playing with weak hands and feet among the large, solemn-sleeping cattle. This was the first time, she told herself, that she had ever been out among the grey-frocked dreams and white-armed fairies. She imagined herself lying asleep in her room, while her own dreams slid out down the moon-beams. She imagined Siegmund sleeping in his room, while his dreams, dark eyed, their blue eyes very dark and yearning at night-time, came wandering over the grey-grass, seeking her dreams.

So she wove her fancies as she walked, until for very weariness she was fain to remember that it was a long way, a long way. Siegmund's arm was about her to support her. She rested herself upon it. They crossed a stile and recognised, on the right of the path, the graveyard of the Catholic chapel. The moon, which the days were paring smaller with envious keen knife, shone upon the white stones in the burial ground. The carved Christ upon his cross hung against a silver-grey sky. Helena looked up wearily, bowing to the tragedy. Siegmund also looked, and bowed his head.

"Thirty years of earnest love; three years Life like a passionate ecstasy,—and it was finished. He was very great and very wonderful. I am very insignificant, and shall go out ignobly. But we are the same: love, the brief ecstasy, and the end. But mine is one rose, and his all the white beauty in the world."

Siegmund felt his heart very heavy, sad and at fault in presence of the Christ. Yet he derived comfort from the knowledge that Life was treating him in the same manner as it had treated the Master, though his compared small and despicable with the Christ-tragedy. Siegmund stepped softly into the shadow of the pine copse.

"Let me get under cover," he thought. "Let me hide in it. It is good, the sudden intense darkness. I am small and futile: my small, futile tragedy..."

Helena shrank in the darkness. It was almost terrible to her, and the silence was like a deep pit. She shrank to Siegmund. He drew her closer, leaning over her as they walked, trying to assure her. His heart was heavy, and heavy with a tenderness approaching grief, for his small, brave Helena.

"Are you sure this is the right way?" he whispered to her.

"Quite, quite sure," she whispered confidently in reply. And presently they came out into the hazy moonlight, and began stumbling down the steep hill. They were both very tired, both found it difficult to go with ease or surety this sudden way down. Soon they were creeping cautiously across the pasture and the poultry farm. Helena's heart was beating, as she imagined what a merry noise there would be should they wake all the fowls. She dreaded any commotion, any questioning, this night. So she stole carefully along till they issued on the high road not far from home.

XIII

In the morning, after bathing, Siegmund leaned upon the sea-wall in a kind of reverie. It was late, towards nine o'clock, yet he lounged, dreamily looking out on the turquoise blue water, and the white haze of morning, and the small, fair shadows of ships slowly realising before him. In the bay were two battle-ships, uncouth monsters lying as naïve and curious as sea-lions strayed afar.

Siegmund was gazing oversea in a half stupid way, when he heard a voice beside him say:

"Where have they come from? Do you know, Sir?"

He turned, saw a fair, slender man of some thirty five years standing beside him and smiling faintly at the battle-ships.

"The men of war?—there are a good many at Spithead," said Siegmund.

The other glanced negligently into his face.

"They look rather incongruous, don't you think? We left the sea empty and shining, and when we come again, behold, these objects keeping their eye on us."

Siegmund laughed.

"You are not an anarchist, I hope," he said jestingly.

"A nihilist, perhaps,"* laughed the other. "But I am quite fond of the Czar, if pity is akin to love—No—but you can't turn round without finding some policeman or other at your elbow—look at them, abominable ironmongery!—ready to put his hand on your shoulder."

The speaker's grey-blue eyes, always laughing with mockery, glanced from the battle-ships and lit on the dark blue eyes of Siegmund. The latter felt his heart lift in a convulsive movement. This stranger ran so quickly to a perturbing intimacy.

"I suppose we are in the hands of—God," something moved Siegmund to say. The stranger contracted his eyes slightly as he gazed deep at the speaker.

"Ah!" he drawled curiously. Then his eyes wandered over the wet hair, the white brow and the bare throat of Siegmund, after which they returned again to the eyes of his interlocutor.

"Does the Czar sail this way?" he asked at last.

"I do not know," replied Siegmund, who, troubled by the other's penetrating gaze,* had not expected so trivial a question.

"I suppose the newspaper will tell us," said the man.

"Sure to," said Siegmund.

"You haven't seen it this morning?"

"Not since Saturday."

The swift blue eyes of the man dilated. He looked curiously at Siegmund.

"You are not alone on your holiday?"

"No." Siegmund did not like this—he gazed over the sea in displeasure.

"I live here—at least for the present—Name Hampson—"*

"Why, weren't you one of the first violins at the Savoy* fifteen years back?" asked Siegmund

They chatted awhile about music. They had known each other, had been fairly intimate, and had since become strangers. Hampson excused himself for having addressed Siegmund:

"I saw you with your nose flattened against the window," he said, "and as I had mine in the same position too, I thought we were fit to be re-acquainted."

Siegmund looked at the man in astonishment.

"I only mean you were staring rather hard at nothing. It's a pity to try and stare out of a beautiful blue day like this, don't you think?"

"Stare beyond it, you mean?" asked Siegmund.

"Exactly!" replied the other, with a laugh of intelligence. "I call a day like this, 'the blue room.' It's the least draughty apartment in all the confoundedly draughty House of Life."

Siegmund look at him very intently. This Hampson seemed to express something in his own soul.

"I mean," the man explained, "that after all, the great mass of life that washes unidentified, and that we call death, creeps through the blue envelope of the day, and through our white tissue, and we can't stop it, once we've begun to leak."

"What do you mean by 'leak'?" asked Siegmund.

"Goodness knows—I talk through my hat. But once you've got a bit tired of the House, you glue your nose to the window pane, and stare for the dark—as you were doing."

"But, to use your metaphor, I'm not tired of the House—if you mean Life," said Siegmund.

"Praise God, I've met a poet who's not afraid of having his pocket picked—or his soul—or his brain," said the stranger, throwing his head back in a brilliant smile, his eyes dilated.

"I don't know what you mean Sir," said Siegmund, very quietly, with a strong fear and a fascination opposing each other in his heart.

"You're not tired of the House—but of your own particular room—say suite of rooms—."

"Tomorrow I am turned out of this 'Blue Room,'" said Siegmund with a wry smile. The other looked at him seriously.

"Dear Lord!" exclaimed Hampson—then: "Do you remember Flaubert's saint, who laid naked against a leper?* I could *not* do it."

"Nor I!"* shuddered Siegmund.

"But you've got to—or something near it—?"

Siegmund looked at the other with frightened, horrified eyes.

"What of yourself?" he said, resentfully.

"I funked—ran away from my leper, and now am eating my heart out, and staring from the window at the dark."

"But can't you *do* something?" said Siegmund.

The other man laughed with amusement, throwing his head back and showing his teeth.

"I won't ask you what *your* intentions are," he said, with delicate irony in his tone. "You know, I am a tremendously busy man: I earn five hundred a year by hard work. But it's no good. If you have acquired a liking for intensity in life, you can't do without it. I mean vivid soul-experience. It takes the place, with us, of the old adventure, and physical excitement."

Siegmund looked at the other man with baffled, anxious eyes.

"Well, and what then?" he said.

"What then? A craving for intense life is nearly as deadly as any other craving. You become a 'concentré';* you feed your normal flame with oxygen, and it devours your tissue. The soulful ladies of romance are always semi transparent."

Siegmund laughed.

"At least, I am quite opaque," he said.

The other glanced over his easy, mature figure and strong throat.

"Not altogether," said Hampson. "And you, I should think, are one whose flame goes nearly out, when the stimulant is lacking."

Siegmund glanced again at him, startled.

"You haven't much reserve. You're like a tree that'll flower till it kills itself," the man continued. "You'll run till you drop, and then you won't get up again. You've no dispassionate intellect to control you and economise."

"You're telling me very plainly what I am and am not," said Siegmund, laughing rather sarcastically. He did not like it.

"Oh, it's only what I think," replied Hampson. "We're a good deal alike, you see, and have gone the same way. You married, and I didn't, but women have always done as they liked with me."

"That's hardly so in my case," said Siegmund.

Hampson eyed him critically:

"Say one woman, it's enough," he replied.

Siegmund gazed, musing, over the sea.

"The best sort of women—the most interesting—are the worst for us," Hampson resumed. "By instinct they aim at suppressing the gross and animal in us. Then they are supersensitive—refined a bit beyond humanity. We who are as little gross as need be, become their instruments. Life is grounded in them, like electricity in the earth; and we take from them the unrealised life, turn it into light or warmth or power for them. The ordinary woman is, alone, a great potential force, an accumulator, if you like, charged from the Source of life. In us her force becomes evident.

"She can't live without us, but she destroys us. These deep, interesting women don't want *us*: they want the flowers of the spirit they can gather of us. We, as natural men, are more or less degrading to them and to their love of us. Therefore they destroy the natural man in us—that is, us altogether."

"You're a bit downright, are you not?" asked Siegmund, deprecatingly. He did not disagree with what his friend said, nor tell him such statements were arbitrary.

"That's according to my intensity," laughed Hampson. "I can open the blue heaven with looking, and push back the doors of day a little and see—God knows what. One of these days I shall slip through. Oh, I am perfectly sane, I only strive beyond myself."

"Don't you think it's wrong to get like it?" asked Siegmund.

"Well, I do—and so does everybody. But the crowd profits by us in the end. When they understand my music, it will be an education to them. And the whole aim of mankind is to render life intelligible."

Siegmund pondered a little.

"You make me feel—as if I were loose, and a long way off from myself," he said slowly.

The young man smiled, then looked down at the wall, where his own hands lay white and fragile, showing the blue veins.

"I can scarcely believe they are me," he said. "If they rose up and refuted me, I should not be surprised. But aren't they beautiful?"

He looked, with a faint smile, at Siegmund.

Siegmund glanced from the stranger's to his own hands, which lay curved on the sea-wall as if asleep. They were small for a man of his stature, but, lying warm in the sun, they looked particularly secure in life. Instinctively, with a wave of self love, he closed his fists over his thumbs.

"I wonder," said Hampson softly, with strange bitterness, "that she can't see it—I wonder she doesn't cherish you. You are full and beautiful enough in the flesh—why will she help to destroy you, when she loves you to such extremity."

Siegmund looked at him with awe-stricken eyes. The frail, swift man, with his intensely living eyes, laughed suddenly.

"Fools—the fools, these women," he said. "Either they smash their own crystal, or it revolts, turns opaque, and leaps out of their hands. Look at me, I am whittled down to the quick. But your neck is thick with compressed life: it is a stem so tense with life that it will hold up by itself. I am very sorry."

All at once he stopped. The bitter despair in his tone was the voice of a heavy feeling of which Siegmund had been vaguely aware for some weeks. Siegmund felt a sense of doom. He laughed, trying to shake it off.

"I wish I didn't go on like this," said Hampson piteously. "I wish I could be normal.—How hot it is already! You should wear a hat. It is really hot—" he pulled open his flannel shirt.

"I like the heat," said Siegmund.

"So do I."

Directly, the young man dashed the long hair on his forehead into some sort of order, bowed, and smiling in his gay fashion, walked leisurely to the village.

Siegmund stood awhile as if stunned. It seemed to him only a painful dream. Sighing deeply to relieve himself of the pain, he set off to find Helena.

XIV

In the garden of tall rose trees and nasturtiums Helena was again waiting. It was past nine o'clock, so she was growing impatient. To herself, however, she professed a great interest in a little book of verses she had bought in St. Martin's Lane for twopence.

> "A late, harsh blackbird smote him with her wings
> As through the glade, dim in the dark, she flew..."*

So she read. She made a curious, pleased sound, and remarked to herself that she thought these verses very fine. But she watched the road for Siegmund.

> "And now she takes the scissors on her thumb...
> Oh then, no more unto my lattice come."*

"H'm!" she said. "I really don't know whether I like that or not."

Therefore she read the piece again before she looked down the road.

"He really is very late. It is absurd to think he may have got drowned. But if he were washing about at the bottom of the sea, his hair loose on the water!"

Her heart stood still as she imagined this.

"But what nonsense!—I like these verses *very* much. I will read them as I walk along the side path, where I shall hear the bees, and catch the flutter of a butterfly among the words. That will be a very fitting way to read this poet."

So she strolled to the gate, glancing up now and again. There, sure enough, was Siegmund coming, the towel hanging over his shoulder, his throat bare and his face bright. She stood in the mottled shade.

"I have kept you waiting!" said Siegmund.

"Well—I was reading, you see."

She would not admit her impatience.

"I have been talking," he said.

"Talking!" she exclaimed in slight displeasure. "Have you found an acquaintance even here?"

"A fellow who was quite close friends in Savoy days—he made me feel queer—sort of Doppelgänger,* he was."

Helena glanced up swiftly and curiously.

"In what way?" she said.

"He talked all the skeletons in the cupboard—such piffle it seems, now!—The sea is like a hare-bell, and there are two battle-ships lying in the bay. You can hear the voices of the men on deck distinctly.—Well, have you made the plans for today—?"

They went into the house to breakfast. She watched him helping himself to the scarlet and green salad.

"Mrs Curtiss," she said, in rather reedy tone, "has been very motherly to me this morning, oh very motherly."

Siegmund, who was in a warm, gay mood, shrank up.

"What, has she been saying something about last night?" he asked.

"She was very much concerned for me—was afraid something dreadful had happened," continued Helena, in the same keen, sarcastic tone which showed she was trying to rid herself of her own mortification.

"Because we weren't in till about eleven," said Siegmund, also with sarcasm.

"I mustn't do it again—Oh no, I mustn't do it again—really."

"For fear of alarming the old lady?" he asked.

"'You know, dear, it troubles *me* a good deal... but if I were your *mother*, I don't know *how* I should feel'," she quoted.

"When one engages rooms, one doesn't usually stipulate for a step-mother, to nourish one's conscience," said Siegmund. They laughed, making jest of the affair. But they were both too thin-skinned. Siegmund writhed within himself, with mortification, while Helena talked as if her teeth were on edge.

"I don't *mind*, in the least," she said. "The poor old woman has her opinions, and I mine."

Siegmund brooded a little.

"I know I'm a moral coward," he said bitterly.

"Nonsense!" she replied. Then, with a little heat: "But you *do* continue to try so hard to justify yourself, as if *you* felt you needed justification."

He laughed bitterly.

"I tell you—a little thing like this—it remains tied tight round something inside me, reminding me for hours—well, what everybody else's opinion of me is."

Helena laughed, rather plaintively.

"I thought you were so sure we were right," she said.

He winced again.

"In myself, I am. But in the eyes of the world— —"

"If you feel so in yourself, is not that enough?" she said brutally.

He hung his head, and slowly turned his serviette ring.

"What is myself?" he asked.

"Nothing very definite," she said, with a bitter laugh.

They were silent. After a while she rose, went lovingly over to him, and put her arms round his neck.

"This is our last clear day, dear," she said.

A wave of love came over him, sweeping away all the rest. He took her in his arms...

"It will be hot today," said Helena, as they prepared to go out.

"I felt the sun steaming in my hair as I came up," he replied.

"I shall wear a hat—you had better do so too."

"No," he said. "I told you I wanted a sun-soaking: now I think I shall get one."

She did not urge or compel him. In these matters he was old enough to choose for himself.

This morning they were rather silent. Each felt the tarnish on their remaining day.

"I think, dear," she said, "we ought to find the little path that escaped us last night."

"We were lucky to miss it," he answered. "You don't get a walk like that twice in a life time, in spite of the old ladies."

She glanced up at him with a winsome smile, glad to hear his words.

They set off, Siegmund bare-headed. He was dressed in flannels and a loose canvas shirt, but he looked what he was, a Londoner on holiday. He had the appearance, a diffident bearing, and the well-cut clothes of a gentleman. He had a slight stoop, a strong shouldered stoop, and as he walked he looked unseeing in front of him.

Helena belonged to the unclassed. She was not ladylike, nor smart, nor assertive; one could not tell whether she were of independent means, or a worker. One thing was obvious about her: she was evidently educated.

Rather short, of strong figure, she was much more noticeably a "concentrée" than was Siegmund. Unless definitely looking at something she always seemed coiled within herself.

She wore a white voile dress made with the waist just below her breasts, and the skirt dropping straight and clinging. On her head was a large, simple hat of burnt straw.

Through the open-worked sleeves of her dress she could feel the sun bite vigorously.

"I wish you had put on a hat Siegmund," she said.

"Why?" he laughed. "My hair is like a hood." He ruffled it back with his hand. The sunlight glistened on his forehead.

On the higher paths, a fresh breeze was energetically chasing the butterflies and driving the few small clouds disconsolate out of the sky. The lovers stood for some time watching the people of the farm in the down below dip their sheep* on this sunny morning. There was a ragged noise of bleating from the flock penned in a corner of the yard. Two red-armed men seized a sheep, hauled it to a large bath that stood in the middle of the yard, and there held it, more or less in the bath, whilst a third man baled a dirty yellow liquid over its body. The white legs of the sheep twinkled as it butted this way and that to escape the yellow douche, the blue-shirted men ducked and struggled. There was a faint splashing and shouting to be heard even from a distance. The farmer's wife and children stood by ready to rush in with assistance if necessary.

Helena laughed with pleasure.

"That is really a very quaint and primitive proceeding," she said. "It is cruder than Theocritus."*

"In an instant, it makes me wish I were a farmer," he laughed. "I think every man has a passion for farming, at the bottom of his blood. It would be fine to be plain-minded, to see no further than the end of one's nose, and to own cattle and land."

"Would it?" asked Helena sceptically.

"If I had a red face, and went to sleep as soon as I sat comfortable, I should love it," he said.

"It amuses me to hear you long to be stupid," she replied.

"To have a simple, slow-moving mind, and an active life is the desideratum."

"Is it?" she asked, ironically.

"I would give anything to be like that," he said.

"That is, not to be yourself," she said pointedly.

He laughed without much heartiness.

"Don't they seem a long way off?" he said, staring at the bucolic scene. "They are farther than Theocritus—down there is farther than Sicily, and more then twenty centuries from us.—I wish it weren't."

"Why do you?" she cried, with curious impatience.

He laughed.

Crossing the down, scattered with dark bushes, they came directly opposite the path through the furze.

"There it is!" she cried. "How could we miss it?"

"Ascribe it to the fairies," he replied, whistling the bird-music out of "Siegfried," then pieces of "Tristan."* They talked very little.

She was tired. When they arrived at a green, naked hollow near the cliff's edge, she said:

"This shall be our house today."

"Welcome home!" said Siegmund.

He flung himself down on the high, breezy slope of the dip, looking out to sea. Helena sat beside him. It was absolutely still, and the wind was slackening more and more. Though they listened attentively, they could hear only an indistinct breathing sound, quite small, from the water below: no clapping, nor hoarse conversation of waves. Siegmund lay with his hands beneath his head, looking over the sparkling sea. To put her page in the shadow, Helena propped her book against him, and began to read.

Presently the breeze, and Siegmund, dropped asleep. The sun was pouring with dreadful persistence. It beat and beat on Helena, gradually drawing her from her book in a confusion of thought. She closed her eyes wearily, longing for shade. Vaguely, she felt a sympathy with Adama in "Adam Cast Forth."* Her mind traced again the tumultuous, obscure strugglings of the two, forth from Eden through the primitive wildernesses, and she felt sorrowful. Thinking of Adam blackened with struggle, she looked down at Siegmund. The sun was beating him upon the face and upon his glistening brow. His two hands, which lay out on the grass, were full of blood, the veins of his wrists purple and swollen with heat. Yet he slept on, breathing with a slight, panting motion. Helena felt deeply moved. She wanted to kiss him, as he lay helpless, abandoned to the charge of the earth and the sky. She wanted to kiss him, and shed a few tears. She did neither, but instead moved her position so that she shaded his head. Cautiously putting her hand on his hair, she found it warm, quite hot, as when you put your hand under a sitting hen and feel the hot-feathered bosom.

"It will make him ill," she whispered to herself, and she bent over to smell the hot hair. She noticed where the sun was scalding his forehead. She felt very pitiful and helpless, when she saw his brow becoming inflamed with the sun-scalding.

Turning weariedly away, she sought relief in the landscape. But the sea was glittering unbearably, like a scaled dragon wreathing. The houses of Freshwater slept, as cattle sleep motionless in the hollow valley. Green Farringford on the slope was drawn over with a shadow of heat and sleep. In the bay below the hill, the sea was hot and restless. Helena was sick with sunshine and the restless glitter of water.

"'And there shall be no more sea,'"* she quoted to herself, she knew not wherefrom.

"No more sea, no more anything," she thought, dazedly, as she sat in the midst of this fierce welter of sunshine. It seemed to her as if all the lightness of her fancy and her hope were being burned away in this tremendous furnace, leaving her, Helena, like a heavy piece of slag seamed with metal. She tried to imagine herself resuming the old activities, the old manner of living.

"It is impossible," she said, "it is impossible. What shall I be when I come out of this? I shall not come out—except as metal to be cast in another shape. No more the same Siegmund, no more the same life. What will become of us, what will happen?"

She was roused from these semi-delirious speculations in the sun-furnace by Siegmund's waking. He opened his eyes, took a deep breath, and looked smiling at Helena.

"It is worth while to sleep," said he, "for the sake of waking like this. I was dreaming of huge ice-crystals."

She smiled at him. He seemed unconscious of fate, happy and strong. She smiled upon him almost in condescension.

"I should like to realise your dream," she said, "This is terrible!"

They went to the cliff's edge, to receive the cool up-flow of air from the water. She drank the travelling freshness eagerly with her face, and put forward her sunburnt arms to be refreshed.

"It is really a very fine sun," said Siegmund lightly. "I feel as if I were almost satisfied with heat."

Helena felt the chagrin of one whose wretchedness must go unperceived, while she affects a light interest in another's pleasure. This time, when Siegmund 'failed to follow her'*—as she put it—, she felt she must follow him.

"You are having your satisfaction complete this journey," she said, smiling; "even a sufficiency of me."

"Ay," said Siegmund, drowsily. "I think I am. I think this is about perfect, don't you?"

She laughed.

"I want nothing more, and nothing different," he continued; "and that's the extreme of a decent time, I should think."

"The extreme of a decent time!" she repeated.

But he drawled on lazily:

"I've only rubbed my bread on the cheese-board until now. Now I've got all the cheese—which is you, my dear."

"I certainly feel eaten up," she laughed, rather bitterly. She saw him lying in a royal ease, his eyes naïve as a boy's, his whole being careless. Although very glad to see him thus happy, for herself, she felt very lonely. Being listless with sun-weariness, and heavy with a sense of impending fate, she felt a great yearning of this sympathy, his fellow-suffering. Instead of receiving this, she had to play to his buoyant happiness, so as not to shrivel one petal of his flower, or spoil one minute of his consummate hour.

From the high point of the cliff where they stood, they could see the path winding down to the beach, and broadening upwards towards them. Slowly approaching up the slight incline came a black invalid's chair, wheeling silently over the short, dry grass. The invalid, a young man, was so much deformed that already his soul seemed to be wilting in his pale sharp face, as if there were not enough life-flow in the distorted body to develop the fair bud of the spirit. He turned his pain-sunken eyes towards the sea, whose meaning, like that of all things, was half obscure to him. Siegmund glanced, and glanced quickly away, before he should see. Helena looked intently for two seconds. She thought of the torn, shrivelled sea-weed flung above the reach of the tide— "the life-tide," she said to herself. The pain of the invalid overshadowed her own distress. She was fretted to her soul.

"Come!" she said quietly to Siegmund, no longer resenting the completeness of his happiness, which left her unnecessary to him.

"We will leave the poor invalid in possession of our green hollow—so quiet," she said to herself.

They sauntered downwards towards the bay. Helena was brooding on her own state, after her own fashion.

"The Mist-Spirit," she said to herself. "The Mist-Spirit draws a curtain round us, it is very kind. A heavy gold curtain sometimes; a thin torn curtain sometimes. I want the Mist-Spirit to close the curtain again: I do not want to think of the outside: I am afraid of the outside, and I am afraid when the curtain tears open in rags. I want to be in our own fine world inside the heavy gold mist-curtain."

As if in answer or in protest to her thoughts, Siegmund said:

"Do you want anything better than this, dear?—Shall we come here next year, and stay for a whole month?"

"If there be any next year," said she.

Siegmund did not reply.

She wondered if he had really spoken in sincerity, or if he too were mocking fate. They walked slowly through the broiling sun towards their lodging.

"There will be an end to this," said Helena, communing with herself. "And when we come out of the mist-curtain, what will it be. No matter—let come what will. All along, Fate has been resolving, from the very beginning, resolving obvious discords, gradually, by unfamiliar progressions; and out of original combinations weaving wondrous harmonies with our lives. Really, the working out has been wondrous, is wondrous, now. The Master-Fate is too great an artist to suffer an anti-climax. I am sure the Master Musician is too great an artist to allow a bathetic anti-climax."

XV

The afternoon of the blazing day passed drowsily. Lying close together on the beach, Siegmund and Helena let the day exhale its hours like perfume, unperceived. Siegmund slept, a light evanescent sleep irised with dreams and with suffering: nothing definite, the colour of dreams without the shape. Helena, as usual, retained her consciousness much more clearly. She watched the far-off floating of ships, and the near wading of children through the surf. Endless trains of thought, like little waves, rippled forward and broke on the shore of her drowsiness. But each thought-ripple, though it ran lightly, was tinged with copper-coloured gleams as from a lurid sunset. Helena felt that the sun was setting on her and Siegmund. The hour was too composed, spell-bound, for grief or anxiety or even for close perception. She was merely aware that the sun was wheeling down, tangling Siegmund and her in the traces, like overthrown charioteers. So the hours passed.

After tea they went eastwards, on the downs. Siegmund was animated, so that Helena caught his mood. It was very rare that they spoke of the time preceding their acquaintance. Helena knew little or nothing of Siegmund's life up to the age of thirty, whilst he had never learned anything concerning her childhood. Somehow, she did not encourage him to self-discovery. Today, however, the painful need of lovers for self-revelation took hold on him.

"It is awfully funny," he said. "I was *so* gone on Beatrice when I married her. She had only just come back from Egypt—her father was an army officer, a very handsome man, and, I believe, a bit of a rake. Beatrice is really well connected, you know. But old FitzHerbert ran through all his money, and through everything else. He was too hot for the rest of the family, so they dropped him altogether.

"He came to live at Peckham when I was sixteen. I had just left school, and was to go into father's business. Mrs FitzHerbert left cards, and very soon we were acquainted. Beatrice had been a good time in a French covent school. She had only knocked about with the army a little while, but it had brought her out. I remember I thought she was miles above me—which she was. She wasn't bad looking, either, and you know men all like her. I bet she'd marry again, in spite of the children.

"At first I fluttered round her. I remember I'd got a little, silky moustache. They all said I looked older than sixteen. At that time I was mad on the violin, and she played rather well. Then FitzHerbert went off abroad somewhere, so Beatrice and her mother half lived at our house. The mother was an invalid.

"I remember I nearly stood on my head one day. The conservatory opened off the smoking room, so when I came in the room, I heard my two sisters and Beatrice talking about good-looking men.

"'I consider Bertram will make a handsome man,' said my younger sister.

"'He's got beautiful eyes,' said my other sister.

"'And a real darling nose and chin,' cried Beatrice. 'If only he was more *solide*.* He is like a windmill, all limbs.'

"'He will fill out. Remember, he's not quite seventeen,' said my elder sister.

"'Ah, he is *doux*—he is *câlin*,'* said Beatrice.

"'I think he is rather *too* spoony for his age,'* said my elder sister.

"'But he's a fine boy for all that: see how thick his knees are,' my younger sister chimed in.

"'Ah *si si*!' cried Beatrice.

"I made a row against the door, then walked across.

"'Hello, is somebody in here?' I said, as I pushed into the little conservatory.

"I looked straight at Beatrice, and she at me. We seemed to have formed an alliance in that look: she was the other half of my consciousness, I of hers. Ha—ha—there were a lot of white narcissus, and little white hyacinths, Roman hyacinths, in the conservatory. I can see them now, great white stars, and tangles of little ones, among a bank of green; and I can recall the keen, fresh scent on the warm air: and the look of Beatrice...her great, dark eyes.

"It's funny, but that Beatrice is as dead—ay, far more dead than Dante's.* And I am not that young fool, not a bit.

"I was very romantic, fearfully emotional, and the soul of honour. Beatrice said nobody cared a thing about her. FitzHerbert was always jaunting off, the mother was a fretful invalid. So I was seventeen, earning half a guinea a week, and she was eighteen, with no money, when we ran away to Brighton and got married. Poor old Pater, he took it awfully well. I have been a frightful drag on him, you know.

"There's the romance—I wonder how it will all end."

Helena laughed, and he did not detect her extreme bitterness of spirit.

They walked on in silence for some time. He was thinking back, before Helena's day. This left her very much alone, and forced on her the idea that, after all, love, which she chose to consider as single and wonderful a thing in a man's life as birth or adolescence or death, was temporary, and formed only an episode. It was her hour of disillusion.

"Come to think of it," Siegmund continued, "I have always shirked. Whenever I've been in a tight corner, I've gone to Pater."

"I think," she said, "marriage has been a tight corner you couldn't get out of to go to anybody."

"Yet I'm here," he answered simply.

The blood suffused her face and neck.

"And some men would have made a better job of it. When it's come to sticking out against Beatrice, and sailing the domestic ship in spite of her, I've always funked. I tell you I'm something of a moral coward."

He had her so much on edge, she was inclined to answer: "So be it." Instead, she ran back over her own history: it consisted of petty discords in contemptible surroundings, then of her dreams and fancies; finally Siegmund.

"In my life," she said, with the fine, grating discord in her tones, "I might say *always*, the real life has seemed just outside—brownies running and fairies peeping—just beyond the common, ugly place where I am. I seem to have been hedged in by vulgar circumstances, able to glimpse outside now and then, and see the reality."

"You are so hard to get at," said Siegmund. "And so scornful of familiar things."

She smiled, knowing he did not understand. The heat had jaded her, so that physically she was full of discord, of dreariness that set her teeth on edge. Body and soul, she was out of tune.

A warm, noiseless twilight was gathering over the downs, and rising darkly from the sea. Fate, with wide wings, was hovering just over her. Fate, ashen grey and black, like a carrion crow, had her in its shadow. Yet Siegmund took no notice. He did not understand. He walked beside her, whistling to himself, which only distressed her the more.

They were alone on the smooth hills to the east. Helena looked at the day melting out of the sky, leaving the permanent structure of the night. It was her turn to suffer the sickening detachment which comes after moments of intense living.

The rosiness died out of the sunset as embers fade into thick ash. In herself, too, the ruddy glow sank and went out. The earth was a cold dead heap, coloured drearily, the sky was dark with flocculent grey ash: and she herself, an upright mass of soft ash.

She shuddered slightly with horror. The whole face of things was to her livid and ghastly. Being a moralist rather than an artist, coming of fervent Wesleyan stock, she began to scourge herself. She had done wrong again. Looking back, no one had she touched without hurting. She had a destructive force: anyone she embraced, she injured. Faint voices echoed back from her conscience. The shadows were full of complaint against her. It was all true, she was a harmful force, dragging Fate to petty, mean conclusions.

Life, and hope were ash in her mouth. She shuddered with discord. Despair grated between her teeth. This dreariness was worse than any her dreary, lonely life had known. She felt she could bear it no longer.

Siegmund was there, surely he could help. He would re-kindle her. But he was straying ahead carelessly whistling the Spring Song from "Walküre."* She looked at him, and again shuddered with horror. Was that really Siegmund, that stooping, thick-shouldered, indifferent man? Was that the Siegmund who had seemed to radiate joy into his surroundings, the Siegmund whose coming had always changed the whole weather of her soul? Was that the Siegmund whose touch was keen with bliss for her, whose face was a panorama of passing God? She looked at him again. His radiance was gone, his aura had ceased. She saw him a stooping man, past the buoyancy of youth, walking and whistling rather stupidly: in short, something of the 'clothed animal on end,' like the rest of men.

She suffered an agony of disillusion. Was this the real Siegmund, and her own, only a projection of her soul? She took her breath sharply. Was he the real clay, and that other, her beloved, only the breathing of her soul upon this. There was an awful blank before her.

"Siegmund," she said in despair.

He turned sharply at the sound of her voice. Seeing her face pale and distorted in the twilight, he was filled with dismay. She mutely lifted her arms to him, watching him in despair. Swiftly he took her in his arms, and asked in a troubled voice:

"What is it, dear? Is something wrong?"

His voice was nothing to her, it was stupid. She felt his arms round her, felt her face pressed against the cloth of his coat, against the beating of his heart. What was all this? This was not comfort or love. He was not understanding or helping, only chaining her, hurting. She did not want his brute embrace—she was most utterly alone, gripped so in his arms. If he could not save her from herself, he must leave her free, to pant her heart out in free air. The secret thud, thud of his heart, the very self of that animal in him she feared and hated, repulsed her. She struggled to escape.

"What is it?—won't you tell me what is the matter?" he pleaded.

She began to sob, dry wild sobs, feeling as if she would go mad. He tried to look at her face, for which she hated him. And all the time he held her fast, all the time she was imprisoned in the embrace of this brute, blind creature, whose heart confessed itself in 'thud, thud, thud.'

"Have you heard anything against us—have I done anything—have I said anything? Tell me, at any rate tell me, Helena."

Her sobbing was like the chattering of dry leaves. She grew frantic to be free. Stifled in that prison any longer, she would choke and go mad. His coat chafed her face: as she struggled, she could see the strong working of his throat. She fought against him: she struggled in panic to be free.

"Let me go!" she cried. "Let me go, let me go." He held her in bewilderment and terror. She thrust her hands in his chest, and pushed him apart. Her face, blind to him, was very much distorted by her suffering. She thrust him furiously away, with great strength.

His heart stood still with wonder. She broke from him, and dropped down, sobbing wildly, in the shelter of the tumuli. She was bunched in a small, shaken heap. Siegmund could not bear it. He went on one knee beside her, trying to take her hand in his, and pleading:

"Only tell me, Helena, what it is. Tell me what it is. At least tell me, Helena, tell me what it is.—Oh, but this is dreadful!"

She had turned convulsively from him. She shook herself, as if beside herself, and at last covered her ears with her hands, to shut out this unreasoning pleading of his voice.

Seeing her like this, Siegmund at last gave in. Quite still, he knelt on one knee beside her, staring at the late twilight. The intense silence was crackling with the sound of Helena's dry, hissing sobs. He remained silenced, stunned by the unnatural conflict. After waiting a while, he put his hand on her. She winced convulsively away.

Then he rose, saying in his heart 'It is enough.' He went behind the small hill, and looked at the night. It was all exposed. He wanted to hide, to cover himself from the openness; and there was not even a bush under which he could find cover.

He lay down flat on the ground, pressing his face into the wiry turf, trying to hide. Quite stunned, with a death taking place in his soul, he lay still, pressed against the earth. He held his breath for a long time before letting it go: then again, he held it. He could scarcely bear, even by breathing, to betray himself. His consciousness was dark.

Helena had sobbed and struggled the life-animation back into herself. At length, weary but comfortable, she lay still to rest. Almost she could have gone to sleep. But she grew chilly, and a ground insect tickled her face. Was somebody coming?

It was dark when she rose. Siegmund was not in sight. She tidied herself, and, rather frightened, went to look for him. She saw him like a thick shadow on the earth. Now, she was heavy with tears good to shed. She stood in silent sorrow, looking at him.

Suddenly she became aware of someone passing and looking curiously at them.

"Dear!" she said softly, stooping and touching his hair. He began to struggle with himself, to respond. At that minute, he would rather have died than face anyone. His soul was too much uncovered.

"Dear, someone is looking," she pleaded.

He drew himself up from cover. But he kept his face averted. They walked on.

"Forgive me dear," she said softly.

"Nay, it's not you," he answered, and she was silenced. They walked on till the night seemed private. She turned to him, and:

"Siegmund!" she said, in a voice of great sorrow and pleading.

He took her in his arms, but did not kiss her, though she lifted her face. He put his mouth against her throat, below the ear, as she offered it, and stood looking out through the ravel of her hair, dazed, dreamy.

The sea was smoking with darkness under half luminous heavens. The stars, one after another, were catching alight. Siegmund perceived first one, and then another dimmer one flicker out in the darkness over the sea. He stood perfectly still, watching them. Gradually he remembered how, in the cathedral, the tapers of the choir-stalls would tremble and set steadily to burn, opening the darkness point after point with yellow drops of flame, as the acolyte touched them, one by one, delicately, with his rod. The night was religious, then, with its proper order of service. Day and night had their ritual, and passed in uncouth worship.

Siegmund found himself in an abbey. He looked up the nave of the night, where the sky came down on the sea like arches, and he watched the stars catch fire. At least it was all sacred, whatever the God might be. Helena herself, the bitter bread, was stuff of the ceremony, which he touched with his lips as part of the service.

He had Helena in his arms, which was sweet company, but in spirit he was quite alone. She would have drawn him back to her, and on her woman's breast have hidden him from fate, and saved him from searching the unknown. But this night he did not want comfort. If he were 'an infant crying in the night,'* it was crying that a woman could not still. He was abroad seeking courage and faith for his own soul. He, in loneliness, must search the night for faith.

"My fate is finely wrought out," he thought to himself. "Even damnation may be finely imagined for me in the night. I have come so far. Now I must get clarity and courage to follow out the theme. I don't want to botch and bungle even damnation."

But he needed to know what was right, what was the proper sequence of his acts. Staring at the darkness, he seemed to feel his course, though he could not see it. He bowed in obedience. The stars seemed to swing softly in token of submission.

XVI

Feeling him abstract, withdrawn from her, Helena experienced the dread of losing him. She was in his arms, but his spirit ignored her. That was insufferable to her pride. Yet she dared not disturb him—she was afraid. Bitterly she repented her of the giving way to her revulsion a little space before. Why had she not smothered it, and pretended? Why had she, a woman, betrayed herself so flagrantly? Now perhaps she had lost him for good. She was consumed with uneasiness.

At last she drew back from him, held him her mouth to kiss. As he gently, sadly kissed her, she pressed him to her bosom. She must get him back, whatever else she lost. She put her hand tenderly on his brow.

"What are you thinking of?" she asked.

"I?" he replied. "I really don't know. I suppose I was hardly thinking anything."

She waited a while, clinging to him, then, finding some difficulty in speech, she asked:

"Was I very cruel, dear?"

It was so unusual to hear her grieved and filled with humility, that he drew her close into him.

"It was pretty bad, I suppose," he replied. "But I should think neither of us could help it."

She gave a little sob, pressed her face into his chest, wishing she had helped it. Then, with 'Madonna' love, she clasped his head upon her shoulder, covering her hands over his hair. Twice she kissed him softly in the nape of the neck, with fond, reassuring kisses. All the while, delicately, she fondled and soothed him, till he was child to her Madonna.

They remained standing with his head on her shoulder for some time, till at last he raised himself to lay his lips on hers in a long kiss of healing and renewal, long, pale kisses of after-suffering.

Someone was coming along the path. Helena let him go, shook herself free, turned sharply aside, and said:

"Shall we go down to the water?"

"If you like," he replied, putting out his hand to her. They went thus with clasped hands down the cliff path to the beach.

There they sat in the shadow of the uprising island, facing the restless water. Around them the sand and shingle were grey; there stretched a long pale line of surf, beyond which the sea was black, and smeared with star-reflections. The deep, velvety sky shone with lustrous stars.

As yet, the moon was not risen. Helena proposed that they should lie on a tuft of sand in a black cleft of the cliff, to await its coming. They lay close together without speaking. Each was looking at a low, large star which hung straight in front of them, dripping its brilliance in a thin streamlet of light along the sea almost to their feet. It was a star-path fine and clear, trembling in its brilliance, but certain upon the water. Helena watched it with delight. As Siegmund looked at the star, it seemed to him a lantern hung at the gate to light someone home. He imagined himself following the thread of the star-track. What was behind the gate?

They heard the wash of a steamer crossing the bay. The water seemed populous in the night-time, with dark, uncanny comings and goings.

Siegmund was considering.

"What *was* the matter with you?" he asked.

She leaned over him, took his head in her lap, holding his face between her two hands as she answered, in a low, grave voice, very wise and old in experience:

"Why, you see dear, you won't understand. But there was such a greyish darkness, and through it—the crying of lives I have touched— —"

His heart suddenly shrank, and sank down. She acknowledged, then, that she also had helped to injure Beatrice and his children. He coiled with shame.

"— — —a crying of lives against me, and I couldn't silence them, nor escape out of the darkness. I wanted you—I saw you in front, whistling the Spring Song, but I couldn't find you—it was not you—I couldn't find you."

She kissed his eyes and his brows.

"No, I don't see it," he said. "You would always be you. I could think of hating you, but you'd still be yourself."

She made a moaning, loving sound. Full of passionate pity, she moved her mouth on his face, as a woman does on her child that has hurt itself.

"Sometimes," she murmured, in a low, grieved confession—"you lose me."

He gave a brief laugh.

"I lose you!" he repeated. "You mean I lose my attraction for you, or my hold over you, and then you— —?"

He did not finish. She made the same grievous, murmuring noise over him.

"It shall not be any more," she said.

"All right," he replied, "since you decide it."

She clasped him round the chest, and fondled him, distracted with pity.

"You mustn't be bitter," she murmured.

"Four days is enough," he said. "In a fortnight I should be intolerable to you. I am not masterful."

"It is not so Siegmund," she said sharply.

"I give way always," he repeated; "—and then—tonight!"

"Tonight, tonight!" she cried in wrath. "Tonight I have been a fool."

"And I?" he asked.

"You, what of you?" she cried. Then she became sad. "I have little perverse feelings," she lamented.

"And I can't bear to compel anything, for fear of hurting it. So I'm always pushed this way and that, like a fool."

"You don't know how you hurt me, talking so," she said.

He kissed her. After a moment he said:

"You are not like other folk. 'Ihr Lascheks seid ein anderes Geschlecht.'* I thought of you when we read it."

"Would you rather have me more like the rest, or more unlike, Siegmund? Which is it?"

"Neither," he said. "You are *you*."

They were quiet for a space. The only movement in the night was the faint gambolling of starlight on the water. The last person had passed, in black silhouette, between them and the sea.

He was thinking bitterly. She seemed to goad him deeper and deeper into life. He had a sense of despair, a preference of death. The German she read with him—she loved its loose and violent romance—came back to his mind: "Der Tod geht einem zur Seite, fast sichtbarlich, und jagt einen immer tiefer ins Leben."*

Well, the next place he would be hunted to, like a hare run down, was home. It seemed impossible the morrow would take him back to Beatrice.

"This time tomorrow night," he said.

"Siegmund!" she implored.

"Why not?" he laughed.

"Don't dear," she pleaded.

"All right, I won't."

Some large steamer crossing the mouth of the bay made the water clash a little as it broke in accentuated waves. A warm puff of air wandered in on them now and again.

"You won't be tired when you go back?" Helena asked.

"Tired!" he echoed.

"You know how you were when you came," she reminded him, in tones full of pity. He laughed.

"Oh, that is gone," he said.

With a slow, mechanical rhythm she stroked his cheek.

"And will you be sad?" she said, hesitating.

"Sad!" he repeated.

"But will you be able to take the old life up, happier, when you go back."

"The old life will take me up, I suppose," he said.

There was a pause.

"I think dear," she said, "I have done wrong."

"Good Lord—you have not," he replied sharply, pressing back his head to look at her, for the first time.

"I shall have to send you back to Beatrice and the babies—tomorrow—as you are now—."

"'Take no thought for the morrow.'* Be quiet, Helena!" he exclaimed as the reality bit him. He sat up suddenly.

"Why?" she asked, afraid.

"Why!" he repeated. He remained sitting, leaning forward on the sand, staring intently at Helena. She looked back in fear at him. The moment terrified her, and she lost courage.

With a fluttered motion she put her hand on his, which was pressed hard on the sand, as he leaned forward. At once he relaxed his intensity, laughed, then became tender.

Helena yielded herself like a forlorn child to his arms, and there lay, half crying, whilst he smoothed her brow with his fingers, and grains of sand fell from his palm on her cheek. She shook with dry, withered sobs, as a child does when it snatches itself away from the lancet of the doctor, and hides in the mother's bosom, refusing to be touched.

But she knew the morrow was coming, whether or not, and she

cowered down on his breast. She was wild with fear of the parting and the subsequent days. They must drink, after tomorrow, separate cups. She was filled with vague terror of what it would be. The sense of the oneness and unity of their fates was gone.

Siegmund also was cowed by the threat of separation. He had more definite knowledge of the next move than had Helena. His heart was certain of calamity, which would overtake him directly. He shrank away. Wildly, he beat about to find a means of escape from the next day, and its consequences. He did not want to go. Anything, rather than go back.

In the midst of their passion of fear, the moon rose. Siegmund started, to see the rim appear ruddily beyond the sea. His struggling suddenly ceased, and he watched, spell-bound, the oval horn of fiery gold come up, resolve itself. Some golden liquor dripped and spilled upon the far waves, where it shook in ruddy splashes. The gold-red cup rose higher, looming before him very large, yet still not all discovered. By degrees the horn of gold detached itself from the darkness at back of the waves. It was immense and terrible. When would the tip be placed upon the table of the sea?

It stood at last, whole and calm, before him. Then the night took up this drinking-cup of fiery gold, lifting it with majestic movement overhead, letting stream forth the wonderful unwasted liquor of gold over the sea, a libation.

Siegmund looked at the shaking flood of gold and paling gold spread wider as the night upraised the blanching crystal, poured out further and further the immense libation from the whitening cup, till at last the moon looked frail and empty.

And there exhaustless in the night the white light shook on the floor of the sea. He wondered how it would be gathered up. "I gather it up into myself," he said. And the stars and the cliffs and a few trees were watching, too. "If I have spilled my life," he thought, "the unfamiliar eyes of the land and sky will gather it up again."

Turning to Helena, he found her face white and shining as the empty moon.

XVII

Toward morning, Siegmund went to sleep. For four hours, until seven o'clock, the womb of sleep received him and nourished him again.

"But it is finest of all to wake," he said, as the bright sunshine of the window, and the lumining green sunshine coming through the lifted hands of the leaves, challenged him into the open.

The morning was exceedingly fair, and it looked at him so gently, that his blue eyes trembled with self-pity. A fragment of scarlet geranium glanced up at him as he passed, so that amid the vermilion tyranny of the uniform it wore, he could see the eyes of the flower, wistful, offering him love, as one sometimes sees the eyes of a man beneath the brass helmet of a soldier, and is startled. Everything looked at him with the same eyes of tenderness, offering him, timidly, a little love.

"They are all extraordinarily sweet," said Siegmund to the full-mouthed scabious and the awkward, down-cast ragwort. Three or four butterflies fluttered up and down, in agitated little leaps, around him. Instinctively Siegmund put his hand forward to touch them.

"The careless little beggars!" he said.

While he came to the cliff-tops there was the morning, very bravely dressed, rustling forward with a silken sound and much silken shining to meet him. The battle-ships had gone, the sea was blue with the panier of diamonds, the sky was full with a misty tenderness, like love. Siegmund had never recognised before the affection that existed between him and everything. We do not realise how tremendously dear and indispensable to us are the hosts of common things, till we must leave them, and we break our hearts.

"We have been very happy together," everything* seemed to say.

Siegmund looked up into the eyes of the morning with a laugh.

"It is very lovely," he said, "whatever happens."

As he went down to the beach his dark blue eyes, darker from last night's experience, smiled always with the pride of love. He undressed by his usual altar-stone.

"How closely familiar everything is," he thought. "It seems almost as if the curves of this stone were rounded to fit in my soul." He touched the smooth white slope of the stone gently, with discovering fingers, in the same way as he touched the cheek of Helena, or of his own babies. He found great pleasure in this feeling of intimacy with things. A very soft wind, shy as a girl, put its arms round him, and seemed to lay its cheek against his chest. He placed his hands beneath his arms, where the wind was caressing him, and his eyes opened with wondering pleasure.

"They find no fault with me," he said. "I suppose they are as fallible as I, and so don't judge," he added, as he waded thigh-deep into the water, thrusting it to hear the mock-angry remonstrance.

"Once more," he said, and he took the sea in his arms. He swam very quietly. The water buoyed him up, holding him closely clasped. He swam towards the white rocks of the headlands. They rose before him like beautiful buttressed gates, so glistening that he half expected to see fan-tail pigeons puffing like white irises in the niches, and white peacocks with dark green feet stepping down the terraces, trailing a sheen of silver.

"Helena is right," he said to himself as he swam, scarcely swimming but moving upon the bosom of the tide, "she is right, it is all enchanted. I have got into her magic at last. Let us see what it is like."

He determined to visit again his little bay. He swam carefully round the terraces, whose pale shadows through the swift-spinning emerald-facets of the water seemed merest fancy. Siegmund touched them with his foot. They were hard, cold, dangerous. He swam carefully. As he made for the archway, the shadows of the headland chilled the water. There underwater, clamouring in a throng at the base of the submerged walls, were sea-women with dark locks, and young sea-girls with soft hair vividly green, striving to climb up out of the darkness into the morning, their hair swirling in abandon. Siegmund was half afraid of their frantic efforts.

But the tide carried him swiftly through the high gate, into the porch. There was exultance in this sweeping entry. The skin-white, full-fleshed walls of the archway were dappled with green lights that danced in and out among themselves. Siegmund was carried along in an invisible chariot, beneath the jewel-stained walls. The tide swerved, threw him as he swam against the inward-curving white rock. His elbow met the rock, and he was sick with pain. He held his breath, trying to get back the joy and magic. He could not believe that the lovely, smooth side of the rock, fair as his own side with its ripple of muscles, could have hurt him thus. He let the water carry him till he might climb out on to the shingle. There he sat upon a warm boulder, and twisted to look at his arm. The skin was grazed, not very badly, merely a ragged scarlet patch no bigger than a carnation petal. The bruise, however, was painful, especially when, a minute or two later, he bent his arm.

"No," said he pitiably to himself, "it is impossible it should have hurt me. I suppose I was careless."

Nevertheless the aspect of the morning changed. He sat on the boulder looking out on the sea. The azure sky and the sea laughed on, holding a bright conversation one with another. The two headlands of the tiny bay gossiped across the street of water. All the boulders and pebbles of the sea-shore played together.

"Surely," said Siegmund, "they take no notice of me; they do not care a jot or a tittle for me. I am a fool to think myself one of them."

He contrasted this with the kindness of the morning as he had stood on the cliffs.

"I was mistaken," he said. "It was an illusion."

He looked wistfully out again. Like neighbours leaning from opposite windows of an overhanging street, the headlands were occupied one with another. White rocks strayed out to sea, followed closely by other white rocks. Everything was busy, interested, occupied with its own pursuit and with its own comrades. Siegmund alone was without pursuit or comrade.

"They will all go on the same. They will be just as gay. Even Helena, after a while, will laugh and take interest in others. What do I matter?"

Siegmund thought of the futility of death.

"We are not long for music and laughter,
  Love and desire and hate;
I think we have no portion in them after
  We pass the gate."*

"Why should I be turned out of the game?" he asked himself, rebelling. He frowned, and answered: "Oh Lord—the old argument!"

But the thought of his own expunging from the picture was very bitter.

"Like the puff from the steamer's funnel, I should be gone."

He looked at himself, at his limbs and his body in the pride of his maturity. He was very beautiful to himself.

"Nothing, in the place where I am," he said. "Gone like a puff of steam that melts on the sunshine."

Again Siegmund looked at the sea. It was glittering with laughter as at a joke.

"And I," he said, lying down in the warm sand, "I am nothing. I do not count. I am inconsiderable."

He set his teeth with pain. There were no tears, there was no relief. A convulsive gasping shook him as he lay on the sands. All the while, he was arguing with himself.

"Well," he said, "if I am nothing dead I am nothing alive."

But the vulgar proverb arose—'Better a live dog than a dead lion'*—to answer him. It seemed an ignominy to be dead. It meant, to be overlooked, even by the smallest creature of God's earth. Surely that was a great ignominy.

Helena meanwhile was bathing for the last time by the same sea-shore with him. She was no swimmer. Her endless delight was to explore, to discover small treasures. For her the world was still a great wonderbox which hid innumerable sweet toys for surprises in all its crevices. She had bathed in many rock-pools' tepid baths, trying first one, then another. She had lain on the sand where the cold arms of the ocean lifted her and smothered her impetuously, like an awful lover.

"The sea is a great deal like Siegmund," she said, as she rose panting, trying to dash her nostrils free from water. It was true, the sea as it flung over her filled her with the same uncontrollable terror as did Siegmund when he, sometimes, grew silent and strange in a tide of passion.

She wandered back to her rock-pools. They were bright and docile: they did not fling her about in a game of terror. She bent over watching the anemones' fleshy petals shrink from the touch of her shadow, and she laughed, to think they should be so needlessly fearful. The flowing tide trickled noiselessly among the rocks, widening and deepening insidiously her little pools. Helena retreated, towards a large cave, round the bend. There the water gurgled under the bladder-wrack of the large stones, the air was cool and clammy. She pursued her way into the gloom, bending though there was no need, shivering at the coarse feel of the sea-weed beneath her naked feet. The water came rustling up beneath the fucus as she crept along on the big stones: it returned with a quiet gurgle which made her shudder, though even that was not disagreeable. It needed, for all that, more courage than was easy to summon before she could step off her stone into the black pool that confronted her. It was festooned thick with weeds that slid under her feet like snakes. She scrambled hastily upwards towards the outlet.

Turning, the ragged arch was before her, brighter than the brightest window. It was easy to believe the light-fairies stood outside in a throng, excited with fine fear, throwing handfuls of light into the dragon's hole.

"How surprised they will be to see me," said Helena, scrambling forward, laughing.

She stood still in the archway, astounded. The sea was blazing with white fire, and glowing with azure as coals glow red with heat below the flames. The sea was transfused with white burning, while over it hung the blue sky in a glory, like the blue smoke of the fire of God. Helena stood still and worshipped. It was a moment of astonishment, when she stood breathless and blinded, involuntarily offering herself for a thank offering. She felt herself confronting God at home in his white incandescence, his fire settling on her like the Holy Spirit. Her lips were parted in a woman's joy of adoration.

The moment passed, and her thoughts hurried forward in confusion.

"It is good," said Helena,—"it is very good." She looked again, and saw the waves like a line of children racing hand in hand, the sunlight pursuing, catching hold of them from behind, as they ran wildly till they fell, caught, with the sunshine dancing upon them like a white dog.

"It is really wonderful, here," said she. But the moment had gone; she could not see again the grand burning of God among the waves. After a while she turned away.

As she stood dabbling her bathing dress in a pool, Siegmund came over the beach to her.

"You are not gone then?" he said.

"Siegmund!" she exclaimed, looking up at him with radiant eyes, as if it could not be possible that he had joined her in this rare place. His face was glowing with the sun's inflaming, but Helena did not notice that his eyes were full of misery.

"I, actually," he said, smiling.

"I did not expect you," she said, still looking at him in radiant wonder. "I could easier have expected—" she hesitated, struggled, and continued—"Eros*—walking by the sea. But you are like him," she said, looking radiantly up into Siegmund's face. "Isn't it beautiful this morning?" she added.

Siegmund endured her wide, glad look for a moment, then he stooped and kissed her. He remained moving his hand in the pool, ashamed, and full of contradiction. He was at the bitter point of farewell; could see, beyond the glamour around him, the ugly building of his real life.

"Isn't the sea wonderful this morning?" asked Helena, as she wrung the water from her costume.

"It is very fine," he answered. He refrained from saying what his heart said, 'It is my last morning, it is not yours. It is my last morning, and the sea is enjoying the joke, and you are full of delight.'

"Yes," said Siegmund, "the morning is perfect."

"It is," assented Helena warmly. "Have you noticed the waves? They are like a line of children chased by a white dog."

"Ay!" said Siegmund.

"Didn't you have a good time?" she asked, touching with her finger-tips the nape of his neck as he stooped beside her.

"I swam to my little bay again," he replied.

"Did you!" she exclaimed, pleased.

She sat down by the pool in which she washed her feet free from sand, holding them to Siegmund to dry.

"I am very hungry," she said.

"And I," he agreed.

"I feel quite established here," she said gaily, something in his position having reminded her of their departure. He laughed.

"It seems another eternity before the 3.45 train, doesn't it?" she insisted.

"I wish we might never go back," he said.

Helena sighed.

"It would be too much for life to give. We have had something Siegmund," she said.

He bowed his head and did not answer.

"It has been something, dear—?" she repeated. He rose and took her in his arms.

"Everything," he said, his face muffled in the shoulder of her dress. He could smell her fresh and fine from the sea. "Everything!" he said. She pressed her two hands on his head.

"I did well, didn't I, Siegmund?" she asked. Helena felt the responsibility of this holiday. She had proposed it; when he had withdrawn, she had insisted, refusing to allow him to take back his word, declaring that she should pay the cost. He permitted her at last.

"Wonderfully well, Helena," he replied.

She kissed his forehead.

"You are everything," he said.

She pressed his head on her bosom.

XVIII

Siegmund had shaved and dressed, and come down to breakfast. Mrs Curtiss brought in the coffee. She was a fragile little woman, of delicate, gentle manner.

"The water would be warm this morning," she said, addressing no one in particular.

Siegmund stood on the hearth-rug with his hands behind him, swaying from one leg to the other. He was embarrassed always by the presence of the amiable little woman; he could not feel at ease, before strangers, in his capacity of accepted swain of Helena.

"It was," assented Helena. "It was as warm as new milk."

"Ay, it would be," said the old lady, looking in admiration upon the experience of Siegmund and his beloved. "And did ye see the ships of war?" she asked.

"No—they had gone," replied Helena.

Siegmund swayed from foot to foot, rhythmically.

"You'll be coming in to dinner today?" asked the old lady.

Helena arranged the matter.

"I think ye both look better," Mrs Curtiss said. She glanced at Siegmund.

He smiled constrainedly.

"I thought ye looked so worn when you came," she said, sympathetically.

"He had been working hard," said Helena, also glancing at him.

He bent his head, and was whistling without making any sound.

"Ay," sympathised the little woman. "And it's a very short time for you. What a pity ye can't stop for the fireworks at Cowes on Monday. They are so grand, so they say."

Helena raised her eyebrows in polite interest. "Have you never seen them?" she asked.

"No," replied Mrs Curtiss. "I've never been able to get. But I hope to go yet."

"I hope you may," said Siegmund.

The little woman beamed on him. Having won a word from him she was quite satisfied.

"Well," she said brightly, "the eggs must be done by now."

She tripped out, to return directly.

"I've brought you," she said, "some of the Island cream, and some white currants, if ye'll have them. You must think well of the Island, and come back."

"How could we help?" laughed Helena.

"We will," smiled Siegmund.

When finally the door was closed on her Siegmund sat down in relief. Helena looked in amusement at him. She was perfectly self-possessed in the presence of the delightful little lady.

"This is one of the few places that has ever felt like home to me," she said. She lifted a tangled bunch of fine white currants.

"Ah!" exclaimed Siegmund, smiling at her.

"One of the few places where everything is friendly," she said—"And everybody."

"You have made so many enemies—?" he asked, with gentle irony.

"Strangers," she replied. "I seem to make strangers of all the people I meet."

She laughed in amusement at this "mot." Siegmund looked at her intently. He was thinking of her left alone amongst strangers.

"Need we go—need we leave this place of friends?" he said, as if ironically. He was very much afraid of tempting her.

She looked at the clock on the mantel-piece and counted—"One-two-three-four-five hours, thirty five minutes. It is an age yet," she laughed.

Siegmund laughed too, as he accepted the particularly fine bunch of currants she had extricated for him.

XIX

The air was warm and sweet in the little lane, remote from the sea, which led them along their last walk. On either side the white path was a grassy margin thickly woven with pink convolvuli. Some of the reckless little flowers, so gay and evanescent, had climbed the trunk of an old yew tree, and were looking up pertly at their rough host.

Helena walked along, watching the flowers, and making fancies out of them.

"Who called them fairies' telephones?" she said to herself. "They are tiny children in pinafores. How gay they are! They are children dawdling along the pavement of a morning. How fortunate they are! See how they take a wind-thrill! See how wide they are set to the sunshine. And when they are tired, they will curl daintily to sleep, and some fairies in the dark will gather them away. They won't be here in the morning, shrivelled and dowdy... If only we could curl up and be gone, after our day— —!"

She looked at Siegmund. He was walking moodily beside her.

"It is good when life holds no anti-climax," she said.

"Ay!" he answered. Of course, he could not understand her meaning.

She strayed into the thick grass, a sturdy white figure that walked with bent head, abstract, but happy.

"What is she thinking?" he asked himself. "She is sufficient to herself—she doesn't want me. She has her own, private way of communing with things, and is friends with them."

"The dew has been very heavy," she said, turning, and looking up at him from under her brows, like a smiling witch.

"I see it has," he answered. Then to himself, he said:

"She can't translate herself into language. She is incommunicable, she can't render herself to the intelligence. So, she is alone and a law unto herself: she only wants me to explore me, like a rock-pool, and to bathe in me. After a while, when I am gone, she will see I was not indispensable..."

The lane led up to the eastern down. As they were emerging, they saw on the left hand an extraordinarily spick and span red bungalow. The low roof of dusky red sloped down towards the coolest green lawn, that was edged and ornamented with scarlet and yellow and white flowers, brilliant with dew.

A stout man in an alpaca jacket and panama hat was seated on the bare lawn, his back to the sun, reading a newspaper. He tried in vain to avoid the glare of the sun on his reading. At last he closed the paper and looked angrily at the house—not at anything in particular.

He irritably read a few more lines, then jerked up his head in sudden decision, glared at the open door of the house, and called:

"Amy! Amy!!"

No answer was forthcoming. He flung down the paper and strode off indoors, his mien one of wrathful resolution. His voice was heard calling curtly from the dining room. There was a jingle of crockery as he bumped the table leg in sitting down.

"He is in a bad temper," laughed Siegmund.

"Breakfast is late," said Helena, with contempt.

"Look!" said Siegmund.

An elderly lady in black and white striped linen, a young lady in holland, both carrying some wild flowers, hastened towards the garden gate. Their faces were turned anxiously to the house. They were hot with hurrying, and had no breath for words. The girl pressed forward, opened the gate for the lady in striped linen, who hastened over the lawn. Then the daughter followed, and vanished also under the shady veranda.

There was a quick sound of women's low, apologetic voices overridden by the resentful abuse of the man.

The lovers moved out of hearing.

"Imagine that breakfast-table," said Siegmund.

"I feel," said Helena, with a keen twang of contempt in her voice "as if a fussy cock and hens had just scuffled across my path."

"There are many such roosts," said Siegmund pertinently.

Helena's cold scorn was very disagreeable to him. She talked to him winsomely and very kindly as they crossed the open down to meet the next incurving of the coast, and Siegmund was happy. But the sense of humiliation, which he had got from her the day before, and which had fixed itself, bled him secretly, like a wound. This hemorrhage of self-esteem tortured him to the end.

Helena had rejected him. She gave herself to her fancies only. For some time she had confused Siegmund with her god. Yesterday, sh had cried to her ideal lover and found only Siegmund. It was the spear in the side of his tortured self-respect.

"At least," he said, in mortification of himself. "At least, someone must recognise a strain of God in me—and who does? I don't believe in it myself."

And moreover, in the intense joy and suffering of his realised passion, the Island, with its sea and sky, had fused till, like a brilliant bead, all their beauty ran together out of the common ore, and Siegmund saw it naked, saw the beauty of everything naked in the shifting magic of this bead. The Island would be gone tomorrow: he would look for the beauty and find the dirt: what was he to do?

"You know, Domine,"* said Helena—it was his old nickname she used, "you look quite stern today."

"I feel anything but stern," he laughed. "Weaker than usual, in fact."

"Yes—perhaps so, when you talk. Then you are really surprisingly gentle. But when you are silent, I am even afraid of you, you seem so grave."

He laughed.

"And shall I not be grave?" he said. "Can't you smell 'Fumum et opes strepitumque Romae'?"* He turned quickly to Helena.

"I wonder if that's right!" he said. "It's years since I did a line of Latin, and I thought it had all gone."

"In the first place, what does it mean?" said Helena calmly—"For I can only half translate. I have thrown overboard all my scrap-books of such stuff."

"Why," said Siegmund, rather abashed, "only 'the row and the smoke of Rome.' But it is remarkable, Helena,"—here the peculiar look of interest came on his face again—, "it is really remarkable that I should have said that."

"Yes, you look surprised," smiled she.

"But it must be twenty"—he counted—"twenty two or three years since I learned that, and I forgot it—goodness knows how long ago. Like a drowning man, I have these memories before— — —" He broke off, smiling mockingly, to tease her.

"Before you go back to London," said she, in a matter-of-fact, almost ironical tone. She was inscrutable. This morning she could not bear to let any deep emotion come uppermost. She wanted rest.

"No," she said, with calm distinctness, a few moments after, when they were climbing the rise to the cliff's edge. "I can't say that I smell the smoke of London. The mist-curtain is thick yet. There it is—" she pointed to the heavy, purple-grey haze that hung like arras on a wall, between the sloping sky and the sea. She thought of yesterday morning's mist-curtain, thick and blazing gold, so heavy that no wind could sway its fringe.

They lay down in the dry grass, upon the golden bits of bird's-foot trefoil of the cliff's edge, and looked out to sea. A warm, drowsy calm dropped over everything.

"Six hours," thought Helena, "and we shall have passed the mist-curtain. Already it is thinning. I could break it open with waving my hand. I will not wave my hand."

She was exhausted by the suffering of the last night, so she refused to allow any emotion to move her this morning, till she was strong. Siegmund was also exhausted: but his thoughts laboured like ants, in spite of himself, striving towards a conclusion.

Helena had rejected him. In his heart, he felt that in this love affair also he had been a failure. No matter how he contradicted himself, and said it was absurd to imagine he was a failure as Helena's lover, yet he felt a physical sensation of defeat, a kind of knot in his breast which reason nor dialectics nor circumstance, not even Helena, could untie. He had failed as lover to Helena.

It was not surprising his marriage with Beatrice should prove disastrous. Rushing into wedlock as he had done, at the ripe age of seventeen, he had known nothing of his woman, nor she of him. When his mind and soul set to develop, as Beatrice could not sympathise with his interests, he naturally inclined away from her, so that now, after twenty years, he was almost a stranger to her. That was not very surprising.

But why should he have failed with Helena?

The bees droned fitfully over the scented grass, aimlessly swinging in the heat. Siegmund watched one gold and amber fellow lazily let go a white clover-head, and boom in a careless curve out to sea, humming softer and softer as he reeled along in the giddy space.

"The little fool!" said Siegmund, watching the black dot swallowed into the light.

No ship sailed the curving sea. The light danced in a whirl upon the ripples. Everything else watched with heavy eyes of heat-entrancement the wild spinning of the lights.

"Even if I were free," he continued to think, "we should only grow apart, Helena and I. She would leave me. This time I should be the laggard. She is young and vigorous: I am beginning to set.

"Is that why I have failed? I ought to have had her in love sufficiently to keep her these few days. I am not quick. I do not follow her or understand her swiftly enough. And I am always timid of compulsion. I cannot compel anybody to follow me.

"So we are here. I am out of my depth. Like the bee, I was mad with the sight of so much joy, such a blue space, and now I shall find no footing to alight on. I have flown out into life beyond my strength to get back. What can I set my feet on, when this is gone?"

The sun grew stronger. Slower and more slowly went the hawks of Siegmund's mind, after the quarry of conclusion. He lay bare-headed looking out to sea. The sun was burning deeper into his face and head.

"I feel as if it were burning into me," thought Siegmund abstractedly. "It is certainly consuming some part of me. Perhaps it is making me ill."—Meanwhile, perversely, he gave his face and his hot black hair to the sun.

Helena lay in what shadow he afforded. The heat put out all her thought-activity. Presently she said:

"This heat is terrible Siegmund. Shall we go down to the water—?"

They climbed giddily down the cliff-path. Already they were somewhat sun-intoxicated. Siegmund chose the hot sand where no shade was, on which to lie.

"Shall we not go under the rocks," said Helena.

"Look," he said, "the sun is beating on the cliffs. It is hotter, more suffocating, there."

So they lay down in the glare, Helena watching the foam retreat slowly with a cool plash, Siegmund thinking. The naked body of heat was dreadful.

"My arms, Siegmund," said she. "They feel as if they were dipped in fire."

Siegmund took them, without a word, and hid them under his coat.

"Are you sure it is not bad for you—your head, Siegmund?—Are you sure?"

He laughed stupidly.

"That is all right," he said. He knew that the sun was burning through him, and doing him harm. But he wanted the intoxication.

As he looked wistfully far away over the sea at Helena's mist-curtain, he said:

"I *think* we should be able to keep together if—" he faltered—"if only I could have you a little longer. I have never had you." Some sound of failure, some tone telling her it was too late, some ring of despair in his quietness, made Helena cling to him wildly, with a savage little cry as if she were wounded. She clung to him, almost beside herself. She could not lose him, she could not spare him. She would not let him go. Helena was, for the moment, frantic.

He held her safely, saying nothing until she was calmer, when, with his lips on her cheek, he murmured:

"I should be able, shouldn't I Helena?"

"You are always able," she cried. "It is I who play with you at hiding."

"I have really had you so little," he said.

"Can't you forget it Siegmund?" she cried. "Can't you forget it? It was only a shadow, Siegmund. It was a lie, it was nothing real. Can't you forget it, dear?"

"You can't do without me?" he asked.

"If I lose you I am lost," answered she with swift decision. She had no knowledge of weeping, yet her tears were wet on his face. He held her safely: her arms were hidden under his coat.

"I will have no mercy on those shadows the next time they come between us," said Helena to herself. "They may go back to hell."

She still clung to him, craving so to have him that he could not be reft away.

Siegmund felt very peaceful. He lay with his arms about her, listening to the backward-creeping tide. All his thoughts, like bees were flown out to sea, and lost.

"If I had her more, I should understand her through and through. If we were side by side we should grow together. If we could stay here, I should get stronger, and more upright."

This was the poor heron of quarry the hawks of his mind had struck.*

Another hour fell like a fox-glove bell from the stalk. There were only two red blossoms left. Then the stem would have set to seed. Helena leaned her head upon the breast of Siegmund, her arms clasping, under his coat, his body which swelled and sank gently, with the quiet of great power.

"If," thought she, "the whole clock of the world could stand still now, and leave us thus, me with the lift and fall of the strong body of Siegmund in my arms...."

But the clock ticked on in the heat, the seconds marked off by the falling of the waves, repeated so lightly, and in such fragile rhythm, that it made silence sweet.

"If now," prayed Siegmund, "death would wipe the sweat from me, and it were dark— —"

But the waves softly marked the minutes, retreating farther, leaving the bare rocks to bleach and the weed to shrivel.

Gradually, like the shadow on a dial, the knowledge that it was time to rise and go crept upon them. Although they remained silent, each knew that the other felt the same weight of responsibility, the shadow-finger of the sundial travelling over them. The alternative was, not to return, to let the finger travel and be gone. But then—! Helena knew she must not let the time cross her: she must rise before it was too late, and travel before the coming finger. Siegmund hoped she would not get up. He lay in suspense, waiting.

At last, she sat up abruptly.

"It is time, Siegmund," she said.

He did not answer, he did not look at her, but lay as she had left him. She wiped her face with her handkerchief, waiting. Then she bent over him. He did not look at her. She saw his forehead was swollen and inflamed with the sun. Very gently, she wiped from it the glistening sweat. He closed his eyes, and she wiped his cheeks and his mouth. Still he did not look at her. She bent very close to him, feeling her heart crushed with grief for him.

"We must go, Siegmund," she whispered.

"All right," he said, but still he did not move.

She stood up beside him, shook herself, and tried to get a breath of air. She was dazzled blind by the sunshine.

Siegmund lay in the bright light, with his eyes closed, never moving. His face was inflamed, but fixed like a mask.

Helena waited, until the terror of the passing of the hour was too strong for her. She lifted his hand, which lay swollen with heat on the sand, and she tried gently to draw him.

"We shall be too late," she said, in distress. He sighed and sat up, looking out over the water. Helena could not bear to see him look so vacant and expressionless. She put her arm round his neck, and pressed his head against her skirt.

Siegmund knew he was making it unbearable for her. Pulling himself together, he bent his head from the sea, and said:

"Why, what time is it?"

He took out his watch, holding it in his hand. Helena still held his left hand, and had one arm round his neck.

"I can't see the figures," he said. "Everything is dimmed, as if it were coming dark."

"Yes," replied Helena, in that reedy, painful tone of hers, "My eyes were the same. It is the strong sunlight."

"I can't," he repeated, and he was rather surprised, "I can't see the time. Can you?"

She stooped down and looked.

"It is half past one," she said.

Siegmund hated her voice as she spoke. There was still sufficient time to catch the train. He stood up, moved inside his clothing, saying: "I feel almost stunned by the heat. I can hardly see, and all my feeling in my body is dulled."

"Yes," answered Helena, "I am afraid it will do you harm."

"At any rate," he smiled as if sleepily, "I have had enough. If it's too much— —what *is* too much?"

They went unevenly over the sand, their eyes sun-dimmed.

"We are going back—we are going back;"—the heart of Helena seemed to run hot, beating these words.

They climbed the cliff-path toilsomely. Standing at the top, on the edge of the grass, they looked down the cliffs at the beach and over the sea. The strand was wide, forsaken by the sea, forlorn with rocks bleaching in the sun, and sand and sea-weed breathing off their painful scent upon the heat. The sea crept smaller, further away; the sky stood still. Siegmund and Helena looked hopelessly out on their beautiful, incandescent world. They looked hopelessly at each other. Siegmund's mood was gentle and forbearing. He smiled faintly at Helena, then turned, and, lifting his hand to his mouth in a kiss for the beauty he had enjoyed: "Addio!"* he said.

He turned away, and looking from Helena landwards, he said, smiling peculiarly:

"It reminds me of 'Traviata'*—an 'Addio' at every verse-end."

She smiled with her mouth in acknowledgment of his facetious irony: it jarred on her. He was pricked again by her supercilious reserve.

"Addi-i-i-o, Addi-i-i-o," he whistled between his teeth, hissing out the Italian's passion-notes* in a way that made Helena clench her fists.

"I suppose," she said, swallowing, and recovering her voice to check this discord, "I suppose we shall have a fairly easy journey—Thursday."

"I don't know," said Siegmund.

"There will not be very many people," she insisted.

"I think," he said, in a very quiet voice, "you'd better let me go by the South Western from Portsmouth, while you go on by the Brighton."

"But why!" she exclaimed in astonishment.

"I don't want to sit looking at you all the way," he said.

"But why should you!" she exclaimed.

He laughed.

"Indeed no!" she said. "We shall go together."

"Very well," he answered.

They walked on in silence towards the village. As they drew near the little post-office, he said:

"I suppose I may as well wire them that I shall be home tonight."

"You haven't sent them any word?" she asked.

He laughed. They came to the open door of the little shop. He stood still, not entering. Helena wondered what he was thinking.

"Shall I?" he asked, meaning 'should he wire to Beatrice.' His manner was rather peculiar.

"Well, I should think so," faltered Helena, turning away to look at the postcards in the window. Siegmund entered the shop. It was dark and cumbered with views, cheap china ornaments, and toys. He asked for a telegraph form.

"My God!" he said to himself bitterly as he took the pencil. He could not sign the abbreviated name his wife used towards him. He scribbled his surname, as he would have done to a stranger. As he watched the amiable, stout woman counting up his words carefully, pointing with her finger, he felt sick with irony.

"That's right," she said, picking up the sixpence and taking the form to the instrument. "What beautiful weather!" she continued. "It will be making you sorry to leave us."

"There goes my warrant," thought Siegmund, watching the flimsy bit of paper under the postmistress' heavy hand.

"Yes—it is too bad, isn't it," he replied, bowing and laughing to the woman.

"It is Sir," she answered pleasantly. "Goodmorning."

He came out of the shop still smiling, and when Helena turned from the postcards to look at him, the lines of laughter remained over his face like a mask. She glanced at his eyes for a sign: his facial expression told her nothing; his eyes were just as inscrutable: which made her falter with dismay.

"What is he thinking of?" she asked herself. Her thoughts flashed back: "And why did he ask me so peculiarly whether he should wire them at home?"

"Well," said Siegmund, "are there any postcards?"

"None that I care to take," she replied. "Perhaps you would like one of these..."

She pointed to some faded looking cards which proved to be imaginary views of Alum Bay, done in variegated sand.* Siegmund smiled.

"I wonder if they dribbled the sand on with a fine glass tube," he said.

"Or a brush—", said Helena.

"She does not understand," said Siegmund to himself. "And whatever I do I must not tell her. I should have thought she would understand."

As he walked home beside her, there mingled with his other feelings resentment against her. Almost he hated her.

XX

At first they had a carriage to themselves. They sat opposite each other, with averted faces looking out of the windows and watching the houses, the downs dead-asleep in the sun, the embankments of the railway with exhausted hot flowers go slowly past, out of their reach. They felt as if they were being dragged away like criminals. Unable to speak or think they stared out of the windows, Helena struggling in vain to keep back her tears, Siegmund labouring to breathe normally.

At Yarmouth the door was snatched open, and there was a confusion of shouting and running; a swarm of humanity clamouring, attached itself at the carriage doorway, which was immediately blocked by a stout man who heaved a leathern bag in front of him, as he cried in German that here was room for all. Faces, innumerable hot, blue-eyed faces strained to look over his shoulders at the shocked girl and the amazed Siegmund.

There entered eight Germans into the second-class compartment, five men and three ladies. When at last the luggage was stowed away they sank into the seats. The last man on either side to be seated lowered himself carefully, like a wedge, between his two neighbours. Siegmund watched the stout man, the one who had led the charge, setting himself between his lady and the small Helena. The latter crushed herself against the side of the carriage. The German's hips came down tight against her. She strove to lessen herself against the window, to escape the pressure of his flesh, whose heat was immediately transmitted to her. The man squeezed in the opposite direction.

"I am afraid I press you," he said, smiling in his gentle, chivalric German fashion. Helena glanced swiftly at him. She liked his grey eyes; she liked the agreeable intonation, and the pleasant sound of his words.

"Oh no," she answered. "You do not crush me."

Almost before she had finished the words she turned away to the window. The man seemed to hesitate a moment, as if recovering himself from a slight rebuff, before he could address his lady with the good-humoured remark, in German: "Well, and have we not managed it very nicely, eh?"

The whole party began to talk in German with great animation. They told each other of the quaint ways of this or the other; they joked loudly over 'Billy',—this being a nickname discovered for the German Emperor*—and what he would be saying of the Czar's trip; they questioned each other, and answered each other concerning the places they were going to see, with great interest, displaying admirable knowledge. They were pleased with everything: they extolled things English.

Helena's stout neighbour, who, it seemed, was from Dresden, began to tell anecdotes. He was a raconteur of the naïf type: he talked with face, hands, with his whole body. Now and again he would give little spurts in his seat. After one of these he must have become aware of Helena,—who felt as if she were enveloped by a soft stove—struggling to escape his compression. He stopped short, lifted his hat, and, smiling beseechingly, said, in his persuasive way:

"I am sorry: I am sorry: I compress you!" He glanced round in perplexity, seeking some escape or remedy. Finding none, he turned to her again, after having squeezed hard against his lady to free Helena, and said:

"Forgive me;—I am sorry."

"You are forgiven," replied Helena, suddenly smiling into his face with her rare winsomeness. The whole party, attentive, relaxed into a smile at this. The good-humour was complete.

"Thank you," said the German gratefully.

Helena turned away. The talk began again like the popping of corn: the raconteur resumed his anecdote. Everybody was waiting to laugh. Helena rapidly wearied of trying to follow the tale. Siegmund had made no attempt. He had watched, with the others, the German's apologies, and the sight of his lover's face had moved him more than he could tell.

She had a peculiar, childish wistfulness at times, and with this an intangible aloofness that pierced his heart. It seemed to him he should never know her. There was a remoteness about her, an estrangement between her and all natural daily things, as if she were of an unknown race that never can tell its own story. This feeling always moved Siegmund's pity to its deepest, leaving him poignantly helpless: this same foreignness, revealed in other ways, sometimes made him hate her. It was as if she would sacrifice him, rather than renounce her foreign birth. There was something in her he could never understand; so that never, never could he say he was master of her as she was of him the mistress.

As she smiled and turned away from the German, mute, uncomplaining, like a child wise in sorrow beyond its years, Siegmund's resentment against her suddenly took fire, and blazed him with sheer pain of pity. She was very small. Her quiet ways, and sometimes her impetuous clinging made her seem small; for she was very strong. But Siegmund saw her now, small, quiet, uncomplaining, living for him who sat and looked at her. But what would become of her when he had left her, when she was alone, little foreigner as she was, in this world, which apologises when it has done the hurt, too blind to see beforehand. Helena would be left behind; death was no way for her. She could not escape thus with him from this house of strangers which she called life. She had to go on, alone, like a foreigner who cannot learn the strange language.

"What will she do?" Siegmund asked himself, "When her loneliness comes upon her like a horror, and she has no one to go to. She will come to the memory of me for a while, and that will take her over till her strength is established. But what then—?"

Siegmund could find no answer. He tried to imagine her life. It would go on, after his death, just in the same way, for a while, and then—? He had not the faintest knowledge of how she would develop. What would she do when she was thirty eight, and as old as himself? He could not conceive. Yet she would not die, of that he was certain.

Siegmund suddenly realised that he knew nothing of her life, her real inner life. She was a book written in characters unintelligible to him and to everybody. He was tortured with the problem of her till it became acute, and he felt as if his heart would burst inside him. As a boy he had experienced the same sort of feeling after wrestling for an hour with a problem in Euclid; for he was capable of great concentration.

He felt Helena looking at him. Turning, he found her steady, unswerving eyes fixed on him so that he shrank confused from them. She smiled: by an instinctive movement she made him know that she wanted him to hold her hand. He leaned forward and put his hand over hers. She had peculiar hands, small, with a strange delightful silkiness: often they were cool or cold; generally they lay unmoved within his clasp, but then they were instinct with life, not inert. Sometimes he would feel a peculiar jerking in his pulse, very much like electricity, when he held her hand. Occasionally it was almost painful, and felt as if a little virtue were passing out of his blood.* But that he dismissed as nonsense.

The Germans were still rattling away, perspiring freely, wiping their faces with their handkerchiefs as they laughed, moving inside their clothing, which was sticking to their sides. Siegmund had not noticed them for some time, he was so much absorbed. But Helena, though she sympathised with her fellow-passengers, was tormented almost beyond endurance by the noise, the heat of her neighbour's body, the atmosphere of the crowded carriage, and her own emotion. The only thing that could relieve her was the hand of Siegmund soothing her in its hold.

She looked at him with the same steadiness, which made her eyes feel heavy upon him, and made him shrink. She wanted his strength of nerve to support her, and he submitted at once, his one aim being to give her out of himself whatever she wanted.

XXI

The tall white yachts in a throng were lounging off the roads of Ryde. It was near the regatta time, so these proud creatures had flown loftily together, and now flitted hither and thither among themselves, like a concourse of tall women,* footing the waves with superb touch. To Siegmund they were very beautiful, but removed from him, as dancers crossing the window-lights are removed from the man who looks up from the street. He saw the Solent and the world of glamour flying gay as snow outside, where inside was only Siegmund tired, dispirited, without any joy.

He and Helena had climbed among coils of rope onto the prow of their steamer, so they could catch a little spray of speed on their faces to stimulate them. The sea was very bright and crowded. White sails leaned slightly and filed along the roads; two yachts with sails of amber floated, it seemed without motion, amid the eclipsed blue of the day; small boats with red and yellow flags fluttered quickly, trailing the sea with colour; a pleasure steamer coming from Cowes swung her soft, stout way among the fleeting ships; high in the back ground were men of war, a long line, each one threading tiny triangles of flags through a sky dim with distance.

"It is all very glad," said Siegmund to himself, "but it seems to me fanciful."

He was out of it. Already he felt detached from life. He belonged to his destination. It is always so: we have no share in the beauty that lies between us and our goal.

Helena watched with poignant sorrow all the agitation of colour on the blue afternoon.

"We must leave it; we must pass out of it," she lamented, over and over again. Each new charm she caught eagerly.

"I like the steady purpose of that brown-sailed tramp," she said to herself, watching a laden coaster making for Portsmouth.

They were still among the small shipping of Ryde. Siegmund and Helena, as they looked out, became aware of a small motor-launch heading across their course towards a yacht whose tall masts were drawn clean on the sky. The eager launch, its nose up as if to breathe, was racing over the swell like a coursing dog. A lady, in white, and a lad with dark head and white jersey were leaning in the bows: a gentleman was bending over some machinery in the middle of the boat, while the sailor in the low stern was also stooping forward attending to something. The steamer was sweeping onwards, huge above the water; the dog of a boat was coursing straight across her track. The lady saw the danger first. Stretching forward, she seized the arm of the lad and held him firm, making no sound, but watching the forward menace of the looming steamer.

"Look!" cried Helena, catching hold of Siegmund. He was already watching. Suddenly the steamer bell clanged. The gentleman looked up, with startled sunburned face, then he leaped to the stern. The launch veered. It and the steamer closed together like a pair of scissors. The lady, still holding the boy, looked up with an expressionless face at the high sweeping chisel of the steamer's bows: the husband stood rigid, staring ahead. No sound was to be heard save the rustling of water under the bows. The scissors closed, the launch skelped forward like a dog from in front of the traffic. It escaped by a yard or two. Then, like a dog, it seemed to look round. The gentleman in the stern glanced back quickly. He was a handsome, dark haired man with dark eyes. His face was as if carven out of oak, set and grey brown. Then he looked to the steering of his boat. No one had uttered a sound. From the tiny boat coursing low on the water, not a sound, only tense waiting. The launch raced out of danger towards the yacht. The gentleman, with a brief gesture, put his man in charge again, whilst he himself went forward to the lady. He was a handsome man, very proud in his movements: and she, in her bearing, was prouder still. She received him almost with indifference.

Helena turned to Siegmund. He took both her hands, and pressed them, whilst she looked at him with eyes blind with emotion. She was white to the lips, and heaving like the buoy in the wake of the steamer. The noise of life had suddenly been hushed, and each heart had heard for a moment the noiselessness of death. How everyone was white and gasping! They strove, on every hand, to fill the day with noise and the colour of life again.

"By Jove, that was a near thing!"

"Ah, that has made me feel bad," said a woman.

"A French yacht," said somebody.

Helena was waiting for the voice of Siegmund. But he did not know what to say. Confused, he repeated:

"That was a close shave."

Helena clung to him, searching his face. She felt his difference from herself. There was something in his experience that made him different, quiet, with a peculiar expression as if he were pained.

"Ah dear Lord!" he was saying to himself. "How bright and whole the day is for them. If God had suddenly put his hand over the sun, and swallowed us up in a shadow, they could not have been more startled. That man, with his fine, white-flannelled limbs and his dark head, has no suspicion of the shadow that supports it all. Between the blueness of the sea and the sky he passes easy as a gull, close to the fine white sea-mew of his mate, amid red flowers of flags, and soft birds of ships, and slow moving monsters of steam-boats.

"For me, the day is transparent and shrivelling. I can see the darkness through its petals. But for him it is a fresh bell-flower, in which he fumbles with delights like a bee.

"For me, quivering in the interspaces of the atmosphere is the darkness, the same that fills in my soul. I can see death urging itself into life, the shadow supporting the substance. For my life is burning an invisible flame. The glare of the light of myself, as I burn on the fuel of death, is not enough to hide from me the source and the issue. For what is a life but a flame that bursts off the surface of darkness and tapers into the darkness again. But the death that issues differs from the death that was the source. At least I shall enrich death with a potent shadow, if I do not enrich life."

"Wasn't that woman fine!" said Helena.

"So perfectly still," he answered.

"The child realised nothing," she said.

Siegmund laughed, then leaned forward impulsively to her.

"I am always so sorry," he said, "that the human race is urged inevitably into a deeper and deeper realisation of life."

She looked at him, wondering what provoked such a remark.

"I guess," she said slowly, after a while, "that the man, the sailor, will have a bad time. He was abominably careless."

"He was careful of something else just then," said Siegmund, who hated to hear her speak in cold condemnation. "He was attending to the machinery or something."

"That was scarcely his first business," said she, rather sarcastic.

Siegmund looked at her. She seemed very hard in judgment, very blind. Sometimes his soul surged against her in hatred.

"So you think the man *wanted* to drown the boat?" he asked.

"He nearly succeeded," she replied.

There was antagonism between them. Siegmund recognised in Helena the world sitting in judgment, and he hated it. 'But, after all,' he thought, 'I suppose it is the only way to get along, to judge the event and not the person. I have a disease of sympathy, a vice of exoneration.'

Nevertheless, he did not love Helena as a judge. He thought rather of the woman in the boat. She was evidently one who watched the sources of life, saw it great and impersonal.

"Would the woman cry, or hug and kiss the boy, when she got on board?" he asked.

"I rather think not. Why?" she replied.

"I hope she didn't," he said.

Helena sat watching the water spurt back from the bows. She was very much in love with Siegmund: he was suggestive, he stimulated her. But to her mind he had not his own dark eyes of hesitation; he was swift and proud as the wind. She never realised his helplessness.

Siegmund was gathering strength from the thought of that other woman's courage. If she had so much restraint as not to cry out, or alarm the boy, if she had so much grace not to complain to her husband, surely he himself might refrain from revealing his own fear to Helena, and from lamenting his hard fate.

They sailed on past the chequered round towers. The sea opened, and they looked out to eastward into the sea-space. Siegmund wanted to flee. He yearned to escape down the open ways before him. Yet he knew he would be carried on to London. He watched the sea-ways closing up. The shore came round. The high old houses stood flat on the right hand. The shore swept round in a sickle reaping them into the harbour. There the old "Victory"—gay with myriad pointed pennons—was harvested, saved for a trophy.

"It is a dreadful thing," thought Siegmund "to remain as a trophy when there is nothing more to do." He watched the landing stage swooping nearer. There were the trains drawn up in readiness. At the other end of the train was London.

He could scarcely bear to have Helena before him for another two hours. The suspense of that protracted farewell, while he sat opposite her in the beating train, would cost too much. He longed to be released from her.

They had got their luggage, and were standing at the foot of the ladder, in the heat of the engines and the smell of hot oil, waiting for the crowd to pass on so that they might ascend and step off the ship on to the mainland.

"Won't you let me go by the South Western, and you by the Brighton?" asked Siegmund hesitating, repeating the morning's question. Helena looked at him, knitting her brows with misgiving and perplexity.

"No," she replied. "Let us go together."

Siegmund followed her up the iron ladder to the quay.

There was no great crowd on the train. They easily found a second-class compartment without occupants. He swung the luggage on the rack and sat down, facing Helena.

"Now," said he to himself, "I wish I were alone."

He wanted to think and prepare himself. Helena, who was thinking actively, leaned forward to him to say:

"Shall I not go down to Cornwall?"

By her soothing willingness to do anything for him, Siegmund knew that she was dogging him closely. He could not bear to have his anxiety protracted.

"But you have promised Louisa, have you not?" he replied.

"Oh well— —!" she said, in the peculiar slighting tone she had when she wished to convey the unimportance of affairs not touching him.

"Then you must go," he said.

"But," she began, with harsh petulance, "I do not want to go down to Cornwall with *Louisa* and *Olive*"*—she accentuated the two names—"—After *this*." She added.

"Then Louisa will have no holiday—and you have promised," he said gravely. Helena looked at him. She saw he had decided that she should go.

"Is my promise so *very* important?" she asked. She glanced angrily at the three ladies who were hesitating in the doorway. Nevertheless the ladies entered, and seated themselves at the opposite end of the carriage. Siegmund did not know whether he were displeased or relieved by their intrusion. If they had stayed out, he might have held Helena in his arms for still another hour. As it was, she could not harass him with words. He tried not to look at her, but to think.

The train at last moved out of the station. As it passed through Portsmouth Siegmund remembered his coming down, on the Sunday. It seemed an indefinite age ago. He was thankful that he sat on the side of the carriage opposite from the one he had occupied five days before. The afternoon of the flawless sky was ripening into evening. The chimneys and the sides of the houses of Portsmouth took on that radiant appearance which transfigures the end of day in town. A rich bloom of light appears on the surfaces of brick and stone.

"It will go on," thought Siegmund, "being gay of an evening—for ever. And I shall miss it all!"

But as soon as the train moved into the gloom of the Town Station, he began again:

"Beatrice will be proud, and silent as steel when I get home. She will say nothing, thank God.—Nor shall I. That will expedite matters: there will be no interruptions— —

"But we cannot continue together after this. Why should I discuss reasons for and against: we cannot. She goes to a cottage in the country. Already I have spoken of it to her. I allow her all I can of my money, and on the rest I manage for myself in lodgings in London. Very good.

"But when I am, comparatively, free, I cannot live alone. I shall want Helena—I shall remember the children. If I have the one, I shall be damned by the thought of the other. This bruise on my mind will never get better. Helena says she would never come to me. But she would, out of pity for me. I know she would— —.

"But then, what then? Beatrice and the children in the country: and me not looking after the children. Beatrice is thriftless. She would be in endless difficulty. It would be a degradation to me. She would keep a red sore inflamed against me: I should be a shameful thing in her mouth. Besides, there would go all her strength. She would not make any efforts. 'He has brought it on us,' she would say. 'Let him see what the result is.' And things would go from bad to worse with them. It would be a gangrene of shame— —.

"And Helena—I should have nothing but mortification. When she was asleep I could not look at her. She is such a strange, incongruous creature. But I should be responsible for her. She believes in me as if I had the power of God. What should I think of myself?"

Siegmund leaned with his head against the window, watching the country whirl past, but seeing nothing. He thought imaginatively, and his imagination destroyed him. He pictured Beatrice in the country.

He sketched the morning, breakfast haphazard at a late hour: the elder children rushing off without food, miserable and untidy, the youngest bewildered under her swift, indifferent preparation for school. He thought of Beatrice in the evening, worried and irritable, her bills unpaid, the work undone, declaiming lamentably, against the cruelty of her husband, who had abandoned her to such a burden of care, while he took his pleasure elsewhere.

This line exhausted or intolerable, Siegmund switched off to the consideration of his own probable life in town. He would go to America: the agreement was signed with the theatre manager. But America would be only a brief shutting of the eyes and closing of the mouth. He would wait for the homecoming to Helena, and she would wait for him. It was inevitable. Then would begin—what? He would never have enough money to keep Helena: even if he managed to keep himself. Their meetings would then be occasional and clandestine. Ah, it was intolerable.

"If I were rich," said Siegmund, "all would be plain. I would give each of my children enough, and Beatrice, and we would go away. But I am nearly forty: I have no genius: I shall never be rich." Round and round went his thoughts like oxen over a threshing floor, treading out the grain. Gradually the chaff flew away; gradually the corn of conviction gathered small and hard upon the floor.

As he sat thinking, Helena leaned across to him, and laid her hand on his knee.

"If I have made things more difficult," she said, her voice harsh with pain, "you will forgive me."

He started. This was one of the cruel cuts of pain that love gives, filling the eyes with blood. Siegmund stiffened himself; slowly, he smiled, as he looked at her childish, plaintive lips, and her large eyes haunted with pain.

"Forgive you!" he repeated. "Forgive you for five days of perfect happiness: the only real happiness I have ever known!" Helena tightened her fingers on his knee. She felt herself stinging with painful joy. But one of the ladies was looking at her curiously. She leaned back in her place, and turned to watch the shocks of corn strike swiftly, in long rows, across her vision.

Siegmund also, quivering, turned his face to the window, where the rotation of the wide sea-flat helped the movement of his thought. Helena had interrupted him. She had bewildered his thoughts from their hawking, so that they struck here and there, wildly, among small pitiful prey that was useless, conclusions which only hindered the bringing home of the final conviction.

"What will she do?" cried Siegmund. "What will she do when I am gone? What will become of her? Already she has no aim in life—then she will have no object. Is it any good my going if I leave her behind? What an inextricable knot this is! But what will she do?"

It was a question she had aroused before, a question which he could never answer. Indeed, it was not for him to answer.

They wound through the pass of the south downs. As Siegmund, looking backward, saw the northern slope of the downs swooping smoothly, in a great broad bosom of sward, down to the body of the land, he warmed with sudden love for the earth. There, the great downs were naked like a breast leaning kindly to him. The earth is always kind: it loves us, and would foster us like a nurse. The downs were big and tender and simple. Siegmund looked at the farm, folded in a hollow, and he wondered what fortunate folk were there, nourished and quiet, hearing the vague roar of the train that was carrying him home.

Up towards Arundel the cornfields of red wheat were heavy with gold. It was evening, when the green of the trees went out, leaving dark shapes proud upon the sky. But the red wheat was forged in the sunset, hot and magnificent. Siegmund almost gloated as he smelled the ripe corn, and opened his eyes to its powerful radiation. For a moment he forgot everything, amid the forging of red fields of gold in the smithy of the sunset. Like sparks, poppies blew along the railway banks, a crimson train. Siegmund waited, through the meadows, for the next wheat-field. It came like the lifting of yellow-hot metal out of the gloom of darkened grass-lands.

Helena was reassured by the glamour of evening over ripe Sussex. She breathed the land now and then, while she watched the sky. The sunset was stately. The blue-eyed day with great limbs, having fought its victory and won, now mounted triumphant on its pyre, and with white arms uplifted took the flames, which leaped like blood about its feet. The day died nobly: so she thought.

One gold cloud, as an encouragement tossed to her, followed the train.

"Surely that cloud is for us," said she, as she watched it anxiously. Dark trees brushed between it and her, while she waited in suspense. It came unswerving from behind the trees.

"I am sure it is for us," she repeated. A gladness came into her eyes.

Still the cloud followed the train. She leaned forward to Siegmund, and pointed out the cloud to him. She was very eager to give him a little of her faith.

"It has come with us quite a long way. Doesn't it seem to you to be travelling with us? It is the golden hand: it is the good omen."

She then proceeded to tell him the legend from "Aylwin."* Siegmund listened, and smiled. The sunset was handsome on his face. Helena was almost happy.

"I am right," said he to himself. "I am right in my conclusions—and Helena will manage by herself, afterwards. I am right: there is the hand to confirm it."

The heavy train settled down to an easy, unbroken stroke, swinging like a greyhound over the level, northwards. All the time Siegmund was mechanically thinking the well-known movement from the Valkyrie Ride,* his whole self beating to the rhythm. It seemed to him there was a certain grandeur in this flight, but it hurt him with its heavy insistence of catastrophe. He was afraid; he had to summon his courage to sit quiet. For a time he was reassured: he believed he was going on towards the right end. He hunted through the country and the sky, asking of everything, "Am I right—am I right?" He did not mind what happened to him, so long as he felt it was right. What he meant by 'right' he did not trouble to think, but the question remained. For a time he had been reassured. Then a dullness came over him, when his thoughts were stupid, and he merely submitted to the rhythm of the train, which stamped him deeper and deeper with a brand of catastrophe.

The sun had gone down. Over the west was a gush of brightness as the fountain of light bubbled lower. The stars, like specks of froth from the foaming of the day clung to the blue ceiling. Like spiders they hung overhead, while the hosts of the gold atmosphere poured out of the hive by the western low door. Soon the hive was empty, a hollow dome of purple, with here and there on the floor a bright brushing of wings,—a village—; then overhead the luminous star-spiders began to run.

"Ah, well!" thought Siegmund—he was tired—"—if one bee dies in a swarm, what is it, so long as the hive is all right? Apart from the gold light, and the hum and the colour of day, what was I?—nothing! Apart from these rushings out of the hive, along with [the] swarm, into the dark meadows of night, gathering God knows what, I was a pebble. Well, the day will swarm in golden again, with colour on the wings of every bee, and humming in each activity. The gold, and the colour, and sweet smell, and the sound of life, they exist, even if there is no bee: it only happens we see the iridescence on the wings of a bee. It exists, whether or not, bee or no bee. Since the iridescence and the humming of life *are*, always, and since it was they who made me, then I am not lost. At least, I do not care. If the spark goes out, the essence of the fire is there in the darkness. What does it matter! Besides, I *have* burned bright; I have laid up a fine cell of honey somewhere—I wonder where. We can never point to it. But it *is* so—what does it matter, then!"

They had entered the north downs, and were running through Dorking towards Leatherhead. Box Hill stood dark in the dusky sweetness of the night. Helena remembered that here she and Siegmund had come for their first walk together. She would like to come again. Presently she saw the quick stilettos of stars on the small, baffled river. They ran between high embankments. Siegmund recollected that these were covered with roses of Sharon—the large golden St. John's wort of finest silk. He looked, and could just distinguish the full-blown, delicate flowers, ignored by the stars. At last he had something to say to Helena.

"Do you remember," he asked, "the roses of Sharon all along here?"

"I do," replied Helena, glad he spoke so brightly. "Weren't they pretty?"

After a few moments of watching the bank, she said:

"Do you know, I have never gathered one. I think I should like to; I should like to feel them, and they should have an orangy smell."

He smiled without answering.

She glanced up at him, smiling brightly.

"But shall we come down here in the morning, and find some?" she asked. She put the question timidly. "Would you care to?" she added.

Siegmund darkened and frowned. Here was the pain revived again.

"No," he said gently. "I think we had better not." Almost for the first time he did not make apologetic explanation.

Helena turned to the window, and remained, looking out at the spinning of the lights of the towns without speaking, until they were near Sutton. Then she rose and pinned on her hat, gathering her gloves and her basket. She was, in spite of herself, slightly angry. Being quite ready to leave the train, she sat down to wait for the station. Siegmund was aware that she was displeased, and again for the first time, he said to himself, "Ah, well, it must be so."

She looked at him. He was sad, therefore she softened instantly.

"At least," she said doubtfully, "I shall see you at the station."

"At Waterloo?" he asked.

"No, at Wimbledon," she replied, in her metallic tone.

"But—!" he began.

"It will be the best way for us," she interrupted, in the calm tone of conviction. "Much better than crossing London from Victoria to Waterloo."

"Very well," he replied.

He looked up a train for her in his little timetable.

"You will get in Wimbledon 10.5—leave 10.40—leave Waterloo 11.30," he said.

"Very good," she answered.

The brakes were grinding. They waited in a burning suspense for the train to stop.

"If only she will soon go—!" thought Siegmund. It was an intolerable minute. She rose: everything was red blur. She stood before him, pressing his hand: then he rose to give her the bag. As he leaned upon the window-frame and she stood below on the platform, looking up at him, he could scarcely breathe. "How long will it be?" he said to himself looking at the open carriage doors. He hated intensely the lady who could not get a porter to remove her luggage: he could have killed her: he could have killed the dilatory guard. At last the doors slammed and the whistle went. The train started imperceptibly into motion.

"Now I lose her," said Siegmund. She looked up at him: her face was white and dismal.

"Goodbye then," she said, and she turned away.

Siegmund went back to his seat. He was relieved, but he trembled with sickness. We are all glad when intense moments are done with: but why did she fling round in that manner, stopping the keen note short: what would she do?

XXII

Siegmund went up to Victoria. He was in no hurry to get down to Wimbledon. London was warm and exhausted after the hot day, but this peculiar luke-warmness was not unpleasant to him. He chose to walk from Victoria to Waterloo.

The streets were like polished gun-metal glistened over with gold. The taxi-cabs, the wild cats of the town, swept over the gleaming floor swiftly, soon lessening in the distance, as if scornful of the other clumsy-footed traffic. He heard the merry click-clock of the swinging hansoms, then the excited whirring of the motor-buses as they charged full tilt heavily down the road, their hearts, as it seemed, beating with trepidation: they drew up with a sigh of relief by the kerb, and stood there panting, great, nervous, clumsy things. Siegmund was always amused by the headlong, floundering career of the buses. He was pleased with this scampering of the traffic: anything for distraction. He was glad Helena was not with him, for the streets would have irritated her with their coarse noise. She would stand for a long time to watch the rabbits pop and hobble along on the common at night: but the tearing along of the taxis, and the charge of a great motor-bus was painful to her: 'discords,' she said, 'after the trees and sea.' She liked the glistening of the streets: it seemed a fine alloy of gold laid down for pavement, such pavement as drew near to the pure gold streets of Heaven. But this noise could not be endured near any wonderland.

Siegmund did not mind it: it drummed out his own thoughts. He watched the gleaming magic of the road, raced over with shadows, project itself far before him into the night. He watched the people. Soldiers, belted with scarlet, went jauntily on in front. There was a peculiar charm in their movement. There was a soft vividness of life in their carriage: it reminded Siegmund of the soft swaying and lapping of a poised candle-flame. The women went blithely alongside. Occasionally in passing one glanced at him. Then, in spite of himself, he smiled; he knew not why. The women glanced at him with approval, for he was ruddy; besides, he had that carelessness and abstraction of despair. The eyes of the women said, 'You are comely, you are lovable,' and Siegmund smiled.

When the street opened, at Westminster, he noticed the city sky, a lovely deep purple, and the lamps in the Square steaming out a vapour of grey-gold light.

"It is a wonderful night" he said to himself. "There are not two such in a year."

He went forward to the Embankment, with a feeling of elation in his heart. This purple and gold-grey world, with the fluttering flame-warmth of soldiers and the quick brightness of women, like lights that clip sharply in a draught, was a revelation to him.

As he leaned upon the Embankment parapet the wonder did not fade, but rather increased. The trams, one after another, floated loftily over the bridge. They went like great burning bees in an endless file into a hive, past those which were drifting dreamily out: while below, on the black distorted water, golden serpents flashed and twisted to and fro.

"Ah!" said Siegmund to himself. "It is far too wonderful for me. Here, as well as by the sea, the night is gorgeous and uncouth. What ever happens, the world is wonderful."

So he went on amid all the vast miracle of movement in the city night, the swirling of water to the sea, the gradual sweep of the stars, the floating of many lofty, luminous cars through the bridged darkness, like an army of angels filing past, on one of God's campaigns; the purring haste of the taxis, the slightly dancing shadows of people: Siegmund went on slowly, like a slow bullet winging into the heart of life. He did not lose this sense of wonder, not in the train, nor as he walked home in the moonless dark.

When he closed the door behind him, and hung up his hat, he frowned. He did not think definitely of anything, but his frown meant to him: "Now for the beginning of Hell!"

He went towards the dining room, where the light was, and the uneasy murmur. The clock, with its deprecating, suave chime was striking ten. Siegmund opened the door of the room. Beatrice was sewing, and did not raise her head. Frank, a tall thin lad of eighteen was bent over a book: he did not look up. Vera had her fingers thrust in among her hair, and continued to read the magazine that lay on the table before her. Siegmund looked at them all. They gave no sign to show they were aware of his entry; there was only that unnatural tenseness of people who cover their agitation. He glanced round to see where he should go. His wicker arm-chair remained empty by the fireplace: his slippers were standing under the sideboard, as he had left them. Siegmund sat down in the creaking chair. He began to feel sick and tired.

"I suppose the children are in bed," he said.

His wife sewed on as if she had not heard him; his daughter noisily turned over a leaf and continued to read, as if she were pleasantly interested and had known no interruption. Siegmund waited, with his slipper dangling from his hand, looking from one to another.

"They've been gone two hours," said Frank at last, still without raising his eyes from his book. His tone was contemptuous: his voice was jarring, not yet having developed a man's fulness.

Siegmund put on his slipper, and began to unlace the other boot. The slurring of the lace through the holes and the snacking of the tag seemed unnecessarily loud. It annoyed his wife. She took a breath to speak, then refrained, feeling suddenly her daughter's scornful restraint upon her. Siegmund rested his arms upon his knees, and sat leaning forward, looking into the barren fireplace, which was littered with paper and orange peel, and a banana skin.

"Do you want any supper?" asked Beatrice, and the sudden harshness of her voice startled him into looking at her. She had her face averted, refusing to see him. Siegmund's heart went down with weariness and despair at the sight of her.

"Aren't *you* having any?" he asked.

The table was not laid. Beatrice's work-basket, a little wicker fruit-skep, overflowed scissors and pins and scraps of holland and reels of cotton on the green serge cloth. Vera leaned both her elbows on the table.

Instead of replying to him, Beatrice went to the sideboard. She took out a table-cloth, pushed her sewing-litter aside, and spread the cloth over one end of the table. Vera gave her magazine a little knock with her hand.

"Have you read this tale of a French convent school in here mother?" she asked.

"In where?" said Beatrice.

"In this month's 'Nash's.'"*

"No" replied Beatrice. "What time have I for reading—much less for anything else."

"You should think more of yourself, and a little less of other people then," said Vera, with a sneer at the 'other people.' She rose.

"Let me do this—you sit down—you are tired, mother," she said.

Her mother, without replying, went out to the kitchen. Vera followed her. Frank, left alone with his father, moved uneasily, and bent his thin shoulders lower over his book. Siegmund remained with his arms on his knees looking into the grate. From the kitchen came the chinking of crockery, and soon, the smell of coffee. All the time, Vera was heard chatting with affected brightness to her mother, addressing her in fond tones, using all her wits to recall bright little incidents to retail to her. Beatrice answered rarely, and then with utmost brevity.

Presently Vera came in with the tray. She put down a cup of coffee, a plate with boiled ham, pink and thin such as is bought from a grocer, and some bread and butter. Then she sat down, noisily turning over the leaves of her magazine, Frank glanced at the table: it was laid solely for his father. He looked at the bread and the meat, but restrained himself, and went on reading, or pretended to do so. Beatrice came in with the small cruet. It was conspicuously bright.

Everything was correct: knife and fork, spoon, cruet, all perfectly clean, the crockery fine, the bread and butter thin. In fact, it was just as it would have been for a perfect stranger. This scrupulous neatness, in a household so slovenly and easy-going, where it was an established tradition that something should be forgotten or wrong, impressed Siegmund. Beatrice put the serving knife and fork by the little dish of ham, saw that all was proper, then went and sat down. Her face showed no emotion: it was calm and proud. She began to sew.

"What do you say, mother?" said Vera, as if resuming a conversation. "Shall it be Hampton Court or Richmond on Sunday?"

"I say as I said before," replied Beatrice. "I cannot afford to go out."

"But you must begin, my dear, and Sunday shall see the beginning. Dîtes donc!"*

"There are other things to think of," said Beatrice.

"Now, maman, nous avons changé tout cela!* We are going out—a jolly little razzle."* Vera, who was rather handsome, lifted up her face and smiled at her mother gaily.

"I am afraid there will be no *razzle*"—Beatrice accented the word, smiling slightly, "for me. You are slangy, Vera."

"Un doux argot, ma mère.*—You look tired." Beatrice glanced at the clock.

"I will go to bed when I have cleared the table," she said.

Siegmund winced. He was still sitting with his head bent down, looking in the grate. Vera went on to say something more. Presently Frank looked up at the table, and remarked, in his grating voice:

"There's your supper, father."

The women stopped and looked round at this. Siegmund bent his head lower. Vera resumed her talk. It died out, and there was silence.

Siegmund was hungry.

"Oh, good Lord, good Lord, bread of humiliation tonight," he said to himself before he could muster courage to rise and go to the table. He seemed to be shrinking inwards. The women glanced swiftly at him and away from him as his chair creaked and he got up. Frank was watching from under his eyebrows.

Siegmund went through the ordeal of eating and drinking in presence of his family. If he had not been hungry, he could not have done it, despite the fact that he was content to receive humiliation this night. He swallowed the coffee with effort. When he had finished he sat irresolute for some time. Then he arose and went to the door.

"Goodnight," he said.

Nobody made any reply. Frank merely stirred in his chair. Siegmund shut the door and went.

There was absolute silence in the room till they heard him turn on the tap in the bathroom. Then Beatrice began to breathe spasmodically, catching her breath as if she would sob. But she restrained herself. The faces of the two children set hard with hate.

"He is not worth the flicking of your little finger, mother," said Vera.

Beatrice moved about with pitiful, groping hands, collecting her sewing and her cottons.

"At any rate, he's come back red enough," said Frank, in his grating tone of contempt. "He's like boiled salmon."

Beatrice did not answer anything. Frank rose, and stood with his back to the grate, in his father's characteristic attitude.

"I *would* come slinking back in a funk!" he said, with a young man's sneer. Stretching forward, he put a piece of ham between two pieces of bread, and began to eat the sandwich in large bites. Vera came to the table, at this, and began to make herself a more dainty sandwich. Frank watched her with jealous eye.

"There is a little more ham, if you'd like it," said Beatrice to him. "I kept you some."

"All right Ma," he replied. "Fetch it in."

Beatrice went out to the kitchen.

"And bring the bread and butter, too, will you?" called Vera after her.

"The damned coward! Ain't he a rotten funker?" said Frank, sotto voce, while his mother was out of the room. Vera did not reply, but she seemed tacitly to agree.

They petted their mother, while she waited on them. At length Frank yawned. He fidgeted a moment or two, then he went over to his mother, and, putting his hand on her arm—the feel of his mother's round arm under the black silk sleeve made his tears rise—he said, more gratingly than ever:

"Ne'er mind, Ma. We'll be all right to you." Then he bent and kissed her.

"Goodnight—mother," he said awkwardly, and he went out of the room. Beatrice was crying.

XXIII

"I shall never re-establish myself," said Siegmund, as he closed behind him the dining room door and went upstairs in the dark. "I am a family criminal. Beatrice might come round: but the children's insolent judgment is too much. And I am like a dog that creeps round the house from which it escaped with joy. I have nowhere else to go. Why did I come back? But I am sleepy. I will not bother to-night."

He went into the bathroom and washed himself. Everything he did gave him a grateful sense of pleasure, notwithstanding the misery of his position. He dipped his arms deeper into the cold water, that he might feel the delight of it a little further. His neck he swilled time after time, and it seemed to him he laughed with pleasure as the water caught him and fell away. The towel reminded him how sore were his forehead and his neck, blistered both to a state of rawness by the sun. He touched them very cautiously to dry them, wincing, and smiling at his own childish touch-and-shrink.

Though his bedroom was very dark, he did not light the gas. Instead, he stepped out into the small balcony. His shirt was open at the neck and wrists: he pulled it further apart, baring his chest to the deliciously soft night. He stood looking out at the darkness for some time. The night was as yet moonless, but luminous, with a certain atmosphere of light. The stars were small. Near at hand, large shapes of trees rose up. Farther, lamps like little mushroom groups shone amid an undergrowth of darkness. There was a vague hoarse noise filling the sky, like the whispering in a shell, and this breathing of the summer night occasionally swelled into a restless sigh as a train roared across the distance.

"What a big night," thought Siegmund. "The night gathers everything into a oneness. I wonder what is in it."

He leaned forward over the balcony, trying to catch something out of the night. He felt his soul like tendrils stretched out anxiously to grasp a hold. What could he hold to in this great, hoarse-breathing night? A star fell. It seemed to burst into sight just across his eyes.

with a yellow flash. He looked up, unable to make up his mind whether he had seen it or not. There was no gap in the sky.

"It is a good sign, a shooting star," he said to himself. "It is a good sign for me. I know I am right. That was my sign."

Having assured himself, he stepped indoors, unpacked his bag, and was soon in bed.

"This is a good bed," he said. "And the sheets are very fresh."

He lay for a little while with his head bending forwards, looking from his pillow out at the stars. Then he went to sleep.

At half past six in the morning he suddenly opened his eyes.

"What is it?" he asked, and almost without interruption answered:

"Well, I've got to go through it."

His sleep had shaped him perfect premonition, which, like a dream, he forgot when he awoke. Only this naïve question and answer betrayed what had taken place in his sleep. Immediately he awoke, this subordinate knowledge vanished.

Another fine day was striding in triumphant. The first thing Siegmund did was to salute the morning, because of its brightness. The second thing was to call to mind the aspect of that bay in the Isle of Wight; 'What would it just be like, now?' said he to himself. He had to give his heart some justification for the peculiar pain left in it from his sleep activity, so he began poignantly to long for the place which had been his during the last mornings. He pictured the garden with roses and nasturtiums: he remembered the sunny way down the shore, and all the expanse of sea hung softly between the tall white cliffs.

"It is impossible it is gone!" he cried to himself. "It can't be gone. I looked forward to it as if it never would come. It can't be gone now. Helena is not lost to me, surely." Then he began a long pining for the departed beauty of his life. He turned the jewel of memory, and facet by facet it wounded him with its brilliant loveliness. This pain, though it was keen, was half pleasure.

Presently he heard his wife stirring. She opened the door of the room next to his, and he heard her:

"Frank, it's a quarter to eight. You *will* be late."

"All right, mother. Why didn't you call me sooner?" grumbled the lad.

"I didn't wake myself. I didn't go to sleep till morning, and then I slept."

She went downstairs. Siegmund listened for his son to get out of bed. The minutes passed.

"The young donkey, why doesn't he get out!" said Siegmund angrily to himself. He turned over, pressing himself upon the bed in anger and humiliation, because now he had no authority to call to his son and keep him to his duty. Siegmund waited, writhing with anger, shame, and anxiety. When the suave, velvety 'Pan-n-n! Pan-n-n-n!' of the clock was heard striking, Frank stepped with a thud onto the floor. He could be heard dressing in clumsy haste. Beatrice called from the bottom of the stairs:

"Do you want any hot water?"

"You know there isn't time for me to shave now," answered her son, lifting his voice to a kind of broken falsetto.

The scent of the cooking of bacon filled the house. Siegmund heard his second daughter, Marjory, aged nine, talking to Vera, who occupied the same room with her. The child was evidently questioning, and the elder girl answered briefly. There was a lull in the household noises, broken suddenly by Marjory, shouting from the top of the stairs:

"Mam!"—she waited—"Mam!"—still Beatrice did not hear her. "Mam!— —Mamma!" Beatrice was in the scullery. "Mamma-a!" The child was getting impatient. She lifted her voice and shouted: "Mam?—Mamma!"—still no answer. "Mam-mee-e!" she squealed.

Siegmund could hardly contain himself.

"Why don't you go down and ask?" Vera called crossly from the bedroom, and at the same moment Beatrice answered, also crossly:

"What do you want?"

"Where's my stockings?" cried the child, at the top of her voice.

"Why do you ask me—are they down here!" replied her mother. "What are you shouting for!" The child podded down stairs. Directly she returned, and as she passed into Vera's room, she grumbled: "And now they're not mended."

Siegmund heard a sound that made his heart beat. It was the crackling of the sides of the crib, as Gwen, his little girl of five, climbed out. She was silent for a space. He imagined her sitting on the white rug and pulling on her stockings. Then there came the quick little thud of her feet as she went downstairs.

"Mam—?" Siegmund heard her say as she went down the hall. "Has Dad come?"

The answer and the child's further talk were lost in the distance of the kitchen. The small, anxious question, and the quick thudding of Gwen's feet made Siegmund lie still with torture. He wanted to hear no more. He lay shrinking within himself. It seemed that his soul was sensitive to madness. He felt that he could not, come what might, get up and meet them all.

The front door banged, and he heard Frank's hasty call: "Good-bye!" Evidently the lad was in an ill humour. Siegmund listened for the sound of the train: it seemed an age: the boy would catch it. Then the water from the wash-hand bowl in the bathroom ran loudly out. That, he supposed, was Vera, who was evidently not going up to town. At the thought of this, Siegmund almost hated her. He listened for her to go downstairs. It was nine o'clock.

The footsteps of Beatrice came upstairs. She put something down in the bathroom—his hot water. Siegmund listened intently for her to come to his door. Would she speak? She approached hurriedly, knocked, and waited. Siegmund, startled, for the moment could not answer. She knocked loudly.

"All right," said he.

Then she went downstairs.

He lay probing and torturing himself for another half hour, till Vera's voice said coldly, beneath his window outside: "You should clear away then. We don't want the breakfast things on the table for a week."

Siegmund's heart set hard. He rose, with a shut mouth, and went across to the bathroom. There he started. The quaint figure of Gwen stood at the bowl; her back was towards him: she was sponging her face gingerly. Her hair, all blowsed from the pillow, was tied in a stiff little pigtail, standing out from her slender, childish neck. Her arms were bare to the shoulder. She wore a bodiced petticoat of pink flannelette, which hardly reached her knees. Siegmund felt slightly amused to see her stout little calves planted so firmly close together. She carefully sponged her cheeks, her pursed-up mouth, and her neck, soaping her hair but not her ears. Then, very deliberately, she squeezed out the sponge and proceeded to wipe away the soap.

For some reason or other she glanced round. Her startled eyes met his. She too had beautiful dark blue eyes. She stood, with the sponge at her neck, looking full at him. Siegmund felt himself shrinking. The child's look was steady, calm, inscrutable.

"Hello!" said her father. "Are you here!" The child, without altering her expression in the slightest, turned her back on him and continued wiping her neck. She dropped the sponge in the water and took the towel from off the side of the bath. Then she turned to look again at Siegmund, who stood in his pyjamas before her, his mouth shut hard, but his eyes shrinking and tender. She seemed to be trying to discover something in him.

"Have you washed your ears?" he said gaily. She paid no heed to this, except that he noticed her face now wore a slight, constrained smile as she looked at him. She was shy. Still she continued to regard him curiously.

"There is some chocolate on my dressing-table," he said.

"Where have you been to?" she asked suddenly.

"To the sea-side," he answered smiling.

"To Brighton?" she asked. Her tone was still condemning.

"Much further than that," he replied.

"To Worthing?" she asked.

"Further— —in a steamer," he replied.

"But who did you go with?" asked the child.

"Why I went all by myself," he answered.

"Twuly?" she asked.

"Weally and Twuly," he answered, laughing.

"Couldn't you take me?" she asked.

"I will next time," he replied.

The child still looked at him, unsatisfied.

"But what did you go for?" she asked, goading him suspiciously.

"To see the sea and the ships and the fighting ships with cannons— —."

"You *might* have taken me," said the child reproachfully.

"Yes, I ought to have done, oughtn't I?" he said, as if regretful.

Gwen still looked full at him.

"You *are* red," she said.

He glanced quickly in the glass, and replied:

"That is the sun. Hasn't it been hot?"

"Mm! It made my nose all peel. Vera said she would scrape me like a new potato;" the child laughed, and turned shyly away.

"Come here," said Siegmund. "I believe you've got a tooth out haven't you?"

He was very cautious and gentle. The child drew back. He hesitated and she drew away from him, unwilling.

"Come and let me look," he repeated.

She drew further away, and the same constrained smile appeared on her face, shy, suspicious, condemning.

"Aren't you going to get your chocolate?" he asked, as the child hesitated in the doorway. She glanced into his room, and answered:

"I've got to go to Mam and have my hair done." Her awkwardness and her lack of compliance insulted him. She went downstairs, without going into his room.

Siegmund, rebuffed by the only one in the house from whom he might have expected friendship, proceeded slowly to shave, feeling sick at heart. He was a long time over his toilet. When he stripped himself for the bath, it seemed to him he could smell the sea. He bent his head and licked his shoulder. It tasted decidedly salt.

"A pity to wash it off," he said.

As he got up dripping from the cold bath he felt for the moment exhilarated. He rubbed himself smooth. Glancing down at himself, he thought: "I look young. I look as young as twenty six."

He turned to the mirror. There he saw himself a mature, complete man of forty, with grave years of experience on his countenance.

"I used to think that, when I was forty," he said to himself, "I should find everything straight as the nose on my face, walking through my affairs easily as you like. Now I am no more sure of myself, have no more confidence than a boy of twenty. What can I do? It seems to me a man needs a mother all his life. I don't feel much like a Lord of Creation."

Having arrived at this cynicism, Siegmund prepared to go downstairs. His sensitiveness had passed off: his nerves had become callous. When he was dressed he went down to the kitchen, without hesitation. He was indifferent to his wife and children. No one spoke to him as he sat to the table. That was as he liked it: he wished for nothing to touch him. He ate his breakfast alone, while his wife bustled about upstairs and Vera bustled about in the dining room. Then he retired to the solitude of the drawing room. As a reaction against his poetic activity, he felt as if he were gradually becoming more stupid and blind. He remarked nothing, not even the extravagant bowl of grasses placed where he would not have allowed it, on his piano; nor his fiddle, laid cruelly on the cold, polished floor near the window. He merely sat down in an arm-chair and felt sick.

All his unnatural excitement, all the poetic stimulation of the past few days had vanished. He sat flaccid, while his life struggled slowly through him. After an intoxication of passion and love, and beauty, and of sunshine, he was prostrate. Like a plant that blossoms gorgeously and madly, he had wasted the tissue of his strength, so that now his life struggled in a clogged and broken channel.

Siegmund sat with his head between his hands, leaning upon the table. He would have been stupidly quiescent in his feeling of loathing and sickness, had not an intense irritability in all his nerves tormented him into consciousness.

"I suppose this is the result of the sun;—a sort of sunstroke," he said, realising an intolerable stiffness of his brain, a stunned condition in his head.

"This is hideous!" he said. His arms were quivering with intense irritation. He exerted all his will to stop them, and then the hot irritability commenced in his belly. Siegmund fidgeted in his chair without changing his position. He had not the energy to get up and move about. He fidgeted like an insect pinned down.

The door opened. He felt violently startled: yet there was no movement perceptible. Vera entered, ostensibly for an autograph album into which she was going to copy a drawing from the "London Opinion";* really to see what her father was doing. He did not move a muscle. He only longed intensely for his daughter to go out of the room, so that he could let go. Vera went out of the drawing room humming to herself. Apparently she had not even glanced at her father. In reality, she had observed him closely.

"He is sitting with his head in his hands," she said to her mother. Beatrice replied:

"I'm glad he's nothing else to do."

"I should think he's pitying himself," said Vera.

"He's a good one at it," answered Beatrice. Gwen came forward and took hold of her mother's skirt, looking up anxiously.

"What is he doing Mam?" she asked.

"Nothing," replied her mother. "Nothing, only sitting in the drawing room."

"But what has he *been* doing?" persisted the anxious child.

"Nothing. Nothing that I can tell *you*. He's only spoilt all our lives."

The little girl stood regarding her mother in the greatest distress and perplexity.

"But what will he do, Mam?" she asked.

"Nothing. Don't bother. Run and play with Marjory now. Do you want a nice plum?"

She took a yellow plum from the table. Gwen accepted it without a word. She was too much perplexed.

"What do you say?" asked her mother.

"Thank you," replied the child, turning away.

Siegmund sighed with relief when he was again left alone. He twisted in his chair, and sighed again, trying to drive out the intolerable clawing irritability from his belly.

"Ah this is horrible!" he said.

He stiffened his muscles to quieten them.

"I've never been like this before. What is the matter?" he asked himself. But the question died out immediately: it seemed useless and sickening to try and answer it. He began to cast about for an alleviation. If he could only do something or have something he wanted, it would be better.

"What do I want?" he asked himself, and he anxiously strove to find this out. Everything he suggested to himself made him sicken with weariness or distaste. The sea-side—a foreign land—a fresh life that he had often dreamed of, farming in Canada.

"I should be just the same there," he answered himself: "Just the same sickening feeling there, that I want nothing."

"Helena!" he suggested to himself, trembling.

But he only felt a deeper horror. The thought of her made him shrink convulsively.

"I can't endure this," he said. "If this is the case I had better be dead. To have no want, no desire: that is death to begin with."

He rested awhile after this. The idea of death alone seemed entertaining. Then:

"Is there really nothing I could turn to?" he asked himself. To him, in that state of soul, it seemed there was not.

"Helena!" he suggested again, appealingly, testing himself. "Ah, no!" he cried, drawing sharply back, as from an approaching touch upon a raw place. He groaned slightly as he breathed, with a horrid weight of nausea. There was a fumbling upon the door-knob. Siegmund did not start. He merely pulled himself together. Gwen pushed open the door, and stood holding onto the door-knob, looking at him.

"Dad, Mam says dinner's ready," she announced. Siegmund did not reply. The child waited, at a loss for some moments, before she repeated, in a hesitating tone:

"Dinner's ready."

"All right," said Siegmund. "Go away."

The little girl returned to the kitchen with tears in her eyes, very crestfallen.

"What did he say?" asked Beatrice.

"He shouted at me," replied the little one, breaking into tears.

Beatrice flushed. Tears came into her own eyes. She took the child in her arms and pressed her to her, kissing her forehead.

"Did he?" she said, very tenderly. "Never mind then, dearie, never mind."

The tears in her mother's voice made the child sob bitterly. Vera and Marjory sat silent at table. The steak and mashed potatoes steamed and grew cold.

XXIV

When Helena arrived home on the Thursday evening, she found everything repulsive. All the odours of the sordid street through which she must pass hung about the pavement, having crept out in the heat. The house was bare and narrow. She remembered children sometimes to have brought her moths shut up in matchboxes. As she knocked at the door she felt like a numbed moth which a boy is pushing off its leaf-rest into his box.

The door was opened by her mother. She was a woman whose sunken mouth, ruddy cheeks and quick brown eyes gave her the appearance of a bird which walks about pecking suddenly here and there. As Helena reluctantly entered, the mother drew herself up, and immediately relaxed, seeming to peck forwards, as she said—"Well?"

"Well—here we are!" replied the daughter in a matter-of-fact tone. Her mother was inclined to be affectionate, therefore she became proportionately cold.

"So I see!" exclaimed Mrs Verden, tossing her head in a peculiar jocular manner. "And what sort of a time have you had?"

"Oh, very good!" replied Helena, still more coolly.

"H'm!"—Mrs Verden looked keenly at her daughter. She recognised the peculiar sulky, childish look she knew so well, therefore, making an effort, she forbore to question.

"You look well," she said. Helena smiled ironically.

"And are you ready for your supper?" she asked, in the playful affectionate manner she had assumed.

"If the supper is ready, I will have it," replied her daughter.

"Well, it's not ready." The mother shut tight her sunken mouth and regarded her daughter with playful challenge. "Because," she continued, "I didn't know when you were coming." She gave a jerk with her arm, like an orator who utters the incontrovertible. "But," she added, after a tedious dramatic pause, "I can soon have it ready. What will you have?"

"The full list of your capacious larder," replied Helena. Mrs Verden looked at her again, and hesitated.

"Will you have cocoa or lemonade?" she asked, coming to the point curtly.

"Lemonade," said Helena.

Presently Mr Verden entered—a small, white-bearded man with a gentle voice.

"Oh, so you are back Nelly!" he said, in his quiet, reserved manner.

"As you see, Pater," she answered.

"H'm!" he murmured, and he moved about at his accounts. Neither of her parents dared to question Helena. They moved about her on tip-toe, stealthily. Yet neither subserved her. Her father's quiet "H'm!", her mother's curt question made her draw inwards like a snail which can never retreat far enough from condemning eyes. She made a careless pretence of eating. She was like a child which has done wrong, and will not be punished, but will be left with the humiliating smear of offence upon it.

There was a quick light palpitating of the knocker. Mrs Verden went to the door.

"Has she come?"—and there were hasty steps along the passage. Louisa entered. She flung herself upon Helena and kissed her.

"How long have you been in?" she asked, in a voice trembling with affection.

"Ten minutes," replied Helena.

"Why didn't you send me the time of the train, so that I could come and meet you?" Louisa reproached her.

"Why— —?" drawled Helena. Louisa looked at her friend without speaking. She was deeply hurt by this sarcasm.

As soon as possible Helena went upstairs. Louisa stayed with her that night. On the next day they were going to Cornwall together for their usual midsummer holiday. They were to be accompanied by a third girl, a minor friend of Louisa, a slight acquaintance of Helena.

During the night, neither of the two friends slept much. Helena made confidences to Louisa, who brooded on these, on the romance and tragedy which enveloped the girl she loved so dearly. Meanwhile Helena's thoughts went round and round, tethered amid the five days by the sea, pulling forwards as far as the morrow's meeting with Siegmund, but reaching no further.

Friday was an intolerable day of silence broken by little tender advances and playful affectionate sallies on the part of the mother, all of which were rapidly repulsed. The father said nothing, and avoided his daughter with his eyes. In his humble reserve there was a dignity which made his disapproval far more difficult to bear than the repeated flagrant questionings of the mother's eyes. But the day wore on. Helena pretended to read, and sat thinking. She played her violin a little, mechanically. She went out into the town, and wandered about.

At last the night fell.

"Well," said Helena to her mother, "I suppose I'd better pack."

"Haven't you done it?" cried Mrs Verden, exaggerating her surprise. "You'll never have it done. I'd better help you. What time does the train go?"

Helena smiled.

"Ten minutes to ten."

Her mother glanced at the clock. It was only half past eight: there was ample time for everything.

Nevertheless, "You'd better look sharp," Mrs Verden said.

Helena turned away, weary of this exaggeration.

"I'll come with you to the station," suggested Mrs Verden. "I'll see the last of you. We shan't see much of you just now."

Helena turned round in surprise.

"Oh, I wouldn't bother," she said, fearing to make her disapproval too evident.

"Yes—I will—I'll see you off."

Mrs Verden's animation and indulgence were remarkable. Usually she was curt and undemonstrative. On occasions like these, however, when she was reminded of the ideal relations between mother and daughter, she played the part of the affectionate parent, much to the general distress.

Helena lit a candle and went to her bedroom. She quickly packed her dress-basket. As she stood before the mirror to put on her hat her eyes, gazing heavily, met her heavy eyes in the mirror. She glanced away swiftly as if she had been burned.

"How stupid I look!" she said to herself. "And Siegmund, how is he I wonder."

She wondered how Siegmund had passed the day: what had happened to him: how he felt, how he looked. She thought of him protectively.

Having strapped her basket, she carried it downstairs. Her mother was ready, with a white lace scarf round her neck. After a short time Louisa came in. She dropped her basket in the passage and then sank into a chair.

"I don't want to go, Nell," she said, after a few moments of silence.

"Why—how is that?" asked Helena, not surprised, but condescending, as to a child.

"Oh—I don't know—I'm tired," said the other petulantly.

"Of course you are—what do you expect, after a day like this?" said Helena.

"And rushing about packing!" exclaimed Mrs Verden, still in an exaggerated manner, this time scolding playfully.

"Oh—I don't know. I don't think I want to go, dear," repeated Louisa dejectedly.

"Well—it is time we set out," replied Helena, rising. "Will you carry the basket or the violin, Mater?"

Louisa rose, and with a forlorn expression, took up her light luggage.

The west opposite the door was smouldering with sunset. Darkness is only smoke that hangs suffocatingly over the low red heat of the sunken day. Such was Helena's longed-for night. The tram-car was crowded. In one corner Olive, the third friend, rose excitedly to greet them. Helena sat mute while the car swung though the yellow, stale lights of a third-rate street of shops. She heard Olive remarking on her sunburned face and arms; she became aware of the renewed inflammation in her blistered arms; she heard her own curious voice answering—everything was in a maze. To the beat of the car, while the yellow blur of the shops passed over her eyes, she repeated "Two hundred and forty miles—two hundred and forty miles."

XXV

Siegmund passed the afternoon in a sort of stupor. At teatime Beatrice, who had until then kept herself in restraint, gave way to an outburst of angry hysteria.

"When does your engagement at the Comedy Theatre* commence?" she had asked him, coldly. He knew she was wondering about money.

"Tomorrow—if ever," he had answered. She was aware that he hated the work. For some reason or other her anger flashed out like sudden lightning at his—"if ever."

"What do you think you *can* do?" she cried—"for I think you have done enough. We can't do as we like altogether, indeed, indeed we cannot. You have had your fling, haven't you? You have had your fling, and you want to keep on? But there's more than one person in the world. Remember that! But there are your children, let me remind you. Whose are they—? You talk about shirking the engagement, but who is going to be responsible for your children, do you think?"

"I said nothing about shirking the engagement," replied Siegmund, very coldly.

"No, there was no need to say. I know what it means. You sit there sulking all day. What do you think *I* do? I have to see to the children, I have to work and slave, I go on from day to day:—I tell you *I'll* stop, I tell you *I'll* do as I like; *I'll* go, as well.—No, I wouldn't be such a coward—you know that. You know *I* wouldn't leave little children—to the workhouse or anything. They're my children—they mightn't *be* yours."

"There is no need for this," said Siegmund, contemptuously. The pressure in his temples was excruciating, and he felt loathsomely sick.

Beatrice's dark eyes flashed with rage.

"Isn't there!" she cried. "Oh, isn't there? No, there is need for a great deal more. I don't know what you think I am. How much further do you think you can go? No, you don't like reminding of us. You sit moping, sulking because you have to come back to your own children. I wonder how much you think I shall stand. What do you think I am, to put up with it. What do you think I am? Am I a servant to eat out of your hand—?"

"Be quiet!" shouted Siegmund. "Don't I know what you are? Listen to yourself."

Beatrice was suddenly silenced. It was the stillness of white hot wrath. Even Siegmund was glad to hear her voice again. She spoke low and trembling.

"You coward, you miserable coward! It is I, is it, who am wrong? It is I who am to blame, is it? You miserable thing. I have no doubt you know what I am— —" Siegmund looked up at her as her words died off. She looked back at him with dark eyes loathing his cowed, wretched animosity. His eyes were bloodshot and furtive: his mouth was drawn back in a half-grin of hate and misery. She was goading him, in his darkness whither he had withdrawn himself like a sick dog, to die or recover as his strength should prove. She tortured him till his sickness was swallowed by anger, which glared redly at her as he pushed back his chair to rise. He trembled too much, however. His chin dropped again on his chest. Beatrice sat down in her place, hearing footsteps. She was shuddering slightly, and her eyes were fixed.

Vera entered with the two children. All three, immediately, as if they found themselves confronted by something threatening, stood arrested. Vera tackled the situation.

"Is the table ready to be cleared yet?" she asked, in an unpleasant tone. Her father's cup was half emptied. He had come to tea late, after the others had left the table. Evidently he had not finished, but he made no reply, neither did Beatrice. Vera glanced disgustedly at her father. Gwen sidled up to her mother and tried to break the tension.

"Mam, there was a lady had a dog, and it ran into a shop, and it licked a sheep, mam, what was hanging up— — —."

Beatrice sat fixed, and paid not the slightest attention. The child looked up at her, waited, then continued softly:

"Mam! —there was a lady had a dog— —"

"Don't bother!" snapped Vera sharply.

The child looked, wondering and resentful, at her sister. Vera was taking the things from the table, snatching them, and thrusting them on the tray. Gwen's eyes rested a moment or two on the bent head of her father. Then deliberately she turned again to her mother, and repeated in her softest and most persuasive tones: "Mam, I saw a dog, and it ran in a butcher's shop and licked a piece of meat.—Mam!—Mam?"

There was no answer. Gwen went forward and put her hand on her mother's knee.

"Mam!" she pleaded timidly. No response.

"Mam?" she whispered. She was desperate. She stood on tip-toe, and pulled with little hands at her mother's breast.

"Mam!!" she whispered shrilly. Her mother, with an effort of self denial, put off her investment of tragedy, and, laying her arm round the child's shoulders, drew her close. Gwen was somewhat reassured, but not satisfied. With an earnest face upturned to the impassive countenance of her mother, she began to whisper, sibilant, coaxing, pleading:

"Mam—there was a lady, she had a dog—." Vera turned sharply to stop this whispering, which was too much for her nerves, but the mother forestalled her. Taking the child in her arms she averted her face, put her cheek against the baby-cheek, and let the tears run freely. Gwen was too much distressed to cry. The tears gathered very slowly in her eyes, and fell without her having moved a muscle in her face. Vera remained in the scullery, weeping tears of rage and pity and shame into the towel. The only sound in the room was the occasional sharp breathing of Beatrice. Siegmund sat without the trace of a movement, almost without breathing. His head was ducked low; he dared never lift it, he dared give no sign of his presence.

Presently Beatrice put down the child and went to join Vera in the scullery. There came the low sound of women's talking, an angry, ominous sound. Gwen followed her mother. Her little voice could be heard cautiously asking:

"Mam—is Dad cross—is he? What did he do?"

"Don't bother," snapped Vera. "You *are* a little nuisance! Here, take this into the dining room, and don't drop it."

The child did not obey. She stood looking from her mother to her sister. The latter pushed a dish into her hand.

"Go along," she said, gently thrusting the child forth.

Gwen departed. She hesitated in the kitchen. Her father still remained unmoved. The child wished to go to him, to speak to him, but she was afraid. She crossed the kitchen slowly, hugging the dish. Then she came slowly back, hesitating. She sidled into the kitchen: she crept round the table inch by inch, drawing nearer her father. At about a yard from his chair she stopped. He, from under his bent brows, could see her small feet, in brown slippers nearly kicked through at the toes, waiting and moving nervously near him. He pulled himself together as a man does who watches the surgeon's lancet suspended over his wound. Would the child speak to him?—Would she touch him with her small hands? He held his breath, and, it seemed, held his heart from beating. What he should do he did not know. He waited in a daze of suspense. The child shifted from one foot to another. He could just see the edge of her white-frilled drawers. He wanted, above all things, to take her in his arms, to have something against which to hide his face. Yet he was afraid. Often, when all the world was hostile, he had found her full of love; he had hidden his face against her; she had gone to sleep in his arms; she had been like a piece of apple blossom in his arms. If she should come to him now—; his heart halted again in suspense; he knew not what he would do. It would open, perhaps, the tumour of his sickness. He was quivering too fast with suspense to know what he feared or wanted or hoped.

"Gwen!" called Vera, wondering why she did not return. "Gwen!"

"Yes!" answered the child, and slowly Siegmund saw her feet lifted, hesitate, move, then turn away. She had gone. His excitement sank rapidly, and the sickness returned stronger, more horrible and wearying than ever. For a moment it was so bad that he was afraid of losing consciousness. He recovered slightly, pulled himself up, and went upstairs. His fists were tightly clenched, his fingers closed over his thumbs, which were pressed bloodless. He lay down on the bed.

For two hours he lay in a dazed condition resembling sleep. At the end of that time, the knowledge that he had to meet Helena was actively at work, an activity quite apart from his will or his consciousness, jogging and pulling him awake. At eight o'clock he sat up. A cramped pain in his thumbs made him wonder. He looked at them, and mechanically shut them again under his fingers, into the position they sought after two hours of similar constraint. Siegmund opened his hands again, smiling.

"It is said to be the sign of a weak, deceitful character," he said to himself.

His head was peculiarly numbed; at the back it felt heavy as if weighted with lead. He could think only one detached sentence at intervals. Betweenwhiles there was a blank, grey sleep or swoon.

"I have got to go and meet Helena at Wimbledon," he said to himself, and instantly he felt a peculiar joy, as if he had laughed somewhere.

"But I must be getting ready. I can't disappoint her," said Siegmund. The idea of Helena woke a craving for rest in him. If he should say to her, 'Do not go away from me; come with me somewhere,' then he might lie down somewhere beside her, and she might put her hands on his head. If she could hold his head in her hands—for she had fine, silken hands that adjusted themselves with a rare pressure, wrapping his weakness up in life—then his head would gradually grow healed, and he could rest. This was the one thing that remained, for his restoration: that she should with long, unwearying gentleness put him to rest. He longed for it utterly, for the hands and the restfulness of Helena.

"But it is no good," he said, starting like a drunken man from sleep. "What time is it?"—it was ten minutes to nine. She would be in Wimbledon by 10.10. It was time he should be getting ready. Yet he remained sitting on the bed.

"I am forgetting again," he said. "—But I do not want to go. What is the good? I have only to tie a mask on for the meeting. It is too much."

He waited and waited, his head dropped forward in a sort of sleep. Suddenly he started awake. The back of his head hurt severely.

"Goodness!" he said, "it's getting quite dark."

It was twenty minutes to ten. He went bewildered into the bathroom to wash in cold water and bring back his senses. His hands were sore, and his face blazed with sun-inflammation. He made himself neat as usual. It was ten minutes to ten. He would be very late. It was practically dark, though these bright days were endless. He wondered whether the children were in bed. It was too late, however to wonder.

Siegmund hurried downstairs and took his hat. He was walking down the path when the door was snatched open behind him, and Vera ran out, crying:

"Are you going out? Where are you going?"

Siegmund stood still and looked at her.

"She is frightened," he said to himself, smiling ironically.

"I am only going a walk. I have to go to Wimbledon. I shall not be very long."

"Wimbledon, at this time!" said Vera sharply, full of suspicion.

"Yes—I am late. I shall be back in an hour."

He was sorry for her. She knew he gave her an honourable promise.

"You need not keep us sitting up," she said.

He did not answer, but hurried to the station.

XXVI

Helena, Louisa and Olive climbed the steps to go to the South Western platform. They were laden with dress-baskets, umbrellas, and little packages. Olive and Louisa at least were in high spirits. Olive stopped before the indicator.

"The next train for Waterloo," she announced, in her contralto voice, "—is 10.30. It is now 10.12."

"We go by the 10.40. It is a better train," said Helena. Olive turned to her with a heavy-arch manner.

"Very well, dear! There is a parting to be got through, I am told. We sympathise, dear, but we regret it. Starting for a holiday is always a prolonged agony. But I am strong to endure it."

"You look it; you look as if you could tackle a bull," cried Louisa, skittish.

"My dear Louisa," rang out Olive's contralto "Don't judge me by appearances. You're sure to be taken in. With me it's a case of 'Oh the gladness of her gladness when she's sad, and the sadness of her sadness when she's glad—'"*

She looked round to see the effect of this. Helena, expected to say something, chimed in sarcastically.

"'They are nothing to her madness— —'"

"'When she's going for a holiday,' dear," cried Olive.

"Oh, go on being mad," cried Louisa.

"What, do you like it? I thought you'd be thanking Heaven that sanity was given me in large doses."

"And holidays in small," laughed Louisa. "Good! No, I like your madness, if you call it such. You are always so serious."

"'It's ill talking of halters in the house of the hanged,'* dear," boomed Olive. She looked from side to side: she felt triumphant. Helena smiled, acknowledging the sarcasm.

"But," said Louisa, smiling anxiously, "I don't quite see it. What's the point?"

"Well, to be explicit, dear," replied Olive, "it is hardly safe to accuse me of sadness and seriousness in *this* trio."

Louisa laughed and shook herself.

"Come to think of it, it isn't," she said.

Helena sighed, and walked down the platform. Her heart was beating thickly; she could hardly breathe. The station lamps hung low, so they made a ceiling of heat and dusty light. She suffocated under them. For a moment she beat with hysteria, feeling, as most of us feel when sick on a hot summer night, as if she must certainly go crazed, smothered under the grey, woolly blanket of heat. Siegmund was late. It was already twenty five minutes past ten.

She went towards the booking-office. At that moment Siegmund came on to the platform.

"Here I am!" he said. "Where is Louisa?"

Helena pointed to the seat, without answering. She was looking at Siegmund. He was distracted by the excitement of the moment, so she could not read him.

"Olive is there, too," she explained.

Siegmund stood still, straining his eyes to see the two women seated amidst pale wicker dress-baskets and dark rugs. The stranger made things more complex.

"Does she—your other friend—does she know?" he asked.

"She knows nothing," replied Helena, in a low tone, as she led him forward to be introduced.

"How do you do?" replied Olive in most mellow contralto. "Behold the dauntless three,* with their traps! You will see us forth on our perils?"

"I will, since I may not do more," replied Siegmund, smiling, continuing: "And how is Sister Louisa?"

"She is very well, thank you. It is *her* turn now," cried Louisa, vindictive, triumphant. There was always a faint animosity in her bearing towards Siegmund. He understood and smiled at her enmity, for the two were really good friends.

"It is your turn now," he repeated, smiling, and he turned away. He and Helena walked down the platform.

"How did you find things at home?" he asked her.

"Oh, as usual," she replied indifferently "And you?"

"Just the same," he answered. He thought for a moment or two, then added: "The children are happier without me."

"Oh, you mustn't say that kind of thing!" protested Helena miserably. "It's not true."

"It's all right dear," he answered. "So long as they are happy, it's all right." After a pause, he added "But I feel pretty bad tonight."

Helena's hand tightened on his arm. He had reached the end of the platform; there he stood, looking up the line which ran dark under a haze of lights. The high red signal-lamps hung aloft in a scarlet swarm: further off, like spangles shaking downwards from a burst sky rocket, was a tangle of brilliant red and green signal-lamps settling. A train with the warm flare on its thick column of smoke came thundering upon the lovers. Dazed, they felt the yellow bar of carriage windows brush in vibration across their faces. The ground and the air rocked. Then Siegmund turned his head to watch the red and the green lights in the rear of the train swiftly dwindle on the darkness. Still watching the distance where the train had vanished, he said:

"Dear—I want you to promise—that, whatever happens to me, you will go on. Remember dear, two wrongs don't make a right."*

Helena swiftly, with a movement of terror, faced him, looking into his eyes. But he was in the shadow, she could not see him. The flat sound of his voice, lacking resonance,—the dead, expressionless tone—made her lose her presence of mind. She stared at him blankly.

"What do you mean?—What has happened?—Something has happened to you. What has happened at home? What are you going to do?" she said sharply. She palpitated with terror. For the first time, she felt powerless; Siegmund was beyond her grasp. She was afraid of him. He had shaken away her hold over him.

"There is nothing fresh the matter at home," he replied wearily. He was to be scourged with emotion again. "I swear it," he added. "And I have not made up my mind—. But I can't think of life without you—and life must go on."

"And I swear," she said wrathfully, turning at bay, "that I won't live a day after you."

Siegmund dropped his head. The dead spring of his emotion swelled up scalding hot again. Then he said, almost inaudibly: "Ah—don't speak to me like that, dear. It is late to be angry.—When I have seen your train out tonight, there is nothing left—." Helena looked at him, dumb with dismay, stupid, angry.

They became aware of the porters shouting loudly that the Waterloo train was to leave from another platform.

"You'd better come," said Siegmund, and they hurried down towards Louisa and Olive.

"We've got to change platforms," cried Louisa, running forward and excitedly announcing the news.

"Yes," replied Helena, pale and impassive.

Siegmund picked up the luggage.

"I say," cried Olive, rushing to catch Helena and Louisa by the arm—"look—look—both of you—look at that hat!"—A lady in front was wearing on her hat a wild and dishevelled array of peacock feathers.—"It's the sight of a lifetime—I wouldn't have you miss it," added Olive in hoarse sotto voce.

"Indeed not!" cried Helena, turning in wild exasperation to look. "Get a good view of it, Olive. Let's have a good mental impression of it, one that will last."

"That's right, dear," said Olive, somewhat nonplussed by this outburst.

Siegmund had escaped with the heaviest two bags. They could see him ahead, climbing the steps. Olive re-adjusted herself, from the wildly animated to the calmly ironical.

"After all, dear," she said as they hurried in the tail of the crowd, "it's not half a bad idea to get a man on the job."

Louisa laughed aloud at this vulgar conception of Siegmund.

"Just now, at any rate," she rejoined.

As they reached the platform the train ran in before them. Helena watched anxiously for an empty carriage: there was not one.

"Perhaps it is as well," she thought. "We needn't talk. There will be three-quarters of an hour at Waterloo. If we were alone, Olive would make Siegmund talk."

She found a carriage with four people, and hastily took possession. Siegmund followed her with the bags. He swung these on the rack, and then quickly received the rugs, umbrellas and packages from the other two. These he put on the seats or anywhere, while Helena stowed them. She was very busy for a moment or two: the racks were full. Other people entered; their luggage was troublesome to bestow.

When she turned round again, she found Louisa and Olive seated, but Siegmund was outside on the platform, and the door was closed. He saw her face move as if she would cry to him. She restrained herself, and immediately called:

"You are coming?—Oh—you are coming to Waterloo?"

He shook his head.

"I cannot come," he said. She stood looking blankly at him for some moments, unable to reach the door because of the portmanteau thrust through with umbrellas and sticks, which stood on the floor between the knees of the passengers. She was helpless. Siegmund was repeating deliriously in his mind:

"Oh—go—go—go—when will she go!"

He could not bear her piteousness. Her presence made him feel insane.

"Would you like to come to the window?" a man asked of Helena kindly.

She smiled suddenly in his direction, without perceiving him. He pulled the portmanteau under his legs, and Helena edged past. She stood by the door leaning forward with some of her old protective grace, her 'Hawwa' spirit evident. Benign and shielding, she bent forward, looking at Siegmund. But her face was blank with helplessness, with misery of helplessness. She stood looking at Siegmund, saying nothing. His forehead was scorched and swollen, she noticed sorrowfully, and beneath one eye the skin was blistered. His eyes were bloodshot and glazed in a kind of apathy; they filled her with terror. He looked up at her because she wished it. For himself, he could not see her; he could only recoil from her. All he wished was to hide himself in the dark, alone. Yet she wanted him, and so far he yielded. But to go to Waterloo he could not yield.

The people in the carriage, made uneasy by this strange farewell, did not speak. There were a few taut moments of silence. No one seems to have strength to interrupt these spaces of irresolute anguish. Finally, the guard's whistle went. Siegmund and Helena clasped hands. A warm flush of love and healthy grief came over Siegmund, for the last time. The train began to move, drawing Helena's hand from his. "Monday," she whispered "Monday,"—meaning that on Monday she should receive a letter from him. He nodded, turned, hesitated, looked at her, turned and walked away. She remained at the window watching him depart.

"Now dear, we are manless," said Olive, in a whisper. But her attempt at a joke fell dead. Everybody was silent and uneasy.

XXVII

He hurried down the platform, wincing at every stride, from the memory of Helena's last look of mute, heavy yearning. He gripped his fists till they trembled; his thumbs were again closed under his fingers. Like a picture on a cloth before him he still saw Helena's face, white, rounded, in feature quite mute and expressionless, just made terrible by the heavy eyes, pleading dumbly. He thought of her going on and on, still at the carriage window looking out: all through the night rushing west and west to the land of Isolde.* Things began to haunt Siegmund like a delirium. He knew not where he was hurrying. Always in front of him, as on a cloth, was the face of Helena, while somewhere behind the cloth was Cornwall, a far-off lonely place where darkness came on intensely. Sometimes he saw a dim, small phantom in the darkness of Cornwall, very far off. Then the face of Helena, white, inanimate as a mask, with heavy eyes, came between again.

He was almost startled to find himself at home, in the porch of his house. The door opened. He remembered to have heard the quick thud of feet. It was Vera. She glanced at him, but said nothing. Instinctively she shrank from him. He passed without noticing her. She stood on the door mat, fastening the door, striving to find something to say to him.

"You have been over an hour," she said, still more troubled when she found her voice shaking. She had no idea what alarmed her.

"Ay!" returned Siegmund.

He went in the dining room and dropped into his chair, with his head between his hands. Vera followed him nervously.

"Will you have anything to eat?" she asked. He looked up at the table, as if the supper laid there were curious and incomprehensible. The delirious lifting of his eyelids showed the whole of the dark pupils and the bloodshot whites of his eyes. Vera held her breath with fear. He sank his head again and said nothing. Vera sat down and waited. The minutes ticked slowly off. Siegmund neither moved nor spoke. At last the clock struck midnight. She was weary with sleep, querulous with trouble.

"Aren't you going to bed?" she asked.

Siegmund heard her, without paying any attention. He seemed only to half hear. Vera waited awhile, then repeated, plaintively:

"Aren't you going to bed, father?"

Siegmund lifted his head and looked at her. He loathed the idea of having to move. He looked at her confusedly.

"Yes, I'm going," he said, and his head dropped again. Vera knew he was not asleep. She dared not leave him till he was in his bedroom. Again she sat waiting.

"Father!" she cried at last.

He started up, gripping the arms of his chair, trembling:

"Yes, I'm going," he said.

He rose, and went unevenly upstairs. Vera followed him close behind.

"If he reels and falls backward he will kill me," she thought,—but he did not fall. From habit he went into the bathroom. While trying to brush his teeth he dropped the tooth-brush onto the floor.

"I'll pick it up in the morning," he said, continuing deliriously: "I must go to bed—I must go to bed—I am very tired." He stumbled over the door mats into his own room.

Vera was standing behind the unclosed door of her room. She heard the sneck of his lock. She heard the water still running in the bathroom, trickling with the mysterious sound of water at dead of night. Screwing up her courage, she went and turned off the tap. Then she stood again in her own room, to be near the companionable breathing of her sleeping sister, listening.

Siegmund undressed quickly. His one thought was to get into bed.

"One must sleep," he said as he dropped his clothes on the floor. He could not find the way to put on his sleeping jacket, and that made him pant. Any little thing that roused or thwarted his mechanical action aggravated his sickness till his brain seemed to be bursting. He got things right at last, and was in bed.

Immediately, he lapsed into a kind of unconsciousness. He would have called it sleep, but such it was not. All the time he could feel his brain working ceaselessly, like a machine running with unslackening rapidity. This went on, interrupted by little flickerings of consciousness, for three or four hours. Each time he had a glimmer of consciousness he wondered if he made any noise.

"What am I doing?—What is the matter?—Am I unconscious?—do I make any noise?—do I disturb them?" he wondered, and he tried to cast back to find the record of mechanical sense-impression. He believed he could remember the sound of inarticulate murmuring in his throat. Immediately he remembered, he could feel this throat producing the sounds. This frightened him. Above all things he was afraid of disturbing the family. He roused himself to listen. Everything was breathing in silence. As he listened to this silence he relapsed into his sort of sleep.

He was awakened finally by his own perspiration. He was terribly hot: the pillow, the bedclothes, his hair, all seemed to be steaming with hot vapour, whilst his body was bathed in sweat. It was coming light. Immediately, he shut his eyes again and lay still. He was now conscious, and his brain was irritably active, but his body was a separate thing, a terrible, heavy, hot thing over which he had slight control.

Siegmund lay still, with his eyes closed, enduring the exquisite torture of the trickling of drops of sweat. First it would be one gathering and running its irregular, hesitating way into the hollow of his neck. His every nerve thrilled to it, yet he felt he could not move more than to stiffen his throat slightly. While yet the nerves in the track of this drop were quivering, raw with sensitiveness, another drop would start from off the side of his chest, and trickle downwards among the little muscles of his side, to drip onto the bed. It was like the running of a spider over his sensitive, moveless body. Why he did not wipe himself he did not know. He lay still and endured this horrible tickling, which seemed to bite deep into him, rather than make the effort to move, which he loathed to do. The drops ran off his forehead down his temples. Those he did not mind: he was blunt there. But they started again, in tiny, vicious spurts, down the sides of his chest, from under his arm pits, down the inner sides of his thighs, till he seemed to have a myriad quivering tracks of a myriad running insects over his hot, wet, highly-sensitised body. His nerves were trembling, one and all, with outrage and vivid suspense. It became unbearable. He felt that, if he endured it another moment he would cry out, or suffocate and burst.

He sat up suddenly, threw away the bedclothes, from which came a puff of hot steam, and began to rub his pyjamas against his sides and his legs. He rubbed madly for a few moments. Then he sighed with relief. He sat on the side of the bed, moving from the hot dampness of the place where he had lain. For a moment he thought he would go to sleep. Then in an instant his brain seemed to click awake. He was still as loth as ever to move, but his brain was no longer clouded in hot vapour: it was clear. He sat, bowing forward on the side of the bed, his sleeping jacket open, the dawn stealing into the room, the morning air entering fresh through the wide-flung window-door. He felt a peculiar sense of guilt, of wrongness, in thus having jumped out of bed. It seemed to him as if he ought to have endured the heat of his body, and the infernal trickling of the drops of sweat. But at the thought of it he moved his hands gratefully over his sides, which now were dry, and soft, and smooth; slightly chilled on the surface, perhaps, for he felt a sudden tremor of shivering from the warm contact of his hands.

Siegmund sat up straight: his body was re-animated. He felt the pillow and the groove where he had lain. It was quite wet and clammy. There was a scent of sweat on the bed, not really unpleasant, but he wanted something fresh and cool.

Siegmund sat in the doorway that gave onto the small veranda. The air was beautifully cool. He felt his chest again to make sure it was not clammy: it was smooth as silk. This pleased him very much. He looked out on the night again, and was startled. Somewhere the moon was shining duskily, in a hidden quarter of sky: but straight in front of him, in the north-west, silent lightning was fluttering. He waited breathlessly to see if it were true. Then, again, the pale lightning jumped up into the dome of the fading night. It was like a white bird stirring restlessly on its nest. The night was drenching thinner, greyer. The lightning, like a bird that should have flown before the arm of day, moved on its nest in the boughs of darkness, raised itself, flickered its pale wings rapidly, then sank again loth to fly. Siegmund watched it, with wonder and delight.

The day was pushing aside the boughs of darkness, hunting. The poor moon would be caught when the net was flung. Siegmund went out on the balcony to look at it. There it was like a poor white mouse, a half moon, crouching on the mound of its course. It would run nimbly over to the western slope, then it would be caught in the net, and the sun would laugh, like a great yellow cat, as it stalked behind playing with its prey, flashing out its bright paws. The moon, before making its last run, lay crouched palpitating. The sun crept forth, laughing to itself as it saw its prey could not escape. The lightning, however, leaped low off the nest like a bird decided to go, and flew away. Siegmund no longer saw it opening and shutting its wings in hesitation amid the disturbance of the dawn. Instead there came a flush, the white lightning gone. The brief pink butterflies of sunrise and sunset rose up from the mown fields of darkness, and fluttered low in a cloud. Even in the west they flew in a narrow, rosy swarm. They separated, thinned, rising higher. Some, flying up, became golden. Some flew rosy gold across the moon, the mouse-moon motionless with fear. Soon the pink butterflies had gone, leaving a scarlet stretch like a field of poppies in the fens. As a wind, the light of day blew in from the east, puff after puff filling with whiteness the space which had been the night. Siegmund sat watching the last morning blowing in across the mown darkness, till the whole field of the world was exposed, till the moon was like a dead mouse which floats on water.

When the few birds had called in the August morning, when the cocks had finished their crowing, when the minute sounds of the early day were astir, Siegmund shivered disconsolate. He felt tired again, yet he knew he could not sleep. The bed was repulsive to him. He sat in his chair at the open door, moving uneasily. What should have been sleep was an ache and a restlessness. He turned and twisted in his chair.

"Where is Helena?" he asked himself, and he looked out on the morning.

Everything out of doors was unreal, like a show, like a peep-show. Helena was an actress somewhere in the brightness of this view. He alone was out of the piece. He sighed petulantly, pressing back his shoulders as if they ached. His arms, too, ached with irritation, while his head seemed to be hissing with angry irritability. For a long time he sat with clenched teeth, merely holding himself in check. In his present state of irritability everything that occurred to his mind stirred him with dislike or disgust. Helena, music, the pleasant company of friends, the sunshine of the country, each, as it offered itself to his thoughts, was met by an angry contempt, was rejected scornfully. As nothing could please or distract him, the only thing that remained was to support the discord. He felt as if he were a limb out of joint from the body of life: there occurred to his imagination a disjointed finger, swollen and discoloured, racked with pains. The question was, how should he re-set himself into joint. The body of life for him meant Beatrice, his children, Helena, the Comic Opera, his friends of the orchestra. How could he set himself again into joint with these: it was impossible. Towards his family he would henceforward have to bear himself with humility: that was a cynicism. He would have to leave Helena, which he could not do. He would have to play strenuously, night after night, the music of "The Saucy Little Switzer," which was absurd. In fine, it was all absurd and impossible. Very well, then, that being so, what remained possible? Why, to depart. 'If thine hand offend thee, cut it off.'* He could cut himself off from life. It was plain and straightforward.

But Beatrice, his young children, without him—? He was bound by an agreement which there was no discrediting to provide for them. Very well, he must provide for them. And then what? Humiliation at home, Helena forsaken, musical comedy night after night. That was insufferable—impossible. Like a man tangled up in a rope, he was not strong enough to free himself. He could not break with Helena and return to a degrading life at home: he could not leave his children and go to Helena.

Very well, it was impossible! Then there remained only one door which he could open in this prison corridor of life. Siegmund looked round the room. He could get his razor, or he could hang himself. He had thought of the two ways before. Yet now he was unprovided. His portmanteau stood at the foot of the bed, its straps flung loose. A portmanteau strap would do. Then it should be a portmanteau strap.

"Very well!" said Siegmund, "it is finally settled. I had better write to Helena, and tell her, and say to her she must go on. I'd better tell her."

He sat for a long time with his note-book and a pencil, but he wrote nothing. At last he gave up.

"Perhaps it is just as well," he said to himself. "She said she would come with me—perhaps that is just as well. She will go to the sea. When she knows, the sea will take her. She must know."

He took a card, bearing her name and her Cornwall address, from his pocket-book, and laid it on the dressing-table.

"She will come with me," he said to himself, and his heart rose with elation.

"That is a cowardice," he added, looking doubtfully at the card, as if wondering whether to destroy it.

"It is in the hands of God: Beatrice may or may not send word to her at Tintagel. It is in the hands of God"—he concluded.

Then he sat down again.

'But for that fear of something after death,'* he quoted to himself.

"It is not fear," he said. "The act itself will be horrible and fearsome—but the after-death—it's no more than struggling awake when you're sick with a fright of dreams. 'We are such stuff as dreams are made of'."*

Siegmund sat thinking of the after-death, which to him seemed so wonderfully comforting, full of rest, and reassurance, and renewal. He experienced no mystical ecstasies. He was sure of a wonderful kindness in death, a kindness which really reached right through life, though here he could not avail himself of it. Siegmund had always inwardly held faith that the heart of life beat kindly towards him. When he was cynical and sulky, he knew that in reality it was only a waywardness of his.

The heart of life is implacable in its kindness: it may not be moved to flutterings of pity: it swings on uninterrupted by cries of anguish or of hate.

Siegmund was thankful for this unfaltering sternness of life. There was no futile hesitation between doom and pity. Therefore he could submit, and have faith. If each man by his crying could swerve the slow, sheer universe, what a doom of guilt he might gain. If Life could swerve from its orbit for pity, what terror of vacillation: and who would wish to bear the responsibility of the deflection?

Siegmund thanked God that life was pitiless, strong enough to take his treasures out of his hands, and to thrust him out of the room: otherwise, how could he go with any faith to death: otherwise, he would have felt the helpless disillusion of a youth who finds his infallible parents weaker than himself.

"I know the heart of life is kind," said Siegmund, "because I feel it. Otherwise I would live in defiance. But Life is greater than me or anybody. We suffer, and we don't know why, often. Life doesn't explain. But I can keep faith in it, as a dog has faith in his master. After all, Life is as kind to me as I am to my dog: I have, proportionally, as much zest. And my purpose towards my dog is good. I need not despair of Life."

It occurred to Siegmund that he was meriting the old gibe of the atheists. He was shirking the responsibility of himself, turning it over to an imaginary God.*

"Well," he said, "I can't help it. I do not feel altogether self-responsible."

The morning had waxed during these investigations. Siegmund had been vaguely aware of the rousing of the house. He was finally startled into a consciousness of the immediate present by the calling of Vera at his door.

"There are two letters for you, father." He looked about him in bewilderment: the hours had passed in a trance, and he had no idea of his time or place.

"Oh—all right," he said, too much dazed to know what it meant. He heard his daughter going downstairs. Then swiftly returned over him the throbbing ache of his head and his arms, the discordant jarring of his body.

"What made her bring me the letters?" he asked himself. It was a very unusual attention. His heart replied, very sullen and shameful: "She wanted to know—she wanted to make sure I was all right."

Siegmund forgot all his speculations on a divine benevolence: the discord of his immediate situation overcame every harmony. He did not fetch in the letters.

"Is it so late?" he said. "Is there no more time for me?"

He went to look at his watch: it was a quarter to nine. As he walked across the room he trembled, and a sickness made his bones feel rotten. He sat down on the bed.

"What am I going to do?" he asked himself.

By this time he was shuddering rapidly. A peculiar feeling, as if his belly were turned into nothingness, made him want to press his fists into his abdomen. He remained shuddering drunkenly, like a drunken man who is sick, incapable of thought or action.

A second knock came at the door. He started with a jolt.

"Here is your shaving water," said Beatrice in cold tones: "It's half past nine!"

"All right," said Siegmund, rising from the bed, bewildered.

"And what time shall you expect dinner?" asked Beatrice. She was still contemptuous.

"Any time—I'm not going out," he answered. He was surprised to hear the ordinary cool tone of his own voice, for he was shuddering uncontrollably, and was almost sobbing. In a shaking, bewildered, disordered condition he set about fulfilling his purpose. He was hardly conscious of anything he did: try as he would, he could not keep his hands steady in the violent spasms of shuddering, nor could he call his mind to think. He was one shuddering turmoil. Yet he performed his purpose methodically and exactly. In every particular he was thorough, as if he were the servant of some stern will. It was a mesmeric performance, in which the agent trembled with convulsive sickness.

XXVIII

Siegmund's lying late in bed made Beatrice very angry. The later it became, the more wrathful she grew. At half past nine she had taken up his shaving water. Then she proceeded to tidy the dining room, leaving the breakfast spread in the kitchen.

Vera and Frank were gone up to town: they would both be home for dinner at two o'clock. Marjory was despatched on an errand, taking Gwen with her. The children had no need to return home immediately, therefore it was highly probable they would play in the field or in the lane for an hour or two. Beatrice was alone downstairs. It was a hot, still morning, when everything out-doors shone brightly, and all indoors was dusked with coolness and colour. But Beatrice was angry. She moved rapidly and determinedly about the dining room, thrusting old newspapers and magazines between the cupboard and the wall, throwing the litter in the grate,—which was clear, Friday having been charwoman's day—, passing swiftly, lightly over the front of the furniture with the duster. It was Saturday, when she did not spend much time over the work. In the afternoon she was going out with Vera. That was not, however, what occupied her mind as she brushed aside her work. She had determined to have a settlement with Siegmund, as to how matters should continue. She was going to have no more of the past three years' life: things had come to a crisis, and there must be an alteration. Beatrice was going to do battle, therefore she flew at her work, thus stirring herself up to a proper heat of blood. All the time, as she thrust things out of sight or straightened a cover, she listened for Siegmund to come downstairs.

He did not come, so her anger waxed.

"He can lie skulking in bed!" she said to herself. "Here I've been up since seven, broiling at it. I should think he's pitying himself. He ought to have something else to do. He ought to have to go out to work every morning, like another man, as his son has to do. He has had too little work. He has had too much his own way. But it's come to a stop now. I'll servant-housekeeper him no longer— —."

Beatrice went to clean the step of the front door. She clanged the bucket loudly, every minute becoming more and more angry. That piece of work finished she went into the kitchen. It was twenty past ten. Her wrath was at ignition point. She cleared all the things from the table and washed them up. As she was so doing, her anger, having reached full intensity without bursting into flame, began to dissipate in uneasiness. She tried to imagine what Siegmund would do and say to her. As she was wiping a cup she dropped it, and the smash so unnerved her that her hands trembled almost too much to finish drying the things and putting them away. At last it was done. Her next piece of work was to make the beds. She took her pail and went upstairs. Her heart was beating so heavily in her throat that she had to stop on the landing to recover breath. She dreaded the combat with him. Suddenly controlling herself, she said loudly at Siegmund's door, her voice coldly hostile:

"Aren't you going to get up?"

There was not the faintest sound in the house. Beatrice stood in the gloom of the landing, her heart thudding in her ears.

"It's after half past ten,—aren't you going to get up?—" she called.

She waited again. Two letters lay unopened on a small table. Suddenly she put down her pail and went into the bathroom. The pot of shaving water stood untouched on the shelf, just as she had left it. She returned and knocked swiftly at her husband's door, not speaking. She waited—then she knocked again, loudly, a long time. Something in the sound of her knocking made her afraid to try again: the noise was dull and thudding: it did not resound through the house with a natural ring,—so she thought. She ran downstairs in terror, fled out into the front garden, and there looked up at his room. The window-door was open—everything seemed quiet.

Beatrice stood vacillating. She picked up a few tiny pebbles and flung them in a handful at his door. Some spattered on the panes sharply; some dropped dully in the room; one chinked on the wash-hand bowl. There was no response. Beatrice was terribly excited. She ran, with her black eyes blazing, and wisps of her black hair flying about her thin temples, out on to the road. By a mercy, she saw the window-cleaner just pushing his ladder out of the passage of a house a little further down the road. She hurried to him.

"Will you come and see if there's anything wrong with my husband?" she asked wildly.

"Why Mum?" answered the window-cleaner, who knew her,

and was humbly familiar. "Is he taken bad or something? Yes, I'll come."

He was a tall thin man with a brown beard. His clothes were all so loose, his trousers so baggy, that he gave one the impression his limbs must be bone, and his body a skeleton. He pushed at his ladders with a will.

"Where is he Mum?" he asked officiously, as they slowed down at the side passage.

"He's in his bedroom, and I can't get an answer from him."

"Then I 's' ll want a ladder," said the window-cleaner, proceeding to lift one off his trolley. He was in a very great bustle. He knew which was Siegmund's room: he had often seen Siegmund rise from some music he was studying and leave the drawing room when the window cleaning began, and afterwards he had found him in the small front bedroom. He also knew there were matrimonial troubles: Beatrice was not reserved.

"Is it the least of the front rooms he's in?" asked the window-cleaner.

"Yes—over the porch," replied Beatrice. The man bustled with his ladder.

"It's easy enough," he said. "The door's open, and we're soon on the balcony."

He set the ladder securely. Beatrice cursed him for a slow, officious fool. He tested the ladder, to see it was safe, then he cautiously clambered up. At the top he stood leaning sideways, bending over the ladder to peer into the room. He could see all sorts of things, for he was frightened.

"I say there!" he called loudly.

Beatrice stood below in horrible suspense.

"Go in!" she cried, "Go in! Is he there?"

The man stepped very cautiously with one foot on to the balcony, and peered forward. But the glass door reflected into his eyes. He followed slowly with the other foot, and crept forward, ready at any moment to take flight.

"Hie! hie!" he suddenly cried in terror, and he drew back.

Beatrice was opening her mouth to scream, when the window-cleaner exclaimed weakly, as if dubious:

"I believe 'e's 'anged 'imself from the door-'ooks."

"No!" cried Beatrice. "No—no—no!"

"I believe 'e 'as!" repeated the man.

"Go in and see if he's dead," cried Beatrice. The man remained in the doorway, peering fixedly.

"I believe he is—," he said doubtfully.

"No—go and see!" screamed Beatrice. The man went into the room, trembling, hesitating. He approached the body as if fascinated. Shivering, he took it round the loins and tried to lift it down. It was too heavy.

"I know!" he said to himself, once more bustling now he had something to do. He took his clasp-knife from his pocket, jammed the body between himself and the door so that it should not drop, and began to saw his way through the leathern strap. It gave. He started, and clutched the body, dropping his knife. Beatrice, below in the garden, hearing the scuffle and the clatter, began to scream in hysteria. The man hauled the body of Siegmund, with much difficulty, onto the bed, and with trembling fingers tried to unloose the buckle in which the strap ran. It was bedded in Siegmund's neck. The window-cleaner tugged at it frantically, till he got it loose. Then he looked at Siegmund. The dead man lay on the bed with swollen, discoloured face, with his sleeping jacket pushed up in a bunch under his arm pits, leaving his side naked. Beatrice was screaming below. The window-cleaner, quite unnerved, ran from the room and scrambled down the ladder. Siegmund lay heaped on the bed, his sleeping suit twisted and bunched up about him, his face hardly recognisable.

XXIX

Helena was dozing down in the cove at Tintagel. She and Louisa and Olive lay on the cool sands, in the shadow, and steeped themselves in rest, in a cool, sea-fragrant tranquillity.

The journey down had been very tedious. After waiting for half an hour in the midnight turmoil of an August Friday in Waterloo Station, they had seized an empty carriage, only to be followed by five north-countrymen, all of whom were affected by whisky. Olive, Helena, Louisa occupied three corners of the carriage: the men were distributed between them. The three women were not alarmed. Their tipsy travelling companions promised to be tiresome, but they had a frank honesty of manner that placed them beyond suspicion. The train drew out westward. Helena began to count the miles that separated her from Siegmund. The north-countrymen began to be jolly: they talked loudly in their uncouth English; they sang the music-hall songs of the day; they furtively drank whisky. Through all this, they were polite to the girls. As much could hardly be said in return of Olive and Louisa: they leaned forward whispering one to another; they sat back in their seats laughing, hiding their laughter by turning their backs on the men, who were a trifle disconcerted by this amusement.

The train spun on and on: little, homely clusters of lamps, suggesting the quiet of country life, turned slowly round through the darkness. The men dropped into a doze: Olive put a handkerchief over her face and went to sleep: Louisa gradually nodded and jerked into slumber. Helena sat weariedly and watched the rolling of the sleeping travellers and the dull blank of the night sheering off outside. Neither the men nor the women looked well asleep. They lurched and nodded stupidly. She thought of Bazarof in "Fathers and Sons," endorsing his opinion on the appearance of sleepers:* all but Siegmund. Was Siegmund asleep? She imagined him breathing regularly on the pillows: she could see the under arch of his eyebrows, the fine shape of his nostrils, the curve of his lips, as she bent in fancy over his face.

The dawn came slowly: it was rather cold; Olive wrapped herself in rugs and went to sleep again; Helena shivered, and stared out of the window. There appeared a wanness in the night, and Helena felt inexpressibly dreary. A rosiness spread out far away. It was like a flock of flamingoes hovering over a dark lake. The world vibrated as the sun came up.

Helena waked the tipsy men at Exeter, having heard them say that there they must change. Then she walked the platform, very jaded. The train rushed on again: it was a most, most wearisome journey. The fields were very flowery, the morning was very bright, but what were these to her? She wanted dimness, sleep, forgetfulness. At eight o'clock, breakfast-time, the 'dauntless three' were driving in a waggonette amid blazing, breathless sunshine, over country naked of shelter, ungracious and harsh.

"Why am I doing this?" Helena asked herself—.

The three friends, washed, dressed, and breakfasted. It was too hot to rest in the house, so they trudged down to the coast, silently, each feeling in an ill humour—.

When Helena was really rested, she took great pleasure in Tintagel. In the first place, she found that the cove was exactly, almost identically the same as the Walhalla scene in "Walküre";* in the second place, "Tristan" was here,* in the tragic country filled with the flowers of a late Cornish summer, an everlasting reality; in the third place, it was a sea of marvellous, portentous sunsets, of sweet morning baths, of pools blossomed with life, of terrible suave swishing of foam which suggested the Anadyomene:* in sum, it was the enchanted land of divided lovers. Helena for ever hummed fragments of "Tristan." As she stood on the rocks, she sang, in her little, half articulate way, bits of Isolde's love, bits of Tristan's anguish, to Siegmund.

She had not received her letter on Sunday. That had not very much disquieted her, though she was disappointed. On Monday she was miserable because of Siegmund's silence, but there was so much of enchantment in Tintagel, and Olive and Louisa were in such high spirits that she forgot most-whiles.

On Monday night, towards two o'clock, there came a violent storm of thunder and lightning. Louisa started up in bed at the first clap, waking Helena. The room palpitated with white light for two seconds: the mirror on the dressing-table glared supernaturally. Louisa clutched her friend. All was dark again, the thunder clapping directly.

"There!—wasn't that lovely!" cried Louisa, speaking of the lightning. "OO—wasn't it magnificent!—glorious!"

The door clicked and opened; Olive entered in her long white night-gown. She hurried to the bed.

"I say, dear," she exclaimed, "—may I come into the fold? I prefer the shelter of your company, dear, during this little lot."

"Don't you like it?" cried Louisa. "I think it's *lovely*—lovely!"

There came another slash of lightning: the night seemed to open and shut: it was a pallid vision of a ghost-world between the clanging shutters of darkness. Louisa and Olive clung to each other spasmodically.

"There!" exclaimed the former, breathless, "That was fine! Helena, did you see that?" She clasped ecstatically the hand of her friend, who was lying down. Helena's answer was extinguished by the burst of thunder.

"There's no accounting for tastes," said Olive, taking a place in the bed. "I can't say I'm struck on lightning. What about you, Helena?"

"I'm not struck yet," replied Helena, with a sarcastic attempt at a jest.

"Thank you dear," said Olive, "you do me the honour of catching hold."

Helena laughed ironically.

"Catching what?" asked Louisa, mystified.

"Why dear," answered Olive, heavily condescending to explain, "I offered Helena the handle of a pun, and she took it. What a flash! You know, it's not that I'm afraid— — —."

The rest of her speech was overwhelmed in thunder.

Helena lay on the edge of the bed, listening to the ecstatics of one friend and to the impertinences of the other. In spite of her ironical feeling, the thunder impressed her with a sense of fatality. The night opened, revealing a ghostly landscape, instantly to shut again with blackness. Then the thunder crashed. Helena felt as if some secret were being disclosed too swiftly and violently for her to understand. The thunder exclaimed horribly on the matter. She was sure something had happened.

Gradually the storm drew away. The rain came down with a rush, persisted with a bruising sound upon the earth and the leaves.

"What a deluge!" exclaimed Louisa. No one answered her. Olive was falling asleep, and Helena was in no mood to reply. Louisa, disconsolate, lay looking at the black window, nursing a grievance, until she too drifted into sleep. Helena was awake: the storm had left her with a settled sense of calamity. She felt bruised: the sound of the heavy rain bruising the ground outside represented her feeling; she could not get rid of the bruised sense of disaster.

She lay wondering what it was, why Siegmund had not written, what could have happened to him. She imagined all sorts of tragedy, all of them terrible, and endued with grandeur—for she had kinship with Hedda Gabler.*

"But no," she said to herself, "it is impossible anything should have happened to him, I should have known. I should have known the moment his spirit left his body; he would have come to me. But I slept without dreams last night, and today I am sure there has been no crisis. It is impossible it should have happened to him: I should have known."

She was very certain that in event of Siegmund's death, she would have received intelligence. She began to consider all the causes which might arise to prevent his writing immediately to her.

"Nevertheless," she said at last, "if I don't hear tomorrow I will go and see."

She had written to him on Monday. If she should receive no answer by Wednesday morning she would return to London. As she was deciding this she went to sleep.

The next day passed without news. Helena was in a state of distress. Her wistfulness touched the other two women very keenly. Louisa waited upon her, was very tender and solicitous. Olive, who was becoming painful by reason of her unsatisfied curiosity, had to be told in part the state of affairs.

Helena looked up a train: she was quite sure by this time that something fatal awaited her.

The next morning she bade her friends a temporary goodbye, saying she would return in the evening. Immediately the train had gone, Louisa rushed into the little waiting room of the station and wept. Olive shed tears for sympathy and self-pity. She pitied herself that she should be let in for so dismal a holiday. Louisa suddenly stopped crying and sat up:

"Oh, I know I'm a pig, dear, am I not!" she exclaimed—. "Spoiling your holiday. But I couldn't help it, dear, indeed I could not."

"My dear Lou!" cried Olive in tragic contralto, "Don't refrain for my sake. The bargain's made, we can't help what's in the bundle."*

The two unhappy women trudged the long miles back from the station to their lodging. Helena sat in the swinging express revolving the same thoughts like a prayer-wheel. It would be difficult to think of anything more trying than this sitting motionless in the train, which itself is throbbing and bursting its heart with anxiety, while one waits hour after hour for the blow which falls nearer as the distance lessens. All the time Helena's heart and her consciousness were with Siegmund in London; for she believed he was ill and needed her.

"Promise me," she had said, "If ever I were sick and wanted you, you would come to me."

"I would come to you from Hell," Siegmund had replied.

"And if you were ill—you would let me come to you?" she had added.

"I promise," he answered.

Now Helena believed he was ill, perhaps very ill, perhaps she only could be of any avail. The miles of distance were like hot bars of iron across her breast, and against them it was impossible to strive. The train did what it could.

That day remains as a smear in the record of Helena's life. In it there is no spacing of hours, no lettering of experience, merely a smear of suspense.

Towards six o'clock she alighted at Surbiton Station, deciding that this would be the quickest way of getting to Wimbledon. She paced the platform slowly, as if resigned, but her heart was crying out at the great injustice of delay. Presently the local train came in. She had planned to buy a local paper at Wimbledon, and if from that source she could learn nothing, she would go on to his house and inquire. She had pre-arranged everything minutely.

After turning the newspaper several times she found what she sought:

"The funeral took place, at two o'clock today at Kingston Cemetery, of—. Deceased was a professor of music, and had just returned from a holiday on the South Coast— —."

The paragraph, in a bald twelve lines, told her everything.

"Jury returned a verdict of suicide during temporary insanity. Sympathy was expressed for the widow and children."*

Helena stood still on the station for some time, looking at the print. Then she dropped the paper and wandered into the town not knowing where she was going.

"That was what I got," she said, months afterwards. "And it was like a brick, it was like a brick."

She wandered on and on, until suddenly she found herself in the grassy lane with only a wire fence bounding her from the open fields on either side, beyond which fields, on the left she could see Siegmund's house standing florid by the road, catching the western sunlight. Then she stopped, realising where she had come. For some time she stood looking at the house. It was no use her going there: it was of no use her going anywhere; the whole wide world was opened, but in it she had no destination, and there was no direction for her to take. As if marooned in the world, she stood desolate, looking from the house of Siegmund over the fields and the hills. Siegmund was gone; why had he not taken her with him?

The evening was drawing on: it was nearly half past seven when Helena looked at her watch, remembering Louisa, who would be waiting for her to return to Cornwall.

"I must either go to her, or wire to her. She will be in a fever of suspense," said Helena to herself, and straightway she hurried to catch a tram-car to return to the station. She arrived there at a quarter to eight: there was no train down to Tintagel that night. Therefore she wired the news:

"Siegmund dead. No train tonight. Am going home." This done, she took her ticket and sat down to wait. By the strength of her will, everything she did was reasonable and accurate. But her mind was chaotic.

"It was like a brick," she reiterated, and that brutal simile was the only one she could find, months afterwards, to describe her condition. She felt as if something had crashed into her brain, stunning and maiming her.

As she knocked at the door of home she was apparently quite calm. Her mother opened to her.

"What, are you alone!" cried Mrs Verden.

"Yes. Louisa did not come up," replied Helena, passing into the dining room. As if by instinct she glanced on the mantel-piece to see if there was a letter. There was a newspaper cutting. She went forward and took it. It was from one of the London papers.

"Inquest was held today upon the body of— —."

Helena read it, read it again, folded it up and put it in her purse. Her mother stood watching her, consumed with distress and anxiety.

"How did you get to know?" she asked.

"I went to Wimbledon, and bought a paper," replied the daughter, in her muted, toneless voice.

"Did you go to the house?" asked her mother sharply.

"No," replied Helena.

"I was wondering whether to send you that paper," said her mother, hesitatingly.

Helena did not answer. She wandered about the house mechanically, looking for something. Her mother followed her, trying very gently to help her.

For some time Helena sat at table in the dining room staring before her. Her parents moved restlessly in silence, trying not to irritate her by watching her, praying for something to change the fixity of her look. They acknowledged themselves helpless; like children, they felt powerless and forlorn, and were very quiet.

"Won't you go to rest, Nelly?" asked the father at last. He was an unobtrusive, obscure man, whose sympathy was very delicate, whose ordinary attitude was one of gentle irony.

"Won't you go to rest Nelly?" he repeated.

Helena shivered lightly.

"Do my dear," her mother pleaded. "Let me take you to bed."

Helena rose. She had a great horror of being fussed or petted, but this night she went dully upstairs, and let her mother help her to undress. When she was in bed, the mother stood for some moments looking at her, yearning to beseech her daughter to pray to God; but she dared not. Helena moved with a wild impatience under her mother's gaze.

"Shall I leave you the candle?" said Mrs Verden.

"No, blow it out," replied the daughter. The mother did so, and immediately left the room, going downstairs to her husband. As she entered the dining room he glanced up timidly at her. She was a tall, erect woman. Her brown eyes, usually so swift and searching, were haggard with tears that did not fall. He bowed down, obliterating himself. His hands were tightly clasped.

"Will she be all right if you leave her?" he asked.

"We must listen," replied the mother abruptly.

The parents sat silent in their customary places. Presently Mrs Verden cleared the supper table, sweeping together a few crumbs from the floor in the place where Helena had sat, carefully putting her pieces of broken bread under the loaf to keep moist. Then she sat down again. One could see she was keenly alert to every sound. The father had his hand to his head: he was thinking and praying.

Mrs Verden suddenly rose, took a box of matches from the mantel-piece, and hurrying her stately, heavy tread, went upstairs. Her husband followed in much trepidation, hovering near the door of his daughter's room. The mother tremblingly lit the candle. Helena's aspect distressed and alarmed her. The girl's face was masked as if in sleep, but occasionally it was crossed by a vivid expression of fear or horror. Her wide eyes showed the active insanity of her brain. From time to time she uttered strange, inarticulate sounds. Her mother held her hands and soothed her. Although she was hardly aware of the mother's presence, Helena was more tranquil. The father went downstairs and turned out the light. He brought his wife a large shawl, which he put on the bedrail, and silently left the room. Then he went and kneeled down by his own bedside, and prayed.

Mrs Verden watched her daughter's delirium, and all the time, in a kind of mental chant, invoked the help of God. Once or twice the girl came to herself, drew away her hand on recognising the situation, and turned from her mother, who patiently waited until, upon relapse, she could soothe her daughter again. Helena was glad of her mother's presence, but she could not bear to be looked at.

Towards morning the girl fell naturally asleep. The mother regarded her closely, lightly touched her forehead with her lips, and went away, having blown out the candle. She found her husband kneeling in his nightshirt by the bed. He muttered a few swift syllables and looked up as she entered.

"She is asleep," whispered the wife hoarsely.

"Is it a—a natural sleep?" hesitated the husband.

"Yes. I think it is. I think she will be all right."

"Thank God!" whispered the father, almost inaudibly.

He held his wife's hand as she lay by his side. He was the comforter. She felt as if now she might cry and take comfort and sleep. He, the quiet, obliterated man held her hand, taking the responsibility upon himself.

XXX

Beatrice was careful not to let the blow of Siegmund's death fall with full impact upon her. As it were, she dodged it. She was afraid to meet the accusation of the dead Siegmund, with the scared jury* of memories. When the event summoned her to stand before the bench of her own soul's understanding, she fled, leaving the verdict upon herself eternally suspended.

When the neighbours had come, alarmed by her screaming, she had allowed herself to be taken away from her own house, into the home of a neighbour. There the children were brought to her. There she wept, and stared wildly about, as if by instinct seeking to cover her mind with confusion. The good neighbour controlled matters in Siegmund's house, sending for the police, helping to lay out the dead body. Before Vera and Frank came home, and before Beatrice returned to her own place, the bedroom of Siegmund was locked.

Beatrice avoided seeing the body of her husband: she gave him one swift glance, blinded by excitement; she never saw him after his death. She was equally careful to avoid thinking of him. Whenever her thoughts wandered towards a consideration of how he must have felt, what his inner life must have been during the past six years, she felt herself dilate with terror, and she hastened to invoke protection.

"The children!" she said to herself, "the children. I must live for the children: I must think for the children."

This she did, and with much success. All her tears and her wildness rose from terror and dismay, rather than from grief. She managed to fend back a grief that would probably have broken her. Vera was too practical minded, she had too severe a notion of what ought to be and what ought not, ever to put herself in her father's place and try to understand him. She concerned herself with judging him sorrowfully, exonerating him in part because Helena, that other, was so much more to blame. Frank, as a sentimentalist, wept over the situation, not over the personae. The children were acutely distressed by the harassing behaviour of their elders, and longed for a restoration of equanimity. By common consent, no word was spoken of Siegmund. As soon as possible after the funeral, Beatrice moved from South London to Harrow. The memory of Siegmund began to fade rapidly.

Beatrice had had all her life a fancy for a more open, public form of living than that of a domestic circle. She liked strangers about the house; they stimulated her agreeably. Therefore, nine months after the death of her husband, she determined to carry out the scheme of her heart, and take in boarders. She came of a well-to-do family, with whom she had been in disgrace owing to her early romantic, but degrading marriage with a young lad who had neither income nor profession. In the tragic, but also sordid, event of his death, the Waltons returned again to the aid of Beatrice. They came hesitatingly, and kept their gloves on. They inquired what she intended to do. She spoke highly and hopefully of her future boarding house. They found her a couple of hundred pounds, glad to salve their consciences so cheaply. Siegmund's father, a winsome old man with a heart of young gold, was always ready further to diminish his diminished income for the sake of his grandchildren. So Beatrice was set up in a fairly large house in Highgate, was equipped with two maids, and gentlemen were invited to come and board in her house. It was a huge adventure, wherein Beatrice was delighted. Vera was excited and interested: Frank was excited, but doubtful and grudging: the children were excited, elated, wondering. The world was big with promise.

Three gentlemen came, before a month was out, to Beatrice's establishment. She hoped shortly to get a fourth or a fifth. Her plan was to play hostess, and thus bestow on her boarders the inestimable blessing of family life. Breakfast was at eight-thirty, and everyone attended. Vera sat opposite Beatrice, Frank sat on the maternal right hand: Mr MacWhirter, who was *superior*, sat on the left hand; next him sat Mr Allport, whose opposite was Mr Holiday.* All were young men of less than thirty years. Mr MacWhirter was tall, fair and stoutish; he was very quietly spoken, was humorous and amiable, yet extraordinarily learned. He never, by any chance, gave himself away, maintaining always an absolute reserve amid all his amiability. Therefore Frank would have done anything to win his esteem, while Beatrice was deferential to him. Mr Allport was tall and broad, and thin as a door; he had also a remarkably small chin. He was naïve, inclined to suffer in the first pangs of disillusionment; nevertheless he was waywardly humorous, sometimes wistful, sometimes petulant, always gentle and gallant: therefore Vera liked him, whilst Beatrice mothered him. Mr Holiday was short, very stout, very ruddy, with black hair. He had a disagreeable voice, was vulgar in the grain,* but officiously helpful if appeal were made to him. Therefore Frank hated him. Vera liked his handsome, lusty appearance, but resented bitterly his behaviour. Beatrice was proud of the superior and skilful way in which she handled him, clipping him into shape without hurting him.

One evening in July, eleven months after the burial of Siegmund, Beatrice went into the dining room and found Mr Allport sitting with his elbow on the window-sill, looking out on the garden. It was half past seven. The red rents between the foliage of the trees showed the sun was setting: a fragrance of evening-scented stocks filtered into the room through the open window: toward the South the moon was budding out of the twilight.

"What, you here all alone!" exclaimed Beatrice, who had just come from putting the children to bed. "I thought you had gone out."

"No—o! What's the use," replied Mr Allport, turning to look at his landlady "of going out? There's nowhere to go—."

"Oh, come! There's the Heath, and the City—and you must join a tennis club. Now I know just the thing—the club to which Vera belongs— —."

"Ah yes! You go down to the City—but there's nothing there—What I mean to say—You want a pal—and even then—well"—he drawled the word—"we-ell, it's merely escaping from yourself—killing time."

"Oh don't say that!" exclaimed Beatrice. "You want to enjoy life."

"Just so!—Ah just so!" exclaimed Mr Allport, "But all the same—it's like this—you only get up to the same thing tomorrow. What I mean to say—what's the good, after all?—it's merely living because you've got to."

"You are too pessimistic altogether for a young man. I look at it differently myself; yet I'll be bound I have more cause for grumbling. What's the trouble, now?"

"We-ell—you can't lay your finger on a thing like that!—What I mean to say— —it's nothing very definite. But after all—what is there to do but to hop out of life as quick as possible?—that's the best way."

Beatrice became suddenly grave.

"You talk in that way, Mr Allport," she said. "You don't think of the others."

"I don't know," he drawled. "What does it matter? Look here—who'd care?—What I mean to say—for long?"

"That's all very easy, but it's cowardly," replied Beatrice, gravely.

"Nevertheless," said Mr Allport "—it's true—isn't it?"

"It is not—and I *should* know," replied Beatrice, drawing a cloak of reserve ostentatiously over her face. Mr Allport looked at her, and waited. Beatrice relaxed towards the pessimistic young man.

"Yes," she said, "I call it very cowardly, to want to get out of your difficulties in that way. Think what you inflict on other people. You men, you're all selfish. The burden is always left for the woman— —."

"Ah but then," said Mr Allport, very softly and sympathetically, looking at Beatrice's black dress, "I've no one depending on *me*."

"No—you haven't—but you've a mother and sister. The women always have to bear the brunt."

Mr Allport looked at Beatrice, and found her very pathetic.

"Yes. They do rather," he replied sadly, tentatively waiting.

"My husband—" began Beatrice. The young man waited—

"My husband was one of your sort: he ran after trouble, and when he'd found it—he couldn't carry it off—and left it—to me."

Mr Allport looked at her very sympathetically.

"You don't mean it!" he exclaimed softly. "Surely he didn't— — —?"

Beatrice nodded, and turned aside her face.

"Yes!" she said. "I know what it is to bear that kind of thing—and it's no light thing, I can assure you."

There was a suspicion of tears in her voice.

"And when was this then?—that he—?" asked Mr Allport, almost with reverence.

"Only last year," replied Beatrice.

Mr Allport made a sound expressing astonishment and dismay. Little by little, Beatrice told him so much: "Her husband had got entangled with another woman. She herself had put up with it for a long time. At last she had brought matters to a crisis, declaring what she should do. He had killed himself—hanged himself—and left her, penniless. Her people, who were very wealthy, had done for her as much as she would allow them. She, and Frank and Vera had done the rest. She did not mind for herself: it was for Frank and Vera, who should be now enjoying their careless youth, that her heart was heavy—."

There was silence for a time. Mr Allport murmured his sympathy, and sat overwhelmed with respect for this little woman who was unbroken by tragedy. The bell rang in the kitchen: Vera entered.

"Oh, what a nice smell! Sitting in the dark Mother?"

"I was just trying to cheer up Mr Allport, he is very despondent."

"Pray do not overlook me," said Mr Allport, rising and bowing.

"Well!—I did not see you!—fancy your sitting in the twilight chatting with the Mater. You must have been an unscrupulous bore, maman."

"On the contrary," replied Mr Allport, "Mrs MacNair has been so good as to bear with me making a fool of myself—."

"In what way?" asked Vera sharply.

"Mr Allport is so despondent.—I think he must be in love," said Beatrice playfully.

"Unfortunately, I am not—or at least I am not yet aware of it," said Mr Allport, bowing slightly to Vera.

She advanced and stood in the bay of the window, her skirt touching the young man's knees. She was tall and graceful. With her hands clasped behind her back she stood looking up at the moon now white upon the richly darkening sky.

"Don't look at the moon, Miss MacNair, it's all rind," said Mr Allport in melancholy mockery. "Somebody's bitten all the meat out of our slice of moon, and left us nothing but peel."

"It certainly does look like a piece of melon shell—one portion," replied Vera.

"Never mind, Miss MacNair," he said—"Whoever got the slice found it raw, I think."

"Oh I don't know—" she said. "But isn't it a beautiful evening? I will just go and see if I can catch the primroses opening."

"What!—primroses?" he exclaimed.

"Evening primroses—there are some."

"Are there?" he said in surprise. Vera smiled to herself.

"Yes—come and look," she said.

The young man rose with alacrity.

Mr Holiday came into the dining room whilst they were down the garden.

"What, nobody in!" they heard him exclaim.

"There is Holiday!" murmured Mr Allport resentfully.

Vera did not answer. Holiday came to the open window, attracted by the fragrance.

"Ho!—that's where you are!" he cried in his nasal tenor, which annoyed Vera's trained ear: she wished she had not been wearing a white dress to betray herself.

"What have you got?" he asked.

"Nothing in particular," replied Mr Allport.

Mr Holiday sniggered.

"Oh well, if it's nothing particular and private—", said Mr Holiday, and with that he leaped over the window-sill and went to join them.

"Curst fool!" muttered Mr Allport. "I beg your pardon," he added swiftly to Vera.

"Have you ever noticed, Mr Holiday?" asked Vera, as if very friendly, "how awfully tantalizing these flowers are. They won't open while you're looking."

"No," sniggered he, "I don't blame 'em. Why should they give themselves away any more than you do? You won't open while you're watched" he nudged Allport facetiously with his elbow—.

After supper, which was late and badly served, the young men were in poor spirits. Mr MacWhirter retired to read. Mr Holiday sat picking his teeth. Mr Allport begged Vera to play on the piano.

"Oh, the piano is not my instrument: mine was the violin, but I do not play now," she replied.

"But you will begin again," pleaded Mr. Allport.

"No, never," she said decisively. Allport looked at her closely: the family tragedy had something to do with her decision, he was sure: he watched her interestedly.

"Mother used to play—" she began—.

"Vera!" said Beatrice reproachfully.

"Let us have a song," suggested Mr Holiday.

"Mr Holiday wishes to sing, mother," said Vera, going to the music-rack.

"Nay—I—it's not me—", Holiday began.

"'The Village Blacksmith'"* said Vera, pulling out the piece. Holiday advanced. Vera glanced at her mother.

"But I have not touched the piano for—for years, I am sure," protested Beatrice.

"You can play beautifully," said Vera.

Beatrice accompanied the song. Holiday sang atrociously. Allport glared at him. Vera remained very calm.

At the end, Beatrice was overcome by the touch of the piano. She went out abruptly.

"Mother has suddenly remembered that tomorrow's jellies are not made," laughed Vera.

Allport looked at her, and was sad.

When Beatrice returned, Holiday insisted she should play again. She would have found it more difficult to refuse than to comply.

Vera retired early, soon to be followed by Allport and Holiday. At half past ten Mr MacWhirter came in with his ancient volume. Beatrice was studying a cookery book.

"You too at the midnight lamp!" exclaimed MacWhirter politely.

"Ah, I am only looking for a pudding for tomorrow," Beatrice replied.

"We shall feel hopelessly in debt if you look after us so well," smiled the young man ironically.

"I must look after you—," said Beatrice.

"You do—wonderfully. I feel that we owe you large debts of gratitude." The meals were generally late, and something was always wrong.

"Because I scan a list of puddings—?" smiled Beatrice, uneasily.

"For the puddings themselves, and all your good things. The piano, for instance! That was very nice indeed." He bowed to her.

"Did it disturb you? But one does not hear very well in the study—."

"I opened the door," said MacWhirter, bowing again.

"It is not fair," said Beatrice. "I am clumsy now—clumsy. I once could play—."

"You play excellently—why that 'once could'?" said MacWhirter.

"Ah—you are amiable. My old master would have said differently," she replied.

"We," said MacWhirter, "are humble amateurs, and to us you are more than excellent."

"Good old Monsieur Fannière, how he would scold me!: he said I would not take my talent out of the napkin.* He would quote me the New Testament: I always think Scripture sounds false in French, do not you?"

"Er—my acquaintance with modern languages is not extensive, I regret to say."

"No?—I was brought up at a convent school near Rouen."

"Ah—that would be very interesting."

"Yes—but I was there six years, and the interest wears off everything."

"Alas—!" assented MacWhirter, smiling.

"Those times were very different from these," said Beatrice.

"I should think so," said MacWhirter, waxing grave and sympathetic.*

XXXI

In the same month of July, not yet a year after Siegmund's death, Helena sat on the top of the tram-car, with Cecil Byrne. She was dressed in blue linen, for the day had been hot. Byrne was holding up to her a yellow backed copy of "Einsame Menschen,"* and she was humming the air of the Russian Folk Song printed on the front page, frowning, nodding with her head and beating time with her hand to get the rhythm of the song. She turned suddenly to him, and shook her head, laughing.

"I can't get it—it's no use. I think it's the swinging of the car prevents me getting the time," she said.

"These little outside things always come a victory over you," he laughed.

"Do they?" she replied, smiling, bending her head against the wind. It was six o'clock in the evening. The sky was quite overcast, after a dim, warm day. The tram-car was leaping along southwards. Out of the corners of his eyes Byrne watched the crisp morsels of hair shaken on her neck by the wind.

"Do you know," she said, "it feels rather like rain."

"Then," said he calmly, but turning away to watch the people below on the pavement, "you certainly ought not to be out."

"I ought not," she said, "for I'm totally unprovided."

Neither however, had the slightest intention of turning back.

Presently they descended from the car, and took a road leading up-hill off the highway. Trees hung over one side, whilst on the other side stood a few villas with lawns upraised. Upon one of these lawns two great sheep-dogs rushed and stood at the brink of the grassy-declivity, at some height above the road, barking and urging boisterously. Helena and Byrne stood still to watch them. One dog was grey, as is usual, the other pale faun. They raved extravagantly at the two pedestrians. Helena laughed at them.

"They are—" she began, in her slow manner.

"Villa sheep-dogs baying us wolves," he continued.

"No," she said, "they remind me of Fafner and Fasolt."*

"Fasolt?—they *are* like that.* I wonder if they really dislike us."

"It appears so," she laughed.

"Dogs generally chum up to me," he said.

Helena began suddenly to laugh. He looked at her inquiringly.

"I remember," she said, still laughing "at Knockholt—you—a half-grown lamb—a dog—in procession." She marked the position of the three with her finger.

"What an ass I must have looked," he said.

"Sort of silent Pied Piper," she laughed.

"Dogs do follow me like that though," he said.

"They did Siegmund," she said.

"Ah!" he exclaimed.

"I remember they had, for a long time, a little brown dog that followed him home."

"Ah!" he exclaimed.

"I remember too," she said, "a little black and white kitten that followed me. Mater *would not* have it in—she would not. And I remember finding it, a few days after, dead in the road. I don't think I ever quite forgave my mater that."

"More sorrow over one kitten brought to destruction, than over all the sufferings of men," he said.

She glanced at him, and laughed. He was smiling ironically.

"For the latter, you see," she replied. "I am not responsible."

As they neared the top of the hill, a few spots of rain fell.

"You know," said Helena, "if it begins, it will continue all night. Look at that!"

She pointed to the great dark reservoir of cloud ahead.

"Had we better go back?" he asked.

"Well—we will go on and find a thick tree, then we can shelter till we see how it turns out. We are not far from the cars here."

They walked on and on: the rain drops fell more thickly, then thinned away.

"It is exactly a year today!" she said as they walked on the round shoulder of the down, with an oak wood on the left hand.—"Exactly!"

"What anniversary is it then?" he inquired.

"Exactly a year today, Siegmund and I walked here—by the day: Thursday. We went through the larch-wood. Have you ever been through the larch-wood?"

"No."

"We will go then," she said.

"History repeats itself," he remarked.

"How?" she asked calmly.

He was pulling at the heads of the cocksfoot grass as he walked.

"I see no repetition," she added.

"No!" he exclaimed bitingly, "You are right."

They went on in silence. As they drew near a farm, they saw the men unloading a last waggon of hay onto a very brown stack. He sniffed the air. Though he was angry, he spoke.

"They got that hay rather damp," he said. "Can't you smell it—like hot tobacco and sandalwood?"

"What—is that the stack?" she asked.

"Yes—it's always like that when it's picked damp."

The conversation was re-started, but did not flourish. When they turned onto a narrow path by the side of the field, he went ahead. Leaning over the hedge, he pulled three sprigs of honeysuckle, yellow as butter, full of scent. Then he waited for her. She was hanging her head, looking in the hedge-bottom. He presented her with the flowers without speaking. She bent forward, inhaled the rich fragrance, and looked up at him over the blossoms with her beautiful, beseeching blue eyes. He smiled gently to her.

"Isn't it nice?" he said. "Aren't they fine bits?" She took them without answering, and put one piece carefully in her dress. It was quite against her rule to wear a flower. He took his place by her side.

"I always like the gold-green of cut fields" he said. "They seem to give off sunshine even when the sky's greyer than a tabby-cat."

She laughed, instinctively putting out her hand towards the glowing field on her right.

They entered the larch-wood. There the chill wind was changed into sound. Like a restless insect he hovered about her, like a butterfly whose antennae flicker and twitch sensitively as they gather intelligence, touching the aura, as it were, of the female. He was exceedingly delicate in his handling of her.

The path was cut windingly through the lofty, dark, and closely serried trees, which vibrated like chords under the soft bow of the wind. Now and again he would look down passages between the trees, narrow, pillared corridors, dusky as if webbed across with mist. All around was a twilight, thickly populous with slender, silent trunks. Helena stood still, gazing up at the tree tops where the bow of the wind was drawn, causing slight, perceptible quivering. Byrne walked on without her. At a bend in the path he stood, with his hand on the roundness of a larch trunk, looking back at her, a blue fleck in the brownness of congregated trees. She moved very slowly down the path.

"I might as well not exist, for all she is aware of me," he said to himself bitterly. Nevertheless, when she drew near, he said brightly:

"Have you noticed how the thousands of dry twigs between the trunks make a brown mist, a brume?"

She looked at him suddenly as if interrupted.

"Hm?—Yes, I see what you mean."

She smiled at him, because of his bright, boyish tone and manner.

"That's the larch-fog," he laughed.

"Yes," she said, "you see it in pictures. I had not noticed it before."

He shook the tree on which his hand was laid.

"It laughs through its teeth," he said, smiling, playing with everything he touched.

As they went along she caught swiftly at her hat. Then she stooped, picking up a hat-pin of twined silver. She laughed to herself as if pleased by a coincidence.

"Last year," she said, "the larch-fingers stole both my pins: the same ones."

He looked at her, wondering how much he was filling the place of a ghost with warmth. He thought of Siegmund, and seemed to see him swinging down the steep bank out of the wood, exactly as he himself was doing at the moment, with Helena stepping carefully behind. He always felt a deep sympathy and kin-ship with Siegmund: sometimes he thought he hated Helena.

They had emerged at the head of a shallow valley, one of those wide hollows in the north downs that are like a great length of tapestry held loosely by four people. It was raining. Byrne looked at the dark-blue dots rapidly appearing on the sleeves of Helena's dress. They walked on a little way. The rain increased. Helena looked about for shelter.

"Here!" said Byrne, "Here is our tent, a black-tartar's, ready pitched."

He stooped under the low boughs of a very large yew tree that stood just back from the path. She crept after him. It was really a very good shelter. Byrne sat on the ledge of a root, Helena beside him. He looked, under the flap of the black branches, down the valley. The grey rain was falling steadily: the dark hollow under the tree was immersed in the monotonous sound of it. In the open, where the bright young corn shone intense with wet green, was a fold of sheep. Exposed in a large pen on the hillside, they were moving restlessly: now and again came the 'tong,-ting-tong' of a sheep bell. First the grey creatures huddled in the high corner, then one of them descended and took shelter by the growing corn lowest down. The rest followed, bleating and pushing each other in their anxiety to reach the place of desire, which was no whit better than where they stood before.

"That's like us all," said Byrne whimsically. "We're all penned out on a wet evening, but we think, if only we could get where someone else is, it would be deliciously cosy."

Helena laughed swiftly, as she always did when he became whimsical and fretful. He sat with his head bent down, smiling with his lips, but his eyes melancholy. She put her hand out to him. He took it without apparently observing it, folding his own hand over it, and, unconsciously, increasing the pressure.

"You are cold," he said.

"Only my hands—and they usually are," she replied gently.

"And mine are generally warm."

"I know that," she said. "It's almost the only warmth I get now—your hands. They really are wonderfully warm and close-touching."

"As good as a baked potato," he said.

She pressed his hand, scolding him for his mockery.

"So many calories per week—isn't that how we manage it?" he asked. "On credit."

She put her other hand on his, as if beseeching him to forego his irony, which hurt her. They sat silent for some time. The sheep broke their cluster and began to straggle back to the upper side of the pen.

"Tong-tong, tong," went the forlorn bell. The rain waxed louder.

Byrne was thinking of the previous week. He had gone to Helena's home to read German with her as usual.—She wanted to understand Wagner in his own language—.

In each of the arm-chairs, reposing across the arms, was a violin-case. He had sat down on the edge of one seat, in front of the sacred fiddle. Helena had come quickly and removed the violin.

"I shan't knock it—it is all right," he had said, protesting. This was Siegmund's violin, which Helena had managed to purchase, and Byrne was always ready to yield its precedence.

"It was all right," he repeated.

"But you were not," she had replied gently. Since that time his heart had beat quick with excitement. Now he sat in a little storm of agitation, of which nothing was betrayed by his gloomy, pondering expression, but some of which was communicated to Helena by the increasing pressure of his hand, which adjusted itself, delicately, in a stronger and stronger stress over her fingers and palm. By some movement he became aware that her hand was uncomfortable. He relaxed. She sighed, as if restless and dissatisfied. She wondered what he was thinking of.

He smiled quietly.

"'The Babes in the Wood,'" he teased. Helena laughed, with a sound of tears. In the tree overhead some bird began to sing, in spite of the rain, a broken evening song.

"That little beggar sees it's a hopeless case, so he reminds us of Heaven. But if he's going to cover us with yew leaves, he's set himself a job."

Helena laughed again, and shivered. He put his arm round her, drawing her nearer his warmth. After this new and daring move, neither spoke for a while.

"The rain continues," he said.

"And will do," she added, laughing.

"Quite content!" he said.

The bird overhead chirruped loudly again.

"'Strew on us roses, roses'," quoted Byrne, adding after a while, in wistful mockery: "'And never a sprig of yew'*—eh?"

Helena made a small sound of tenderness and comfort for him, and weariness for herself. She let herself sink a little closer against him.

"Shall it not be so—no yew?" he murmured.

He put his left hand, with which he had been breaking larch twigs, on her chilled wrist. Noticing that his fingers were dirty, he held them up.

"I shall make marks on you," he said.

"They will come off," she replied.

"Yes—we come clean after everything. Time scrubs all sorts of scars off us."

"Some scars don't seem to go," she smiled, and she held out her other arm, which had been pressed warm against his side. There, just above the wrist, was the red sun-inflammation from last year. Byrne regarded it gravely.

"But it's wearing off—even that," he said wistfully.

Helena put her arms round him, under his coat. She was cold. He felt a hot wave of joy suffuse him. Almost immediately she released him, and took off her hat.

"That is better," he said.

"I was afraid of the pins," said she.

"I've been dodging them for the last hour," he said, laughing, as she put her arms under his coat again for warmth.

She laughed, and making a small, moaning noise, as if of weariness and helplessness, she sank her head on his chest. He put down his cheek against hers.

"I want rest and warmth," she said, in her dull tones.

"All right!" he murmured.

EXPLANATORY NOTES

EXPLANATORY NOTES

The Trespasser

41:3 **Louisa,** Character based upon Agnes Louise Eliza Mason (1871–*c.* 1950), intimate friend of Helen Corke in Croydon. See *Letters*, i. 194 n.

41:4 **Helena** See Introduction, pp. 33–4.

42:9 **On the mantel-piece...of sea-weed.** The objects described here were on Helen Corke's mantelpiece when DHL visited her; the lustres were two iridescent white vases.

42:28 **Byrne** For this self-portrait, DHL borrowed the surname of a Croydon teaching colleague, Algernon M. Byrne (1889–1928). See *Letters*, i. 194 n. DHL's uncertainty about the name of a minor character is evident here: 'Cecil Byrne' in the extant pages of chapter I of MSI is 'Ernest Lambert' in the last chapter of MSI, which was revised to 'Cecil Byrne' at or before the time that the pages of the last chapter were incorporated in MSII. ('Ernest Lambert' is the name of the main character in *A Collier's Friday Night*, and 'Cecil Byrne' is similar to 'Cyril Beardsall' in *The White Peacock*.)

44:5 **"'Ye did run well—what hath hindered you?'"** Galatians v. 7. ['...well; who did hinder you...?' (AV)]

46:5 **Siegmund,"** See Introduction, p. 10.

47:3 **heard the discord.** DHL revised this phrase twice in the final MS (MSII): 'heard the discord fretting' became 'heard the discord of life fretting on life' and, finally 'heard the discord of life fretting on death'.

48:4 **Beatrice** Character based upon Herbert Baldwin Macartney's wife, Alice née Edwardes.

48:23 **the season,** The opera season was over at the end of July.

49:11 **the flowers...the market-hall.** The outdoor flower market near the Covent Garden Opera House. See letter to Frederick Atkinson, 24 June 1910, where DHL described 'The Saga' as 'horribly poetic: Covent Garden market, floral hall' (*Letters*, i. 167).

49:35 **casting him forth.** An allusion to Charles M. Doughty, (1843–1926) *Adam Cast Forth* (1908). See notes on 103:24 and 118: 25.

51:24 **Gwen and Marjory, aged nine and twelve,** DHL was inconsistent about the ages of Siegmund's daughters. On p. 176, Marjory is referred to as the 'second daughter...aged nine'; Gwen is said to be 'five'. He does not tell us the age of Irene,

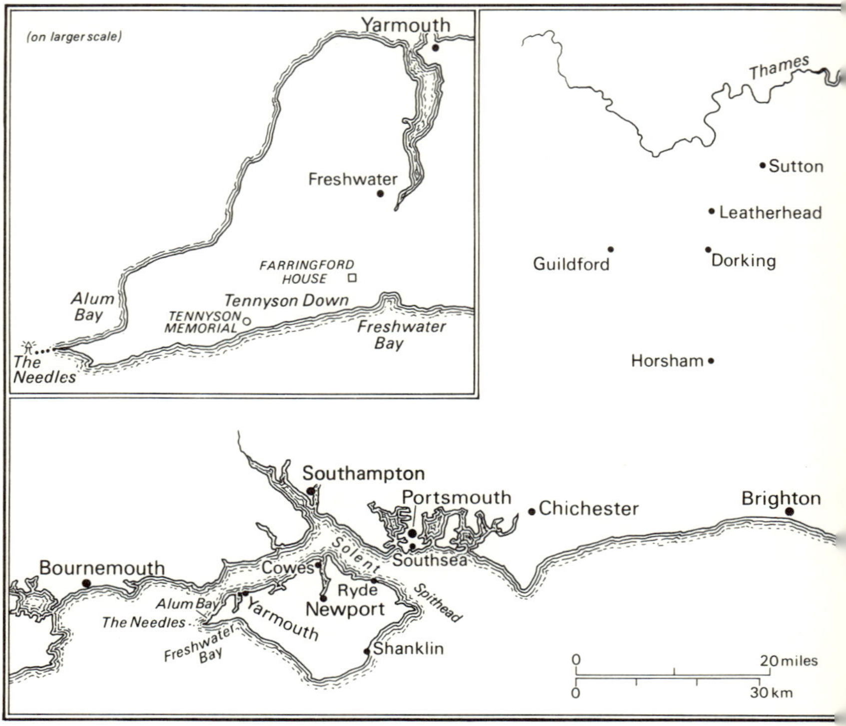

The Isle of Wight and the Solent.

who appears on p. 54, nor does he refer to her again. In the final manuscript, he referred to Marjory as 'Minna' in the later scenes.

52:26 **de Beriot concerto** Charles de Beriot (1802–70), Belgian violinist and composer whose compositions have a natural flow designed to display the characteristics of the violin.

52:37 **score of "Pelléas."** *Pelléas et Mélisande* (1902): opera by Claude Debussy (1862–1918) based on the drama by Maurice Maeterlinck (1862–1949). DHL may have intended an allusion to the theme of infidelity, thwarted love and death.

53:29 **Isle of Wight,** See map.

54:11 **sneck** A sharp clicking sound (dialect).

55:11 **it was Romance, going back to Tristan.** DHL seems to be using the term 'Romance' to suggest the period and subject-matter of the verse and prose Romances of the Middle Ages. For a note on the opera *Tristan und Isolde*, by Richard Wagner (1813–83), see below, p. 325.

56:3 **the old "Victory"...and scarlet:** *Victory* was the flagship of Admiral Lord Nelson at the Battle of Trafalgar. When Helen Corke and H. B. Macartney (and DHL) visited the Isle of Wight in 1909, *Victory* was moored off Gosport, west of Portsmouth, and decked with flags to honour the visiting Czar. (Cf. *Letters*, i. 133–4.)

56:6 **the battle-ships** Portsmouth was the headquarters of the Home Fleet and an important naval dockyard. On royal occasions the Fleet was drawn up for review off Spithead.

56:9 **the round fortress,** The Round Tower was built early in the fifteenth century at the mouth of Portsmouth Harbour; Southsea Castle was built about a mile east of it by Henry VIII. DHL was probably referring to the Round Tower as a part of the Castle site.

56:17 **Sieglinde's island** This one instance of the name 'Sieglinde' in the first edition may have been an oversight. More probably, it is part of Siegmund's fantasy. MSII reads: 'In front ⟨Sieglinde's island⟩ ⟨⟨⌜Helena's⌝⟩⟩ ⌜Sieglinde's island⌝ drew near, and nearer, creeping towards him, bringing him Helena' (40). See Introduction, note 183, p. 35 for an explanation of transcription practices. DHL's revision of 'Helena' to 'Sieglinde' suggests that, unlike the other occurrences of 'Sieglinde' in MSII, DHL intended to use the Wagnerian name here. Sieglinde was not, however, associated with an island. See below, p. 326 and Introduction, pp. 33–4.

58:5 **—not Wotan's wrath, nor Siegfried's dragon..."** DHL appears to be alluding to the musical motifs representing Wotan's wrath in *Walküre* and the dragon Fafner in *Siegfried*, comparing them with the sound of the foghorn, which seems to threaten happiness.

58:17 **It's something...to Tristan."** In *Tristan und Isolde* III, the shepherd stationed to watch for the ship that brings Isolde to the dying Tristan plays his pipe, represented in a cor anglais solo. DHL may have mistakenly remembered the call as coming *from* the ship (thus 'across the sea'), as he did in a 1913 letter: 'It was like the horn of Tristan sounding across the sea – I mean of Isolda' (*Letters*, i. 535). In Act II the lovers hear the distant horns of the King's hunting party as they profit by his absence. The two sounds may be conflated.

59:40 **They were on the downs,** Just above Freshwater Bay is an area called Tennyson Downs, after the poet Alfred, Lord Tennyson (1809–92), whose house, Farringford, was nearby.

60:5 **the siren from the Needles** The Needles are a series of pointed, white chalk rocks jutting from the western end of the Isle of Wight, on which there is a lighthouse.

60:24 **the note in 'Tristan'?"** Refers to the horn call in *Tristan und Isolde* III. See note on 58:17.

61:26 **It was...to Helena.** The reference appears to be to Act III of *Siegfried* where the hero approaches Brünnhilde in her circle of fire; but DHL does not carry through with the allusion. Instead, Siegmund interprets the sunset through a Beethoven symphony.

62:1 **"The Grail music, in 'Lohengrin'—"** The motive ('motif') is a repeated phrase thematically central to a musical composition and here represents the Grail in Wagner's opera, *Lohengrin* (first performed 1848). DHL may have intended to suggest the possibility of Helena's losing Siegmund as Elsa loses Lohengrin.

64:14 **the only Hermaphrodite.** The nymph Salmacis fell in love with Hermaphroditus, son of Hermes and Aphrodite. She prayed to the gods to keep him with her forever, and the two were united in one body.

64:16 **that class of 'Dreaming Women',** Rachel Annand Taylor, 'The Epilogue of the Dreaming Women', *The Hours of Fiammetta* (1910). See Introduction, p. 18. See note on 119: 37.

66:16 **Nietzsche** Friedrich Wilhelm Nietzsche (1844–1900). German philospher whose works Helen Corke began reading in 1908 (Corke, *Infancy* 157).

67:39 **Mr MacNair** Siegmund's surname is a variation of the spelling of H. B. Macartney's mother's maiden name, McNair.

75:28 **fancy more than imagination.** A reference to the distinction made by Samuel Taylor Coleridge (1772–1834) between 'fancy', a mechanical process of reordering sense impressions, and the unifying creative power of 'imagination' (*Biographia Literaria* (1817), chaps. 13–14). The reference was added at proof-stage.

75:39 **Rhine Maidens...to sun.** General allusion to Wagner's opera, *Das Rheingold* I, i.

77:11 **a tall cross,...iron fence.** A Cornish granite cross was erected in 1897 as a monument to Lord Tennyson (see note on 59:40).

77:19 **peacocks and princesses** Probably a reference to Tennyson's poem 'The Princess' (1847), which contains the line that may have inspired the title of DHL's first novel: 'Now droops the milk-white peacock like a ghost' (vii. 181). Cf. *Letters*, i. 167.

77:39 **the Sagas** See Introduction, p. 10 for a discussion of the word *saga*.

81:4 **saluting the Czar.** Nicholas II (1894–1918), Czar of Russia, reviewed the English fleet in the Solent on 2 August 1909. See letter to Mabel Limb [3 August 1909], *Letters*, i. 134: 'We saw the fleet as we walked along – heard them saluting the Czar's vessel as he passed.' See also note on 56:3.

82:37 **he [almost] laughed to himself.** Although the manuscript reading is 'always' DHL probably intended to write 'almost'.

84:37 **Wotan is so clumsy** Wotan is a character in Wagner's *Der Ring des Nibelungen*. The allusion seems to make no sense except as another example of Helena's whimsy.

86:32 **"The Watch on the Rhine."** 'Die Wacht am Rhein' (1840), poem by Max Schneckenburger (1819–49), set to music in 1854 by Karl Wilhelm (1815–73) and became a popular German national song. Its popularity dates from 1870.

92:9 **Francis Thompson's poems,** Francis Thompson (1859–1907) was rescued from ill-health and poverty by Alice Meynell and her husband Wilfrid (who subsequently edited his *Works*, 1913). Thompson's life, however, remained lonely and painful; his shyness and suffering kept him on the outskirts of society. 'A few poppies here and there among the wild rye' may refer to 'poppies 'mid the wheat' in Thompson's poem, 'July Fugitive' (1897) (line 18) or to 'The Poppy' (1891), where 'the sleep-flower sways in the wheat its head' (line 64).

92:14 **"Think of Wagner,"** In 'The Letter', Helen Corke said of Wagner: 'He suffered as we do' (p. 285, below), the 'we' indicating Macartney and herself.

98:10 **"'Here on this mole-hill— —'"** *3 Henry VI*, II. v. 14.

100:6 **"'Carpe diem',"** Horace (65–8 B.C.), *Odes*, I. xi. 8: 'carpe diem, quam minimum credula postero' ['seize today, and trust as little as possible in tomorrow']. Reference to "the 'postero'" in 100:9 shows that DHL knew the full quotation.

100:11 **a Rose not many men have plucked."** May be an allusion to a well-known poem on the theme of 'carpe diem', 'To The Virgins, To Make Much of Time' (1648) by Robert Herrick (1591–1674), which begins: 'Gather ye rosebuds while ye may...'

100:20 **stars. He bent** The sentence removed at proof-stage had already undergone fairly heavy revision: 'stars. His eyes were steady, fixed with a strange calm and happiness; yet his heart was hurting badly with tears. He bent' MSII (148). See textual apparatus for final MSII reading.

101:23 **"Tiefe Stille... das Meer— —."** Poem by Johann Wolfgang von Goethe (1749–1832), 'Meeresstille' (1827): ['Deep stillness rules in the water, / Without movement rests the sea' (lines 1–2).] All the German poems quoted in *The Trespasser* are included in the anthology, *German Poetry for Schools* (see Introduction p. 9n).

101:26 **Heine and Uhland** Heinrich Heine (1797–1856), Johann Ludwig Uhland (1787–1862): German poets, including Goethe, whose work DHL and Helen Corke read together.

101:28 **"Die Luft... der Rhein."** Heine, 'Lorelei' (1827). ['The air is cool and it is growing dark / and the Rhine is flowing quietly' (lines 5–6).]

101:34 **"Wie Träume... Weihnachtsgaben——."** Heine, 'Meergruss' (referred to as *Thalatta* by Helen Corke, *Portrait* 170):

> I see it glistening like dreams of childhood
> In the province of your billowing waves,
> And old memory tells me once again
> Of all those dear, glorious toys
> Of all those gleaming Christmas gifts. (lines 20–4)

102:8 **"Aus alten... Zauberland."** Heine, 'Aus alten Märchen winkt es' (1827):

> From ancient fairy tales it beckons
> To us with a pale hand
> There is the singing and the ringing
> Of a magical land. (lines 1–4)

102:21 **"'Die grosse Blumen schmachten,'"** Heine, 'Aus alten Märchen winkt es'. ['Wo grosse Blumen schmachten': 'Where big flowers languish' (line 5).]

102:33 **"'Und Liebesweisen tönen'** Heine, 'Aus alten Märchen winkt es'. ['And love-songs resound' (line 13).]

103:24 **"Hawwa,—Eve—Mother!"** In *Adam Cast Forth*, Adam's wife, Adama, after her childbearing is named 'Hawwa' by Adam. 'Hawwa', according to a note to the 1908 Duckworth edition, is Hebrew and Arabic (the root, *breathe*, *live*), from which 'Eva' or 'Eve' derives. DHL read this verse play while in Croydon, *Letters*, i. 95.

105:19 **"l'agonie."** Literally, 'the pangs of death' (French). Siegmund deliberately avoids the figurative meaning – anguish, torture – commonly associated with the English word 'agony'.

106:39 **where Brünnhilde...of fire.** Wagner's *Die Walküre* III, and *Siegfried* III.

107:4 **manna must...Arabian deserts.** Food miraculously provided for the Israelites' journey through the wilderness, which DHL refers to as the Arabian deserts. Exodus xvi. 14–15.

109:21 **an anarchist...nihilist,** nineteenth-century revolutionary groups: anarchists advocated voluntary social organization in place of government; nihilists, destruction of all government. Endorsement of terrorism by both groups led to the assassination of Czar Alexander II in 1881.

110:3 **penetrating gaze,** When 'intimate' was removed in proof from the phrase 'penetrating, intimate gaze', the comma was mistakenly left.

110:13 **Hampson—"** See pp. 319–23, below for the original version of this chapter.

110:14 **the Savoy** London theatre known particularly for its performances of Gilbert and Sullivan light opera.

111:11 **Flaubert's saint...a leper?** Gustave Flaubert (1821–80), 'La Légende de Saint Julien l'Hospitalier' (1877). It is through the act to which Hampson refers that Julien becomes a saint, despite his seemingly irredeemable sin of having killed his own parents.

111:12 **"Nor I!"** "Nor I?" in the manuscript does not make sense. It seems probable that DHL meant to write an exclamation mark; his eyes may have caught the question mark directly above the word 'I'.

111:30 **'concentré';** One who has an extreme inner orientation (French).

114:7 **"A late,...she flew..."** Walter Ramal [pseudonym of Walter de la Mare (1873–1956)], *Songs of Childhood* (1902), 'The Pedlar', lines 31–2. ['...dark in the dim, she flew;']. See letter to De la Mare, 1 March 1912: 'I delighted in that first little book of poems, by Walter Ramal' (*Letters*, i. 370).

114:12 **"And now...lattice come."** 'The Pedlar', lines 49–50.

115:2 **Doppelgänger,** Ghostly counterpart of a living person (German).

117:11 **dip their sheep** To kill ticks (using a liquid with a sulphuric base, hence the tawny colour).

117:23 **cruder than Theocritus."** Theocritus, third-century B.C. Greek poet, generally considered the father of bucolic or pastoral poetry. In the earliest extant manuscript (MSI), the reference differs significantly: '"It is very primitive," said Sieglinde, and laughing, she added, "it is ⟨quite⟩ a scene from Theocritus"' (151). Helena's perception of the scene as 'cruder than Theocritus' (which appeared when DHL wrote MSII) is in keeping with the altered characterisation elsewhere. See Introduction, pp. 33–5.

118:7 **whistling the bird-music...of "Tristan."** Wagner's *Siegfried* and *Tristan und Isolde*. The former reference is to the music of Siegfried's conversations with the Forest Bird, which protects and guides him and from whom he learns of Brünnhilde.

118:25 **Adama in "Adam Cast Forth."** See 103:24. Both Satan and the Chorus in *Adam Cast Forth* refer to Adam's sin or fall as his 'trespass'.

119:10 **"'And there shall be no more sea,'"** Revelation xxi. 1 ['and there was...' (AV)].

119:37 **'failed to follow her'** DHL sometimes used single quotation marks to distinguish thoughts or ideas from conversation; this convention has been reproduced in this text.

123:15 ***solide.*** 'Strong, sturdy' (French).

123:18 ***doux...câlin.'*** 'Charming, winning...coaxing' (French).

123:19 ***too* spoony for his age,'** Spoony: soft, silly, especially in the sense of sentimentally amorous.

123:34 **Beatrice is...than Dante's.** Dante Alighieri (1265–1321) as a young man fell in love with the woman he celebrated as 'Beatrice' – after her death, it is believed – in the *Vita nuova* and the *Divina Commedia*.

125:20 **the Spring Song from "Walküre."** Musical motive at the conclusion of Act I, in which Siegmund and Sieglinde discover their love for each other.

128:12 **'an infant crying in the night,'** Tennyson, *In Memoriam* (1850), LIV. 18.

131:26 **'Ihr Lascheks seid ein anderes Geschlecht.'** Gerhart Hauptmann (1862–1946), *Elga* (1901), scene v ['You Lascheks are a breed apart']. The words are spoken to Elga, the unfaithful wife, by her mother-in-law, who continues: '...self-willed, light-hearted, always ready to risk everything. Therefore, also, you lost everything'.

131:37 **"Der Tod...ins Leben."** *Elga*, scene v ['Death goes at one's side almost visibly, and always forces one deeper into life.'] The words are Elga's. DHL used part of this quotation in a letter to Helen Corke, 21 June 1910, *Letters*, i. 164; they had read Grace Crawford's copy of *Elga* together (see Corke, *Infancy* 236).

132:26 **"'Take no thought for the morrow.'** Matthew vi. 34 ['Take therefore no thought for the morrow: for the morrow shall take thought for the things of itself.' (AV)]

134:28 **the affection that...together," everything** The original reading of the passage in MSI 246 was:

the ⟨sweet⟩ affection that everything bore him. The sky was like a sister, who, on the morning of his departure, had ⟨put smiling over her grief and ⟩ ⌜covered her grief with smiling and put⌝ bright words upon her trembling lips, and was slipping into his purse fair coin of love to last him on the journey.

"You must set out bravely, dear heart," everything

See textual apparatus for later MSII reading. The deletion of sentences from the proofs here is in keeping with DHL's achievement of greater economy found elsewhere.

136:32 **"We are...the gate."** Ernest Dowson (1867–1900), 'Vitae summa brevis spem nos vetat incohare longam' (1896):

> They are not long, the weeping and the
> laughter,
> Love and desire and hate:
> I think they have no portion in us after
> We pass the gate. (lines 1–4)

137:12 **'Better a live dog than a dead lion'** The proverb stems from Ecclesiastes ix. 4 ['a living dog is better than a dead lion' (AV)].

138:40 **Eros** God of love. MSII 244 reads: ⟨Jesus⟩ Eros – walking by the sea. – But you are like ⟨Him⟩ him,".

145:12 **Domine,"** Master, professor (Latin). This was an affectionate name Helen Corke used for Macartney; also the name of the character representing him in her novel, *Neutral Ground*.

145:21 **'Fumum et opes strepitumque Romae'?"** Horace, *Odes*, III. xxix. 12 ['The smoke and the grandeur and the noise of Rome'].

148:29 **had struck.** The sentence following this was deleted from the proofs (see textual apparatus) and had already been revised and shortened in MSII (266–7). It originally read: 'Further off, still flying and singing a now inaudible song, was the fatal white wild swan which, hearing again, he would have to bring down.'

150:28 **"Addio!"** 'Farewell, goodbye' (Italian), frequently used by DHL as a complementary close to his letters.

150:31 **'Traviata'** *La Traviata* (1853), opera by Giuseppe Verdi (1813–1901), based on the play *La Dame aux Camélias* by Alexandre Dumas fils (1824–95).

150:36 **the Italian's passion-notes** Reference to Verdi's passionate expression of the lovers bidding each other farewell. (On 'Addio' and *Traviata*, *Letters*, i. 253.)

152:8 **Alum Bay, done in variegated sand.** Alum Bay is famous for its unusual geological formation of brightly coloured sands, samples of which are available for tourists.

154:4 **the German Emperor** Wilhelm II, emperor of Germany 1888–1918.

155:39 **a little virtue...his blood.** An allusion to the healing of the woman with 'an issue of blood', Mark v. 30: 'And Jesus, immediately knowing in himself that virtue had gone out of him, turned him about in the press, and said, Who touched my clothes?' (AV)

157:5 **of tall women,** This is the only instance of revision marked on the uncorrected page proofs. A line has been drawn through 'white' and a deletion sign placed in the margin. This mark cannot be positively identified as DHL's.

161:29 ***Olive*"** Character based upon Violet Mary Babbage – 'Vio' in 'The Cornwall Writing' (see below, p. 303) – who accompanied Helen Corke and Agnes Mason to Cornwall.

165:6 **the legend from "Aylwin."** *Aylwin* (1898), a novel by Walter Theodore Watts-Dunton (1832–1914). Gipsy lore maintains that a golden cloud shaped like a hand – dukkeripen, the golden hand – brings luck.

165:15 **the well-known movement from the Valkyrie Ride,** *Die Walküre* III. i. Music which accompanies the appearance of the Valkyries on horseback.

170:36 **this month's 'Nash's.'"** London magazine which later merged with *Pall Mall.*

171:30 **Dîtes donc!"** 'Look here!' (French).

171:32 **nous avons changé tout cela!** (French). Possibly a reference to *Le Médecin malgré lui* (1666) by Molière (1622–73): 'Oui, cela était autrefois ainsi, mais nous avons changé tout cela' (II. vi). ['Yes, it was once so, but we have changed all that.'] Molière's point, however, is unrelated to DHL's.

171:33 **razzle"** Abbreviation of 'razzle-dazzle': a spree.

171:37 **"Un doux argot, ma mère.** 'A charming (or pleasant) slang, mother' (French).

180:19 **"London Opinion";** London weekly magazine.

187:5 **the Comedy Theatre** A London theatre that featured comic or light opera, similar to the London Gaiety Theatre, in which H. B. Macartney played.

192:18 **'Oh the gladness...when she's glad—'"** J. M. Barrie (1860–1937), *Rosalind* (1912) in *The Plays of J. M. Barrie* (New York, 1945):

> Oh the gladness of her gladness when she's glad,
> And the sadness of her sadness when she's sad,
> But the gladness of her gladness
> And the sadness of her sadness
> Are as nothing, Charles,
> To the badness of her badness when she's bad. (p. 701)

192:28 **"'It's ill talking of halters in the house of the hanged,'** English proverb, ironic in the circumstances. M. P. Tilney, *A Dictionary of Proverbs in England*, 1950, H59.

193:24 **the dauntless three,** Thomas Babington Macaulay (1800–59), 'Horatius', xxxi.

194:16 **"Dear—I...a right."** Helen Corke quoted Macartney's words in 'The Cornwall Writing' as: 'Whatever happens to me – you must go on —' (see below, p. 303). In 'The Letter', however, his words are much closer to those DHL used in *The Trespasser*: '"Sieglinde dear, I want you to promise that, whatever happens to me, you will go on... Remember dear, two wrongs do not make a right...."'.

197:9 **the land of Isolde.** Wagner's *Tristan und Isolde*. Isolde actually came from Ireland; Cornwall was the land of King Mark, to whom she was betrothed.

202:4 **'If thine hand offend thee, cut it off.'** Matthew v. 30, ['And if thy right hand offend thee, cut it off, and cast *it* from thee: for it is profitable for thee that one of thy members should perish, and not *that* thy whole body should be cast into hell.' (AV)]

202:37 **'But for that fear of something after death,'** *Hamlet*, III. i. 46, ['But that the dread of...']

202:41 **'We are such stuff as dreams are made of'."** *The Tempest*, III. i. 146–7, ['...made on'].

203:31 **an imaginary God.** Originally DHL had written 'a mythical God' – which he later revised to 'a suppository God'. A note to 'suppository' (in Edward Garnett's hand) reads: '? suppositious' (MSII 416). The proofs retain 'suppository'; but the first edition (perhaps an actual revision by Garnett or one prompted by him) reads 'an imaginary god'.

209:29 **his opinion on the appearance of sleepers**: Bazarof, the hero of *Father and Sons* (1862) by Turgenev (1818–83), makes the judgment: 'every man's face is stupid when he's asleep' (ed. Ralph E. Matlaw, New York, 1966, p. 103).

210:19 **the Walhalla scene in "Walküre"**; No part of *Die Walküre* is set in Walhalla, the new home of the gods. The whole action takes place on earth. Acts II and III may be thought of as in the neighbourhood of Walhalla, or DHL may have been thinking of the closing scene of the preceding opera in the cycle, *Das Rheingold*.

210:20 **"Tristan" was here,** See note on 197:9.

210:24 **foam which suggested the Anadyomene**: Anadyomene, an epithet used of Aphrodite, alludes to the legend of her birth out of sea foam at the island, Cythera – an interesting reference relative to a title suggested by DHL for this novel in a letter of 30 December 1911: 'Trespassers in Cythera' (*Letters*, i. 343).

212:6 **kinship with Hedda Gabler.** Tragic, psychotic heroine of the play *Hedda Gabler* (1890) by Henrik Ibsen (1828–1906).

212:37 **The bargain's...the bundle."** A variant of the proverb, 'A bargain is a bargain'. See Tilney, *Dictionary of Proverbs*, B76.

213:33 **"The funeral took...widow and children."** *The Surrey Comet*, 11 August 1909, reported the inquest on Herbert Baldwin Macartney. See below, p. 324.

217:4 **scared jury** This was mis-transcribed by the compositor as 'sacred jury', possibly because 'scared' is not written clearly (and might also be read as 'seared').

218:29 **Mr MacWhirter...Mr Allport...Mr Holiday.** All three boarders were modelled upon DHL's colleagues at Davidson Road School: Arthur William McLeod, Robert Henry Aylwin and Ernest Arthur Humphreys, respectively. See *Letters*, i. 136n. and 194n.

219:1 **vulgar in the grain,** Ernest Humphreys recognised himself as 'Mr Holiday' and objected to the description. Writing to Arthur McLeod, on 29 October 1912, DHL defended himself: 'Do persuade Ernie he's not vulgar in the grain. Tell him I say I said that for contrast – a sheer bit of fiction altogether' (*Letters*, i. 465).

222:30 **"'The Village Blacksmith'"** The poem (1841) by Henry Wadsworth Longfellow (1807–82) was set to music by several people; among the most popular versions is the one by Willoughby Hunter Weiss (1820–67), his only well-known composition.

223:28 **I would...the napkin.** Luke xix. 20. 'And another came, saying, "Lord, behold, *here* is thy pound, which I kept laid up in a napkin"' (AV). DHL had considered 'The Talent in the Napkin' for the title of his first novel. See *Letters*, i. 163.

223:40 **and sympathetic.** An additional passage, which followed the paragraph about 'Beatrice Félicité' (see textual apparatus) and discussed the contrast between her life before and after marrying Siegmund, was heavily revised in MSII and then crossed out.

224:5 **"Einsame Menschen,"** [*Solitary People* (1891)] play by Gerhart Hauptmann (1862–1946). DHL borrowed a copy of this play from Grace Crawford in July 1910: see *Letters*, i. 171. *Einsame Menschen* is a particularly appropriate allusion for *The Trespasser*. It dramatises a man's choice between his wife and another woman, and his apparent suicide after that woman's decision to leave him for the sake of his wife.

224:34 **Fafner and Fasolt."** The two giants in *Das Rheingold*. DHL wrote 'Fasner' in MSII, and that error was preserved in the first edition.

225:1 **"Fasolt...like that.** DHL had originally written in a page transferred to MSII (473): '"No," she said, "like Fasner and what's the other——?" "Fasolt?—they *are* like that."' Byrne's repeating the name 'Fasolt' as a question makes more sense in this context.

229:22 **"'Strew on us...a sprig of yew'** Matthew Arnold (1822–88), 'Requiescat' (1853), ['...a spray of yew', lines 1–2].

TEXTUAL APPARATUS

TEXTUAL APPARATUS

The Trespasser

The following symbols are used to distinguish states of the text:

MS = Final manuscript (MSII in introduction)
UP = Uncorrected page proofs
E1 = First English edition

All subsequent impressions, including the American editions, in Lawrence's lifetime reproduce *E1*.

Whenever the *MS* reading is adopted, it appears within the square bracket with no symbol. Corrupt readings follow the square bracket, in chronological sequence, with their first source denoted. In the absence of information to the contrary, the reader should assume that a particular variant recurs in all subsequent states. When a *UP* or *E1* reading has been preferred, it appears with its source-symbol within the square bracket. The *MS* reading always follows.

The following symbols are used editorially:

Ed. = Editor
P = Paragraph
/ = Line break resulting in hyphenation ambiguity; or line break in poem
~ = Repeated word in recording an accidental variant

41:4 violinist. Helena] ~. *P* Helena *UP*

41:7 apathetic] a pathetic *UP*

41:18 'Allegro'] *Allegro UP*

41:21 arm-chairs] arm-/chairs *UP*

41:25 sitting room *Ed.*] sitting-room *MS*

41:28 trams,] ~ *UP*

41:30 foliage,] ~; *UP*

41:30 carpet] ~, *UP*

41:31 floor] ~, *UP*

41:31 like a square *UP*] like square *MS*

41:34 look:] ~; *UP*

41:35 arm-chairs] armchairs *UP*

42:1 recess,] ~ — *UP*

42:5 mantel-piece] mantelpiece *UP*

42:5 soap-stone] soapstone *UP*

42:9 rock crystals] rock-crystals, *UP*

42:9 sea-weed] seaweed *UP*

42:13 fern] ~, *UP*

42:17 but] ~, *UP*

42:26 shoulders,] ~ *UP*

42:27 floated] ~, *UP*

42:30 soap-stone] soap stone *UP*

42:30 candle light] candle-light *UP*

42:31 front,] ~ *UP*

42:34 right?" Helena *Ed.*] ~." Helena *MS* ~?" *P* Helena *UP*

43:1 violin-case *UP*] violin case *MS*

43:2 full of *E1*] of full *MS*

43:13 music,] ~. *UP*

43:21 arm] ~, *UP*

43:22 long red-burned] ~, red-/burned *UP*

43:23 flesh,] ~ *UP*

43:24 arm,] ~ *UP*
43:28 it? *UP*] ~. *MS*
43:31 said,] ~ *UP*
43:34 come,] ~ — *UP*
43:37 answered,] ~ *UP*
43:39 gently,] ~ — *UP*
44:5 "'Ye] " ~ *UP*
44:5 you?'"] ~?" *UP*
44:5 Byrne. *E1*] Byrne, caressingly. *MS*
44:6 Oh] ~, *UP*
44:9 Oh] ~, *UP*
44:10 dear, *UP*] ~ *MS*
44:10 laughing brief] laughing briefly *UP*
44:10 You] you *UP*
44:15 sign;] ~, *UP*
44:18 the pavement. *E1*] the pavement, like the boom and rush of the wind and the patter of raindrops. *MS*
44:37 dullness] dulness *UP*
44:40 Oh—OO—Oh] Oh—o-o-oh *UP*
45:1 slept together] ~ ~, *UP*
45:2 played together] ~ ~, *UP*
45:4 closed. "If] ~, "if *UP*
45:15 friend.] ~? *UP*
45:17 see] ~, *UP*
45:21 'danse macabre'— —.] *danse macabre*——*UP*
45:23 coldly.] ~, *UP*
45:24 pleaded. "No] ~, "no *UP*
45:25 blow,] ~ *UP*
45:30 again,] ~ *UP*
45:35 dead...] ~.... *UP*
46:7 fire. *P* "You] ~. "You *UP*
46:12 Dead.] ~! *UP*
46:15 her;] ~, *UP*
46:16 gaze,] ~ *UP*
46:22 sick,] ~ *UP*
46:24 good,] ~; *UP*
46:26 Folks are better than a garden *E1*] Folk are flowers that make the street like a garden *MS* Folks are flowers...garden *UP*
46:30 last] ~ — *UP*
46:37 simplest,] ~ — *UP*
46:37 love,] ~ — *UP*
46:38 most,] ~ *UP*
46:40 said,] ~ *UP*
47:3 discord. *E1*] discord of life fretting on death. *MS see explanatory note*
47:3 him, sometimes,] ~ ~ *UP*
48:3 portmanteau,] ~ *UP*
48:3 lumber room,] lumber-room *UP*
48:4 £20] twenty pounds *UP*
48:6 up] ~, *UP*
48:7 hasty] ~, *UP*
48:8 months,] ~ *UP*
48:18 heart,] ~ *UP*
48:19 beloved,] ~ *UP*
48:19 being,] ~ *UP*
48:20 dead,] ~; *UP*
48:21 him,] ~ *UP*
48:22 before,] ~ *UP*
48:25 hurt too] ~, ~, *UP*
48:26 opera, *MS*, *E1*] ~ *UP*
48:26 pity,] ~ *E1*
49:1 opera house] opera-house *UP*
49:4 years,] ~ *UP*
49:5 years,] ~ *UP*
49:5 opera house] opera-house *UP*
49:6 comrades'] comrade's *UP*
49:10 violin-case,] ~ *UP*
49:11 gas-light] gaslight *UP*
49:12 spaces,] ~ *UP*
49:14 thing,] ~; *UP*
49:16 faces,] ~; *UP*
49:19 moonglitter] moon-glitter *UP*
49:21 train] ~, *UP*
49:25 years,] ~ *UP*
49:30 blood ties] blood-ties *UP*
49:32 carriage window] carriage-window *UP*
49:34 Slowly,] ~ *UP*
49:34 the body *E1*] the karmic body *MS*
49:37 now,] ~ *UP*
49:40 moonlight] moon-/light *UP*
50:1 elms,] ~' *UP*
50:1 shadows, *MS*, *E1*] ~ *UP*
50:4 effort,] ~ *UP*
50:5 road,] ~ *UP*
50:7 heavens,] *UP*
50:13 garden gate] garden-gate *UP*

50:16 drawing room] drawing-room *UP*
50:17 moonlight] moon-/light *UP*
50:22 moonshine.—] ~. *UP*
50:23 quietly,] ~; *UP*
50:23 room,] ~ *UP*
50:26 broad,] ~ *UP*
50:27 arm-chair *Ed.*] armchair *MS* arm-chair, *UP*
50:29 cloth,] ~ *UP*
50:30 saucer, *MS*, *E1*] ~ *UP*
50:31 plate *MS*, *E1*] ~, *UP*
50:32 red-bordered] ~, *UP*
50:33 cocoa tin] cocoa-tin *UP*
50:37 oilcloth] oil-cloth *UP*
51:1 and rubbish *E1*] and pink and blue and white rubbish *MS*
51:1 paper] papers *UP*
51:2 he crushed *E1*] he had crushed *MS*
51:3 dresser,] ~ *UP*
51:4 slippers:] ~; *UP*
51:5 Beatrice,] ~ *UP*
51:8 joy,] ~ *UP*
51:11 teddy-bear,] ~ *UP*
51:12 life:] ~— *UP*
51:13 tugged] lugged *UP*
51:30 children,] ~ *UP*
51:34 cross *MS*, *E1*] across *UP*
51:37 moustache, was full with youth. *E1*] moustache was full, rich with appeal. *MS* moustache, was...appeal. *UP*
51:40 glamourous *Ed.*] glamorous *MS*
52:5 calm,] ~ *UP*
52:6 love,] ~ *UP*
52:8 and manna *E1*] and fair white manna, *MS* and fair white manna *UP*
52:9 things,] ~ *UP*
52:12 bed,] ~ *UP*
52:16 undressed,] ~ *UP*
52:18 himself. "And] ~, "and *UP*
52:21 brain] ~, *UP*
52:21 hive *E1*] hive in spring *MS*
52:22 thoughts] ~, *UP*
52:22 him] ~, *UP*
52:23 a pond *E1*] a dark pond *MS*
52:24 him,] ~; *UP*
52:25 de Beriot *Ed.*] 'de Beriot' *MS* De Beriot *UP*
52:30 hasty,] ~; *UP*
52:37 "Pelléas." *UP*] ~. *MS*
52:39 'Pelléas' *UP*] ~ *MS*
53:1 fashion] ~, *UP*
53:2 humiliating—] ~, *UP* ~; *E1*
53:2 her,] ~ *UP*
53:4 Then,] ~ *UP*
53:7 home:] ~; *UP*
53:7 together:] ~; *UP*
53:14 eyes,] ~: *UP*
53:20 lap,] ~ *UP*
53:29 to the Isle *E1*] on the Isle *MS*
53:31 solitary; *E1*] solitary, free from yearning; *MS*
53:34 the downs *E1*] the turfy downs *MS*
54:4 wife,] ~ *UP*
54:7 convent school *UP*] Convent School *MS*
54:10 self-respect. *E1*] self respect, till he could scarcely rouse himself from a lethargy like a moping bird's. *MS*
54:12 hall door] hall-door *UP*
54:13 worn-out] worn out *UP*
54:19 finger nails] finger-/nails *UP*
54:21 chuff-chuff-chuff] "Chuff-chuff-chuff" *UP*
54:24 dead—] ~! *UP*
54:24 down,] ~! *UP*
54:26 who lay with *E1*] who slept with *MS*
55:4 Town,] ~ *UP*
55:11 time,] ~; *UP*
55:11 Tristan. *E1*] Tristan. Siegmund was in a grand bright space beyond the allotting of days. *MS*
55:12 crocus flowers] crocus-flowers, *UP*
55:13 the small *E1*] the brilliant small *MS*
55:15 all,] ~ *UP*
55:26 moment,] ~ *UP*
55:29 upon its blueness] upon the blueness *UP*
55:31 sails,] ~— *UP*

55:32 sea noon] sea-moon *UP*
55:34 White,] ~ *UP*
56:2 birds:] ~; *UP*
56:2 "Victory" *Ed.*] ~ *MS Victory UP*
56:3 scarlet:] ~; *UP*
56:6 battle-ships] battleships *UP*
56:14 trailed myriads *E1*] trailed like myriads *MS*
56:15 battle-ships *Ed.*] battle ships *MS* battleships *UP*
56:17 near,] ~ *UP*
56:20 him,] ~; *UP*
56:28 Newport,] ~ *UP*
56:29 station] Station *UP*
56:31 Island] island *UP*
56:36 afternoon,] ~ *UP*
56:36 second-class *UP*] second class *MS*
57:3 station then!] ~, ~. *UP*
57:18 are then!] ~, ~. *UP*
57:19 hat] ~, *UP*
57:21 teatime,] ~ *UP*
57:26 to him,] ~ ~ *UP*
57:30 forehead] ~, *UP*
57:31 thick,] ~ *UP*
57:36 white] ~, *UP*
57:36 strong] ~, *UP*
57:37 him. *E1*] him, like the presence of God. *MS*
58:4 mean?—] ~? *UP*
58:4 fog horn *Ed.*] fog-horn *MS*
58:4 dear,—] ~— *UP*
58:5 dragon...] ~.... *UP*
58:12 sound,] ~ *UP*
58:13 fog horn] fog-horn *UP*
58:18 softly—] ~, *UP*
58:23 Yet,] ~ *UP*
58:23 fog horn] fog-horn *UP*
58:29 often,] ~ *UP*
58:32 inwardly,] ~ *UP*
58:34 present." At] ~." *P* At *UP*
58:34 moment,] ~ *UP*
58:34 rose,] ~ *UP*
58:38 dress,] ~ *UP*
58:39 eyes,] ~ *UP*
58:40 blind to...self urged *E1*] blind to his extremity. But the other part of himself urged *MS*
59:4 breast] ~, *UP*
59:9 tea,] ~ *UP*
59:15 tired?—] ~? *UP*
59:15 are tired,] ~ ~— *UP*
59:19 relief. "No] ~—"no *UP*
59:22 go to bed *UP*] go bed *MS*
59:23 soft,] ~ *UP*
59:25 her,] ~ *UP*
59:34 It puts us *E1*] It wraps you and me *MS*
59:34 together,] ~ *UP*
59:36 us,] ~ *UP*
59:38 She] she *UP*
59:40 look!" He] ~!" *P* He *UP*
59:40 were on the downs, so *E1*] were in an open space, so *MS*
60:1 man,] ~ *UP*
60:2 Suddenly,] ~ *UP*
60:5 place,] ~ *UP*
60:9 horizontal?—] ~? *UP*
60:9 scale—] ~, *UP*
60:15 fog horn *Ed.*] foghorn *MS* fog-horn *UP*
60:19 F♯] F sharp *UP*
60:24 'Tristan' *UP*] ~ *MS*
60:26 said,] ~ *UP*
60:34 itself. *E1*] itself its eternal lullaby. *MS*
60:39 Siegmund, glancing *E1*] Siegmund, ironically glancing *MS*
61:1 front!] ~? *UP*
61:9 no...] ~.... *UP*
61:11 said,] ~ *UP*
61:21 golflinks] golf-links *UP*
61:22 tired] ~, *UP*
61:27 this same glory. *E1*] this tremendous glory of farewell. *MS*
61:37 symphony] Symphony *UP*
61:40 steady—] ~; *UP*
62:1 music,] ~ *UP*
62:1 'Lohengrin'— *Ed.*] ~— *MS* '~,' *UP*
62:3 displeased her *E1*] distressed her *MS*
62:5 sky!] ~? *UP*
63:4 dense,] ~ *UP*
63:12 Pleadingly,] ~ *UP*
63:12 tightly *MS*, *E1*] lightly *UP*

63:13 soft,] ~ *UP*
63:14 big,] ~ *UP*
63:14 whispered,] ~ *UP*
63:21 See,] ~! *UP*
63:29 him,] ~— *UP*
64:1 her,] ~ *UP*
64:14 being, Two-in-one, the *E1*] being, like a real God, Two-in-one, an angel, the *MS*
64:16 'Dreaming Women',] "dreaming women" *UP*
64:20 breast] ~, *UP*
64:24 her,] ~ *UP*
64:26 dream—] ~, *UP*
64:30 centuries,] ~ *UP*
64:31 'animal'] "~" *UP*
64:36 passively, subtly drew *E1*] passively, quite passively drew *MS*
65:2 he was her *UP*] he her *MS*
65:8 dear,] ~; *UP*
65:8 coaxed,] ~ *UP*
65:12 loth] loath *UP*
65:15 me— —] ~—— *UP*
65:19 forward] ~, *UP*
65:23 Siegmund] ~, *UP*
65:25 known...] ~.... *UP*
65:26 her] ~, *UP*
66:3 cottage,] ~ *UP*
66:4 sitting room] sitting-room *UP*
66:7 good looking] good-/looking *UP*
66:8 back...] ~.... *UP*
66:12 smile,] ~ *UP*
66:15 dress. "I] ~. *P* "I *UP*
66:16 Curtiss *E1*] Brinton *MS*
66:17 brought— —.] ~—— *UP*
66:18 answer,] ~ *UP*
66:20 a balked animal. *E1*] a wild animal at hunt. *MS*
66:21 bubbles,] ~— *UP*
66:24 swiftly, as sparks *E1*] swiftly, like sparks *MS*
66:29 him] ~, *UP*
67:1 tenderness,] ~ *UP*
67:4 love. *UP*] love them. *MS*
67:13 cloth] ~, *UP*
67:16 lamp-light] lamplight *UP*
67:17 sweet peas] sweet-peas *UP*
67:18 shoulders,] ~ *UP*
67:22 gentle,] ~; *UP*
67:32 out] ~, *UP*
67:35 coming] ~, *UP*
67:36 Curtiss' *E1*] Brinton's *MS*
67:37 Goodnight dear—Goodnight Sir] Good-night, dear—good-night, sir *UP*
68:2 arm-chair *Ed.*] arm chair *MS* armchair *UP*
68:6 asked,] ~ *UP*
68:18 time,] ~ *UP*
68:30 Curtiss *E1*] Brinton *MS*
68:32 Ah] ~, *UP*
68:32 you—] ~. *UP*
68:32 Goodnight!"—they] Good-night!" They *UP*
68:39 with desire *E1*] with fire *MS*
69:11 shone rosily. *E1*] shone like two long, soft flames. *MS*
69:17 arms] ~, *UP*
69:18 arm-chair] armchair *UP*
69:19 feverish] ~, *UP*
69:19 half hour] half-hour *UP*
69:25 said. *P* She] ~. She *UP*
69:26 him] ~, *UP*
69:26 her,] ~ *UP*
69:27 his stillness *E1*] his perfect stillness *MS*
69:28 him,] ~; *UP*
69:31 new,] ~ *UP*
69:37 still:] ~; *UP*
70:4 arm] ~, *UP*
70:12 sea, and the moonlight. *E1*] sea and the dark and white night. *MS*
70:14 Siegmund,] ~? *UP*
70:16 an easiness *E1*] a great easiness *MS*
70:18 moon-path *Ed.*] moonpath *MS*
70:19 land,] ~ *UP*
70:23 replied,] ~ *UP*
70:24 and rocking *E1*] and to be rocking *MS*
70:29 now] ~, *UP*
70:30 at home here, *E1*] at home in this night, *MS*
70:30 home,] ~ *UP*
70:35 night—] ~, *UP*
70:36 us—] ~, *UP*
70:36 rags.] ~? *UP*

70:37 want!] ~? *UP*
71:1 is a sort of mother *E1*] is mine for a mother *MS*
71:1 moon a...a brother: *E1*] moon for sister, and the stars for children, and sometimes, the sea for brother: *MS* moon for...sometimes the...brother: *UP*
71:5 among the moonlit *UP*] among moonlit *MS*
71:8 The key of the castle, *E1*] What more than what you are? *MS*
71:14 remained] ~, *UP*
71:16 together, gazing *E1*] together, with pale faces rising like a rock from their quivering, heaving breasts, and gazing *MS*
72:3 was,] ~; *UP*
72:4 Fairy tales] Fairy-tales *UP*
72:4 true] ~, *UP*
72:7 sleep drenched] sleep-drenched *UP*
72:10 window, as a *E1*] window, and a *MS*
72:18 cattle] ~, *UP*
72:20 window ledge] window-ledge *UP*
72:21 sleeping jacket] sleeping-jacket *UP*
72:26 sunshine] ~, *UP*
72:26 honeysuckle] honey-/suckle *UP*
72:27 woodbine,] ~ *UP*
73:1 headland. *Ed.*] head-land, dark with shadow. *MS* head-/land. *E1*
73:3 naked white] naked-white *UP*
73:5 bathing place] bathing-place *UP*
73:22 morning; he] ~. He *UP*
73:25 where] ~, *UP*
73:30 onto] on to *UP*
73:30 sand,] ~ *UP*
73:30 heart] ~, *UP*
73:30 brain] ~, *UP*
73:34 his body *E1*] his white, masculine body *MS*
73:37 wet] ~, *UP*
74:11 not,] ~; *UP*
74:12 baboon,] ~ *UP*
74:13 firm plating *E1*] firm, white plating *MS* firm white plating *UP*
74:15 long,] ~ *UP*
74:20 of a pink] of pink *UP*
74:20 But] ~, *UP*
74:20 Jove,] ~! *UP*
74:22 show...] ~.... *UP*
74:22 me—?] ~? *UP*
74:25 dining room] dining-room *UP*
74:29 bathed—?] ~? *UP*
74:32 said,] ~; *UP*
74:32 smelled] smelt *UP*
74:34 No—] ~; *UP*
74:34 what—?] ~—— *UP*
75:9 said,] ~ *UP*
75:9 sarcastically. Whistling] ~. P Whistling *UP*
75:11 asked,] ~ *UP*
75:14 Oh] ~, *UP*
75:17 said,] ~ *UP*
75:19 throat,] ~ *UP*
75:21 dark-faced] dark-/faced *UP*
75:24 things:] ~— *UP*
75:24 barbaric,] ~ *UP*
75:25 and pink *E1*] and small, pink *MS* and small pink *UP*
75:25 convolvuli,] ~; *UP*
75:25 flowers] ~, *UP*
75:26 dew] ~, *UP*
75:27 and fancy more than imagination. *E1*] and the detail more than the great morning. *MS*
75:32 lowest,] ~ *UP*
75:33 down:] ~; *UP*
75:34 in fancy *E1*] in fancy or fantasy *MS* in fancy of fantasy *UP*
75:36 fairies,] ~ *UP*
75:36 towzled...,] ~... *UP*
75:37 horns,] ~ *UP*
75:37 day fairies *Ed.*] day-fairies *MS*
75:39 Maidens] maidens *UP*
75:39 hair to sun] hair to the sun *UP*
76:2 stupid] ~, *UP*
76:8 cool] ~, *UP*
76:12 its own game *E1*] its own immense game *MS*
76:15 its passions *E1*] its great passions *MS*
76:17 bare-headed] bare headed *UP*

76:18 cornflowers, rather;] ~ ~, *UP*
76:20 grey,] ~ *UP*
76:21 stone,] ~ *UP*
76:25 sun] ~, *UP*
76:25 wind] ~, *UP*
76:26 herself,] ~ *UP*
76:27 that,] ~ *UP*
76:39 said,] ~; *UP*
77:2 Ah] ~, *UP*
77:8 so;—] ~; *UP*
77:9 psychically,] ~ *UP*
77:14 fence-in] fence in *UP*
77:15 indefinitely. He] ~. *P* He *UP*
77:17 Yes—] ~, *UP*
77:19 princesses—] ~, *UP*
77:19 things—] ~. *UP*
77:26 again,] ~ *UP*
77:27 edge] ~, *UP*
77:30 poetry,] ~ *UP*
77:34 fate] Fate *UP*
77:38 Death] death *UP*
77:38 her,] ~ *UP*
77:39 Sagas] sagas *UP*
77:39 grand] ~, *UP*
77:40 sweeping] ~, *UP*
78:1 sand,] ~ *UP*
78:2 all,] ~ *UP*
78:21 headland,] ~; *UP*
78:27 en route] *en route* *UP*
78:29 spheres] ~, *UP*
78:31 sea-bird] sea-/bird *UP*
78:37 sails—] ~—— *UP*
78:39 yes—] ~? *UP*
78:40 —That] ~ *UP*
78:40 schooner—you] ~. You *UP*
78:40 and— —.] ~—— *UP*
79:8 time—?] ~? *UP*
79:12 sun] ~, *UP*
79:12 sand] ~, *UP*
79:13 the flowers *E1*] the noon-day flowers *MS* the noonday flowers *UP*
79:14 shadows startled *E1*] shadows of clouds startled *MS*
79:16 Yes—] ~; *UP*
79:21 Yes,] ~; *UP*
79:24 real] ~, *UP*
79:24 manifest] ~, *UP*
79:28 lay] ~, *UP*
79:32 a half-dream *E1*] a blissful half-dream *MS*
79:34 sea] ~, *UP*
79:34 heart-beats] heart-/beats *UP*
79:35 island,] ~ *UP*
79:37 heart?—] ~? *UP*
79:38 Heart] heart *UP*
79:39 not:] ~, *UP*
81:3 shaggy,] ~ *UP*
81:13 the shore *E1*] the yielding shore *MS*
81:14 with chalk débris *E1*] with white débris *MS*
81:15 side,] ~ *UP*
81:18 a headland *E1*] a great headland *MS*
81:22 skins,] ~ *UP*
81:24 white-dashed] white-/dashed *MS*
81:27 over head] overhead *UP*
81:27 him,] ~— *UP*
82:1 the boulders *E1*] the white boulders *MS*
82:5 Really] ~, *UP*
82:8 sea:] ~; *UP*
82:9 great,] ~ *UP*
82:11 massed,] ~ *UP*
82:13 west. Smiling] ~. *P* Smiling *UP*
82:22 Then—?] ~? *UP*
82:22 then] ~, *UP*
82:22 suppose] ~, *UP*
82:22 teatime] tea-/time *UP*
82:26 said,] ~; *UP*
82:28 followed:] ~; *UP*
82:36 he [almost] laughed *Ed.*] he always laughed *MS see explanatory note*
82:37 silence,] ~; *UP*
83:5 this ledge,] this ridge, *UP*
83:6 them] ~, *UP*
83:7 furious,] ~; *UP*
83:7 two,] ~ *UP*
83:18 heart,] ~ *UP*
83:30 beach,] ~ *UP*
83:31 small figure *E1*] small, white figure *MS*
83:33 her,] ~ *UP*
83:34 young,] ~ *UP*

83:40 hillock,] ~ *UP*
84:15 that way *E1*] any way *MS*
84:19 combings,] ~ *UP*
84:20 electric-light] electric-/light *UP*
84:27 fine fingered] fine-fingered *UP*
84:36 said—] ~. *UP*
84:37 flap-flap flap] flap-flap-flap *UP*
84:38 pizzicato] *pizzicato* *UP*
84:38 sea—!] ~— *UP*
85:2 disagree,] ~ *UP*
85:17 this?—] ~? *UP*
85:19 eyes,] ~ *UP*
85:25 sea-weed] sea-/weed *UP*
85:26 fingers—!] ~— *UP*
85:31 had,] ~! *UP*
86:3 downlands] ~, *UP*
86:11 other,] ~ *UP*
86:14 humble-minded;] ~, *UP*
86:24 motion,] ~; *UP*
86:24 she rested on *E1*] she leaned on *MS*
87:3 happiness,] ~ *UP*
87:6 him:] ~, *UP*
87:8 That night...seemed blasted. *E1*] That night, she met his love with love as blazing as his own. They were not themselves, but transfigured in pure, fiery passion which they themselves merely held located, like the burning bush. They far transcended their own beings. It was a wonderful night to achieve. *MS* That night she... to achieve. *UP*
87:17 All,] All things, *UP*
87:18 was] were *UP*
87:19 texture;] ~, *UP*
87:25 shadow] ~, *UP*
87:39 feet fluttered *E1*] feet, two moths, fluttered *MS*
88:1 Siegmund,] ~? *UP*
88:6 water] ~, *UP*
88:14 the corner *E1*] the white corner *MS*
88:19 was pure as *E1*] was white as *MS*
88:20 archway,] ~ *UP*
88:21 glistening petal *E1*] glistening white petal *MS*
88:26 white,] ~ *UP*
88:28 breast] ~, *UP*
88:28 belly] ~, *UP*
88:31 the warm *E1*] the white, warm *MS*
88:32 sand:] ~; *UP*
88:34 Helena,] ~; *UP*
88:37 smooth,] ~ *UP*
88:38 surface,] ~ *UP*
88:39 end,] ~ *UP*
89:3 like a bee in a flower *E1*] like a white bee in a white flower *MS*
89:7 sand] ~, *UP*
89:10 child,] ~ *UP*
89:10 fair,] ~— *UP*
89:18 himself clean. *E1*] himself white. *MS*
89:23 free,] ~— *UP*
89:26 dirt of misery were *E1*] dirt of city years were *MS*
89:28 felt,] ~— *UP*
89:34 sideways] ~, *UP*
89:35 laburnum tree] laburnum-tree *UP*
89:38 grey:] ~; *UP*
90:1 antennae] antennæ *UP*
90:9 Siegmund was *E1*] Siegmund had come to her, and was *MS*
90:18 bay—just] ~, ~ *UP*
90:18 virgin bay—] ~ ~, *UP*
90:24 cliffs] ~, *UP*
90:27 and inscrutable. *E1*] and inscrutable as floating foam. *MS*
90:27 him:] ~; *UP*
90:27 earnest *UP*] ~, *MS*
90:38 joy] ~, *UP*
91:5 glad. *E1*] glad. Her softly heaving bosom could receive and hide his own agitation, so that he could rise bright, self-possessed. *MS*
92:3 chalk-roads] chalk roads *UP*
92:5 bare-headed] bareheaded *UP*
92:6 hearth,] ~ *UP*
92:7 scarlet,] ~ *UP*
92:7 like blood-drops *E1*] like lotus *MS*

92:11 Siegmund] ~, *UP*
92:15 heaven] ~, *UP*
92:17 them:] ~— *UP*
92:19 rockery] ~, *UP*
92:20 ragwort] ~, *UP*
92:21 overhead; among] ~. Among *UP*
92:27 ripples] ~, *UP*
92:27 beetles] ~, *UP*
93:5 eye.] eyes. *UP*
93:10 them,] ~ *UP*
93:13 preciously,] ~; *UP*
93:16 experience,] ~; *UP*
93:18 Helena,] ~; *UP*
93:18 on,] ~ *UP*
93:20 lightly,] ~ *UP*
93:24 spread] ~, *UP*
93:30 her. *E1*] her more gently and more beautifully even than the blue of the sea and the sky. *MS*
93:32 do. And] ~; and *UP*
93:37 hand. He] ~. *P* He *UP*
94:9 with blossoms of red anemones *E1*] with red blossoms of anemones *MS*
94:11 pebbles] ~, *UP*
94:18 stone] ~, *UP*
94:28 beneath,] ~— *UP*
94:29 cognisance] cognizance *UP*
94:32 inscrutable;] unscrutable, *UP*
95:1 Helena,] ~ *UP*
95:5 said,] ~ *UP*
95:10 wet," she] ~." She *UP*
95:12 finger-tips] finger-/tips *UP*
95:21 shout,] ~; *UP*
95:21 rushed barking] ~, ~, *UP*
95:23 Dadda] dadda *UP*
95:25 kitten,] ~ *UP*
95:28 Tissie,] ~; *UP*
95:28 on, have] ~; ~ *UP*
95:34 tiny as *E1*] tiny and forlorn, as *MS*
95:37 kitten and smiling. *E1*] kitten with a peculiar smile. *MS*
95:38 Crying because *E1*] Crying just because *MS*
96:1 I," he] ~." He *UP*
96:3 pinafores...] ~.... *UP*
96:5 why!] ~? *UP*
96:9 right,] ~ *UP*
96:10 waist deep] waist-deep *UP*
96:14 slowly,] ~; *UP*
97:3 cross *Ed.*] Cross *MS*
97:3 downs] ~, *UP*
97:6 copses,] ~— *UP*
97:10 sign-post] signpost *UP*
97:11 dusk,] ~ *UP*
97:14 higher,] ~ *UP*
97:14 a bearskin *E1*] a black bearskin *MS*
97:17 chalk pit] chalk-pit *UP*
97:18 farm-house] farmhouse *UP*
97:26 Siegmund. *E1*] Siegmund; a black wall of prickles. *MS* Siegmund—a...prickles. *UP*
97:27 said he, *E1*] said Siegmund, *MS*
97:29 the walls *E1*] the black-caved walls *MS* the black carved walls *UP*
97:30 farm-house] farmhouse *UP*
97:32 road-way] roadway *UP*
98:3 seemed only *UP*] seemed to only *MS*
98:8 rabbit run] rabbit-run *UP*
98:10 mole-hill— —] ~, *UP*
98:10 he quoted mockingly. *E1*] quoted Siegmund, mockingly. *MS* quoted Siegmund mockingly. *UP*
98:14 honeysuckle *Ed.*] honey-suckle *MS*
98:14 bracken-scent] bracken scent *UP*
98:18 I would not *E1*] I could not *MS*
98:21 thigh. *E1*] thigh. It hurt, but he did not stir. *MS*
98:23 round— —] ~. *UP*
98:33 time we take *E1*] time we are swinging in our tide, Sieglinde, and we take *MS* time...tide, Helena,...take *UP*
99:1 separate:] ~; *UP*
99:2 all in a symphony *E1*] all swimming and shining and marching in a symphony *MS*
99:2 motive,] ~ *UP*

99:5 this,] ~— *UP*
99:8 murmured,] ~— *UP*
99:9 bright—] ~ *UP*
99:10 beyond!] ~. *UP*
99:19 hazel-nuts *UP*] hazel-/nuts *MS*
99:19 opium— —] ~.... *UP*
99:22 murmured,] ~ *UP*
99:25 them."—] ~." *UP*
99:26 still—] ~. *UP*
99:28 about—,"—then] ~." Then *UP*
99:29 him—] ~: *UP*
99:32 her,] ~ *UP*
99:33 stars,] ~ *UP*
99:34 constellations;] ~, *UP*
99:34 plants:] ~. *UP*
99:37 on,] ~— *UP*
99:38 here,] ~ *UP*
100:6 'Carpe diem'] *Carpe diem UP*
100:7 Hell] hell *UP*
100:8 Hell] hell *UP*
100:9 'postero'.] *postero. UP*
100:10 Day] day *UP*
100:10 Rose] rose *UP*
100:12 in quick] in a quick *UP*
100:15 matter!—] ~? *UP*
100:20 stars. He bent *E1*] stars. His eyes were steady, smiling a strange calm and assurance: yet he was pained by her tears. He bent *MS* stars. His...assurance; yet... He bent *UP see explanatory note*
100:23 hers *UP*] her's *MS*
100:23 hair,] ~ *UP*
100:24 his face burn *E1*] his salt cheek burn *MS*
100:25 asked,] ~ *UP*
100:25 last, "why] ~. "Why *UP*
100:28 you] ~, *UP*
100:29 I!] ~? *UP*
101:1 what he thought] what she thought *UP*
101:3 something,] ~ *UP*
101:5 an unreasonable *UP*] a unreasonable *MS*
101:5 obsession,] ~ *UP*
101:15 farm-house] farmhouse *UP*
101:16 shone on the] shone in the *UP*
101:18 stars:] ~; *UP*
101:23 Meer— —.] ~... *UP*
101:24 was very fond] was fond *UP*
101:34 Weihnachtsgaben— —.] ~... *UP*
101:35 and he *E1*] and Siegmund *MS*
102:2 unfelt] ~, *UP*
102:4 gates.] ~: *UP*
102:9 moon lifted slowly *UP*] Moon lifted herself slowly *MS*
102:10 aloud,] ~ *UP*
102:11 sing-song *Ed.*] singsong *MS*
102:14 sing-song] singsong *UP*
102:14 tone; he] ~. He *UP*
102:19 forehead,] ~ *UP*
102:20 mystery,] ~ *UP*
102:21 said to herself, curiously *E1*] said, curiously *MS*
102:22 joyous:] ~. *UP*
102:24 bridegroom] bride-/groom *UP*
102:24 flesh-petalled *UP*] flesh-/petalled *MS*
102:25 Siegmund;] ~— *UP*
102:26 magic-land] magic land *UP*
102:27 ecstasy,] ~ *UP*
102:29 heavily:] ~; *UP*
102:38 in you—] ~ ~, *UP*
102:38 dear—] ~, *UP*
102:38 wonderlove] wonder-love *UP*
102:39 Siegmund—"] ~!" *UP*
103:1 slow,] ~ *UP*
103:2 drops,] ~ *UP*
103:4 Rocked thus on *E1*] Swinging thus gently on *MS*
103:8 death,] ~! *UP*
103:14 breath,] ~ *UP*
103:15 him,] ~— *UP*
103:16 for ever. *E1*] for good. *MS*
103:18 too: "No] to—"no *UP*
103:23 her,] ~ *UP*
103:24 murmured "Hawwa,] ~: "Hawwa *UP*
103:25 him,] ~ *UP*
103:27 woman] ~, *UP*
103:31 he dreamed *UP*] his dreamed *MS*
104:3 hillside *UP*] hill-side *MS*

104:6 he said *E1*] said Siegmund *MS*
104:12 still,] ~ *UP*
104:15 moon-path *Ed.*] moon path *MS*
104:15 down hill] downhill *UP*
104:16 joyously] ~, *UP*
104:20 lightly,] ~ *UP*
104:23 anguish,] ~ *UP*
104:25 phrases] ~, *UP*
104:26 Betweenwhiles *Ed.*] Between-/whiles *MS* Between whiles *UP*
104:28 also,] ~ *UP*
104:30 down hill] downhill *UP*
104:32 over,] ~ *UP*
105:3 body,] ~— *UP*
105:18 sickness] ~, *UP*
105:18 was,—] ~— *UP*
105:25 lost,] ~! *UP*
105:27 her,] ~ *UP*
105:29 No, see] ~. See *UP*
105:29 emotion,—] ~— *UP*
105:32 Well] ~, *UP*
105:34 down] ~, *UP*
105:35 clouds,] ~ *UP*
105:37 alone:] ~; *UP*
106:1 another,] ~— *UP*
106:1 glamourous *Ed.*] glamorous *MS* glamorous, *UP*
106:3 I have lived too intensely *E1*] I have housed too many *MS*
106:9 here—] ~, *UP*
106:14 wine,] ~ *UP*
106:16 along his limbs] along the limbs *UP*
106:32 said,] ~ *UP*
106:37 experience:] ~— *UP*
106:38 Brünnhilde] Brünhild *E1*
106:40 Freshwater.] ~? *UP*
107:3 moon-lit] moonlit *UP*
107:6 miles." She] ~." *P* She *UP*
107:7 wandered;] ~, *UP*
107:8 night,] ~ *UP*
107:18 night:] ~; *UP*
107:19 hinterlandt] hinterland *UP*
107:22 dream-faces *UP*] dream-/faces *MS*
107:23 windows:] ~; *UP*
107:25 fancy of wayward *E1*] fancy of the wayward *MS*
107:31 dark eyed] dark-eyed *UP*
107:32 grey-grass,] grey grass *UP*
107:35 way,] ~— *UP*
107:36 her. She] ~; she *UP*
107:39 burial ground] burial-ground *UP*
107:40 silver-grey] silver-/grey *UP*
108:3 years Life] ~' life *UP*
108:4 ecstasy,—] ~— *UP*
108:5 same:] ~; *UP*
108:6 his] His *UP*
108:8 sad] ~, *UP*
108:8 fault] ~, *UP*
108:9 Life] life *UP*
108:13 it. It] ~; it *UP*
108:15 tragedy...] ~! *UP*
108:29 night. So] ~, so *UP*
108:30 high road] highroad *UP*
109:2 sea-wall] sea wall *UP*
109:6 battle-ships *Ed.*] battleships *MS*
109:6 monsters] ~, *UP*
109:7 sea-lions] sea-/lions *UP*
109:8 half stupid] half-stupid *UP*
109:10 from? Do] ~; do *UP*
109:10 Sir] sir *UP*
109:11 thirty five years *Ed.*] thirty years *MS* thirty-five years *E1*
109:12 battle-ships *Ed.*] battleships *MS*
109:13 war?—there] ~? There *UP*
109:13 at Spithead *E1*] in the Spithead *MS*
109:18 us.] ~! *UP*
109:20 anarchist] Anarchist *UP*
109:20 hope,] ~? *UP*
109:21 nihilist] Nihilist *UP*
109:22 love—No—] ~. ~; *UP*
109:24 ironmongery!— *E1*] ~— *MS*
109:26 battle-ships *Ed.*] battleships *MS*
109:33 brow] ~, *UP*
109:33 the bare *E1*] the full, bare *MS*
109:34 interlocutor. *P* "Does] ~. "Does *UP*
110:3 penetrating gaze *Ed.*] penetrating, intimate gaze *MS* penetrating, gaze *E1*
110:4 us,] ~? *UP*
110:13 Name Hampson—] name, ~ —— *UP*

110:21 re-acquainted *E1*] acquainted *MS*

110:26 replied *E1*] flashed *MS* flushed *UP*

110:27 this,] ~ *UP*

110:35 leak'?] ~?' *UP*

110:37 House] house *UP*

111:1 God,] ~! *UP*

111:2 soul—] ~, *UP*

111:2 brain,] ~! *UP*

111:4 mean Sir] ~, sir *UP*

111:6 House—] ~, *UP*

111:7 say] ~, *UP*

111:7 rooms—.] ~—— *UP*

111:8 Blue Room] blue room *UP*

111:10 Hampson—] ~; *UP*

111:12 I! *Ed.*] ~? *MS see explanatory notes*

111:13 it—?] ~! *UP*

111:16 leper, and *E1*] leper like fury—and *MS* leper like fury, and *UP*

111:22 man:] ~. *UP*

111:23 work. But] ~ ; but *UP*

111:25 soul-experience] soul experience *UP*

111:32 semi transparent] semi-transparent *UP*

112:6 married,] ~ *UP*

112:7 didn't,] ~; *UP*

112:9 critically:] ~. *UP*

112:10 woman,] ~; *UP*

112:15 We] ~, *UP*

112:17 the unrealised] their unrealized *UP*

112:18 great potential *E1*] great inert potential *MS* great inert, potential *UP*

112:19 Source] source *UP*

112:22 *us*:] ~; *UP*

112:24 us. Therefore] ~; therefore *UP*

112:31 what.] ~! *UP*

112:32 sane,] ~; *UP*

112:32 myself.] ~! *UP*

112:34 do—] ~, *UP*

112:34 everybody. But] ~; but *UP*

112:36 them. And] ~; and *UP*

113:4 refuted] refused *UP*

113:9 self love] self-love *UP*

113:12 it—] ~; *UP*

113:14 loves] loved *UP*

113:14 extremity.] ~? *UP*

113:17 women,] ~! *UP*

113:19 quick. But] ~; but *UP*

113:20 life:] ~; *UP*

113:27 normal.—] ~. *UP*

113:28 hot—" he] ~." He *UP*

113:28 his flannel *E1*] his fine flannel *MS*

113:31 Directly,] ~ *UP*

113:32 his gay *E1*] his poignantly gay *MS*

114:6 wings] ~, *UP*

114:7 flew...] ~.... *UP*

114:13 said.] ~, *UP*

114:16 drowned. But] ~; but *UP*

114:19 nonsense!—] ~! *UP*

114:25 bare] ~, *UP*

114:26 waiting!] ~, *UP*

114:27 Well—] ~, *UP*

115:1 days—] ~; *UP*

115:6 now!—] ~! *UP*

115:6 battle-ships *Ed.*] battleships *MS*

115:7 distinctly.—] ~. *UP*

115:8 today—?] to-day? *UP*

115:12 morning, oh] ~; "~, *UP*

115:12 motherly.] ~! *UP*

115:17 tone] ~, *UP*

115:19 eleven,] ~? *UP*

115:21 again—Oh] ~. ~ *UP*

115:21 again—really. *Ed.*] ~—~.. *MS* ~, ~. *UP*

115:24 feel', *Ed.*] ~'.. *MS* ~,' *UP*

115:25 rooms,] ~ *UP*

115:26 step-mother,] ~ *UP*

115:27 affair. But] ~; but *UP*

115:28 himself,] ~ *UP*

115:30 *mind*,] ~ *UP*

116:1 laughed,] ~ *UP*

116:4 myself,] ~ *UP*

116:4 world— —] ~—— *UP*

116:11 said. *E1*] said piteously. *MS*

116:13 arms...] ~.... *UP*

116:17 sun-soaking:] sun-/soaking; *UP*

116:26 life time] lifetime *UP*

116:29 was,] ~— *UP*

116:31 strong shouldered] strong-shouldered *UP*
116:34 assertive; one] ~. One *UP*
116:35 means,] ~ *UP*
117:5 hat] ~, *UP*
117:8 paths,] ~ *UP*
117:24 instant,] ~ *UP*
117:25 farming,] ~ *UP*
117:32 mind,] ~ *UP*
117:34 asked,] ~ *UP*
117:40 us.—] ~. *UP*
118:6 bird-music] bird music *UP*
118:7 "Siegfried," *Ed.*] '~,' *MS Siegfried, UP*
118:7 "Tristan." *Ed.*] ~. *MS Tristan. UP*
118:17 clapping,] ~ *UP*
118:19 him,] ~ *UP*
118:24 Vaguely,] ~ *UP*
118:30 which lay *E1*] which now lay *MS*
118:33 him,] ~ *UP*
118:35 instead] ~, *UP*
118:37 hen] ~, *UP*
119:1 helpless,] ~ *UP*
119:6 slope] ~, *UP*
119:7 hill,] ~ *UP*
119:10 "'And *UP*] "~ *MS*
119:10 sea,'" *UP*] ~," *MS*
119:12 thought,] ~ *UP*
119:18 said,] ~; *UP*
119:18 impossible.] ~! *UP*
119:19 out—] ~, *UP*
119:21 us,] ~— *UP*
119:23 sun-furnace] sun furnace *UP*
119:26 ice-crystals] ice-/crystals *UP*
119:27 seemed unconscious *E1*] seemed so unconscious *MS*
119:29 said,] ~. *UP*
119:37 'failed] "~ *UP*
119:37 her'—] ~," *UP*
119:37 it—,] ~, *UP*
119:39 this journey *E1*] this time *MS*
120:1 Ay,] ~! *UP*
120:1 Siegmund,] ~ *UP*
120:4 more,] ~ *UP*
120:21 short,] ~ *UP*
120:28 sea-weed] seaweed *UP*
120:29 life-tide] life tide *UP*
120:37 Mist-Spirit,] Mist Spirit, *UP*
120:37 Mist-Spirit] Mist Spirit *UP*
120:38 us,] ~— *UP*
120:39 thin] ~, *UP*
120:39 Mist-Spirit] Mist Spirit *UP*
120:40 again:] ~. *UP*
120:40 outside:] ~. *UP*
121:4 dear?—] ~? *UP*
121:8 he too] ~, ~, *UP*
121:12 be.] ~? *UP*
121:13 along,] ~ *UP*
121:17 wondrous,] ~ *UP*
121:17 Master-Fate] master, Fate, *UP* Master-Fate, *E1*
122:6 without the shape] without shape *UP*
122:10 thought-ripple] thought-/ripple *UP*
122:11 copper-coloured] copper-/coloured *UP*
122:16 eastwards,] ~ *UP*
122:20 Somehow,] ~ *UP*
122:21 self-discovery *Ed.*] self discovery *MS*
122:24 Egypt—her] ~. Her *UP*
122:32 about with the *E1*] about in the *MS*
122:34 bad looking] bad-looking *UP*
123:9 smoking room] smoking-room *UP*
123:14 chin,] ~! *UP*
123:15 *solide.*] ~! *UP*
123:20 that: see] ~. See *UP*
123:22 Ah *si si*!] ~, ~, ~! *UP*
123:26 to have *UP*] to be have *MS*
123:28 Ha—ha—] ~, ~! *UP*
123:31 air:] ~; *UP*
123:32 great,] ~ *UP*
123:33 dead] ~— *UP*
124:1 romance—] ~. *UP*
124:7 birth] ~, *UP*
124:7 adolescence] ~, *UP*
124:11 corner,] ~ *UP*
124:19 edge,] ~ *UP*
124:19 answer:] ~, *UP*
124:22 fancies;] ~, *UP*
124:22 finally] ~— *UP*

124:27 see the reality. *E1*] see great halls of dignity. *MS*
124:33 downs,] ~ *UP*
125:6 ash:] ~, *UP*
125:6 herself,] ~ *UP*
125:11 force:] ~; *UP*
125:11 embraced,] ~ *UP*
125:15 Life,] ~ *UP*
125:18 there, surely] ~. Surely *UP*
125:18 help.] ~? *UP*
125:18 re-kindle] rekindle *UP*
125:19 ahead] ~, *UP*
125:20 "Walküre." *Ed.*] ~. *MS* *Die Walküre.* *UP*
125:21 thick-shouldered] thick-/shouldered *UP*
125:28 stupidly:] ~— *UP*
125:28 'clothed] "~ *UP*
125:29 end,'] ~," *UP*
125:31 own,] ~ *UP*
125:34 Siegmund,] ~! *UP*
125:40 her,] ~— *UP*
126:6 free,] ~ *UP*
126:9 it?—won't] ~? Won't *UP*
126:13 this brute, blind *E1*] this strong, blind *MS*
126:13 'thud] ~ *UP*
126:14 thud.'] ~. *UP*
126:15 us—have] ~? Have *UP*
126:15 anything—have] ~? Have *UP*
126:16 me, at] ~—~ *UP*
126:19 face:] ~; *UP*
126:19 struggled,] ~ *UP*
126:20 him:] ~; *UP*
126:22 go, let] ~! Let *UP*
126:22 go.] ~! *UP*
126:23 chest,] ~ *UP*
126:25 away,] ~ *UP*
126:26 him,] ~ *UP*
126:31 Helena, tell] ~; ~ *UP*
126:31 is.—] ~. *UP*
126:35 in. Quite still, he *E1*] in. White and without a movement in his body, he *MS*
126:40 heart 'It] ~, "~ *UP*
126:40 enough.'] ~." *UP*
127:2 openness;] ~, *UP*
127:7 go:] ~, *UP*
127:7 again,] ~ *UP*
127:10 life-animation] life animation *UP*
127:16 Now,] ~ *UP*
127:21 himself,] ~ *UP*
127:21 minute,] ~ *UP*
127:24 He drew himself *E1*] He wrenched himself *MS*
127:26 me] ~, *UP*
127:28 and: *P* "Siegmund] ~ "Siegmund *UP*
127:33 half luminous] half-/luminous *UP*
127:35 one] ~, *UP*
127:40 delicately,] ~ *UP*
128:4 sea like] sea-like *UP*
128:12 'an infant] "~ ~ *UP*
128:12 night,'] ~," *UP*
128:13 soul. He *E1*] soul. She must not stand between him and the stars, nor hide from him the preparation of the sky for night-worship. He *MS*
129:6 it,] ~ *UP*
129:10 her,] ~ *UP*
129:19 humility,] ~ *UP*
129:24 'Madonna'] ~ *UP*
129:31 renewal,] ~— *UP*
130:5 long pale line *E1*] long, white line *MS* long white line *UP*
130:5 black,] ~ *UP*
130:8 yet,] ~ *UP*
130:9 cliff,] ~ *UP*
130:12 light along *E1*] light which came along *MS*
130:12 to their *E1*] to touch their *MS*
130:16 the star-track *E1*] the white star-track *MS*
130:23 answered,] ~ *UP*
130:25 see] ~, *UP*
130:27 touched— —] ~.... *UP*
130:28 shrank,] ~ *UP*
130:31 — — —a] ...A *UP*
131:1 confession—] ~, *UP*
131:5 you— —] ~—— *UP*
131:6 grievous,] ~ *UP*
131:10 chest,] ~ *UP*
131:15 so] ~, *UP*

131:16 repeated; "—and] ~. "And *UP*
131:17 fool.] ~! *UP*
131:32 passed,] ~ *UP*
131:32 silhouette,] ~ *UP*
132:4 Don't] ~, *UP*
132:18 back.] ~? *UP*
132:21 think] ~, *UP*
132:22 not,] ~! *UP*
132:25 now—.] ~.... *UP*
132:33 sand,] ~ *UP*
132:39 doctor,] ~ *UP*
133:8 Wildly,] ~ *UP*
133:9 day,] ~ *UP*
133:9 Anything,] ~ *UP*
133:11 fear,] ~ *UP*
133:12 started,] ~ *UP*
133:14 gold come *UP*] gold came *MS*
133:19 tip be *E1*] tip of the horn be *MS*
133:20 him. Then] ~; then *UP*
133:21 drinking-cup *UP*] drinking-/cup *MS*
133:23 sea,] ~— *UP*
133:28 there] ~, *UP*
133:28 night] ~, *UP*
133:30 up into myself *E1*] up myself *MS*
134:7 gently,] ~ *UP*
134:10 wore,] ~ *UP*
134:16 down-cast] down-/cast *UP*
134:17 down,] ~ *UP*
134:20 cliff-tops] cliff tops *UP*
134:22 battle-ships] battleships *UP*
134:22 gone,] ~; *UP*
134:23 panier] *panier* *UP*
134:23 diamonds,] ~; *UP*
134:23 tenderness,] ~ *UP*
134:24 the affection..."We have been] the affection that existed between him and everything. The world is a family that long familiarity has blinded. We do not realise how tremendously dear and indispensable to us are the hosts of common things, till we must leave them, and we break our hearts. The morning was slipping into Siegmund's purse the fair coin of love, to speed him. *P* "We have been *MS*
134:32 As he] So he *UP*
134:32 beach] ~; *UP*
135:2 soul." He] ~." *P* He *UP*
135:3 gently,] ~ *UP*
135:15 headlands. They] ~; they *UP*
135:17 fan-tail] fantail *UP*
135:20 swimming] ~, *UP*
135:21 tide,] ~; *UP*
135:22 magic at *E1*] magic place at *MS*
135:23 little bay *E1*] little white bay *MS*
135:24 emerald-facets] emerald facets *UP*
135:26 foot. They] ~; they *UP*
135:29 sea-girls] ~, *UP*
135:30 hair] ~, *UP*
135:33 gate,] ~ *UP*
135:37 jewel-stained *UP*] jewel-/stained *MS*
135:38 inward-curving *UP*] inward-/curving *MS*
135:38 rock. His] ~; his *UP*
135:39 and he *E1*] and Siegmund *MS*
136:6 however, *Ed.*] ~ *MS*
136:10 Nevertheless] ~, *UP*
136:14 sea-shore] seashore *UP*
136:26 same. They] ~; they *UP*
136:28 death.] ~: *UP*
136:32 gate." *P* "Why *UP*] ~."/"Why *MS*
136:34 Oh Lord] ~, ~! *UP*
136:37 the puff *E1*] the white puff *MS*
136:38 the pride of his maturity *E1*] the handsome pride of his just perfect maturity *MS*
137:1 Gone] ~, *UP*
137:1 of steam *E1*] of white steam *MS*
137:5 warm sand *E1*] warm white sand *MS*
137:6 count.] ~; *UP*
137:8 while,] ~ *UP*
137:11 'Better] "~ *UP*
137:12 lion'—] ~," *UP*
137:15 Helena meanwhile] ~, ~, *UP*
137:15 bathing] ~, *UP*
137:15 time] ~, *UP*
137:16 sea-shore] seashore *UP*

137:24 true,] ~; *UP*
137:26 he, sometimes,] ~ ~ *UP*
137:28 rock-pools. They] ~; they *UP*
137:28 docile:] ~; *UP*
137:31 laughed,] ~ *UP*
137:33 retreated,] ~ *UP*
137:33 cave,] ~ *UP*
137:34 bladder-wrack] bladder-/wrack *UP*
137:35 stones,] ~; *UP*
137:36 bending] ~, *UP*
137:37 sea-weed *Ed.*] seaweed *MS*
137:38 stones:] ~; *UP*
138:9 me,] ~! *UP*
138:17 thank offering] thank-/offering *UP*
138:17 his white] His ~ *UP*
138:18 his fire] His ~ *UP*
138:22 Helena,—] ~; *UP*
138:27 wonderful, here,] ~ ~! *UP*
138:27 she. But] ~; but *UP*
138:32 gone] ~, *UP*
138:36 his eyes were full of misery. *E1*] his eyes were like two caves where the water ran in the dark, and the weeds waved cold. *MS*
138:39 expected—" she] ~" —~ *UP*
138:40 Eros—] ~ *UP*
139:11 said, 'It] ~: "~ *UP*
139:11 morning, it] ~; ~ *UP*
139:12 delight.'] ~." *UP*
139:15 white dog. *E1*] white dog on the downs—. *MS* white...downs. *UP*
139:20 you!] ~? *UP*
139:21 pool] ~, *UP*
139:26 departure. He] ~. *P* He *UP*
139:27 3.45] three forty-/five *UP*
139:31 something] ~, *UP*
139:33 head] ~, *UP*
139:34 dear—?] ~, *UP*
139:34 repeated. He] ~. *P* He *UP*
139:37 said. She] ~. *P* She *UP*
140:2 cost *E1*] costs *MS*
140:5 everything, *E1*] everything, Sieglinde, *MS* everything, Helena! *UP*
141:7 hearth-rug] hearth rug *UP*
141:9 ease,] ~ *UP*
141:11 was," assented *E1*] was," warmly assented *MS*
141:15 No—] ~, *UP*
141:22 said,] ~ *UP*
141:32 get. But] ~; but *UP*
142:1 him] ~, *UP*
142:6 Island *UP*] island *MS*
142:16 said—] ~. *UP*
142:18 enemies—?] ~? *UP*
142:21 "mot."] *mot. UP*
142:25 mantel-piece *Ed.*] mantel piece *MS* mantelpiece *UP*
142:25 counted—"One-two-three-four-five] ~: "One, two, three, four, five *UP*
143:5 flowers, so gay and evanescent, had *E1*] flowers, that are gay and evanescent as butterflies, had *MS*
143:6 yew tree] yew-tree *UP*
143:6 rough *UP*] ~, *MS*
143:9 fairies' telephones?"]'~' ~?'" *UP*
143:13 sunshine.] ~! *UP*
143:15 dowdy...] ~.... *UP*
143:16 day— —!] ~... *UP*
143:24 own,] ~ *UP*
143:28 himself,] ~ *UP*
143:28 said: *P* "She] ~: "She *UP*
143:29 incommunicable,] ~; *UP*
143:30 So,] ~ *UP*
143:31 rock-pool *Ed.*] rock pool *MS*
143:33 indispensable...] ~.... *UP*
144:1 bungalow. *E1*] bungalow surprising that rough place. *MS*
144:3 scarlet] ~, *UP*
144:3 yellow] ~, *UP*
144:4 flowers,] ~ *UP*
144:11 Amy!!] Amy! *UP*
144:14 dining room] dining-room *UP*
144:17 Helena,] ~ *UP*
144:29 breakfast-table,] breakfast table! *UP*
144:33 him winsomely *E1*] him very winsomely *MS*
144:37 like a wound. *E1*] like a wound under the feathers of a bird. *MS*
144:37 hemorrhage] hæmorrhage *UP*

144:38 self-esteem] self-/esteem *UP*
144:40 Yesterday,] ~ *UP*
145:1 lover] ~, *UP*
145:3 himself. "At] ~—"at *UP*
145:6 And] ~, *UP*
145:7 Island] island *UP*
145:10 Island] island *UP*
145:11 dirt: what] ~. What *UP*
145:11 do?] ~?" *UP*
145:13 used,] ~— *UP*
145:16 Yes—] ~, *UP*
145:17 you,] ~— *UP*
145:20 'Fumum et opes strepitumque Romae'] *Fumum et opes strepitumque Romæ UP*
145:21 Helena. *P* "I] ~. "I *UP*
145:22 right!] ~, *UP*
145:24 calmly—"For] ~, "for *UP*
145:28 Helena,"] ~" *UP*
145:29 again—,] ~— *UP*
145:34 before— — —] ~ . . . *UP*
145:39 rest. *P* "No] ~. "No *UP*
146:2 mist-curtain *UP*] mist curtain *MS*
146:2 is—"] ~ "—*UP*
146:7 golden bits] gold bits *UP*
146:15 exhausted:] ~; *UP*
146:17 heart,] ~ *UP*
146:21 reason] ~, *UP*
146:21 dialectics] ~, *UP*
146:33 clover-head] clover-/head *UP*
146:37 The light *E1*] The white light *MS*
146:38 heat-entrancement] heat entrancement *UP*
147:2 vigorous:] ~; *UP*
147:10 on,] ~ *UP*
147:12 bare-headed] ~, *UP*
147:16 ill."—] ~." *UP*
147:20 terrible] ~, *UP*
147:20 water—?] ~? *UP*
147:21 cliff-path] cliff path *UP*
147:22 the hot *E1*] the white, hot *MS*
147:22 sand] ~, *UP*
147:24 rocks,] ~? *UP*
147:25 Look,] ~! *UP*
147:28 plash,] splash; *UP*
147:33 Siegmund?—] ~? *UP*
147:37 harm. But] ~, but *UP*
147:40 if—"] ~ "— *UP*
147:41 you." Some *Ed.*] ~.." Some *MS* ~ . . ." *P* Some *UP*
148:1 of despair in his quietness, made *E1*] of intense despair in his quietness, his wistfulness, made *MS*
148:8 I Helena *Ed.*] I Sieglinde *MS* I, Helena *UP*
148:9 able,] ~! *UP*
148:18 safely:] ~; *UP*
148:24 bees] ~, *UP*
148:25 sea,] ~ *UP*
148:28 stronger,] ~ *UP*
148:29 struck. *E1*] struck. Further off, still flying and singing a now inaudible song, was that bird of Fate which he hunted. *MS see explanatory notes*
148:30 fox-glove] foxglove *UP*
148:33 body] ~, *UP*
149:2 dark— —] ~ . . . *UP*
149:10 then—!] ~ . . . *UP*
149:10 her:] ~; *UP*
149:14 last,] ~ *UP*
149:19 gently,] ~ *UP*
149:32 said,] ~ *UP*
149:32 distress. He] ~. *P* He *UP*
149:33 water. Helena *Ed.*] water. Sieglinde *MS* water. *P* Helena *UP*
150:3 hers,] ~. *UP*
150:5 surprised,] ~— *UP*
150:8 half past] half-past *UP*
150:15 much— —] ~— *UP*
150:16 the sand *E1*] the velvet sand *MS*
150:16 sun-dimmed] sun-/dimmed *UP*
150:17 back;] ~! *UP*
150:19 cliff-path] cliff path *UP*
150:22 sea-weed *UP*] sea weed *MS*
150:28 enjoyed:] ~, *UP*
150:29 and] ~, *UP*
150:31 'Traviata' *Ed.*] ~ *MS*
150:33 irony:] ~; *UP*
150:35 Addi-i-i-o,] ~! *UP*
150:39 discord,] ~— *UP*
151:3 South Western] South-Western *UP*
151:3 Portsmouth,] ~ *UP*

151:5 why!" *Ed.*] ~!", *MS* ~?" *UP*
151:7 you!"] ~?" *UP*
151:12 post-office,] ~ *UP*
151:17 meaning 'should] ~, ~ *UP*
151:17 Beatrice.'] ~. *UP*
151:19 so, *UP*] ~ .. *MS*
151:35 is Sir] ~, sir *UP*
151:37 him,] ~ *UP*
151:38 sign:] ~; *UP*
151:39 inscrutable:] ~, *UP*
152:2 back:] ~. *UP*
152:4 postcards *UP*] post-cards *MS*
152:6 these...] ~? *UP*
152:7 faded looking] faded-looking *UP*
152:8 Bay,] ~ *UP*
152:12 brush—",] ~," *UP*
152:14 would understand. *E1*] would have understood. *MS*
152:16 her,] ~ *UP*
152:17 hated her. *E1*] hated her: she did not understand. *MS* hated her. She...understand. *UP*
153:2 other,] ~ *UP*
153:3 faces] ~, *UP*
153:4 dead-asleep] dead asleep *UP*
153:5 past,] ~ *UP*
153:7 think] ~, *UP*
153:10 humanity] ~, *UP*
153:12 him,] ~ *UP*
153:13 Faces,] ~ *UP*
153:13 innumerable] ~— *UP*
153:14 faces] ~— *UP*
153:27 eyes;] ~, *UP*
153:33 good-humoured *Ed.*] good humoured *MS* good-/humoured *UP*
153:33 remark,] ~ *UP*
154:3 'Billy',] "~" *UP*
154:7 everything:] ~; *UP*
154:9 was a *E1*] was an admirable *MS*
154:9 raconteur] *raconteur* *UP*
154:12 Helena,—] ~— *UP*
154:14 said,] ~ — *UP*
154:15 sorry: I am sorry:] ~. ~ ~ ~. *UP*
154:19 me;—] ~, *UP*
154:24 corn:] ~; *UP*
154:25 raconteur] *raconteur* *UP*
154:35 helpless: this] ~. This *UP*
154:37 him,] ~ *UP*
154:38 understand;] ~, *UP*
155:3 fire, and *E1*] fire, as a choking, inflammable gas will do, and *MS*
155:10 beforehand.] ~? *UP*
155:12 life.] "~." *UP*
155:12 on,] ~ *UP*
155:14 When] when *UP*
155:17 then—?] ~? *UP*
155:19 then—?] ~? *UP*
155:22 die, of *E1*] die herself, of *MS*
155:28 Euclid;] ~, *UP*
155:31 him] ~, *UP*
155:34 strange] ~, *UP*
155:35 silkiness: often] ~. Often *UP*
156:10 steadiness,] ~ *UP*
157:5 of tall *E1*] of white tall *MS* *see explanatory notes*
157:7 window-lights] window lights *UP*
157:9 Siegmund] ~, *UP*
157:11 onto] on to *UP*
157:17 soft,] ~ *UP*
157:18 back ground] background *UP*
157:18 men of war] men-of-war *UP*
157:23 it. *E1*] it all. *MS*
157:30 brown-sailed *UP*] brown-/sailed *MS*
158:3 bows:] ~; *UP*
158:7 the dog *E1*] the white dog *MS*
158:13 startled] ~, *UP*
158:13 face,] ~; *UP*
158:16 bows:] ~; *UP*
158:21 dark haired] dark-haired *UP*
158:28 movements:] ~; *UP*
158:31 hands,] ~ *UP*
158:32 emotion. She *E1*] emotion. Siegmund sighed. She *MS*
158:39 bad,] ~! *UP*
159:3 a close shave *E1*] a near shave *MS*
159:7 Ah] ~, *UP*
159:8 them.] ~! *UP*
159:8 his] His *UP*
159:13 sea-mew] sea-/mew *UP*

159:14 steam-boats] steam-/boats *UP*
159:16 me,] ~ *UP*
159:19 the interspaces *E1*] the blue interspaces *MS*
159:19 atmosphere] ~, *UP*
159:20 darkness,] ~ *UP*
159:24 darkness] ~, *UP*
159:26 least] ~, *UP*
160:1 judgment,] ~— *UP*
160:6 'But] "But *UP*
160:6 all,'] ~," *UP*
160:7 'I] "~ *UP*
160:9 exoneration.'] ~." *UP*
160:13 boy,] ~ *UP*
160:18 Siegmund: he] ~. He *UP*
160:18 suggestive,] ~; *UP*
160:32 hand. *E1*] hand of the ship like cliffs. *MS* hand...ship-like cliffs. *UP*
160:32 sickle] ~, *UP*
160:33 "Victory"—] *Victory*, *UP*
160:34 pennons—] ~, *UP*
160:35 Siegmund] ~, *UP*
160:36 landing stage] landing-stage *UP*
161:5 on] ~, *UP*
161:7 South Western] South-Western *UP*
161:8 Siegmund] ~, *UP*
161:9 question. Helena] ~. *P* Helena *UP*
161:17 himself. Helena] ~. *P* Helena *UP*
161:24 Oh well— —!] ~, ~! *UP*
161:30 —After *this*." She] after ~," she *UP*
161:32 gravely. Helena *Ed.*] gravely. Sieglinde *MS* gravely. *P* Helena *UP*
161:35 Nevertheless] ~, *UP*
162:2 Portsmouth] ~, *UP*
162:9 evening—] ~, *UP*
162:14 God.—Nor] ~—nor *UP*
162:15 interruptions— —] ~... *UP*
162:17 against: we] ~? We *UP*
162:21 am, comparatively, free,] ~ ~ ~ *UP*
162:22 Helena—] ~; *UP*
162:24 me. But] ~; but *UP*
162:25 would— —.] ~. *UP*
162:26 country:] ~, *UP*
162:29 me:] ~; *UP*
162:31 say. 'Let] ~; 'let *UP*
162:33 shame— —.] ~. *UP*
163:1 morning,] ~— *UP*
163:1 hour:] ~; *UP*
163:3 preparation for] preparations for *UP*
163:5 lamentably,] ~ *UP*
163:6 care,] ~ *UP*
163:9 own probable life] own life *UP*
163:10 America:] ~; *UP*
163:12 homecoming] home-coming *UP*
163:13 inevitable. Then] ~; then *UP*
163:14 Helena:] ~, *UP*
163:16 intolerable.] ~! *UP*
163:18 away. But] ~; but *UP*
163:19 forty:] ~; *UP*
163:19 genius:] ~; *UP*
163:28 slowly,] ~ *UP*
163:31 you!] ~? *UP*
163:32 happiness:] ~; *UP*
163:32 known!" Helena] ~!" *P* Helena *UP*
163:34 joy. But] ~; but *UP*
163:37 Siegmund] ~, *UP*
163:37 also,] ~ *UP*
163:40 small] ~, *UP*
164:2 final conviction.] final convictions. *UP*
164:5 life—] ~; *UP*
164:8 answer. Indeed] ~; indeed *UP*
164:11 great] ~, *UP*
164:12 earth. There,] ~; there *UP*
164:13 were] ~, *UP*
164:13 breast] ~, *UP*
164:14 kind:] ~; *UP*
164:16 wondered what *E1*] wondered wistfully what *MS*
164:21 sky. But] ~; but *UP*
164:31 day] ~, *UP*
164:34 nobly:] ~, *UP*
164:39 came] ~, *UP*
164:39 unswerving] ~, *UP*
165:1 Siegmund,] ~ *UP*
165:5 hand:] ~; *UP*
165:6 Aylwin." Siegmund] ~." *P* Siegmund *UP*
165:7 face. Helena] ~. *P* Helena *UP*

165:9 conclusions—] ~, *UP*
165:10 herself,] ~ *UP*
165:10 right:] ~; *UP*
165:11 it." *E1*] it." *P* He was wonderfully gladdened to think that the unknown gave a sign of approval of his half-winnowed resolution. *MS*
165:13 level,] ~ *UP*
165:17 insistence] insistance *UP*
165:18 reassured:] ~; *UP*
165:20 right—] ~? *UP*
165:22 'right'] "~" *UP*
165:23 reassured. Then] ~; then *UP*
165:29 day] ~, *UP*
165:33 wings,] ~ *UP*
165:33 village—;] ~— *UP*
165:33 then] ~, *UP*
165:33 overhead] ~, *UP*
165:33 star-spiders] star-/spiders *UP*
165:35 —if] ~ *UP*
165:37 I?—nothing] ~? Nothing *UP*
165:38 with [the] swarm *Ed.*] with swarm *MS*
166:1 gold,] ~ *UP*
166:2 colour,] ~ *UP*
166:2 smell,] ~ *UP*
166:3 bee:] ~; *UP*
166:4 exists,] ~ *UP*
166:5 *are*,] ~ *UP*
166:7 matter!] ~? *UP*
166:9 where.] ~? *UP*
166:9 it. But] ~; but *UP*
166:16 river. They] ~; they *UP*
166:20 Helena.] ~: *UP*
166:26 one.] ~? *UP*
166:28 smiled] ~, *UP*
166:34 gently.] ~; *UP*
167:1 again] ~, *UP*
167:7 But—!"] ~—!", *MS* ~——" *UP*
167:18 go—!] ~! *UP*
167:19 rose:] ~; *UP*
167:20 hand:] ~; *UP*
167:23 himself] ~, *UP*
167:25 luggage:] ~; *UP*
167:25 her:] ~; *UP*
167:28 Siegmund. She] ~ *P* She *UP*
167:28 him:] ~; *UP*
167:30 Goodbye] ~, *UP*
167:30 then,] ~! *UP*
167:32 with:] ~; *UP*
167:34 short:] ~; *UP*
168:4 luke-warmness] luke-/warmness *UP*
168:11 full tilt] full-tilt *UP*
168:12 trepidation:] ~; *UP*
168:13 panting,] ~— *UP*
168:15 traffic:] ~; *UP*
168:18 night:] ~; *UP*
168:19 taxis,] ~ *UP*
168:20 her: 'discords,'] ~. "Discords," *UP*
168:20 'after] "~ *UP*
168:20 sea.'] ~." *UP*
168:21 streets:] ~; *UP*
168:23 Heaven. But] ~; but *UP*
168:25 it:] ~; *UP*
168:30 carriage:] ~; *UP*
168:32 Occasionally] ~, *UP*
168:32 passing] ~, *UP*
168:32 him. Then] ~; then *UP*
168:34 that carelessness and abstraction of despair. *E1*] that winsome happiness which is circled round with sorrow, distinct on his face. *MS* that winsome...sorrow distinct...face. *UP*
169:1 The eyes *E1*] The bright eyes *MS*
169:1 said, 'You] ~: "~ *UP*
169:2 lovable,'] ~," *UP*
169:6 night"] ~," *UP*
169:14 great burning bees *E1*] great gold-burning bees *MS* great gold burning bees *UP*
169:14 file into *E1*] file sweeping gently into *MS*
169:15 out:] ~, *UP*
169:16 black] ~, *UP*
169:18 himself. "It] ~; "it *UP*
169:19 Whatever] Whatever *UP*
169:24 past,] ~ *UP*
169:24 campaigns;] ~, *UP*
169:25 people:] ~. *UP*
169:29 him,] ~ *UP*
169:29 hat,] ~ *UP*
169:29 he frowned. *E1*] he sighed. *MS*

169:30 his frown *E1*] his sigh *MS*
169:31 "Now for the beginning of Hell!" *E1*] "Now we shut the door on the beauty of life. It all roams outside, but we shut it out. Now we are shut in this box full of ugliness." *MS*
169:32 dining room *Ed.*] dining-room *MS*
169:33 chime] ~, *UP*
169:35 tall] ~, *UP*
169:35 eighteen] ~, *UP*
169:36 book: he] ~. He *UP*
170:1 arm-chair] armchair *UP*
170:2 fireplace:] ~; *UP*
170:3 chair. He] ~; he *UP*
170:11 contemptuous:] ~, *UP*
170:19 paper] ~, *UP*
170:19 orange peel] orange-peel *UP*
170:19 banana skin] banana-skin *UP*
170:21 her. She] ~. *P* She *UP*
170:26 scissors] ~, *UP*
170:26 pins] ~, *UP*
170:30 table-cloth] tablecloth *UP*
170:30 sewing-litter] sewing litter *UP*
170:36 'Nash's' *Ed.*] ~ *MS Nash's UP*
170:37 No] ~, *UP*
170:37 reading—] ~, *UP*
170:38 else.] ~? *UP*
170:40 'other people.'] "~ ~." *UP*
170:40 rose. *P* "Let] ~. "Let *UP*
171:1 this—you] ~: You *UP*
171:1 down—] ~; *UP*
171:5 knees] ~, *UP*
171:6 soon,] ~ *UP*
171:6 time,] ~ *UP*
171:11 thin] ~, *UP*
171:12 bread and butter] bread-/and-butter *UP*
171:13 table:] ~; *UP*
171:16 cruet. It] ~; it *UP*
171:18 thin. In] ~—in *UP*
171:20 easy-going] easygoing *UP*
171:22 Siegmund. *E1*] Siegmund keenly. *MS*
171:23 was proper, *E1*] was correct, *MS*
171:24 emotion:] ~; *UP*
171:27 say] ~, *UP*
171:27 Beatrice.] ~: *UP*
171:33 razzle.] ~! *UP*
171:36 slightly,] ~— *UP*
171:37 mère.—] ~. *UP*
171:37 tired." Beatrice] ~." *P* Beatrice *UP*
172:2 remarked,] ~ *UP*
172:7 Lord, bread] ~! ~ *UP*
172:7 tonight,] to-night! *UP*
172:16 time. Then] ~; then *UP*
172:17 Goodnight,] Good-night! *UP*
172:21 bathroom. Then] ~; then *UP*
172:33 sneer. Stretching] ~. *P* Stretching *UP*
172:35 table,] ~ *UP*
172:38 you some. *E1*] you a little. *MS*
172:39 right Ma] ~, ma *UP*
173:1 bread and butter] bread-and-butter *UP*
173:3 a rotten *E1*] a damned *MS*
173:3 sotto voce] *sotto voce UP*
173:4 room. Vera] ~. *P* Vera *UP*
173:11 Ma. We'll] ma; we'll *UP*
173:12 her. *P* "Goodnight—] ~. "Good-night, *UP*
173:14 room. Beatrice] ~. *P* Beatrice *UP*
174:2 Siegmund,] ~ *UP*
174:3 dining room *Ed.*] dining-room *MS*
174:4 round:] ~, *UP*
174:12 further] farther *UP*
174:18 dark,] ~ *UP*
174:20 wrists: he] ~. He *UP*
174:20 further] farther *UP*
174:22 luminous,] ~ *UP*
174:29 night,] ~! *UP*
174:34 eyes,] ~ *UP*
175:3 sign,] ~— *UP*
175:10 stars. Then] ~, then *UP*
175:11 half past] half-past *UP*
175:12 answered: *P* "Well] ~: "Well *UP*
175:16 awoke,] ~ *UP*
175:21 Wight;] ~. *UP*
175:21 'What] "~ *UP*
175:21 like, now?' *Ed.*] ~, ~?" *MS* ~ ~?" *UP*
175:25 nasturtiums:] ~; *UP*

176:7 'Pan-n-n! Pan-n-n-n!'] "~! pan-n-n-n!" *UP*
176:8 onto] on to *UP*
176:15 Marjory *E1*] Minna *MS*
176:18 Marjory *E1*] Minna *MS*
176:20 Mam!"—she] ~!" She *UP*
176:20 waited—"Mam!"—still] ~. "~!" Still *UP*
176:21 Mam!— —] ~! *UP*
176:23 Mam?—Mamma!"—still] ~? ~!" Still *UP*
176:27 bedroom, and] ~. *P* And *UP*
176:27 crossly: *P* "What] ~: "What *UP*
176:29 child,] ~ *UP*
176:30 me—are] ~? Are *UP*
176:30 here!] ~? *UP*
176:31 for!" The] ~?" *P* The *UP*
176:31 down stairs] downstairs *UP*
176:39 Mam—?] ~, *UP*
176:39 hall. "Has] ~, "has *UP*
176:40 Dad] dad *UP*
177:3 feet] ~, *UP*
177:4 shrinking within *E1*] shrinking and shrinking within *MS*
177:8 ill humour] ill-/humour *UP*
177:9 train:] ~; *UP*
177:9 age:] ~; *UP*
177:21 half hour] half-hour *UP*
177:21 till Vera's *UP*] till he Vera's *MS*
177:22 outside: "You] ~: *P* "You *UP*
177:23 away] ~, *UP*
177:27 bowl;] ~, *UP*
177:27 him:] ~; *UP*
177:34 hair] ~, *UP*
177:37 She too] ~, ~, *UP*
177:40 here!" The] ~!" *P* The *UP*
178:1 him] ~, *UP*
178:7 gaily. She] ~. *P* She *UP*
178:8 slight,] ~ *UP*
178:13 sea-side *Ed.*] seaside *MS*
178:13 answered] ~, *UP*
178:15 further] farther *UP*
178:17 Further— —] Farther— *UP*
178:19 Why] ~, *UP*
178:21 Twuly] twuly *UP*
178:27 cannons— —.] ~—. *UP*
178:35 potato;" the] ~." The *UP*
178:35 laughed,] ~ *UP*
179:1 further] farther *UP*
179:4 doorway. She] ~. *P* She *UP*
179:5 Mam] mam *UP*
179:5 done." Her] ~." *P* Her *UP*
179:6 downstairs,] ~ *UP*
179:14 bath] ~, *UP*
179:19 think that, when *E1*] think when *MS* think, when *UP*
179:19 "I *E1*] "that I *MS*
179:21 affairs easily] affairs as easily *UP*
179:23 Lord of Creation] lord of creation *UP*
179:26 off:] ~; *UP*
179:27 kitchen,] ~ *UP*
179:29 it:] ~; *UP*
179:31 dining room] dining-room *UP*
179:32 drawing room *Ed.*] drawing-/room *MS* drawing-room *UP*
179:35 it,] ~— *UP*
179:37 arm-chair *Ed.*] armchair *MS* armchair, *UP*
179:39 days] ~, *UP*
179:40 After an intoxication *E1*] After a magnificent intoxication *MS*
180:6 sickness,] ~ *UP*
180:8 sun;—] ~— *UP*
180:16 startled:] ~; *UP*
180:18 "London Opinion"; *Ed.*] '~ ~'; *MS* *London Opinion*, *UP*
180:21 drawing room *Ed.*] drawing-/room *MS*
180:24 mother. Beatrice] ~ *P* Beatrice *UP*
180:25 replied: *P* "I'm] ~: "I'm *UP*
180:28 Beatrice. Gwen] ~. *P* Gwen *UP*
180:30 doing Mam] ~, mam *UP*
180:31 mother. "Nothing,] ~—"nothing; *UP*
180:32 drawing room] drawing-room *UP*
180:34 Nothing. Nothing] Nothing—nothing *UP*
180:38 Mam] mam *UP*
180:39 Marjory *E1*] Minna *MS*
181:8 Ah] ~, *UP*

181:11 himself. But] ~. *P* But *UP*
181:11 immediately: it] ~. It *UP*
181:13 do something] ~ ~, *UP*
181:16 out. Everything] ~. *P* Everything *UP*
181:17 distaste. The] ~: the *UP*
181:17 sea-side—] seaside, *UP*
181:17 land—] ~, *UP*
181:19 himself:] ~ *UP*
181:25 desire:] ~—*UP*
181:27 Then: *P* "Is] ~ "Is *UP*
181:28 himself. To] ~. *P* To *UP*
181:30 appealingly,] ~ *UP*
181:32 a raw place. He *Ed.*] a raw-/red place. He *MS* a raw red place. *P*. He *UP* a raw place. *P* He *E1*
181:35 onto] on to *UP*
181:35 door-knob,] ~ *UP*
181:37 Mam] mam *UP*
181:37 announced. Siegmund] ~. *P* Siegmund *UP*
182:1 said Siegmund *E1*] snapped Siegmund *MS*
182:8 said,] ~ *UP*
182:8 mind] ~, *UP*
182:8 dearie,] ~— *UP*
182:11 Marjory *E1*] Minna *MS*
183:2 evening,] ~ *UP*
183:10 cheeks] ~, *UP*
183:12 entered,] ~ *UP*
183:13 forwards,] ~ *UP*
183:13 said—"Well] ~: *P* "Well *UP*
183:14 Well—] ~, *UP*
183:14 tone. Her] ~. *P* Her *UP*
183:17 see!] ~, *UP*
183:19 good!] ~, *UP*
183:20 H'm!"—Mrs] ~!" *P* Mrs. *UP*
183:23 said. Helena] ~. *P* Helena *UP*
183:24 playful] ~, *UP*
183:26 ready,] ~ *UP*
183:27 mouth] ~, *UP*
183:33 Helena. Mrs] ~. *P* Mrs. *UP*
184:4 white-bearded *Ed.*] white-/bearded *MS*
184:6 back] ~, *UP*
184:6 Nelly *Ed.*] Nellie *MS*
184:9 accounts. Neither] ~. *P* Neither *UP*
184:11 tip-toe] tiptoe *UP*
184:12 H'm!",] ~!" *UP*
184:12 question] ~, *UP*
184:17 quick] ~, *UP*
184:19 come?"—and] ~?" *P* And *UP*
184:26 Why— —?] ~? *UP*
184:26 Helena. Louisa] ~. *P* Louisa *UP*
184:30 midsummer] mid-/summer *UP*
184:31 girl,] ~— *UP*
184:32 night,] ~ *UP*
184:33 made confidences *E1*] made a few brief confidences *MS*
184:34 Meanwhile] ~, *UP*
184:38 silence] ~, *UP*
184:39 playful] ~, *UP*
185:13 half past] half-/past *UP*
185:13 eight: there] ~. There *UP*
185:15 Nevertheless, "You'd] "~, you'd *UP*
185:33 he] ~, *UP*
185:33 wonder.] ~? *UP*
185:34 day:] ~, *UP*
185:35 him:] ~, *UP*
185:39 passage] ~, *UP*
186:2 Why—] ~, *UP*
186:4 Oh—] ~, *UP*
186:4 know—] ~; *UP*
186:5 are—what] ~. What *UP*
186:7 packing!] ~, *UP*
186:9 Oh—] ~, *UP*
186:11 Well—] ~, *UP*
186:13 with a forlorn *UP*] with forlorn *MS*
186:13 expression,] ~ *UP*
186:17 tram-car] tramcar *UP*
186:19 mute] ~, *UP*
186:20 third-rate] third-/rate *UP*
186:20 Olive *E1*] Vera *MS*
186:23 answering—everything] ~. Everything *UP*
186:24 repeated] ~: *UP*
187:2 teatime *UP*] tea-time *MS*
187:6 him,] ~ *UP*
187:6 coldly. He] ~. *P* He *UP*
187:8 answered. She] ~. *P* She *UP*
187:10 his—] ~ *UP*
187:11 cried—"for] ~. "For *UP*
187:12 altogether,] ~— *UP*
187:14 on?] ~. *UP*

187:15 that!] ~. *UP*
187:16 they—?] ~? *UP*
187:22 day:—] ~. *UP*
187:23 like;] ~. *UP*
187:23 go,] ~ *UP*
187:23 well.—] ~. *UP*
187:24 coward—] ~, *UP*
187:25 children—to] ~; ~ *UP*
187:26 *be*] be *UP*
187:27 Siegmund,] ~ *UP*
187:27 contemptuously. The] ~. *P* The *UP*
187:32 further] farther *UP*
187:33 sulking] ~, *UP*
187:34 stand.] ~? *UP*
188:2 hand—?] ~? *UP*
188:4 yourself.] ~! *UP*
188:5 white hot] white-hot *UP*
188:9 thing.] ~! *UP*
188:10 am— —" Siegmund] ~." *P* Siegmund *UP*
188:12 furtive:] ~, *UP*
188:16 he pushed *E1*] he feebly pushed *MS*
188:20 three,] ~ *UP*
188:23 asked,] ~ *UP*
188:24 tone. Her] ~. *P* Her *UP*
188:27 mother] ~, *UP*
188:29 up— — —.] ~. *UP*
188:32 Mam!—] ~, *UP*
188:32 dog— —] ~—— *UP*
188:37 father. Then] ~; then *UP*
188:38 tones: "Mam] ~: *P* "Mam *UP*
188:40 meat.—Mam!—Mam?] ~. ~, ~! *UP*
189:3 timidly. No] ~. *P* No *UP*
189:4 Mam?] ~! *UP*
189:4 whispered. She] ~. *P* She *UP*
189:4 tip-toe *Ed.*] tiptoe *MS*
189:6 Mam!!] ~! *UP*
189:6 shrilly. Her] ~. *P* Her *UP*
189:6 self denial] self-denial *UP*
189:12 Mam—] ~, *UP*
189:12 dog—." Vera] ~——" *P* Vera *UP*
189:14 arms] ~, *UP*
189:15 baby-cheek] baby cheek *UP*
189:18 rage] ~, *UP*
189:18 pity] ~, *UP*
189:23 child] ~, *UP*
189:24 talking,] ~— *UP*
189:27 Mam—] ~, *UP*
189:27 Dad] dad *UP*
189:28 bother,] ~! *UP*
189:29 dining room] dining-room *UP*
189:35 dish. Then] ~; then *UP*
189:36 kitchen:] ~; *UP*
189:39 feet,] ~ *UP*
189:39 slippers] ~, *UP*
190:1 together] ~, *UP*
190:2 him?—] ~? *UP*
190:4 know. He] ~. *P* He *UP*
190:6 white-frilled *UP*] white-/frilled *MS*
190:9 love;] ~, *UP*
190:10 her;] ~, *UP*
190:10 arms;] ~, *UP*
190:11 apple blossom] apple-blossom *UP*
190:11 now—;] ~— *UP*
190:12 suspense;] ~— *UP*
190:14 feared] ~, *UP*
190:14 wanted] ~, *UP*
190:16 Yes!] ~, *UP*
190:17 away. She] ~. *P* She *UP*
190:21 tightly clenched *E1*] tight clenched *UP*
190:24 time,] ~ *UP*
190:25 work,] ~— *UP*
190:28 fingers,] ~ *UP*
190:33 heavy] ~, *UP*
190:35 Betweenwhiles] Between whiles *UP*
190:38 somewhere. *P* "But] ~. "But *UP*
190:40 Siegmund. The] ~. *P* The *UP*
191:1 'Do] "~ *UP*
191:2 somewhere,'] ~," *UP*
191:7 remained,] ~ *UP*
191:7 restoration:] ~— *UP*
191:8 utterly,] ~— *UP*
191:10 sleep. *P* "What] ~. "What *UP*
191:11 it?"—it] ~?" *P* It *UP*
191:14 "—But] "~ *UP*
191:17 waited,] ~; *UP*
191:19 Goodness!] ~, *UP*
191:19 dark.] ~! *UP*

191:22 sun-inflammation *Ed.*] sun-/inflammation *MS* sun inflammation *UP*
191:25 however] ~, *UP*
191:28 out,] ~ *UP*
191:35 Yes—] ~, *UP*
191:36 honourable *UP*] honorable *MS*
192:2 Louisa] ~, *UP*
192:2 South Western] South-Western *UP*
192:4 Louisa] ~, *UP*
192:4 least] ~, *UP*
192:7 "—is] "~ *UP*
192:8 10.40. It] ~; it *UP*
192:8 Helena. Olive] ~. *P* Olive *UP*
192:10 dear!] ~. *UP*
192:13 it; you] ~. You *UP*
192:15 contralto "Don't judge] ~, don't "~ *UP* ~, "don't ~ *E1*
192:16 of 'Oh] ~ *P* "' ~ *UP*
192:20 sarcastically.] ~: *UP*
192:21 madness— —] ~—— *UP*
192:22 "'When] "~ *UP*
192:22 holiday,'] ~, *UP*
192:28 hanged,' dear, *UP*] ~, ~', *MS*
192:29 Olive. She] ~. *P* She *UP*
192:29 side: she] ~. She *UP*
193:10 Siegmund came on to *E1*] Siegmund rushed onto *MS* Siegmund rushed on to *UP*
193:12 said. *E1*] said breathlessly. *MS*
193:13 seat,] ~ *UP*
193:18 dress-baskets *UP*] dress baskets *MS*
193:21 Helena,] ~ *UP*
193:27 is Sister *E1*] is our Sister *MS*
193:29 triumphant. There] ~. *P* There *UP*
193:30 understood] ~, *UP*
193:30 enmity, for the two were really good friends. *E1*] enmity, feeling always kindly disposed towards Helena's friend. *MS*
193:32 away. He] ~. *P* He *UP*
193:35 indifferently] ~. *UP*
193:36 He thought..."The children *E1*] He thought of the merry sound of the children's playing in the afternoon. *P* "The children *MS*
193:40 right] ~, *UP*
194:1 pause,] ~ *UP*
194:1 added] ~: *UP*
194:4 platform; there] ~. There *UP*
194:6 swarm:] ~; *UP*
194:6 sky rocket] sky-rocket *UP*
194:7 signal-lamps *UP*] signal lamps *MS*
194:9 carriage windows *Ed.*] carriage-windows *MS*
194:14 Dear—] ~, *UP*
194:14 promise—] ~ *UP*
194:15 Remember] ~, *UP*
194:19 resonance,—] ~— *UP*
194:21 mean?—] ~? *UP*
194:21 happened?—] ~? *UP*
194:23 time,] ~ *UP*
194:24 powerless;] ~. *UP*
194:28 mind—.] ~. *UP*
194:33 again. Then *E1*] again. He made a small sound, between a sigh and a gasp. Then *MS*
194:33 Ah—] ~, *UP*
194:34 angry.—] ~. *UP*
194:35 tonight,] to-night *UP*
194:35 left—." Helena] ~." *P* Helena *UP*
195:6 arm—] ~, *UP*
195:6 hat!"—] ~!" *UP*
195:8 feathers.—] ~. *UP*
195:8 lifetime—] ~. *UP*
195:9 sotto voce] *sotto voce* *UP*
195:12 it,] ~— *UP*
195:13 nonplussed] non-/plussed *UP*
195:16 re-adjusted] readjusted *UP*
195:16 herself,] ~ *UP*
195:18 said] ~, *UP*
195:23 carriage: there] ~. There *UP*
195:29 umbrellas] ~, *UP*
195:31 two:] ~; *UP*
195:32 luggage was troublesome to bestow. *E1*] luggage could not go on the racks. *MS*
195:33 again,] ~ *UP*
195:37 coming?—Oh—] ~? ~, *UP*
195:39 said. She] ~. *P* She *UP*

196:4 go!] ~? *UP*
196:11 door] ~, *UP*
196:12 'Hawwa'] "~" *UP*
196:26 Siegmund,] ~ *UP*
196:27 his. "Monday] ~. *P* "Monday *UP*
196:28 whispered] ~— *UP*
196:32 Now] ~, *UP*
196:32 Olive,] ~ *UP*
197:8 out:] ~; *UP*
197:20 door mat *Ed.*] door-mat *MS*
197:24 Ay! *Ed.*] ~!, *MS* ~, *UP*
197:25 in the] into the *UP*
197:25 dining room] dining-room *UP*
197:27 asked. He] ~. *P* He *UP*
197:30 bloodshot *Ed.*] blood-/shot *MS* blood-shot *UP*
197:30 whites] white *UP*
198:2 her,] ~ *UP*
198:3 repeated,] ~ *UP*
198:11 trembling:] ~. *UP*
198:15 backward] backwards *UP*
198:15 thought,—] ~, *UP*
198:17 onto] on to *UP*
198:20 door mats] door-mat *UP*
198:26 listening. *P* Siegmund] ~. Siegmund *UP*
198:29 sleeping jacket] sleeping-jacket *UP*
198:33 Immediately,] ~ *UP*
198:39 doing?—] ~? *UP*
198:39 matter?—] ~? *UP*
198:39 unconscious?—do] ~? Do *UP*
198:40 noise?—do] ~? Do *UP*
199:1 sense-impression *Ed.*] sense-/impression *MS* sense impression *UP*
199:4 things] ~, *UP*
199:9 hot: the] ~. The *UP*
199:11 Immediately,] ~ *UP*
199:22 onto] on to *UP*
199:29 arm pits] armpits *UP*
199:31 highly-sensitised *Ed.*] highly-/sensitised *MS* highly-sensitized *UP*
199:33 moment] ~, *UP*
199:40 Then] ~, *UP*
200:1 loth] loath *UP*
200:10 surface,] ~ *UP*
200:16 onto] on to *UP*
200:18 clammy: it] ~. It *UP*
200:20 sky:] ~; *UP*
200:26 day, moved *E1*] day, was outreached towards it, moved *MS* day, was outstretched towards it, moved *UP*
200:27 loth] loath *UP*
200:28 it,] ~ *UP*
200:30 the net *E1*] the white net *UP*
200:31 was like] ~, ~ *UP*
200:32 half moon] half-moon *UP*
200:36 crouched] ~, *UP*
201:34 how] How *UP*
201:35 re-set] reset *UP*
201:35 joint.] ~? *UP*
201:37 these: it] ~? It *UP*
201:39 humility: that] ~. That *UP*
202:3 'If] "~ *UP*
202:4 off.'] ~." *UP*
202:6 him—?] ~! *UP*
202:10 impossible.] ~! *UP*
202:12 home:] ~; *UP*
202:19 strap.] ~! *UP*
202:23 note-book] notebook *UP*
202:29 pocket-book *UP*] pocket-/book *MS*
202:29 dressing-table *UP*] dressing table *MS*
202:34 God:] ~. *UP*
202:35 God"—] ~," *UP*
202:37 'But] "'~ *UP*
202:37 after death,'] ~ ~,'" *UP* after-death,'" *E1*
202:39 fearsome—] ~, *UP*
202:41 of'."] ~.'" *UP*
203:1 after-death *UP*] after-/death *MS*
203:5 it. Siegmund *E1*] it. The prodigal son, among foreigners, too sulky and bitter-spirited to ask for the bread which would not have been denied his asking, was all the time aware of the heart of love beating for him steadily many miles away. Never for one moment, in his heart of hearts, did he disbelieve in the ultimate kindness of his home-folk. So Siegmund *MS*

203:7 sulky,] ~ *UP*
203:7 his. *E1*] his. The heart of life beat steadily on, kindly, as the heart of the father never swerved from the stroke of love for his prodigal. *MS*
203:8 kindness: it] ~. It *UP*
203:9 flutterings] fluttering *UP*
203:9 pity:] ~; *UP*
203:12 Therefore] ~, *UP*
203:13 submit,] ~ *UP*
203:15 vacillation:] ~; *UP*
203:18 room:] ~; *UP*
203:19 death:] ~, *UP*
203:26 dog:] ~. *UP*
203:28 Life *E1*] life *MS*
203:31 an imaginary God *Ed.*] a suppository God *MS* a suppository god *UP* an imaginary god *E1 see explanatory note*
203:38 father." He] ~." *P* He *UP*
203:39 bewilderment:] ~; *UP*
204:1 Oh—] ~, *UP*
204:7 know—] ~; *UP*
204:8 benevolence: the] ~. The *UP*
204:12 watch: it] ~. It *UP*
204:21 shaving water] shaving-water *UP*
204:21 tones:] ~. *UP*
204:22 half past] half–past *UP*
204:22 nine!] ~. *UP*
204:26 time—] ~. *UP*
204:26 answered. He] ~. *P* He *UP*
204:30 did:] ~; *UP*
205:3 half past *Ed.*] half-past *MS*
205:4 shaving water] shaving-/water *UP*
205:4 dining room *Ed.*] dining-room *MS*
205:6 town:] ~; *UP*
205:7 Marjory *E1*] Millicent *MS*
205:13 dining room *Ed.*] dining-room *MS*
205:15 grate,—] ~, *UP*
205:16 day—,] ~, *UP*
205:19 as she brushed *UP*] as brushed *MS*
205:22 life:] ~; *UP*
205:33 servant-housekeeper *Ed.*] servant-/housekeeper *MS*
205:33 longer— —.] ~. *UP*
206:6 uneasiness. She...her. As *E1*] uneasiness. Beatrice commenced to wonder. She tried to remember if she had heard any sound of Siegmund. As *MS*
206:7 cup] ~, *UP*
206:12 breath. She dreaded the combat with him. Suddenly *E1*] breath. Suddenly *MS*
206:18 half past *Ed.*] half-past *MS*
206:18 ten,—] ~— *UP*
206:18 up?—"] ~?" *UP*
206:22 shaving water] shaving-water *UP*
206:24 waited—] ~, *UP*
206:25 again: the] ~. The *UP*
206:27 ring, —] ~, *UP*
206:32 room; one] ~. One *UP*
206:32 chinked] clinked *UP*
206:35 mercy,] ~ *UP*
206:40 Why Mum] ~, mum *UP*
207:7 he Mum] ~, mum *UP*
207:10 I 's' ll] I 's'll *UP* Is'll *E1*
207:10 window-cleaner *UP*] window cleaner *MS*
207:13 drawing room] drawing-room *UP*
207:13 window cleaning] window-cleaning *UP*
207:18 window-cleaner *UP*] window cleaner *MS*
207:19 Yes—] ~, *UP*
207:19 Beatrice. The] ~. *P* The *UP*
207:30 cried,] ~. *UP*
207:35 Hie!] ~, *UP*
207:38 door-'ooks.] ~! *UP*
207:39 No—no—] ~, ~, *UP*
208:1 dead,] ~! *UP*
208:1 Beatrice. The] ~. *P* The *UP*
208:3 is—,] ~, *UP*
208:4 Beatrice. The] ~. *P* The *UP*
208:9 clasp-knife] clasp-/knife *UP*
208:14 onto] on to *UP*
208:19 sleeping jacket] sleeping-jacket *UP*

208:19 arm pits] arm-pits *UP*
208:22 sleeping suit] sleeping-suit *UP*
209:3 sands,] ∼ *UP*
209:4 sea-fragrant] sea-/fragrant *UP*
209:8 north-countrymen] north-/countrymen *UP*
209:9 Louisa] ∼, *UP*
209:9 carriage: the] ∼. The *UP*
209:14 north-countrymen *UP*] north countrymen *MS*
209:16 this,] ∼ *UP*
209:18 Louisa: they] ∼. They *UP*
209:18 another; they] ∼. They *UP*
209:21 on: little,] ∼. Little *UP*
209:23 doze:] ∼. *UP*
209:24 sleep:] ∼. *UP*
209:31 pillows:] ∼; *UP*
209:33 slowly: it] ∼. It *UP*
209:33 cold;] ∼. *UP*
209:34 again;] ∼. *UP*
210:7 again: it] ∼. It *UP*
210:10 breakfast-time *Ed.*] breakfast-/time *MS* break-/fast time *UP*
210:10 'dauntless three'] "∼ ∼" *UP*
210:13 herself—.] ∼. *UP*
210:16 humour—.] ∼. *UP*
210:19 Walhalla *E1*] Walhall *MS*
210:19 "Walküre" *E1*] '∼' *MS* "Walkua" *UP*
210:20 "Tristan" *UP*] '∼' *MS*
210:24 Anadyomene: in] ∼. In *UP*
210:24 sum,] sun *UP*
210:25 "Tristan." *UP*] '∼.' *MS*
210:26 rocks,] ∼ *UP*
210:26 half articulate] half-articulate *UP*
210:32 spirits] ∼, *UP*
210:32 most-whiles] most whiles *UP*
210:35 seconds: the] ∼; The *UP* ∼; the *E1*
210:38 There!—] ∼, *UP*
210:39 OO—] Oo, *UP*
211:1 opened;] ∼: *UP*
211:2 night-gown] nightgown *UP*
211:3 dear,] ∼! *UP*
211:3 "—may] "∼ *UP*
211:6 lightning: the] ∼. The *UP*
211:7 shut: it] ∼. It *UP*

211:10 breathless,] ∼. *UP*
211:11 that?" She] ∼?" *P* She *UP*
211:18 you dear] ∼, ∼ *UP*
211:18 Olive,] ∼; *UP*
211:20 Helena laughed ironically *E1*] Helena sniggered ironically *MS*
211:22 Why] ∼, *UP*
211:24 afraid— — —.] ∼.... *UP*
211:29 with blackness. *E1*] with level blackness. *MS* with level blackiness. *UP*
211:36 Louisa. No] ∼. *P* No *UP*
211:39 she too] ∼, ∼, *UP*
211:39 awake:] ∼; *UP*
211:40 bruised: the] ∼. The *UP*
212:5 grandeur—] ∼, *UP*
212:8 him,] ∼— *UP*
212:25 train: she] ∼. She *UP*
212:29 waiting room] waiting-room *UP*
212:33 not!] ∼? *UP*
212:33 exclaimed—.] ∼. *UP*
212:37 made,] ∼; *UP*
212:40 same thoughts] same thought *UP*
213:1 this sitting] thus sitting *UP*
213:5 London;] ∼, *UP*
213:6 If] if *UP*
213:8 Hell,] hell! *UP*
213:25 pre-arranged] pre-/arranged *UP*
213:27 sought:] ∼. *UP*
213:29 of—.] ∼——. *UP*
213:30 Coast— —.] ∼.... *UP*
213:35 town] ∼, *UP*
213:37 afterwards. "And] ∼; "and *UP*
213:39 on, until *E1*] on for some miles until *MS* on...miles, until *UP*
214:1 left] ∼, *UP*
214:4 there:] ∼; *UP*
214:9 gone; why had he not taken her with him? *E1*] gone; his nest was dragged; where was left for her to go? *MS*
214:10 on:] ∼; *UP*
214:10 half past] half-past *UP*
214:16 eight:] ∼; *UP*
214:17 news: *E1*] news, with crude brevity *MS* news,...brevity *UP*

214:18 home." This] ~." *P* This *UP*
214:19 will,] ~ *UP*
214:28 alone!] ~? *UP*
214:30 dining room] dining-room *UP*
214:37 Wimbledon,] ~ *UP*
214:37 bought a *E1*] got a *MS*
214:39 her mother] the mother *UP*
215:2 mother,] ~ *UP*
215:3 answer.] answer her. *UP*
215:6 dining room *Ed.*] dining-room *MS* dining-/room *UP*
215:11 Nelly] Nellie *UP*
215:14 rest Nelly] ~, Nellie *UP*
215:15 shivered lightly.] shivered slightly. *UP*
215:16 Do] ~, *UP*
215:19 bed,] ~ *UP*
215:26 dining room *Ed.*] dining-room *MS*
215:37 head:] ~; *UP*
216:20 syllables] ~, *UP*
216:28 man] ~, *UP*
217:4 scared jury] sacred jury *UP see explanatory note*
217:9 house,] ~ *UP*
217:16 husband:] ~; *UP*
217:20 been] ~, *UP*
217:22 herself,] ~— *UP*
217:23 children:] ~; *UP*
217:25 dismay,] ~ *UP*
217:27 practical minded] practical-minded *UP*
217:32 personae] personæ *UP*
217:33 of their elders] of the elders *UP*
217:34 consent,] ~ *UP*
218:1 funeral,] ~ *UP*
218:8 romantic,] ~ *UP*
218:13 boarding house] boarding-house *UP*
218:18 Highgate *E1*] Child's Hill *MS*
218:20 interested:] ~; *UP*
218:21 grudging:] ~; *UP*
218:28 hand:] ~; *UP*
218:30 fair] ~, *UP*
218:37 nevertheless] ~, *UP*
218:39 gallant: therefore] ~. Therefore *UP*
219:7 dining room] dining-room *UP*
219:8 window-sill] window-/sill *UP*
219:8 half past] half-past *UP*
219:10 setting:] ~; *UP*
219:10 stocks filtered into *E1*] stocks filled into *MS*
219:11 window:] ~; *UP*
219:11 South] south *UP*
219:16 landlady] ~, *UP*
219:16 go—.] ~. *UP*
219:19 belongs— —.] ~. *UP*
219:20 Ah] ~, *UP*
219:21 What] what *UP*
219:21 You] you *UP*
219:24 Oh] ~, *UP*
219:25 so!—Ah] ~! ~, *UP*
219:25 Allport,] ~. *UP*
219:27 all?—it's] ~? It's *UP*
219:31 trouble,] ~ *UP*
219:32 that!—] ~! *UP*
219:33 say— —] ~— *UP*
219:33 But] ~, *UP*
219:34 possible?—that's] ~? That's *UP*
219:39 care?—] ~? *UP*
219:40 Beatrice,] ~ *UP*
220:1 Allport "—it's] ~, "~ *UP*
220:3 her,] ~ *UP*
220:5 cowardly,] ~ *UP*
220:8 woman— —.] ~. *UP*
220:9 Ah but] ~, ~, *UP*
220:9 Allport,] ~ *UP*
220:14 Yes. They] ~, they *UP*
220:15 waited— *P* "My] ~. "My *UP*
220:20 didn't— — —?] ~——? *UP*
220:22 Yes!] ~, *UP*
220:25 this then?] ~, ~— *UP*
220:25 he—?] ~——? *UP*
220:29 little,] ~ *UP*
220:32 her,] ~ *UP*
220:34 She,] ~ *UP*
220:37 heavy—.] ~. *UP*
220:40 kitchen:] ~. *UP*
221:1 dark Mother] ~, mother *UP*
221:2 Allport,] ~; *UP*
221:4 Well!—] ~! *UP*
221:4 you!—fancy] ~! Fancy *UP*
221:5 Mater] mater *UP*
221:8 myself—.] ~. *UP*

221:10 despondent.—] ~. *UP*
221:16 moon] ~, *UP*
221:20 but peel. *E1*] but rind. *MS*
221:21 melon shell] melon-shell *UP*
221:23 said—"Whoever *Ed.*] ~ "— " ~ *MS* ~. " ~ *UP*
221:25 Oh] ~, *UP*
221:25 know—] ~, *UP*
221:27 What!—] ~! *UP*
221:30 Yes—] ~, *UP*
221:32 dining room *Ed.*] dining-room *MS*
221:35 Holiday!] ~, *UP*
221:38 Ho!—] ~! *UP*
221:39 ear: she] ~. She *UP*
222:4 Oh] ~, *UP*
222:4 private—",] ~——" *UP*
222:9 Holiday?] ~, *UP*
222:10 are.] ~? *UP*
222:14 watched" he] ~." He *UP*
222:14 elbow—.] ~. *UP*
222:17 teeth.] ~; *UP*
222:17 play on the] play the *UP*
222:18 instrument:] ~; *UP*
222:21 never,] ~! *UP*
222:21 closely: the] ~. The *UP*
222:22 sure: he] ~. He *UP*
222:24 play—] ~—— *UP*
222:24 began—.] ~. *UP*
222:29 me—",] ~," *UP*
222:30 Blacksmith'] ~,' *UP*
222:37 end,] ~ *UP*
223:5 half past *Ed.*] half-past *MS*
223:6 cookery book] cookery-book *UP*
223:7 You too] ~, ~, *UP*
223:12 you—,] ~, *UP*
223:15 puddings—?] ~? *UP*
223:15 Beatrice,] ~ *UP*
223:17 instance!] ~. *UP*
223:18 study—.] ~. *UP*
223:21 play—.] ~. *UP*
223:22 excellently—why] ~. Why *UP*
223:23 Ah—] ~, *UP*
223:25 are more than excellent. *E1*] are par-excellent. *MS* are par excellent. *UP*
223:27 me!: he] ~! He *UP*
223:29 Testament:] ~. *UP*
223:33 No?—] ~. *UP*
223:33 convent school *UP*] Convent School *MS*
223:35 Yes—] ~, *UP*
223:37 Alas—!] ~! *UP*
223:40 sympathetic. *E1*] sympathetic. *P* "They, used to call me Félicité — they said I had everything I wanted, those poor meagre French girls! I was Beatrice Félicité." *MS see explanatory note*
224:3 tram-car,] tramcar *UP*
224:5 yellow backed] yellow-/backed *UP*
224:5 "Einsame Menschen," *UP*] '~,' *MS*
224:6 Folk Song] folk-song *UP*
224:7 head] ~, *UP*
224:16 tram-car] tramcar *UP*
224:23 Neither] ~, *UP*
224:25 up-hill] uphill *UP*
224:27 grassy-declivity] grassy declivity *UP*
224:32 are—] ~—— *UP*
224:34 Fafner *Ed.*] Fasner *MS see explanatory note*
225:1 Fasolt?—they] ~? They *UP*
225:5 laughing] ~, *UP*
225:8 looked,] ~! *UP*
225:10 that] ~, *UP*
225:13 remember] ~, *UP*
225:13 had,] ~ *UP*
225:13 time,] ~ *UP*
225:16 black and white] black-and-/white *UP*
225:20 destruction,] ~ *UP*
225:22 him,] ~ *UP*
225:23 replied.] ~, *UP*
225:24 hill,] ~ *UP*
225:25 begins,] ~ *UP*
225:29 Well—] ~, *UP*
225:29 tree,] ~; *UP*
225:31 on: the] ~. The *UP*
225:33 today!] to-day, *UP*
225:33 said] ~, *UP*
225:34 down,] ~ *UP*

225:34 oak wood] oak-wood *UP*
225:34 hand.—] ~. *UP*
225:35 it] ~, *UP*
225:36 day:] ~, *UP*
225:38 larch-wood] larch-/wood *UP*
225:40 go] ~, *UP*
226:5 No!] ~, *UP*
226:5 bitingly, "You] ~; "you *UP*
226:5 right.] ~! *UP*
226:6 farm,] ~ *UP*
226:7 onto] on to *UP*
226:10 sandalwood] sandal-wood *UP*
226:11 What—] ~, *UP*
226:12 Yes—] ~, *UP*
226:13 re-started] restarted *UP*
226:14 onto] on to *UP*
226:14 field,] ~ *UP*
226:16 scent. Then] ~; then *UP*
226:21 bits?" She] ~?" *P* She *UP*
226:24 fields"] ~," *UP*
226:30 antennae] antennæ
226:35 trees, narrow,] ~—~ *UP*
226:38 tree tops] tree-tops *UP*
227:1 larch trunk] larch-trunk *UP*
227:4 near,] ~ *UP*
227:8 Hm?—] H'm? *UP*
227:9 bright,] ~ *UP*
227:10 larch-fog] larch fog *UP*
227:15 hat. Then] ~; then *UP*
227:18 pins:] ~— *UP*
227:22 wood,] ~ *UP*
227:24 kin-ship] kinship *UP*
227:24 Siegmund:] ~; *UP*
227:26 valley,] ~— *UP*
227:27 north downs] North Downs *UP*
227:28 dark-blue] dark blue *UP*
227:31 Here!] ~, *UP*
227:31 Byrne, "Here] ~—"here *UP*
227:31 tent,] ~— *UP*
227:31 black-tartar's,] black tartar's— *UP*
227:33 yew tree] yew-tree *UP*
227:35 looked,] ~ *UP*
227:36 branches,] ~ *UP*
227:37 steadily:] ~; *UP*
227:40 restlessly:] ~; *UP*
228:1 'tong,-ting-tong'] "tong-ting-tong" *UP*
228:1 sheep bell] sheep-bell *UP*
228:12 and, unconsciously,] ~ ~ *UP*
228:15 hands—] ~, *UP*
228:20 baked potato," he *E1*] baked-potato. I'll call myself your baked potato stall," he *MS* baked potato...baked-potato ...he *UP*
228:26 cluster] ~, *UP*
228:29 read German *UP*] read a German *MS*
228:29 usual.—] ~. *UP*
228:30 language—.] ~. *UP*
228:31 arm-chairs *Ed.*] arm chairs *MS* armchairs *UP*
228:32 violin-case *UP*] violin case *MS*
228:32 seat,] ~ *UP*
228:34 protesting. This] ~. *P* This *UP*
228:36 its precedence. *E1*] it precedence. *MS*
228:38 gently. Since] ~. *P* Since *UP*
229:2 itself, delicately,] ~ ~ *UP*
229:6 of. *P* He] ~. He *UP*
229:8 "'The *Ed.*] "~ *MS*
229:8 Wood,'" *Ed.*] ~," *MS*
229:8 teased. Helena] ~. *P* Helena *UP*
229:12 Heaven] heaven *UP*
229:12 yew leaves] yew-leaves *UP*
229:15 move,] ~ *UP*
229:19 content!] ~, *UP*
229:21 roses',"] ~,'" *UP*
229:26 larch twigs] larch-twigs *UP*
229:31 Yes—] ~, *UP*
229:31 Time scrubs all sorts of scars off us." *E1*] Time scrubs the scars off us—with cloudy ammonia and cold cream,—Grief and sympathy—" *MS* Time...us with...cream. Grief...sympathy——" *UP*
229:33 smiled, and] ~. *P* And *UP*
229:38 him,] ~ *UP*
230:5 and making] ~, ~ *UP*
230:8 her dull *E1*] her rough, dull *MS*

In this edition the following compound words are hyphenated at the end of a line; these hyphenated forms occur in the base-text (MSII) and should be retained in quotation:

76:15	self-sufficient
107:26	solemn-sleeping
135:15	full-mouthed
135:24	emerald-facets
146:39	heat-entrancement
159:14	steam-boats
165:33	star-spiders
200:4	window-door
203:32	self-responsible
206:35	window-cleaner
224:27	grassy-declivity

APPENDIXES

Appendix 1

FROM 'THE LETTER': THE DIARY OF HELEN CORKE (WRITTEN 5 SEPTEMBER 1909 – 8 MAY 1910)*

Aug. 6th [19]09

'Sieglinde dear, I want you to promise that, whatever happens to me, you will go on...Remember dear, two wrongs do not make a right....

'I swear I will not live one day after you are dead –'

Sept. 5th

Chaos – still chaos – no light anywhere – Am I guilty of breaking my word, dear? Why did you leave me – why did you do what even you contemplated as wrong?

Was it that you could not bear the physical longing for me – Had those five days of unbroken intercourse made the prospect of limitation so unbearable that right and wrong – your own responsibility and others' pain weighed as nothing against the chance of cessation from all feeling. If so may God forgive my foolishness and pity my stupidity –I thought I understood...

Was it that only – or had you thought the matter out, and decided that death was the best course? I will believe that rather, unless you contradict me. I like to think that you were willing to sacrifice the body, because you felt that in the fight between it and your mind, it ignominiously held more than its own. I remember your words on Thursday morning 'Now, strangely, I wish I had'nt let you – and yet it was'nt all your fault.' Did you, looking into the future, see that we should both be in bondage to our passions, and that our lives meant the birth of miseries and wrongs yet unknown: O my darling, if this was your conviction – if you were willing to leave all these seeming certainties – to endure the fear and agony with which the strength of your physical nature must have approached death—I in my weakness can only hope that some day your strong hands may draw me up to your side again.

I don't know whether you anticipated anything more than oblivion. Probably you did not – else why were you willing to go alone – You might have taken me with you. I have always been unreasonably afraid of death till now, but I think if you had given me the choice, I should not have let you go without me. I should have tried to dissuade you from your purpose.

It may be that you expected me – that you believed our minds so attuned that even at Treknow you would be able to come to me and call me to you. Did I not swear to you that I would not live without you – not a day. Yet I was in ignorance

* The diary, in the form of a letter addressed to Herbert Baldwin Macartney, is in the possession of the Humanities Research Center, University of Texas at Austin. Helen Corke refers to this diary in *Portrait* as 'the long letter which there seems no need to end'(171).

for more than a week – anxious, certainly – for you did not write – but still hoping that it was only a matter of a lost address – planning what to do should you be ill.

'I think I had better not come back from Tintagel.' I remember saying that – too lightly saying it perhaps. Apart from the one great reason for suicide – the avoidance of what I told you I considered a greater crime – I had no desire or thought in its favour. I was indeed a little afraid that it might be my lot. But the bill was paid dear – you were right. I need not have worried about it. I hear now your despairing tones – oh those awful last few minutes. 'If I lose you I lose everything!'

If I have lost you, I have lost everything – Your vitality was my life. I clung to you in times of mental weakness, for under all the tempestuous surface water of your nature there was – oh may I say is – a calm depth of strength and self reliance which steadied me. I have not lost the sense of your personality. Tonight I feel scarcely different towards you from what I would feel if we were just separated for the usual week. But if I do lose that sense – if the increasing demands of what must now be a life of devotion to the commonplace, gradually rob me of the aura surrounding our intercourse – if you in short are to become a memory, thought – abstraction only, then life, as I have conceived it, no longer exists. Nothing remains but the 'permanent possibility of sensation'.

My darling, my Siegmund, *mine* now – if indeed you are aught but a dream – I want your warm passionate humanity – Madness, to write it, when the dear white hands I kissed are stiff and cold, and will never again send the music that throbbed in your brain through every fibre of your beloved fiddle. Where is it now, I wonder – silent in its case – or answering to the touch of a stranger. I would like to look at it sometimes – but it is right that a better player than I should succeed you as its owner. I am...

I stopped – I don't know what should have been written there – but what comes now is this. *I am the cause* of your misery and death, of Alice's horror and pain – I have made your children orphans. I loved to feel my power over you. I wanted you to love me – selfishness all – what did the others matter. O – they were welcome to the second place – so that the first was mine. Once you were drifting away from me – I myself had half broken the bonds – but I called you back. We would be *friends* – I flattered myself that I meant no more, then, and we have drifted together since. We will help each other, I said, and when the passion that touched me only racked and seared you I added fuel to flame and told myself that I was helping you to cultivate self control – Why did I not realise what I was doing. 'This will end in tragedy:' I said once, but there was almost pleasure in a thought not realised – What did I know of tragedy: *We* were together, I loved you, I love you now – oh the selfishness of that love. Not for your good – mine – mine always – persuading myself that my good was yours – How much of my sorrow now is self pity?

Do you despise me now dear? If you are – if your mind sees me now, now that you have put away the lust of the flesh for ever – pity me – pity me and forgive – I feel that I could bear very much now if I might just hear once more 'Sieglinde dear!' Perhaps some day before I die, when my poor little soul has grown –

My *soul* – yours – what do I mean? It is not easy to reject any kind of abstraction which may seem to offer the filmiest strand of hope to cling to. Comfort there is in the Celtic mysticism of Yeats – but can my reason accept such consolation – If I were only convinced that we each have an imperishable essence, which untouched by mortality will express itself in ever changing forms of increasing beauty – if I could also believe that our love has bound us indissolubly – that I might keep my finger on its golden thread, knowing that it would certainly lead me at last through death to you – then I could work and wait and be happy.

But I cannot at present have faith in anything tangible – hopes, wonders – wishes – no firm ground.

The beautiful conception of Nirvana – the absorption of the unit in the whole – the drop in the ocean – does not satisfy me at all. *I want you.* You as the individual. It was your cry for me once – have you forgotten dear? Have you forgotten it all – music – sun and sky and sea – and me? I would fain think not.

Why do I not ask of death?

I am surely not afraid now. At least I could defy the natural fear – but – you asked me to go on – for the sake of Agnes [Mason] and the others. Even were I sure of finding you in that dim world of mind, to shirk my penance were further selfishness. I may not pass on to my little friend who leans on me, this suffering which is mine. I want to share *your* responsibility. Those of yours whom I have injured – perhaps it will be in my power to help.

Ah no, I do not *want* to work out any sort of salvation in this way – I am tired, tired, dear – surely as tired as you were. With no self confidence, no faith in the virtue of the course I follow – no inspiration – how can I *want* to go on. I fear a kind of mental paralysis, bred of absolute hopelessness. In my work is no self expression – I am a machine. Irritable – depressing – moody – or assuming an optimism which is a sham – what good am I to the children I teach. 'Can the blind lead the blind – shall they not both fall into the ditch?'

Yet I live, and these three people who love me and who want to keep me with them are pleased when I can seem interested in the small commonplaces of the life from which I have wandered so far. There are no terribly obvious discords in this life; it is only a little mean tune full of wearyingly persistent repetitions.

I stop my ears and fall asleep, but even in my dreams I am still conscious that I am dreaming.

To sleep always – to stop this grinding thought which is not thought, but only the asking of unanswerable questions, and the cry for a little light. To be awake in the darkness and alone – .

'I can always sleep when I am miserable,' you said. How I comforted myself that night, when the miles were lengthening between us, saying that you were asleep, and had forgotten our misery for the time. I hoped that the sun would not wake you up early. But when my journey was done and I was lying in a half sleep, half stupor on the couch in that Treknow cottage – then you woke, and remembered everything. It had been so good to forget – even to forget Sieglinde. No unsatisfied desire – no sickening pretence – peace. And your weary soul braced itself for one last effort – the effort to attain an eternal peace – 'for there is no God found greater than Death – and death is a sleep'.

Have you found it – O my darling? When I, duly masked, was playing my part at Tintagel – and longing for Monday that I might get a message to quiet the fears which had haunted me since we parted – you were stretched again on your bed and the room was very silent. Was it peace, my Siegmund? You and yet not you. Love and desire never again to burn into my soul from those closed, faded blue eyes. I could not have kissed you awake as I did in our nest on the cliffs three days before. Strong, sensitive white hands, so limp now that they had finished their last terrible work as well as they had carried out every detail of their master's mind.

I went over to Malden on Sunday and looked at the empty house I had loved because it held you. It and Malden seemed not familiar – the personality of both had departed – you were gone. Had I stood by your bedside – should I have felt the same? Was your body only your house: Is there indeed a wise owner of houses who will 'let you a better'? If so I will find you yet. Sleep, dear – and rest. When I can feel that I have earned my night, and I slip away into the darkness, let me find your arms round me.

Five weeks tonight – our parting. How many more weeks – I wonder –

. . .

Sept. 26th

'Hope springs eternal'. I have started to work – not with any intelligent aim – but that my will is in training. Day by day I plan the time out and record whether the work so planned has been carried through. There is a satisfaction in getting physically weary and yet feeling that the will can force mind and body to finish its task. There is yet more content in the discovery that I can throw all my powers into the moment's business, and yet, as soon as it is over, feel myself again by your side on the cliffs by the sea, wrapped soul and body in the warm golden mist of our last Thursday morning. The intervening weeks vanish as soon as they are past.

Some sort of plan I seem sometimes to trace faintly. Looking back over our past road I fancy I see sign posts unseen before. Half forgotten dreams and fancies have taken significance almost prophetic. At times I am half convinced that we have been walking steadily forward in an appointed path when we thought we were lost children, aimlessly wandering. That we had helped each other as much as we could do at our present stage, and had to be separated for a while in order that we might not hinder each other. That we shall grow strong and self reliant, and find each other again, knowing, when we look into one another's eyes, that the love which Music suggested, and which we sought, was indeed beyond human conception, and experience.

Oct. 1st

Another Friday. The weeks pass, and all the trifles and the labour with which the days are filled are forgotten as soon as gone. My spirit stands looking over your grave into that little eternity of summer and joy. 'No one can rob us of our memories' you said. 'Ah, but if *you* have forgotten I shall also forget.'

I would wish to forget that Friday night and the cursed sense of convention which caused me to fail you in that crisis, the vain, vain thoughts of what I might have done – the lack of comprehension I showed, which strengthened Despair's hold upon you. My agony is keenest when I feel that I might have you yet, had I understood and acted without fear. Useless – foolish – maddening regret – born as you looked from a hell of pain into my eyes for the last time – and turned from the moving train;

growing when the journey was fairly started and the express flashed through Malden station – giving me a glimpse of the darkened windows of your home: always growing through the night – the pale wan night of mist and waning moon, till a shrouded morning broke –

Siegmund, Siegmund dearest – it will always grow till death brings me either that oblivion which is the end of all individuality – or in what state I know not and care not – you.

I had a dream last night in which I was happy once more. Your eyes looked at me out of a white mist – No more of you could I see, but I felt your passionate clasp again. *You* were the same – form mattered nothing.

Sunday, Oct. 3rd

I cannot work today, my brain is drained of energy. The weather is close and wet. I sit in this room of mine and endure the fearful piano din which comes from all around. If only there was *music* from any one of those pianos – I would be patient with the rest. I showed my impatience unwisely just now and was reproved and reminded that other people have to put up with my playing – Heavens! so they do – and to what end? Is any more *music* ever likely to emanate from my disordered mind. Work, work – endless Schradiek and Kreutzer trill studies are strengthening my fingers – but how can I ever play music who cannot think it? Agnes says that she can feel a disturbing unsettling influence which increases her nervousness when I play with her. Shall I give up?

Indeed I am inclined to wonder whether there be not the show of a braver spirit in the act of laying down a task which is obviously and indisputably beyond one's powers, than in continuing to beat oneself upon it. But I know that while I live I shall still seek relief from thought with my fiddle, and venture to hope that the beings who perpetrate the din from which I suffer – feeling no discomfort therefrom themselves, may not be too much troubled by me.

Today, however the strings will not even afford me any satisfaction. I put the fiddle in its case and try to read. I have the 6th volume of Wagner's biography and letters edited by Ashton Ellis. It is deeply interesting, tho' over weighted with small unimportant personalities. I feel less lonely in reading it. He suffered as we do – the Master – and 'Tristan' he calls 'Child of our sorrows'.

Of 'Tristan' I know nothing as yet – but I shall come to the opera when it is produced. Do you remember how much we said we both wished to hear it – I *wonder* whether you will be there?

. . .

Friday, Oct. 8th

Nine weeks – and tonight I am once more on Wimbledon station. I have been patting the earth which covers all that is left of that loved, troublesome, exacting body of yours. I have crowned it with great bunches of mountain ash berries. Then I went once more to Malden, and looked again at the locked windows of your drawing room, and the window of your room above it. Is it foolish of me to behave like a poor ghost whose being is only a shadow of what is past?

The Coombe lay dark and restful under a tranquil sunset, and the fields all round were as richly, youthfully green as on our night in the Spring when, after our lesson I walked that way and listened to all the thrushes singing the Spring song. I remember a line from one of your letters at that time. 'And my thoughts turn to August, and the realisation of a dream.' Oh, to know how many of your dreams August realised.

Sunday Oct. 10th

I have the score of 'Die Walküre'. I cannot play it, but a few chords here and there, and the chief motives, suggest the whole to me. I don't know whether it gives me the more pleasure or pain. The darkened opera house – and you down in the orchestra – the light from your desk illumining your earnest face. I watch tireless fingers and the masterful motion of a perfectly controlled bow. I know that you are happy, feeling that I am near you, and yet that your concentration is yet undisturbed – nay perhaps strengthened by my presence. I feel the Siegmund and Sieglinde motive bring you closer to me; the spell of the master magician is upon us both – we are children in the childhood of the world – and it is Spring flooded in moonlight. The first notes of the Spring Song – you are looking straight into my eyes – we are one, dear – and in more intimate union than when sometimes in each other's arms.

Sunday Oct. 17th

I spent last evening in the cosy dining room at Purley. Laura and your father welcome me, I think, *because* I love you. I want to be quite unselfish where they are concerned – I will try and say nothing to worry or vex them.

I am wondering exactly what you meant by pinning the card on which I wrote our address, to the note you left Alice. Was it only irony, or had you some dim idea that the bird, freed from its cage would make straight for the nest it loved. I think of your bitter words upon the journey back. 'The string is being pulled, and the bird is going back to its cage' – and I know how you scorned yourself as you said them.

Poor Alice – she hates me – and yet I still do not know whether she loves you. She and I are antitheses. I thought to help her – but it seems impossible. 'Til I regard our love as a sin, and all which has lifted me out of materialism – all that has given me beauty for ashes and linked the ideal and the real, as suitable fuel for her burning, there can be no true sympathy between us. Her suffering seems to me the most unexplained part of the tragedy.

After March I shall know how to act – At present the way seems to lead straight towards 'August, and the realisation of a dream'. I will work hard and earn my liberty.

The dream is so sweet that it interferes with the business today. I cannot put it into music. I remember on the Sunday evening at Treknow, sitting on a great black rock watching the tide come roaring and foaming up the gulleys of Trebawith Strand. In the fiery red of the sunset I noticed a lonely white gull perched motionless upon the same rock. The red light glowed on his white feathers, and he sat on the very edge, apparently oblivious of the noisy water just beneath, looking out over the sea towards the sunset. No other bird was to be seen. Was it because you had said 'I shall be very often with you in spirit' that I thought of you with the personality of the bird? Once since I have dreamed of flying over the surf – I think at Compton

Bay. I don't think it occurred to me to wonder whether I had become a seagull – the motion was perfectly natural.

Oct. 20th

...I am going to try and do a little German with the help of David so that I may get more insight into Wagner's philosophy. I used to find David a mental stimulus – he is so eager for experience, so self confident and clear headed, so fearless in criticism. He holds the cup of life before him and contemplates it with great satisfaction – he is going to drain it before putting it down. He stimulates me to greater misery now – I who stand holding a broken cup – bearing my famishing thirst as best I may. 'Courage and more wine' he says and laughs when I turn tired eyes to seek the shadow of a kind angel who may have in keeping, tho' still hidden, a perfect cup to replace my useless one.

Oct. 24th

...Come to me dear – just your old self, and let me be Sieglinde again. For I cannot yet shake off responsibility to fulfil my own words. I will write them and realise afresh the joy of your face, and the sun on the sea and the wind blowing through my hair – and the warm sand under my bare feet.

'You look now as if you belong to the sea', you said. 'I do – and someday I shall go back to it.'

Sunday Oct 31st

Hallow'een. I have heard 'Tristan' for the second time: Sat on Friday night near my old place – saw your seat filled by another – it was Covent Garden, but...how long must I stay with dead things: The strangeness seemed not so much in your absence as in my presence. As for the music – surely you must be familiar with it. For I am Isolt as well as Sieglinde – but a more unfortunate Isolt. I came from Cornwall to find my Tristan – but I found only his grave. Little of real tragedy, it seems to me, lies in the last act – Fate was kind to both. My lot is harder. 'Where Tristan now is going – wilt thou Isolda, follow?' Ah, if you could but tell me, dear, why you did not wait for me? Come quickly March. Those dreary rainy October days have dragged away at last. Last year – the glory of the woods in the vale and on the Common – how inexpressibly content I was then.

Nov. 3rd

The search for something real – the essence of things – I remember writing to you from Rye, four years ago – 'When I am quite tired, and have given up looking for anything real, I will go back to Mermaid Street and drowse away the residue of life in one of its red tiled cottages, where the bees drone over the hanging window boxes, and the chant of the nuns in the tiny chapel, mingles with the drone of the bees. And where, from the upper window I could see away over the plain below, a dark blue line which is the sea' – Something like that I wrote, in the days when with the characteristic humbug which has ruined our lives, I heaped petty kindnesses upon Alice and the children to salve my conscience for drawing you nearer to myself.

Two real things I have found: the joy of our five days and the pain which has succeeded them, and which stretches before me indefinitely. But, like the little mermaid in Andersen's tale, I will welcome suffering if it will only confirm the hope of the sole immortality I covet – life with you.

Sunday Nov. 7th

My brain is getting numbed. The self which lived only through you is starving. It is growing feeble, and the host of smaller, meaner selves which it dominated, are fighting above it. I loathe them; those little selves – so content with the scraps thrown to them – so cowardly.

'Put on your mask, as I do mine,' you said once. I replied, 'I have no mask. It is only one of my faces.'

Monday

More strength of mind, more concentration and grip, dear – I look behind too much. And death rather than the paralysis of materialism.

Nov. 17th

I came by the old 8-55 train to Wimbledon on Saturday and walked over the Common, through the Warren and to Kingston. The serenest autumn glory hovered over the woods. I could see Malden from the Common – even distinguish your home – I came to the stile half way down the path leading into the Vale, and thought of that first walk – in May, more than two years ago, when you introduced me to the Common and the Park. I remembered resting on the stile, and watching thick lowering clouds over Malden. 'We shall be drenched,' I said 'Oh no' you replied indifferently 'it will clear'. And the stars came out as the night closed. We were very happy that night: all around the thrushes sang the Spring Song.

Horrible Kingston: and they put you there under eight feet of clay, in a cemetery surrounded by mean streets and overlooked by a factory chimney. On the slope of Putney Heath you might have lain. There even the inevitable ugly monuments are half hidden by trees. When I die, if the sea is not my grave, I want the fire to have my body, and then let the ashes be scattered over the sea.

Ah well: perhaps it matters not at all. I find no angel to say to me 'Why seek ye the living among the dead', as I kneel to make a grave into a garden, and shudder as I throw aside the writhing earth creatures I find. But I do not realise that *you* are below. Certainly if Siegmund exists, he does not waste any time in such surroundings. Yet, when the thrushes sing the Spring Song in the two big willow trees near, I want that little mound to be covered with flowers. So much beauty – at least we will produce – by the help of Death.

...

Nov. 26th

I am writing the story of our five days. It is good to live it all over again in the writing of it. At present every detail is clear – I write but enough to suggest the whole – how much I want to show it you – to ask whether you think I have succeeded in catching the beauty of our Utopia.

...

Dec: 2nd

It is a black stormy night – dark before I took off my abhorred school mask and came home in the reeking car. The wind recalls a night late last autumn, when we tore up and down the road over Mitcham Common, pursued by all the winds of Dante's First Circle. Your letters of that time – I was secretly proud of my power, dear, – the power that wrung such pleading from the soul of my king and star – Did I know whether, in all this lonely, deaf, dumb and sightless universe ought remains of your conscious life, I would call you as you called me – 'Come to me dear – come to me – I cannot live without you. I cannot go through this desert alone' –

Dec: 5th

'Tristan' is becoming as familiar to me as 'Die Walküre'. I have been looking through the score today. Sometimes my tortured imagination will picture what might have been if I had understood, and held you back from death. I see three months more of growing misery for you, my darling, of misery and perhaps of terror for me – then the message of 'Tristan', and oblivion for both of us.

I cannot say that you did not do right. Perhaps it is good that I now wear a mask to cover a living death and smile and play and work incessantly without hope or wish. The flies are all dead now. I watched many of them when first the frost came. They hurried about with a tremendous show of blind energy. Almost as aimless as my efforts seem.

Dec: 8th

I am feeling stifled. Siegmund, for one breath of your spontaneous life. David has lent me a book called 'Evelyn Innes'. The greater part of it is full of music and passion, and set me aching again with physical longing for you. They have buried you, dear, deep and quiet, but is'nt it worse to have left the consciousness of Life's pulse beating against one's dead self. I want to kiss the throbbing veins upon your temples, dear – to look into the blue night of your eyes, and to be hurt by your passionate, seeking hands.

Oh – that – or to sleep – 'deep, unending, all, oblivion' Tristan's Kingdom – and yours. Are not the Powers that guide men's destinies weary of the unceasing cry?

Even at night when my body sleeps my mind wanders on in squalid suffocating ways.

...

Dec. 30th

Do you remember Christmas Eve last year. It was nearly dark when I reached Malden, and came up the road past the field. The house had a deserted look, and I almost felt afraid – an indefinite fear. But though all the windows were dark, the little red shaded, oriental lamp on the hall table was burning, and you brought me into our drawing room and put me into the arm chair by the fire. Then we had tea – we two in the silent house – by fire light and candle light. We talked – you standing upon the rug with your back to the fire looking down upon me curled up luxuriously in the arm chair; while I finished my tea very slowly – loving and yet fearing the light in your eyes and the restless energy you were trying hard to keep under control. But as soon as I could not even pretend to eat more, there was a minute's silence, and you were down by my chair, your head in my lap. Our fiddles were not touched that evening. It was the only time we allowed even music to take nothing of our concentration upon each other –

This year I wanted to creep up to the door again – if only to fancy the dim red light shining in the hall. I walked over the Common, deserted, and soaked with almost incessant rain – It was so still that even the fir trees stood stiff as children's toys – and the unborn, folded Spring could discern unconsciously the redness of warmth and light. I sat on the stile by the Malden path waiting, looking stupidly at dead leaves under an oak tree – I did not want to reach Malden before twilight.

The house is let –

Jan. 9th [1910]

The vacation is over. I have kept my body working, and taken a walk nearly every day. I have practised, with what interest I could, regularly. I have prepared my school work for next term. My home mask now fits very well – indeed I have pressed it on so tightly that to raise it would cause discomfort. I suppose it will only collapse when all it covers has wasted. The story of our last week is not yet finished. I snatch some crumbs of contentment from memory, for I only write a little each time; it is possible to forget the present entirely in the past.

Jan: 16th

Last night I took my fiddle and played to Laura and your father – the Seitz concerto – and we tried the Gade Sonata, but the accompaniment proved too difficult. I hear that Alice is well and seems her old self. She and the children can do without us both, dear.

Talk, talk, talk, – the smell of the toadstools covering the fallen tree.

'I would come to you from hell': you said once – but no glimpse of you brightens for an instant this hell of mine. Yet I must not be too despairing – who have not sought you through death.

I have been reading again the libretto of 'Madam Butterfly'. Do you remember the last time you played in it – Act One – all brightness, colour and life, ending with 'Night of Rapture' – then I ran down the stairs and we had five minutes talk chiefly over the final arrangement for going to Freshwater. Acts Two and Three – the development and climax of Butterfly's pitiful story – the simplicity of Emmie Destinn's realisation of the part – the sympathy of her glorious voice.

> 'Too much light outside
> And too much smiling Spring.'

And I, making a sort of personal application of the tragedy, told myself that I ought to feel like a guilty supplanter. So when you overtook us afterwards I let the others talk to you and only looked, very seriously into your eyes. They answered with complete understanding, and the joy of that silent sympathy and the sense of our complete unity, made me fear lest I should be drugging my conscience with an affectation of remorse.

...

Feb. 3rd Thursday –

A year today 'Rheingold'. That grand, all comprehending E Major chord, climbing its way from inaudible depths to inaudible heights – Wagner's symbol of the fundamental realities.

The arrangements for the season at Covent Garden are made public – Two cycles of the Ring – and 'Tristan' – Again 'Pelleas' and 'Tess', 'Samson', 'Madame Butterfly' – but you know the list, surely. 'That will be something to look forward to' you said, when you had told me of the signing of your contract. I shall do my best to get cycle tickets for the 'Ring'. I remember telling you that I should like us to hear 'Valkyrie' 'when you were not playing'. But I have now no hope of finding you, nor of feeling your presence, on this side death.

Feb: 16th

Dearest, it is only play now – only pretence to write to you. For I am dead – that I which had its life centred in your personality – which bound you to itself with a cobweb of idealism. This Self which now is all that has taken Our place, knows Us only indirectly. To it We are romance. Our bodies of woven dream stuff belong to the world of word and colour and sound. It is flesh and blood and appetite. It uses your name to summon a mental image of its own fashioning – which has indeed scarce a resemblance of you.

Feb. 20th Sunday

A tempest of wind and rain is booming the menacing motive of storm. The rain lashes my window, and I suppose, the lonely little snowdrops on your grave. I went to see them last week – just two were in bloom, and I picked one and brought it home with me. It still peeps its tiny shrivelled face over the top of its vase. One or two tulips and some crocuses showed strong green shoots above the soil, but the hyacinths and irises and daffodils are yet underneath. They are stretching long white fingers down towards you – they are my only messengers. Only they dare come through the dark clay where the earth creatures hide – and you – are lying even deeper than they may push their way. I will plant roses later, and a little birch tree from the Common. It may be, that in the sight of Those Who Know, your body is yet as fair as mine. So I, who do not know, slip my fingers under the earth, and send my desire down by the white, fearless root-fingers.

You came to me I think, a year ago today. It was dark, and I kept the blinds up till you should be guided by the firelight. When you came I was afraid of unrestrained intercourse and we were unhappy.

I would that your free spirit could come to me tonight. The gale is sweeping in fury from the South. If anywhere on the shore of our home you are yet lingering, ride the wind and come and claim me, Siegmund, my Siegmund.

The living would laugh at me for a foolish dreamer – but indeed it is no more difficult to feel that such a dream might be realised, than to realise that the past is not a dream.

...

March 25th

It is Good Friday. I have escaped from the dragging home ties, to Sevenoaks for the weekend. I am free to play and write and read as I choose. I have my fiddle with me, and the Beethoven Sonatas, and my harmony exercises – so long neglected: also German exercises and some folios of David's story which I am revising for him.

So I wait, and watch your decaying image. Every morning I wake with the thought 'Siegmund is dead', and always, always, my brain peers into the blank page of death to find even the faintest, most unintelligible record of you. Hope's flame has ceased to give any light: at the most it flickers uselessly for an instant, now and then. I suppose I shall yet go on living, as long as my mind will bear the strain of an existence devoid of love, hope and faith. Art is left to me, indeed, but I feel too weary to pursue it. David tries to spur me on – he believes I have the power of creative art – but he is young and lusty and I am old, and the well of life is low and muddy for me. I am afraid of leaning upon him – afraid of discovering yet more unworthiness in my own nature.

April 13th

Thunder in Spring – a grey blue gloom of cloud from the southwest – all the windows blurred by lashing rain driven before a shrieking wind – The flicker of rosy lightning, and the steady rolling of a smooth black thunder surge. Beyond the storm a lake of palest green, skimmed by cloud puffs of whipped black froth.

A thrush sings the passing of the storm from a sleeping ash-tree near. The great silent cloud shapes move grandly on towards the darkness of the evening's eastern road, from twilight through the heavy glow that hangs above the hearth of the sun.

Do you see dear – Once I wrote you only the hot thoughts of a mind full of ache and fever – now I am lingering over words – comforting myself with the beauty of words, and the satisfaction of being able to bring from them the only harmony I understand. They come to me with their delicate suggestions – and build themselves into chords – broken perhaps, but yet living – real – intelligible – Through you dear, the Real spoke in terms of music – I envied you that power of expression, and stooped to imitation. O Domine – how your dull pupil must have chafed you. I love my violin still, but I know now that it will never yield to me.

May 8th

The season has begun – and in spite of myself, life and spring claim me still. Siegmund! wo bist du? – are you awake and glad? Do you still bid me go on? Tell me if Love and Death are one.

I have drawn another life into mine – to hold as I hold you dear. What can I do?

> Thou art too far off for wings of words to follow
> Far too far off for thought or any prayer
> What ails us gazing where all seen is hollow –

It seems so – O Destiny, if this is my waking time – this year – put no more dreams into my sleep – for even in my sleep I shall laugh at the dreams.

Appendix 2

THE FRESHWATER DIARY (WRITTEN 1909–10), BY HELEN CORKE*

I will not dress too early this morning altho' the sun and the dancing green boughs outside the open window invite me to get up – I will try and sleep again – there are seven long hours to wait.

It is now nearly half past ten – how to make the walk to Yarmouth – a little over three miles – last till three oclock – I consider – and start strolling slowly up the lane towards Farringford.

Where is Siegmund now? – Perhaps he has reached Portsmouth?

I linger under the noble trees which shelter the home Tennyson loved – then on past farm and cottage till a stretch of sunlit baked road makes me long for shade. There is none and the road winds up and up.

At the top – I stand and look over the valley and down – the Solent shines blue to the north – I am not yet in sight of Yarmouth – but I am more than half way there. It lies somewhere at the bottom of this winding hill road which is the next stage of the journey. There is a little brick chapel standing near and I listen to the congregation within singing the hymn 'O Paradise' – I hum the tune and laugh happily and think how supremely foolish of people to shut themselves up in an ugly little building to sing about a mythical heaven when here outside the Lord God has planted a garden of delight.

Downwards now – I arrive at a pleasant green, shaded by trees. I will rest and read. A clock in the cottage opposite strikes twelve – O Time – if I could only treat you in Wonderland fashion – Three more hours!

Half an hour passes. 'Romola' is hard reading today. I stroll on down the hill. A soldier on a bicycle sings out a cheery 'Good-morning', which I return.

I am at the bottom of the hill and the sea is close – but Yarmouth itself half a mile further on. Through a gate I pass down a path on to the shore. I sit down close to the water, but the sun is very hot and here there seems no breeze.

Well. I will reach Yarmouth – the half mile of road is not interesting. Half way along it I cross a bridge and an official comes forth from a cottage at the side and demands a toll. I pay and ask for information about a big liner at present passing noiselessly very close in shore.

Yarmouth – the place is in its Sunday sleep. I am tired, and the sky is getting overcast. It is only twenty minutes past one.

I will go on the jetty – at present deserted. At least there is a seat at the end, and I can read. I try to induce an automatic machine to surrender me some chocolate,

* The manuscript is in the possession of the Humanities Research Center, University of Texas at Austin.

but it obstinately refuses. Patience: Siegmund is waiting at Newport – only twelve miles away.

Grey sky. Chilly wind – even a spot of rain. Perhaps I had better find the station.

There is the train – going to Newport. The clock of that grey church has just struck two. The station is in view – it lies close to the marshes.

Two small boys clamber over a gate at the side and suggest to me a similar course. But the gate is higher than I anticipated, and so I cross the metals, and sit down in a corner of the shelter on the down side of the station. I *must* read, and I do, only disturbed by the screaming of the restless, wheeling swallows.

By three oclock I am feeling damp and chilly – the draught is laden with mist. But there is only ten minutes longer to wait. The station master, who is also signalman, booking clerk and porter, proceeds to signal the train through. I cross to the opposite side, get my ticket, and return.

The little train is in sight. I am shivering with cold, and a vague doubt as to whether, after all, Fate is going to let us – –

'You *here*!' I am dragged into a carriage, shaking almost too much to answer that familiar voice, with an unfamiliar ring of gladness in it. But the train has started, and Siegmund's arms are round me, holding me close enough to hurt.

'Is it a dream *now*, dear?' he whispers.

Ah yes! it *is* all a dream – and bad dreams have clouded my brain since then. It is very dark, and I have lost my Siegmund. In this night I am afraid to walk alone, so I crouch down and wait. With the greyest dawn I will seek him. But I am very tired –

Aug. 1st

The foghorn warning comes to us, muffled by the mist. We are together on the cliffs for the first time. We have hardly a regret for the vanished beauty of the morning – and it matters not at all that we can scarcely see five yards before us. The sunlight of the inner vision is unclouded – after nearly six years of waiting Fate has granted us five days of each other. Of this eternity the unseen sea is singing below us. Wrap us closer – grey damp shroud of mist. White, singing sea, lure us closer. Take us by the steep cliff pathway into the dark – let our last consciousness be the tighter clasp of each other's arms. For Fate is already setting upon her favours a price to be paid in agony.

We stand at the cliff edge and see how the smooth white chalk slope vanishes beneath. 'Shall we go down here and end all our troubles?' says one. But there is no sincerity in the suggestion. It is too absurd in the face of that illimitable five days prospect.

The foghorn in F, or in F♯ – we disagree about the pitch – still calls from westward. We wander on in that direction. The Mist Spirit who has her home above the Lethe stream has dropped a beautiful cloud round our souls. So kind is she. Neither past nor future have we, but an infinite content.

Suddenly and strangely rises in our path, and but a few steps before us, the great dim outline of a Cross. The Mist Spirit has no veil thick enough to hide its form. It stands like a shadow of itself: a gigantic, menacing shadow. We turn back and presently descend the cliffs to the Bay. It is nearing sunset time, and breaking masses of fog flying from cliff to cliff uncover a still sky of mottled gold. We will go eastward now.

Beyond the links lie green mounds and turfed banks of earth. I am tired, and choose the driest to rest against.

'Children,' says Apollo, 'I give you the beauty of peace. You are mine, and the day is mine. Look, and worship!'

The curtains of the Mist Spirit become but transparent golden films through which we gaze into the light which satisfies. The light which can only be seen by those into whose souls it has been born. Greatly blessed and greatly cursed are they, for seldom is the light unobscured – and the black shadows are terrible.

Siegmund asks what music holds the best interpretation of the sunset. I am silent, but he is thinking of a Beethoven symphony. Afterwards, for me it blends itself into the sustained harmonies of the strings in the Grail music from 'Lohengrin'.

The glory is very transient: the fog thickens again, and our visible world is limited to a small circular patch of wet grass. We will go home.

I look out at eleven o'clock. The moon is wading through shallows into a clear depth of blue. We walk down the white road to the Bay, and stand at the beginning of the Moonpath across the full tide.

Aug. 2nd Monday

The morning breeze is fresh, and the stems of the creeper outside my window wake me with imperative tapping. It will be a day of alternate cloud and sun – but with more sun than cloud.

At nine o'clock it is good to lean over the low sea wall and spread one's fingers out upon the warm stones. There is much content, and satisfaction unspoiled by satiety in the curling of the deep blue water round the little rocks below. But soon the breeze from over the green hill calls us westward. Upon the highest point stands clearly out the Tennyson Cross. No mysticism wraps it this morning: it is just a shining white stone monument – an admirable landmark, and memorial to the poet whose name it bears. We regret that it should be necessary to surround the cross with an ugly iron railing painted red.

Westward still! We are nearing the Needles. How the gulls scream and moan. Hundreds live in these cliffs.

'Come back dear! Oh *don't* go so near the edge', Siegmund pleads, when I creep close as possible to the beautiful birds. But I laugh and feel proud of my steady brain – just for a moment – Only play! a kind of play with the possibility of separation which makes the joy of the reality of possession more intense.

This is the mighty cliff which terminates the south-western corner of the island. A slippery path of dazzling chalk ends in a sheer descent of something like four hundred feet. West of this bends Alum Bay. We enquire the nearest way down, and the coast-guard directs us to the Path of the Hundred Steps. Siegmund counts the steps, being sceptical about the number and reduces it to sixty eight.

The water laps quietly in upon the beach. We lie down to rest upon the sloping terrace of beach nearest it, and look out through half closed fingers. One or two lazy sailing ships idle down the Solent. Siegmund attempts to classify them, and I listen and laugh, not at all respectfully – for he probably knows rather less about them than his pupil.

Clouds and sun, but more sun than cloud. Yet of any cloud Siegmund is impatient. I am not, for I know the good north west wind controls those big black masses and that their day's journey is far.

We do not talk much, and our thoughts are heavy winged and have no desire to fly above the cliffs. I can hear the curling splash and retreat of sleepy little waves, and the strong beat of Siegmund's heart.

Later in the afternoon we decide to walk on to Colwell Bay. The way of the shore is strewn with crumbling cliffs. We climb heaps of slippery stone and jump running water; we scramble up half obliterated paths and creep round dangerous corners; we halt for breath upon reaching a grass crowned mound midway. Siegmund holds me tightly and breathes hard – I cannot speak. It is full tide.

We are alone upon the shore but for three children, who are searching for treasures. They are presently enriched by the gift of an electric light bulb which Siegmund finds. Curious that the frail thing of the city should lie there intact, where the sea has strewn wide the ruins of the land.

The way home lies across country. We pass a little Catholic church in the fields: a carved Christ looks down from his cross over the mounds of the dead. Our path, skirting the churchyard wall, leads through a fir copse, and down a very steep tree-shadowed hill. At the bottom of this, we have much argument as to the right direction – but presently find our way through a pasture bordered by great elms, out behind a poultry farm. Then we see the woodlands of Farringford. Somewhere in the distance a band is playing the 'Watch on the Rhine'.

As we pass under the beeches by the Tennyson bridge, I wonder, carelessly, what next Monday will bring for us. It hardly matters – being so immense a distance away. But Siegmund grips me as if parting were imminent, though his laugh is quite natural.

'Quick curtain!' he says joyously.

August 3rd Tuesday

The little waves run up the beach full and clear and foamless. I lie in the deliciously cool water and look lazily round the Bay – its rocks and cliffs – and out over the shining sea. It is seven in the morning. Existence is a calm perfection of delight.

We decide, an hour later, that today we will explore eastward in Eden.

The sand of Compton Bay is firm and white. A narrow strip is beyond high water mark. We descend by means of a gap in the high cliffs, where a landslip has crumbled them.

The breeze is left behind, up on the hills. Down here is glowing heat quivering from sand and stones. When my bare feet feel scorched I run into the water to cool them. We have no desire to walk further – but sit down upon the sand, leaning against a smooth, flat bar of glistening brown stone.

We are silent. Even thought fades in the compelling, enthralling sunshine.

So we lie for hours, and the sea creeps close up to us and sinks again: sinks till a boulder strewn way is opened for us, along the shore. Late in the afternoon a breeze finds its way down. I stand up and shake the sand out of my loose hair – and let the wind comb out its tangles – and feel a wonderful sense of harmony and happiness. Siegmund smiles up at me, then rouses himself to say 'You look now as if you belong to the sea!' 'I do – and someday I shall go back to it', is my instant answer.

Our progress among the rocks is slow. We have to climb them and it is easy to slip off into sand and water. We linger over lovely rock pools, seaweed curtained and full of red anemones, and meanwhile the sun is slanting down beyond the Cross. At last Siegmund, looking doubtfully at two miles more of glistening sunlit boulders, suggests ascending the cliffs. I am in no hurry to put on stockings: and sit upon a rock looking at pink toes in a warm little pool.

'Come!' says Siegmund, holding out his arms. 'You are only six years old today.'

The sand is being invaded by way of the cliff path. A whole family, including the kitten, which the youngest child liberates upon the beach. Poor bewildered little atom! it scampers mewing after the dog.

We stand upon the edge of the cliff and see the two bays. On our left, blue water and the House of the Brown Stones. On our right a rippled, sun-gold sea, and Freshwater in partial shadow from the west cliff. Siegmund lingers over the view.

'I want to absorb it *all* into my memory', he says earnestly after a long silence.

Yes, we can retain the details of our vision – it may be an exquisite photograph – but what, for want of a clearer definition we call 'atmosphere' fades as quickly and surely as the scent of a dying rose.

The moon rises late this evening. We think to find our way through the lanes to Alum Bay, and eventually, keeping the Cross in sight, to return over the down, with the Moonpath before us.

The twilight dims more rapidly than we anticipate. The lane winds, and we have lost our landmark. By the time we reach the next sign post there is barely light enough to show its wording. The Down, its slope darkened by furze, is to the left.

We approach it by a path leading to a disused chalk pit and ascend till we reach the lower edge of the furze. Then Siegmund tries vainly to find a way through. It seems an impenetrable forest of black prickles.

He comes back to me at last. 'I'm afraid we must give it up tonight,' he says. So we sit down on the sloping grass. Northward, over the trees below, we can see the little lights of the moving ships in the Solent, and the big fixed light on Lymington pier. After a little while, intense quiet is over everything, and the lamps are put out in the farmhouse which we passed on our way up.

We take a wrong turning, upon the way home. When the moon shines above the Down behind us, she is still struggling through cloud barriers. Being lost, we simply keep as directly as possible to the eastward, but the lanes wind. We walk on, thinking.

'We may be on the road to Newport,' I say presently, as the country develops yet more unfamiliar features. 'And the distance is ten miles.'

I laugh, not caring in the least whether we are really going further astray. I am drunk with freedom. Let the lane turn about as it will, and let us wander on through scented fields and past sleeping farms till we are quite tired. There is no one to question us, even in look or thought. The Dreams only share with us this island of peace: the dreams of those in the locked and darkened cottages. So have we often sent our dreams forth, but all that their weak willing little hands gather to bring back for us they lose upon the way, and only the scent of Night's flowers still clings round them.

We cross a stile, and recognise, on the right of the path the graveyard of the Catholic chapel. The shrinking moon has slipped between the clouds, and shines upon the white stones. The carved Christ upon his cross hangs black against a silver grey sky. The path before us disappears into the pine copse.

We step softly into the darkness – intense darkness to our vision. Siegmund's arm is round me, but I cannot see him. No cathedral ever enshrined such a depth of silence.

'Are you quite sure that this is the way?' Siegmund whispers.

I am quite sure – and presently we come out into the hazy moonlight, and stumble down the steep hill, and very cautiously cross the pasture and the poultry farm. A merry noise would there be should we wake all the fowls.

But this does not happen, and we are presently safe upon the Farringford road.

Aug. 4th Wednesday

The garden in front of our house is long and crooked with a sunken flagstone pavement running up to the door by the side of the lawn. The high fence screening the garden on either side is heavy with mingling clematis and honeysuckle. A bushy little laburnum shades the seat where I sit, tracing out the course of our wanderings upon the map.

Siegmund's hand upon the latch startles me. He is standing at the gate in the sunshine. We greet each other across the tall roses.

The people of the farm below the Down are busy dipping their sheep this morning. The process is quite primitive. In the middle of the yard is a big zinc bath, half full of a dirty yellow liquid. Two men seize a fat sheep from the little group penned in a corner, and with difficulty hold him more or less in the bath, while the third bales the yellow stuff over his back with an old tin bowl. The farmer's family stands ready to assist, if necessary.

We pass on to the slope of the Downs, and directly in front is the path through the furze which last night we missed. The sun is hot and a stiff breeze is energetically chasing the few little white clouds. We climb slowly and gain the highest point near the Cross.

A green hollow, by the edge of the cliff, shall be our house today. I make a book-rest of Siegmund, and read, while he, with hands crossed behind his head looks lazily over the sparkling sea.

The sun scorches and the breeze and Siegmund drop asleep. I change my position and try to shade his head, which he *will* bare in defiance of the strongest sun. The veins in his wrists are blue and swollen with the heat.

There lies Freshwater, tucked down in the valley, and the little Bay below the hill, and green Farringford on the slope, all asleep too.

I long for shade.

'It is worth while to sleep, for the sake of a waking like this!' says Siegmund, when he rouses. 'I was dreaming of huge glittering ice-crystals!'

At the cliff's edge the wind comes fresh from the water, cool against my sunburnt face and arms. We can see the path from this point. An invalid's chair is being wheeled over the short grass, and its misshapen and helpless occupant turns pain-sunken eyes towards the sea. We look once only, and then leave him the quiet of our green hollow. Torn, shrivelled, seaweed, beyond reach of the tide! the life-tide in which we exult, in whose infinity our self consciousness is lost.

The curtain of the Mist Spirit is thinning. Siegmund sees beyond it more clearly than I!

'Do you want anything better than this, dear,' he says, as we walk slowly home. 'Shall we come here next year, and stay for a whole month?'

I wonder if he himself feels the unreality of his apparently commonplace suggestion – whether his words are a protest against the conviction that has come to *me* with a strength forbidding question, and yet with a calm dispelling all fear. The conviction that the Fate who has been, since the beginning, resolving obvious discords gradually, by unfamiliar progressions, and out of original combinations weaving wondrous harmony with our lives, is too great an artist to suffer an anti-climax.

'If there be any next year,' I say carelessly, and Siegmund needs no explanation for the reply.

But later, in the warm gloaming, when a dusky stillness is rising from the sea, and we are alone on the eastern downs, I feel myself slipping into an unforeseen valley of shadows. There is void and darkness around me, and out of it comes only the distant crying of many lives that have touched mine. These I know, but beyond them, low and plaintive, I hear the complaint of a little unknown voice. What have I done to hurt it so?

Siegmund, in an irresponsible mood, is whistling the 'Spring Song' from 'Die Walküre'. He is very far away from me – indeed, I half wonder if I have loved only a dream woven soul – and no reality. I call to him, despairingly – only he can silence with comfort those wailing voices. If my Siegmund exists, I must send him back into their darkness.

I cannot find him. I drag myself free from the passionate grip of his arms, and drop down sobbing, in the shelter of the tumuli – trying to shut out the unreasoning pleading of his voice.

He is beaten at last. There is quiet, and I become conscious that a stranger, passing along the cliff, is looking curiously towards us.

Thursday. Aug. 5th

The flowing tide trickles noiselessly among the rocks, widening and deepening insidiously the little pools. Only an occasional gurgle, at once subdued, tells of its return, as it takes possession of this dim, clammy cave I am exploring. From the shiny boulders upon the floor the seaweeds stretch down their fingers into the dark water. I climb and wade towards the ragged arch at the entrance, and so come again into the sunshine of the early morning.

Warm and sweet is the air of this lane, remote from the sea: the belt of dewy grass on either side is thick with little pink and white convolvuli. They have climbed half way up the dwarf fir trees in the hedge – the still old trees, keeping forever their winter mourning and winter thoughts. It is a perfect day to which these flower children have been born, and in sun-glow and wind-thrill its hours will pass uncounted by them. When it is over and the dainty cups curl sleepily, night will touch and seal them against the possible gloom of tomorrow.

'It is good when life holds no anti-climax,' I say softly to Siegmund.

He agrees, but fails to find the path of my thought. He cares nothing for the details of Nature's working. He stands apart, in her holy places, till her soul bends to his blind worship. With spirit and sense he adores her and only through music does he seek to interpret her.

The lane leads upwards to the freedom of the eastern down. At the end of it stands a low bungalow, roofed with dusky red, in the midst of a large square of the coolest green lawn. The flowers and bushes in the border touching the lawn on all sides are sparkling with sunlit dew.

On a garden seat, with his face turned from the sun, sits the owner of the house, reading a paper. As we pass, he flings it irritably down, calls twice a name we do not catch, and hurries indoors.

'Isn't he in a bad temper!' says Siegmund, much amused. 'And all because breakfast is a little late. Look – here come his wife and daughter.'

They look flurried and anxious. They push open the gate, rush across the lawn and enter the house by the shady verandah.

'It's pitiful,' says Siegmund, still smiling, but with much regret in his voice. 'Imagine the things he is saying – the life inside that house – even this morning.'

I feel as if a fussy cock and two hens had just scurried across my path.

Our little kingdom dreams on. There is no thought in its dream, but only the consciousness of all satisfying light and colour and heat. The mist curtain, thick and golden, wraps it heavily – so heavily that no wind from beyond can even sway its fringe.

In six hours we shall be exiles. We shall have passed the curtain. I can thin it with a wave of my hand. But the present is a warm drowsy calm. There is something of the quiet of exhaustion in it. We suffered so last night.

Sometimes a bee drones softly, aimlessly, over the scented grass. No ship sails the sea; the white light dances fitfully, leaping to and fro over the blue ripples.

Presently we climb down the cliff's edge and seek the House of the Three Brown Stones. At midday the sun scorches very fiercely. I hide my smarting arms under Siegmund's coat. Something in his voice makes me cling to him half savagely when he says, looking wistfully away, 'I *think* I should be able to follow your moods, if – if only I could have you a little longer.'

I will have no mercy on those shadows, the next time they come between us. They may go back to hell.

An hour passes – fleeting before us in sea-woven blue and gold: or perhaps three sister hours, playing on the edge of the foam; or maybe none of these, but a Life, in sheen of countless softened hues. Our eyes are sun-dimmed, and we can scarcely trust our vision.

When the ebbing tide has left the rocks, and the sun has bleached them white, we turn at last from the lonely, lovely shore. Standing silently above, on the grass, we look hopelessly at our beautiful world, and hopelessly at each other.

'Addio!' says Siegmund presently.

Appendix 3

FROM 'THE CORNWALL WRITING' (WRITTEN 1911–12) BY HELEN CORKE*

On the opposite side of the railway carriage there is a yellow map with red lines crossing and curving and intersecting over its shaking surface – It would be well if they would lie straight – those lines. I try to straighten them out, with my eyes, but they become more tangled than before, and they look something like worms – I wish it were not so hot: the red things are swelling – rising.

I see Agnes's face for an instant: then a black oblong slides before me. I look into it steadily. I like it: it is so deep. Points of light pass through it, orderly and slow – from left to right they swim in lines far distant: from out of it presses a sense of coolness upon the thick heat around me. It is strange that this yellow glare above my head can lay no intrusive finger into the black oblong. Ah – the still darkness is good – and the rhythmic passing of the dull white star – 'For now we see through a glass darkly'...

...

Now – I must keep things real. I must hold something very fast. But Siegmund's face: framed in that carriage window – how long ago – oh – ten minutes! The absurdity of these real things. Siegmund's distorted face – that does not seem real either – only like a reflection from a bad glass. And now the light has been turned out and I see only the wide darkness where he hides, and the pale march of the city lamps.

Oh, I want to hide also. I want to slip out of this train so that I may stand quietly in the dark somewhere – out of Agnes' sight. Then I could think – and presently I would turn and go back to Siegmund. It is all play, this – all temporizing – all foolishness. In Siegmund's presence alone there is reality – and I have left him.

What will he do: I must think out all he said at the station. It was cruel of him to hint at suicide. Not that – no, not that. He is not brave enough. I am so glad he is not very brave. He could not die alone. He will go home and sink into sleep. 'I can always sleep when I am miserable,' he said once. And tomorrow he will write – He promised. But –

...

I am too weak to change the course of fate; to speak wounding words to her: to refuse, now that we are at Waterloo, to go further. We leave the local platform for the main, and soon the long journey is begun. We run towards Cornwall and daylight – and the air of the great station at midnight is a forgotten nightmare. Back

* The manuscript of 'The Cornwall Writing' is in the possession of the Humanities Research Center, University of Texas at Austin.

through Wimbledon, through Malden. I press my face against the window, and lower the sash as we rush through Malden station. The last local train has arrived: the station lights are out. Beyond I see the outline of the house where Siegmund lies – he will be asleep now: his head ached very badly, I know, but one can sleep when one's head aches. Yet perhaps he would listen for the passing of my train. The late risen moon faintly whitens the front of the house: the train rushes past: Malden is left in the night.

We share a carriage with four men: they appear to be mechanics of the better class: they are from Lancashire or the Midlands. They are beginning their holiday, and affect the usual ostentatious enjoyments of their type. They got into the carriage at Waterloo, with loud apologies, displaying a large bottle of whiskey. They eat and drink and sing and shout banalities at each other. They work painfully at the duty of merriment: their affectation makes me loathe them. Vio's gaiety has gone – she sits in the corner opposite me, very quietly – Two of the men separate Vio from Agnes, who lies in the further corner, rolled in her great coat. Just above Vio's head is a picture of Freshwater Gate, blue and calm as yesterday – When I look up at it I am happy: it is like being sprinkled with spray flung far inland from the breaking of a great wave – I had never dared before to hope that any fulfilment could redeem the preceding promise – never, since, a little child – the early morning had drawn me into itself, and shown me the spinning of its delicate illusions. But now I see that there is nothing so real as happiness – and fate can tear that knowledge from me.

My blistered arms burn, and the blood beats in them uncomfortably. I stand to slip off my jacket, and lean forward to find out whether the picture indicates the exact spot where lies that little hollow at the cliff's edge – our sunbath of Wednesday. How in its depth, Siegmund lay asleep, caring nothing for the heat: giving his face freely to the fierce stress of the intolerable sunlight: and how I, afraid, took his limp white hand and stroked the swollen veins, and kissed his scorched forehead – and woke him.

I should have waked him sooner. I ought to have taken more thought for him – The sun has hurt his head, or he would not have looked so strangely tonight. And then, 'Whatever happens to me – you must go on –' he said that – Ah, hush, dear, don't call me over all the miles – you can never overtake me – this train is pulling the spaces of eternity between us. Make him sleep. Oh God, put Siegmund to sleep.

The sky is faded with the thin light of the small waned moon. The pines of Brookwood are blackened, but in Dorset the rough, wide pasture land stretches indefinitely away. We are nearing Salisbury – North westward is Salisbury plain: somewhere, just beyond the hills that rise in that direction stand the Great Stones. I think of Tess – of Hardy. The film of days flits backward. I see Hardy for an instant before the curtain in the opera house – it is the giving of the verdict upon the first performance of *Tess* – the audience is pleased and calls for author and composer. The orchestra applauds in a leisurely good humoured way: its members stand chatting in little groups, but Siegmund has slipped out after wishing the dark boy, who sits next him, goodnight. The July night breathes warm in the streets: the smooth floor of the Strand gleams beneath the clear soft showing of blending colour: the motor cars pass, with steady bright eyes, purring quietly. We stand a moment at the corner, and I introduce Tina and Siegmund: there is delight in watching the meeting of the suddenly lifted bright brown eyes of Tina and the grave blue ones of Siegmund as they greet each other. So, humming the *Tess* motive, we pass through the thrilled life of the Strand to Charing Cross.

The opera house is dark tonight –

We feel the check of the brakes as the train rounds Salisbury Curve – then slides into the half lighted station. The door flies open – there are shouts from the porters: we wait here ten minutes.

The four men go to the bar to refill their whiskey bottle. I walk up and down the platform, glad of the movement. There is just light enough to show the clockhands indicating five minutes past two. There is little noise – groups of travellers, looking pale and sleepy stand at their carriage doors, chatting in a subdued way: the great express, nearly empty, stretches curving backward into the darkness beyond the few lighted lamps.

'Take your seats please' – the monotonous voice passes along the length of the train: the groups disperse – there is a sudden rush of those who linger at the bar, and the train starts with a jerk – The Northerners for a little, drink and talk as before, but stupidly and mechanically. Two of them drop asleep, in spite of the prodding of the noisiest of the party, who rambles on long after his companion has ceased to listen to him.

They are all asleep at last. Vio and Agnes, with their heads pillowed on their rolled cloaks, in the corners: the men doubled in awkward uncomfortable attitudes; their bodies swaying with the rocking train: the light beats down upon them and pours itself out on to the darkness of the embankment: the train gathers its strength and leaps westward.

I sit straight – pressing my hands against my back. I have a new and curious feeling there that stays like a recollection, when there is no pain. But now the train jars and hurts.

It is as if I hear my own voice, from a wide starlit down by the sea – 'I hold it a crime to bring a child into the world for whom the world has no place. I will never have an illegitimate child.'

And again, from another racing train – 'I don't know – I'm not quite sure – Perhaps I had better not come back from Tintagel' –

I need not have said those things: they have troubled him. I could not have said them except in the security his presence lent me. Only he covers me from all harm so completely that there is no fear even in Death. I wonder – is there only a little while left – But I shall not see death till it comes too near for a thought of escape.

'I will not live a single day after you are dead.' Why did that sound so insincere. It was like a petulant lie. Poor Siegmund – I was angry with you for one moment: was it not hard enough without –

But in three weeks time we will have a long day at Leith Hill – as we said.

I have pencil and paper, and sitting hard back in my corner I begin to write. 'Wait till you hear from me,' – Siegmund said, but I shall have his letter on Monday morning. I write slowly. Long, long strings of beads are my thoughts, and only one here and there which shines for Siegmund. I drop the rest gladly into the silence.

The train tears on. The complaint of the wheels, rising and sinking in the monotonous cadence, seems akin to silence. Sometimes the thick breathing of one of the men, sounds over it.

'– you must never again speak of leaving me. I cannot live alone – If it be death – we will go together –'

...

I feel lonely and lost. I try to call warmth from the picture of Freshwater, but I cannot forget. I settle back into my corner and write of the dawn to Siegmund. He will not know how cold it was, though I describe it – and he is asleep now. I am less lonely in telling him about it.

...

The stopping of the train at Exeter wakes Agnes and Vio – but the men sleep on – This is their destination, so we try to rouse them. They understand only when the porter shouts loudly at them, and then, looking dazed and wretched, collect their things and depart almost in silence. We walk up and down the platform for a little and then lie down upon the carriage seats. It is only when the train is about to start that we find we are in the wrong section – that for Newquay.

We jump up and hurry forward. Later I discover that I have left 'Romola' and with it Siegmund's letter, behind me.

...

It will wake Siegmund early – this sun – I hate it. It will not shine in at his bedroom window, for that faces westward – but the heat will wake him, in that little close back room. It is six o'clock. I hope he is not awake yet.

Something spinning round in my brain is beginning to run as noisily as the wheels of the carriage. There is a kind of duet between the two pieces of machinery: sometimes argumentative, but generally in unison, and from both I hear as before over and over, with varying degree of emphasis, 'two hundred and forty miles – two hundred and forty miles – two hundred and –

'No, not yet', I say, 'only a hundred and ninety' – But the voices persist.

...

I get up from the breakfast table deliberately and go to fetch the letters. There is nothing from Siegmund. I stand a moment by the door turning four post cards over and over. Within me there is a dragging, sucking sensation – like that of the wave pull – only cold, very cold. I shiver in the sunshine, and watch the postman pass down to the gate. Mrs Dawes has spread linen out to dry over the bushes of clipped rose – 'One for you – Agnes – yes, two cards – Vio – and a card for me.'

'Why – oh God – Siegmund – why? You told me Monday...' I cannot talk to him – I cannot ask him anything – because he looks at me still as at Wimbledon, with terrible eyes.

It will come tomorrow – He wrote yesterday, and posted yesterday evening – Two hundred and forty miles – and the letter must wait at Camelford and at Tintagel before it is carried here – I shall get it tomorrow.

...

When the postman has passed the gate and disappeared down the sandy lane on the next morning – I get pen and ink and sit down to write. I write very distinctly

Thorn Cottage
Treknow
Tintagel
Cornwall.

Then as it is necessary to speak, I say to Agnes, again with the sense of cutting the words in metal with a machine, 'Siegmund is ill – or he is dead – or he has lost this address.'

Agnes assures me that the last named explanation is by far the most probable. I write a brief note – three or four lines only – signing it 'Sieglinde', and fling it over for Agnes's inspection while I address the envelope.

'You are not going to send that to Malden?' she queries.

'I am.'

'It is silly of you. He told you to wait till he had written.'

I take the letter to the post box at the head of the village. It will remain in the box till evening.

...

I think of the letter in the box. It should reach Malden perhaps by the first – perhaps by the second delivery tomorrow – Then my answer must come on Thursday morning. It is indeed possible that Siegmund may have lost my address. I gave it him on a loose slip of paper which he put in his pocket book. But someone else's address similarly written, was so lost during our holiday. I remember Siegmund's search for it.

I shall be answered even if he does not write – Then I must go to him because he is ill...

...

When the postman has passed the cottage on Thursday morning I enquire for a railway time table. Mrs Dawes does not own one, neither does she know where I can obtain one, except at the station.

It is an eight hours journey – I must reach Malden in the daylight – I must find somewhere to stay – somewhere near him. I cannot go home – I think I can never go home again.

If I start today at the earliest it will be night when the journey is finished. If I find the time of the first express, and go tomorrow morning, it will surely make little difference. That will be the better way. We will go to Delabole station and determine the time of the departure of the train. Yes, for even tomorrow morning the letter may come.

And it does not: yet at Agnes's entreaty I still wait.

...

We reach Delabole station half an hour before the train should be due.

At the booking office I discover that the express does not stop at Delabole: it will be necessary to go to Camelford, a mile and a half distant, and the train will be at Camelford in twenty minutes. I explain to Mr Dawes – enquire if it can be done at any price, and at last he shows signs of some activity. The road between the stations is fairly level, and presently the pony's little hoofs rap along it with determination.

When the old man comes to the window of the carriage later, I thank him very sincerely.

Mid-day brings Exeter. The stop is long. There are sudden flashes of fierce sunlight upon the red walls. The clouds are blacker now, but broken into indeterminate wind tossed masses.

...

It is four o'clock at Salisbury. I must change – the express makes no call at Malden – I wander to the bookstall and buy a green pencil and a postcard. The card bears a picture of Salisbury cathedral spire. I dispatch it to Agnes.

The train is late in leaving Salisbury and tears over Dorset and through the pine country. Hail rattles upon the windows: a sharp thunder flies over us, showering blinding light of silver from the edge of its cloud carpet. When the panes clear I see the towers of Woking.

Since leaving Treknow I have not thought of Siegmund: there is no good in thinking – in speculating. It is time to act, and necessarily I must act blindly – I cannot examine possibilities nor consider plans of action. I must first go to him – the rest shall take care of itself. I feel free; curiously detached from all my world. I am not conscious of the claim of any. I am glad that every face I see is strange, and that never from one of these will a glance of recognition greet me.

Yet now there are ugly thoughts pressing hard upon me.

When I stand upon the platform at Surbiton waiting for a train that has one more stage to carry me I begin to realise to what end I have come. There is a bleakness in the air and all movement around me becomes connected and coordinate – the action of an intolerable piece of mechanism, childish and without significance. I know that my thoughts may be destructive – it is of no consequence – I know that the force which controlled them has been diverted and is working in waste. I think to buy a local paper, but the train runs in – Well – to Malden – it does not matter.

In five minutes I am standing on Malden station platform, wondering what made me bring on a journey a dress basket too heavy for me to carry. The thing must be disposed of. I have it taken to the parcels office and descend the station steps to the road below.

I realise that I am shaking with cold: that my knees are stiff and that my mind is set upon a colour suggestion of blurred white and grey – that I have suddenly a great fear of falling. I wish it were dark. These people, with whom I have nothing to do, would come round me curiously if I should fall. Then I should not be free any more. I must eat something at once. There is a little dairy where I have often lunched on Saturday mornings after my lesson. Next door to the dairy is a stationer's shop with local papers displayed in a rack outside. I buy a paper and enter the dairy, ordering tea – then I sit down by a little marble table and turn over the pages of the paper...to find that which I set out to find.

It is in good type and large. I read but two lines, and stand up, very shuddering and sick. The shop woman who had taken the order for tea stands behind the counter, staring dreamily out through the open door into the street. She starts when I speak to her.

'I am sorry. I shall not want that tea – Please let me pay you for it.'

She looks frightened. It is because I cannot stand quite steadily, and my face looks strange. I can see it reflected in the glass which runs the length of the shop behind the counter. The woman glances at the paper in my hand, saying quickly, 'You have had bad news – won't you sit down – let me get you something....'

I thank her, declining. I beg her to take the money, and then I am again in the street, and walking rapidly and uncertainly along the road towards Coombe.

'Siegmund dead – Siegmund dead – Siegmund dead!' So a hundred times – the words soon become quite meaningless.

My promise to Agnes occurs to me – I would telegraph to her this evening. The post office is near: it is a march rhythm that my feet beat out 'Siegmund dead – Siegmund dead!' – all the time.

I write the words upon the telegraph form.

I want to know about him – all about what he has been doing this week. We would always compare times and happenings. I have written him my doings – only the letter is not yet posted. I must know his – I must read more from the paper – If he is dead he cannot write to me – this printing is the form of his message.

Along the green lane which runs by the farm, which is overlooked by the window of our drawing room and Siegmund's bedroom, there is quiet. I read, very many times, what he has chosen I shall read. The reading is difficult because there is a red mist before my eyes and because my breath is torn into long sobs. All the time I walk, now and again conscious of some creature quivering and shapeless that passes quickly, sliding behind between the grey road and the grey sky.

I look beyond the farm to the house on the slope. His window is locked, and bare of curtains and stands outlined, a black oblong against the red brick – Below, I trace the pattern of the stained glass in the French doors of the drawing room – my eyes obeying the effort – Inside, his fiddle stands on the arms of the wicker chair facing the little black piano. I know – There is my copy of Nietzsche on the lid of the piano, and his correction pencil hanging from the music stand.

And Siegmund is not indoors – and he is not at rehearsal nor at the opera – nor reading in the train – to look above his book at growing shadows in a warm twilight and long for freedom and the woods – and me – Siegmund is *not*.

Nay, but I am: how can it be that there is no Siegmund. He has cast himself forth beyond the grasp of all that would hold him: he has disowned the body that would not obey him: he has dared to explore the great darkness in quest of a larger freedom, and to venture it alone; he who would call himself coward always. What has become of That which spoke in Siegmund's violin and Siegmund's eyes and worked through Siegmund's will – surely it is that I love. That which purposed the destruction of Siegmund's body – how could it destroy itself....

'Unto dying eyes the window slowly grows
A glimmering square'

The words lift themselves into memory. My thought follows those tortured eyes.

They were dying – but the spirit that lived holding the body to the agony of those hours – what of it?

No physical contact was more intimate than the touch of his soul upon mine. Ah but without some kind of physical medium there is no form of expression. How may he show himself to me?

'I shall be often with you in spirit' – So – just before I left him. But why did he not come sooner – I call his name softly – Out of a world of emptiness creeps a rustling of oak leaves and the startled scurry of a sparrow's wings.

'Only play – only play – only play!' The march rhythm takes up a new burthen, but my feet will not answer to its insistence. It is my body that will call Siegmund, and Siegmund will never hear – Nay – Death keep Siegmund from the crying of the coward thing. It will bear no thought: it will be but a shrinking, sobbing misery, clinging with its arms about the bar of the old shaking meadow gate.

The lights of a train passing along the embankment beyond the fields shine out through the half dark. I will go and get into the train again: as it runs into the night I shall sleep.

I have been dreaming – I will find a sleep deep enough to drown this dream.

Agnes's fear for me suggests itself. It is disturbing: I do not want anyone to be concerned about me. Noone must think of me at all, else the thought will spoil my sleep. I wire to Agnes that I am returning by the first train. When I leave Malden, it is already dark.

'Camelford – single' –

The booking clerk looks attentively at me and says sharply. 'Camelford! There's no train till the morning.'

'How far can I go tonight?' I ask.

'You can't go at all tonight – you could only get to Salisbury and you'd have to wait there for the morning train' –

I turn away and walk slowly out of the booking office and up the slope. The main road is full of people and yellow with gaslight. In a corner a little out of the gas light I stand and listen to the tramping of their feet – the feet of all those people crossing the bridge – There is a rhythm that they keep – I know it well. Black shapes striped yellow in the gas glare – not real – not real at all, but they worry me just now....

I can get up the hill to the Common. It is still there – I might sleep. If it would stay dark long enough – I cannot have the light find me on the Common...

A sudden chill breath of air passes round me. The street and the station and the people stand out clearly, insisting upon my recognition. I must go away.

I climb upon the next tramcar which approaches. I am going home.

Tooting passes – two smears of yellow. How slowly the car moves –

Longley Road is asleep in shadow. Its night lights burn very tiny and still. Out of its sleep many old expressions rise and fleet over its face – I stand afar and watch – impersonally. The marking of the day – I did not know before that the poor little mean road had been sometimes so fine. I had passed quickly, gladly out of it – yet the road has shared Siegmund.

At the other end of Longley Road I take the car which passes through Mitcham into Croydon. The stars glitter through torn cloud and the air is soft and damp.

I lean back and shut my eyes and the atmosphere of the eastern down comes upon me very tenderly and generously, because I am so tired.

The car has stopped. There is the tearing of gas jets in the wind and the rant of a merry go round. It is the end of Mitcham Fair. I see, indistinctly, by the roadside, an empty stage – the gilt figures above it partly visible by the glare of a side gas jet. Three children race about it, chasing one another stamping loudly upon the flooring boards – Beyond, one or two swingboats pass up and down among a number still and empty: men stand in a little group under the gas upon the trampled grass.

It is all past. The Common is silent and dark. There is a little flicker of lightning leaping round the horizon – the car swings forward.

There is a light in the hall at home – I ring the bell. I wish there were no light and that I could creep upstairs to my bed...God, for darkness – real, utter darkness to drown in.

They ask questions in shaking nervous tones...I have given them the paper...They might let me go...I tell them I am asleep but it is a false sleep...how can one sleep when one is always moving: They bar the way to the staircase...they make me sit down in the lamp light...I hate them – why won't they let me go. What is she saying – my mother – she would have saved me – saved me *this*...There is a tickling in my head that makes me beat it against the wall...I will not stay here...there is no sleep. I tell them I will not stay...and then.

Ah, they are such pitiful children. I need not hurt them.

'Please will you let me go to bed. I do not indeed want anything else. I will not hurt myself – I shall be better in the morning...

My mother will come upstairs – she will light the candle while I undress. When I am lying down my father comes, clasping the bed rail with both hands.

'Now try and sleep – If you count the sheep jumping a hedge you know, it's a good way. I used to get myself to sleep in that way – Fancy a large flock in a field and count them as they jump the hedge...' It is all said jerkily, broken by nervous coughs. The words...he used to say them to me when he would come into the loneliness of sleepless hours, long years ago, when I was a little child. But now, as I watch his twitching hands, and the strange motions of his shadow on the wall, and see my mother standing close beside him, looking anxiously at me out of the great hollows of her eyes...I feel that I am very old and very calm.

'Yes...I think I shall go to sleep...and now you will go downstairs – won't you, and not worry.'

'Shall I sit beside you?' My mother comes round to me and places her hand on my head. I beg her to go away. They both kiss me and then, uncertainly, go downstairs.

The blind is close drawn. I do not want the eye of one star to look at me tonight – for no star looks into Siegmund's sleep. Let mine be like his. I stretch out my arms to him in the darkness which seems to press thick and soft down – calling him, telling him things he wanted always to hear, which I might never say before – He is mine utterly now, if I can only reach to him. I remember his promise and its making –

'Siegmund – if I should ever call you – if I were very ill and should send for you – would you come to me in spite of everything and everybody?'

'I would come to you from hell.'

The passion of his voice seems to linger with me, quivering, caught in the darkness. I lie quiet, and for a moment forget.

The sound of rain half wakes me – and when I stir there is a responsive movement from the bedside. My mother is sitting there. It is still quite dark and I sleep again.

The grey of dawn is creeping under the blind. I see it in my sleep and try to shut it out with my hands – failing, the sound of my own moaning rouses me. I start up suddenly and turn and see my mother. She has slipped to the side of her chair dozing from weariness: her head, bent forward touches the edge of the pillow. Her face is grey and hollow and shadowy. I lie down again and draw the bed clothes high over my head, shivering. She moves, conscious that I am awake.

'Won't you go to bed, mater. I wish you would go to bed.'

She comes round, near me, trying to see my face.

'Is there anything you would like now – will you drink some tea if I make it?' She tries to pull the sheets lower, but I clutch them.

'No, no – nothing – Only keep the light out – keep it away.' She fastens the thick blue blind down to the window frame – but still on either side a long thread of light winds in. I hold desperately to the sleep that is slipping from me, but slowly my mind unwraps its covering and all force of life concentrates itself upon the consideration of the immediate: there is no escape.

Only Siegmund's way – I think of it. I want Siegmund – without him life is meaningless. But death seems more meaningless. There is surely but one key, the same, for the unlocking of life or death. Siegmund knew more than I, very much more than I know. 'Remember, dear, whatever happens – you must go on.' He had seen very far to say that – I would have said with Death but a step from me 'Siegmund – come with me.'

Years ago – at the beginning – when we had only touched hands in friendship, there came a dream of him. We were running, he and I, over a wide sandy shore. The clasp of his hand was strong and firm and warm – never had mine been so held in waking. We ran swiftly, and in running plunged upon a mound of loose drifted sand which sank beneath us: the dream faded into a vague sense of loss.

The key – dream – so placed at the beginning. Ay – perhaps – anything we will seize upon when we would look over into Death – yet keeping a footing upon the shore of Life – any shadowy branch that seems to stretch out towards us.

But why must I go on? Why try to bind me to life in that way? If you looked for non-existence simply – Siegmund, why should you deny it to me. You give me back to the others... why? you were not often thinking of them before. And which for me is easier?

Millions of tiny pin points of light pierce the blind: the shape of each object in the room is visible: children come out to play in the neighbouring gardens: I hear them calling to one another above the whirring of a steam saw which has begun the day's work in a shed beyond the gardens. There is no familiar sound that does not come unfamiliarly to me: with all these things I have no part – no understanding. I am as completely isolated as if indeed death had cut all bonds and given it me to stand alone in a purely passionless contemplation of human activity.

My mother has gone downstairs: there is the clatter of dishes and the smell of breakfast in the house. I drink the tea brought me and lie down again, drawing the bed clothes close about my head. There come knocks and ringing at the house door. The voices of tradespeople – the shouting of milk-boys in the street – the shunting of trains upon the railway – a jingle upon a neighbour's piano. And louder than these, the throbbing of life within me – the beating of my heart and of those answering pulses in my back. I clench my hands and fight the strangling sobs that come of fierce resentment against the insistent voices of the Little Things – I would hear no voice but Siegmund's.

Never – unless in the silence he sought – but lying here is foolishness – I get up and set the water running into the bath. I will cool the fever in my body. Downstairs, the noise of the running water reaches my mother's ears: as I turn the key of the bathroom door, there is an anxious call from the foot of the staircase: it ends in a suppressed wail – 'Don't – oh don't lock yourself in there.'

I laugh, feeling as if the veins in my throat will burst, and unlock the door at once. She does not know how impossible it is for me to die so, here where the Little Things crowd about me. She waits in my bedroom.

The heat goes out of me, and my strength. I slip back into my room, cold and sick, and bent with shuddering. Instead of the old throbbing is the pull of a cold hand that is wrenching at all the life cords of my body – then comes a sudden snapping – –

My mother helps me on to the bed – she has saved me a fall. She wraps me up carefully. I do not now mind her touch – she and all things that were pressing round me have become remote and insubstantial. I lie and talk softly to Siegmund. From all known things we are detached, he and I.

The weakness passes and desire drags me out of sleep. I cannot lie still. I must hold at least something he has touched – I grope downstairs and get my violin. Its pale golden varnish shines like a little child's hair. I pass my fingers over its easily curving surface. It is very cold. I tuck it under the bedclothes to warm it.

Someone has brought a large bunch of fresh lavender. I devour the scent, and draw the stalks out by twos and threes scattering them over the bed. My mother gathers them all up again.

So the day turns slowly. When it is nearly dark Agnes comes. There is talking in low voices outside my door: my father thinks she should not see me tonight.

I tell them to let her come. She comes and bends over me, kissing me gently; then kneels by the bedside. I turn and look at her: she is tired – very tired – I ask about her journey: she makes light of it: she rises and arranges the folds of the bed-clothes telling me to be silent and go to sleep. Then she puts her arms about me, saying passionately 'What can I do? You know I must be everything to you now – just everything.'

Oh, my God!

She sleeps beside me at night. I listen to the rain falling straight and heavy out of the dark. I remember that they have buried Siegmund: a superficial consciousness, carrying no realisation imposes this upon me – yet I wish I could cover his grave from the rain. A lonely dog is howling – his voice rises into my half sleep ever and again like a long horn call. So, when I was a child, a dog would call my shivering soul out to hunt shadows through a night world that was yet only the image of the vaster, nearer night, whose strange stars would sometimes flash through the human web of cowering daylight.

I am not afraid now. I think I never shall be afraid again, because I have seen the face of that world reflected in Siegmund's eyes. Out of his eyes the things I have hunted look at me – they stand quiet to look at me, and I know them, but they are all shapen and beautiful. And of them he and I are kin. Because of this, and because I have taken of his hand something of the freedom he won, I shall never run in terror to hide among the Little Things. They will hold me for a while – they may tie me close down and cover my eyes, but I shall never look to them for protection.

Something of Siegmund they have buried. Just that which I repudiated: such was my justice. Nay, but there was nothing else of you which was not mine beyond all repudiation – and had this not been so, what beside your body could Alice hold? Yet I have given up very much, and you, surely you have also. I must find out where the gain lies – I will not believe you lost.

Agnes and I wander in and out between rows of new graves in a large cemetery. Beyond the railing press straight streets of poor houses, and the blank windows of a high school building overlook from one corner. Opposite, from a little distance, the red funnel of a factory chimney smokes slowly. 'Here it is' – Agnes speaks reverently, brokenly. I step beside her and look curiously down upon a narrow, long mound, the last of a line of similar mounds. I read Siegmund's home name upon cards attached to fading wreaths and his public names upon that sent with a floral harp, broken stringed – subscribed by the Gaiety orchestra. I laugh, thinking how even Siegmund with his hatred of irony, would laugh: knowing the fretting energy for so long wasted upon its detested banalities. I laugh, so foolish everything seems, and then I do not laugh, because I took his white hands once and hid them from the fierce sun, and because I know they will never throb to the sunlight any more.

'Shall I leave you a little while – shall I come back for you presently?' I hear Agnes say.

'No, why?' I stare down at this sanded earth heap. It is no more than any other – there are dozens all round – I kneel down to look more closely, and let the grains of sand run between my fingers. This earth heap is instead of Siegmund. Then how is it I am not changed? It is very difficult to understand. But my head feels like a big empty room. I press it hard against the earth.

There is a little blind street of artisan's cottages in Sevenoaks – terminated by the boundary fence of an orchard. Before each cottage the nasturtiums creep out to touch the pavement, unprotected by palings. We came here, Agnes and I, yesterday or the day before. We stay in one of these cottages, using the parlour which fronts the street. I like to be here: here one can so easily sleep. And now I cannot do anything – there is only to wait and sleep.

In the stillness of Sunday afternoon I sit and watch the clock hands moving. They will soon tell three. It is easy, very easy, to close my eyes upon today and to slip back into the Sunday afternoon of three weeks ago: to be waiting upon the little station by the marsh for the train that is to bring Siegmund. To hear the screaming swallows about the roof, and the little rumble of the train in the distance: to see it at last, a tiny thing creeping below the great green shoulder of the down under its grey cloak of mist.

I know the sense of cold and dread during the moment before the train slows into the station: the feeling that I have desired this thing too much – it will not be – and then sudden stupifying surprise at the sound of his voice, low and quivering full of joy – 'You – here', as he takes my hands and draws me in beside him –

'Siegmund!' – as soon as I can speak – 'I was so afraid – I didn't think our fate would let us –'

The clock strikes three – I look up and listen to its steady ticking – Agnes – upon the couch is asleep, her book has dropped from her hands. I am all alone – Perhaps he will come to me, the train is due in ten minutes – I wait – straining towards the shadow of his soul.

The small thick door set deeply in the wall which in Seal Hollow bounds Knole stands ajar:

> Spirit, nearing yon dark portal, at the limit of thine earthly state.
> Fear not thou the hidden purpose of that Power which alone is great.
> Nor the myriad worlds, His shadow – nor the silent opener of the gate.

The sight of the door starts this jingle in my brain, which goes on long repeating it. I am irritated – a pretentious lie – God does not show me any significance in death. Surely to me it is near. I should see something of its meaning.

We sit under the great grey beeches, where each stands lapped in a deep pool of its own dead leaves: the leaves of many summers. My book opens at the page where lie sheets of note paper, closely written – Siegmund cannot have that letter. I need not finish it. I tear the sheets into tiny pieces and scatter them among the beech leaves. Will any, I wonder, find their way into the nests of next spring?

Why has chance put into my hands just today *The Secret Rose* – of Yeats – with its strange binding and cover design – but of the dead who lie together in decay, rise twining branches in a golden network, springing from sinister hungry roots – woven and interwoven in intricate ordered working – ultimately to bud and flower in human shape. I remember reading some three months since – other thoughts of Yeats. I remember.

> Come near – come near – yet leave me still
> A little space for the world's breath to fill
> Lest I no more see common things that crave
> The weak worm hiding down in his small cave
> The fieldmouse running by me on the grass
> And heavy human hopes that toil and pass –

So – to the *Secret Rose* – the symbol of the Whole Beauty, in the seeking of which we lose our humanity.

I wonder if Siegmund understood Yeats as I – He made no comment when I showed him the passage. But why did I read to him from the end of the book –

> The years like great black oxen tread the world
> And God the herdsman goads them on behind
> And I am broken by their passing feet.

I read this new book, and would fain see prophesy in its mysticism, and a wavering intention instead of chance as the means of its production. I begin to look back also, through the years of our intercourse for the indications of a definite plan – the development of an ordered destiny.

The Friday evening brings rain. I should rather be alone, but Agnes, when she sees I am going out – will come, though she would prefer that we stayed in. We walk between dripping pine trees. Agnes is thinking of home, and that the holidays are over, and of the school life that will reopen next week, and draw her again into its easy routine of absorbing little duties – she is glad – She is anticipating also that it will take me, and with all its little imperious demands claim me, and with all its strong tiny hands hold me in the ever moving present day life of the Little Things. And how, in time, I shall wrap myself in the warmth that is nearest to me, and, closing the curtains of my windows against the night in which Siegmund is lost shall play seriously the small games for the counters of comfort – forgetting.

I am silent: not thinking, only seeing passing pictures, grey and fugitive, through the falling rain, a lonely moon standing over the sea, slashing its blackness with one long white stroke – the Malden house, its casement windows wide open, their soft frilled curtains shaken outward by the draught – Hanrahan sowing rose petals into the abyss – myself with all doors shut behind me, watching the stars fade and the Cross dissolve, feeling the Down sink beneath me, knowing the slow lapping of the encroaching darkness.

I think Agnes has been talking before and that I have sometimes answered but I do not know what has been said. And then I hear her plainly – She is talking, in a cheerful matter of fact tone, slightly tinged with forbearance about the possibilities and prospects of the coming term of school. She enquires of my plans.

A headlong – foolish anger stiffens me – half chokes me. I rush forward along the road. Agnes following.

'I!' – suddenly I stop and turn to her. 'Do you think that I am going back – after this – do you think that I can teach – now?' My voice is thick with hate and with fear of the power of the Little Things.

Agnes draws her breath in a shrill sob. She clutches my arm, shaking it. 'Not going back – What do you mean – what do you mean by it – tell me – you shall tell me what you mean.' Her voice rises in hysteric gasps, and her fingers clench themselves into the flesh of my arm.

'There! Agnes, nothing. It will be all right. Let's go in now.'

'No – tell me – what – what are you going to do?'

'I am not' – I say bitterly 'going to do anything – I did not mean – what you think –'

It is true. I have been putting the possibility of death between myself and the sight of a small and dreary life these many days – that my dreams might show clear against its dimness. But I have not been able to place upon my desire that seal of my will which should annul all the claims of the banded Little Things. So they may force me back among them, and I am angry and afraid, when they speak in Agnes's voice.

Yet *one* may silence them.

I know that if I have Siegmund's child – when it wakes – nay, before it wakes – I shall take it back to him – There is no place for it among the Little Things – and I should love it.

So – waiting, I am still again, feeling my destiny speeding me like the train, out into the dark – while the things of the life I knew pass like points of light in the distance. I lie watching them – I ask no meaning of them – they pass in order – vivid against the darkness. Only of the whispers that come like echoes of forgotten, essential harmonies out of the night I ask – yet not daring to hope for any intelligible answer.

...

I walk the way we walked on a day six weeks ago.

We plan our holiday. Siegmund has many difficulties to face. He tells me some, but there are many more than those he tells me. But I am happy and I will have no difficulties. Siegmund shall have his holiday somehow – anyhow, he has worked for it and longed for it and talked about it since early spring. Every Saturday he would speak of it – and it is now many weeks since I would answer 'Summer holidays – nay – no plan yet – why, the laburnum is still in full bloom' – and, in fun 'Your Utopia – remember Utopia means nowhere.' So I attack the difficulties and defeat them one after another, and Siegmund is drawn from the contemplation of those more serious obstacles of which he cannot speak. He puts them aside – he refuses for the last time to consider them – he looks along the short, bright way I have made so easy for him. At the worst there is death at the end of that little path – but he does not fear death and he knows that as his capacity for the fullness of life is increasing so do his circumstances more and more tend to limit his opportunities of exhaustion.

He lifts his face to the wind of the down and all the sense of responsibility drifts away from him – I – I am so free – and I have called him – he will be for a little, free too, quite free – and he laughs me back the greeting that out of my eyes the summer brings him.

We turn off the down and skirt the larch wood, looking for the path that dips between its brown boughs down towards Sanderstead valley. The entrance to the path shows like a small black hole between the trees that stand in close rows with boughs interlaced. But a few steps into the wood and there is a dusk at midday. They are of our kin of one thought, these trees, standing close with slender bare limbs entwined – so intimate that at only a short distance from the eye their individual outlines fade and one's vision is bounded by an impenetrable brown mist. We stay – midway down the path, listening to the noise of the trees as the light breeze sways them, and they rub each other's limbs gently.

'It is like the calm sea upon a fine shingle' says Siegmund, glancing at me suddenly.

I smile back at him, very satisfied – 'I'm thinking of the Wood of the Dead, that is upon High Peak in Devon. It's like that' – I say.

'Look!' says Siegmund pointing upward as the pale green of the larch summits point upward round a little pool of still blue sky.

I know that is the earnest of the sea for him. His eyes are so dark and eager – but their blue comes out of a night that is full of stars. It is not the blue of any daylight. We pass on down the slope till we reach the other side of the wood, where the path opens upon a green valley. Then Siegmund stops.

'Shall we have a rest – And what is beyond this path – let's explore.'

We turn in among the trees, parting with difficulty their knotted branches. Soon the brown mist of larch twigs has closed behind us and hidden the path – closed before us – locked by dry black boughs. We push on and the snapping of the twigs strikes sharply upon the stillness of the wood. We see daylight in front and emerge upon the first ranks of a great field of white oats that stand rustling – tall and full eared, in the shadow of the larches. My hat slips off. 'The larch fingers have pulled out its pins' I say laughing 'Don't come – I'll go back and find them.'

The wood baffles me: as soon as its brown veil drops round me I am uncertain of my direction. I turn, struggling through the boughs towards the sound of snapping twigs which tells me that Siegmund has followed.

'What a weird place! I did'nt like to let you go out of my sight', he says, pulling apart the fencing of branches that separates us. He is standing in a little green glade. The enclosing trees let in upon us here a tiny glimpse of blue sky.

'Come and sit down', says Siegmund – 'I don't want to much' I say doubtfully — 'The grass is damp.' He spreads his waterproof coat out for me to sit upon. 'Now come, that will be all right.'

But I do not like the grating of suppressed passion in his voice and the gleam of his eyes and the flush that has come upon his brow, usually so white. It is wrong for Siegmund to want me with his body, which is Alice's. I am sorry, it hurts me to see him lose his self control – he has fought for it so – I have held his hands and tried to help him to conquer his desire so often – it is pain and tears for me and shame for him – 'You will yet save me from myself' – he said one evening, when the grip of my fingers was red upon his wrists, – and I shall not forget – I must not. Yet the long strife – it is wearing him so – and I cannot leave him – I cannot. I try, and when he calls me like a child that has lost its way, I go back – too glad to reason the right or wrong of another submission, and begin anew the fight with the demands of his desire.

'Siegmund – dear – This will end in tragedy.' It is one evening when after my lesson the struggle has been fiercer than usual – when his face is flushed and drawn and I am breathless –

'Tragedy! This *is* the tragedy' – he says bitterly.

I know that we shall not strive any longer: nay, I know that I am losing fear of defeat – and yet today I grudge that passion should disturb the calm of my happiness – even though that calm is the outcome of tacit surrender.

'No. Siegmund, listen. I have no desire to come now – It is wrong that I should submit, when I cannot come willingly – Let us go.'

'Oh!' he speaks hoarsely, with a twitching face – 'You are cruel – oh you are cruel.' The words anger me a little – do I not endure much as well as he – But the sight of his face hurts me, and I stretch out my hands: his own close upon them like steel.

I kiss the tense fingers softly.

'Sieglinde – Sieglinde dear – come –'

And I am glad he wants me so. I am glad, and I do not care. I do not care what is the issue, but I know subconsciously that some thread spun into our lives at a stress too high – has given its warning – and that there is a very near limit to the strain of such spinning.

We walk slowly up the opposite hill when the long after glow of the July sunset lies upon the corn. Siegmund is silent, walking as if he were by himself – I also, until

I see suddenly how still he is, and how far he has slipped into the negation of the twilight – Then I would wake him – being restless...

'Tell me – what has taken you away – You seem such a long distance.'

He turns to me, smiling a little – and so standing, the pale glow of the sky touches his calm face, and the long dark lashes shadow his eyes.

'No – it's all right. There's such peace and harmony – Always – when I am with you – really.' The words come slowly, as if dropping from his cloudy thought.

Ah yes. I do not care what comes – it is very good to have lived.

And now I walk again into the larch wood, and turn at the little bend midway down the path, looking for Siegmund.

...

No, Siegmund is dead.

Within the green circle, crouching against a tree I repeat this, foolishly, for I do not know what it means. Above the decay of the wood the young life of the larches sends pale spray into the light. I claim clothing for the soul of Siegmund and voice for his silence – these things from the spirit of life that moves upward among the larches.

...

The closed door is fast closed – It gives no invitation – nay, there is refusal in every hard line. There is no means of opening and no promise of sunlight beyond threading the spaces about it. I should surely see above it the trace of an ancient writing. 'Mors janua vitae.' But there is no writing. Neither is there from behind it, any sound of voice or of movement.

I turn towards the open door. From the further side the jangling voices of the Little Things reach me. But I hear also Siegmund's children, and Alice. They call the Little Things about them – playing in their midst. They would shrink away if I should go near them. Neither do I wish to go near, but at a distance I watch them. Sometimes, when the children look at one another, standing a moment still, they may show me something of Siegmund that he gave them.

They play recklessly, and the road before is rough. I will go their way a little while.

Appendix 4

FROM LAWRENCE'S MSI: CHAPTER 12 ('THE STRANGER') OF 'THE SAGA OF SIEGMUND'

In the morning, after bathing, Siegmund leaned upon the sea-wall, languidly. It was late, towards nine oclock, and yet he lounged dreamily looking out at the turquoise blue water, at the white haze of the morning and the small fair shadows of ships slowly realising before him. ⟨Out⟩ ⟨o⟩ ⌜O⌝ff the bay ⟨lay⟩ ⌜were⌝ two battleships, ⟨strange⟩ wild monsters ⟨lying tame, quiet and curious as mild sea lions which, having wandered beyond their regions of wrath ⟨beyond their⟩ survey with naïve wonder the new shores.⟩ ⌜lying as naïve and curious as sea-lions which have wandered out of bounds.⌝ ⟨of wrath.⟩

Siegmund looked out ⟨absorbedly, unconscious of everything⟩ ⌜unconscious⌝ even of the thought of experience which was happening in his soul. He was not startled, ⟨yet⟩ ⌜though⌝ he was surprised to hear a voice from his side, saying:

"We leave the sea empty and shining: when we come to it again, it is inhabited ⟨, and we don't know ⟨these bogeys[?]⟩ when or how they came.⟩ ⌜by these monsters. Where have they come from?⌝

Siegmund smiled dimly. There was a mystical note in the speech which pleased him. He turned slowly to the speaker. This was a fair; slender man of thirty or so, who was smiling to himself ⟨thoughtfully⟩, as he looked out at the battleships ⟨lying⟩ ⌜half-absorbed⌝ in the morning-haze.

"You mean the men-of-war?" said Siegmund. The other glanced negligently into his face.

"Yes, they have stolen ⟨in⟩ upon us during the night, ⟨all unawares[?]⟩ ⌜and⌝ ⟨we lie in their power. How many things powers stand⟩ ⌜now they have us. What next shall we find at our elbows,⌝ ready to lay hand on our shoulders."

The speaker's grey-blue eyes, always smiling ⟨inscrutably⟩ ⌜betwixt two meanings,⌝ lit on the dark blue eyes of Siegmund, who felt his ⌜heart⌝ lift in a convulsive movement. ⟨like the throe of an unborn bird which is ⟨⌜thing⌝⟩ ⟨⌜struggling out of the shell⌝⟩ beginning to force itself from the shell.⟩ "I suppose ⟨We⟩ ⌜we⌝ are in the hands of—God," said Siegmund, hesitating at the last word, ⟨as if tempted to supply some ⟨⌜one⌝⟩ more meaningless word, ⟨⌜"the gods" or "Fate"⌝⟩ such as "Fate."⟩.

The stranger contracted his eyes slightly and looked again at him, so that Siegmund felt another strange throe. Then the grey-blue eyes wandered over the wet hair, the white brow, and the full bare throat of ⟨the other ⟩ ⌜Siegmund⌝. ⟨⌜"In the hand of God—⌝⟩ ⟨Like half fledged thrushes in the hands of a bird-nester?," ⟨⌜boys⌝⟩⟩ "You've been bathing?", asked the stranger, smiling brilliantly, yet with ⟨his eyes sad and inscrutable.⟩ ⌜an unchanging despair in his eyes.⌝ Siegmund smiled back ⟨meaningly⟩.

"I suppose the Czar will be sailing this way," said the stranger quietly.

"I do not know," replied Siegmund.

"Nor I," continued the other. "We must be the two most ill-informed persons on the island. It's a bad sign, when one ceases to care for the news." He smiled again, his flashing smile that ⟨made⟩ ⌜set⌝ the heart of Siegmund ⟨wildly, sadly⟩ ⌜anxiously⌝ questioning itself.

"A sign of what?" asked Siegmund.

⟨"That you'd rather listen to the wind outside the night, than to the tales round the fire.⟩ ⌜The stranger laughed, as if mocking⌝ ⟨⌜his own pain⌝⟩ himself:

⌜"That you're tired of the gossip round the fire," he said, "and want to listen to the night outside.⌝ We sit and watch pictures in the fire"—he made a motion with his eyes and his brows to signify the sea and the shore, a picture in the sunfire;—"and we listen to the tales—," he glanced at Siegmund, ⟨significantly⟩—"—⟨until the voices⟩ ⌜until we're sick, and the sounds⌝ outside ⟨call⟩ ⌜cry⌝ too loud, then we flatten our noses against the window—."

Siegmund laughed.

"You also?" he said, in a dramatic manner.

"The ⟨h⟩ ⌜H⌝ouse of Life is pretty draughty," replied the stranger, smiling brilliantly, then looking away at the sea. Siegmund did not answer.

"For you and me and the Czar," continued the other, still smiling. "A draught blows under the doors of Life, pretty cold to our feet. Even in this great, blue brilliant room of a day, ⟨of a life-day⟩—there's a draught of death under the door, and an ⟨eternal wandering outside in the darkness⟩ ⌜answer to the wandering night ⟨⌜singing⌝⟩ sung by our hearts in spite of us."⌝ He laughed, and looked quizzically at Siegmund, who was staring ⟨thoughtfully⟩ at the battleships.

"But it is so," went on the Stranger sadly. "When the tales round the fire become foolish, stale things, reiterated ⟨inanely⟩, then one listens to the night ⟨sweeping⟩ ⌜going⌝ round the warm blue room."

Siegmund looked at him.

"I suppose," said the stranger, suddenly laughing, showing his teeth and opening his heavy brows, "I suppose this is the effect, the result of getting specially drunk last night. The last phase of a 'drunk' is ⟨always⟩ ⌜usually⌝ sublime poetry, have you noticed? ⟨"⟩ ⌜You sit on the doorstep and sing 'Lead Kindly Light'."⌝ Siegmund was offended ⟨at⟩ ⌜by⌝ this cynicism.

"No," he replied. "I didn't know—and certainly I shouldn't have thought it."

"You are a romantic, you know," laughed the other. "So am I, for that matter.—But once you have found the eternal roaring night which is the very core of you, once you have gone in there—you ⟨are a strong man if you can⟩ ⌜don't easily⌝ come back into the ⟨small⟩ ⌜blue⌝ rooms."

"I am afraid" said Siegmund gravely, ⟨that you were *very* drunk last night⟩ ⌜"it must have been very bad, your 'last night'."⌝ Yet he smiled gently, so that the other should not be offended.

"Oh ⟨It⟩ ⌜it⌝ was," replied the Stranger, ⟨relaxing⟩ ⌜changing⌝ his laughter, his wistfulness, his contracted thought for a look of weariness. "I was ⌜very far gone⌝.

But then, so were you, also. You think I am talking round my hat. Straight talk, as you call it—it's only throwing a stone at the looking-glass. But however— —." ⟨Now look here, we're each one of us like a house,—a temple if you like, built round a roaring dark space. This roaring dark space sets us going like machinery, miller and mill-stones and mill machinery all rumbling and busy, but the ghastly black hole where the black water roars, that's the origin. Now you look too long in the black ⟨horror⟩ ⌜terror⌝ of⟩ ⌜He was silent for a time, till he began to recite in a whimsical manner: "Would God no Argo e'er had Crossed the seas to Colchis through the blue Sempligades— —" He smiled with his handsome, mobile mouth, never with his eyes, and sighed. Then he continued in a didactic tone: "No—it's like this. We're like a mill, built round a roaring dark space. There the black water roars and keeps you going like machinery, miller and mill-stones and mill-machinery all rumbling busily. But the heart of it all is the roaring dark hole, where you never look, which you don't know. If once you stare a long time ⟨⌜into your⌝⟩⌝ ⌜in the⌝ water-sluice, ⟨and⟩ you forget yourself, your mill and your grist—everything. All the rest seems clanking clattering foolery: there's the roaring black space."

He looked at Siegmund with his ⟨terrible⟩ ⌜dreadful⌝ blue-grey eyes, where ⟨agony seemed pouring⟩ ⌜pain swam thick⌝ in the black, large pupils, ⟨roaring hoarsely⟩ ⌜sounding low⌝ among all the chatter and brilliant laughter. Siegmund felt very sorry for him.

"It is a pity to drink so much," he said, very quiet and sad, so that the other could not be angry. The ⟨other⟩ ⌜man⌝ flashed into sudden, startling laughter.

"*That* I should tell *you*" he said, very deep, ⟨and, meaningful.⟩ ⌜and pointedly.⌝ "That I should tell you. It is a pity for *you* to drink so much, you so beautiful, with a thick neck firm with an enormous strong pressure of life: it's a pity for *you* to drink so much—what?—love?"

Siegmund felt a slight fear, a self-pity, a⌜n⌝ ⟨great⟩ urging of tears.

"Because," continued the stranger, very slowly, very sadly, "You will not be able to ⟨live⟩ ⌜work⌝ in your ⟨roo⟨m[?]⟩⟩ mill: you will be drawn back there, to the dark ⟨roaring space⟩ ⌜sluice⌝ whence your ⟨life⟩ ⌜activity⌝ issues: you ⌜will⌝ see."

Both were silent for some time. Siegmund looked out to the ⟨pearl-mist⟩ ⌜bloom⌝ on the horizon over the sea. His heart was panting with dread; he wanted to get away from this stranger, who, he said to himself, was surely mad. ⟨or delirious with drinking.⟩

"Women—one sort of women," resumed the strange man reflectively, "when they love us, they are—jealous of everything. They lift our hands off the machinery, they take us away from the dribbling corn and the puffing of flour, they say 'Listen, listen, listen', and they draw no nearer the dark roar. They make us open the doors that were not made to open, and sheltering behind us they watch, ⟨watch⟩ ⌜fascinated,⌝ the black raving of ⟨incoherent⟩ life-water at it pours ⟨darkly⟩ in us, watch us as we ⟨whiten⟩ ⟨⌜darken⌝⟩ ⌜wilt⌝ and grow sick: and they exult. They have a passion for this. We men are the actors, the agonistes, they are the ⟨spectators⟩ ⌜onlookers⌝ who gather the experience and ⟨weave⟩ ⌜store⌝ it up in ⟨to world⟩ ⌜blood-⌝wisdom: but they kill us, they can't help it."

Siegmund watched the battle-ships. He could see movement aboard them; he could see the sharp hulls becoming a livid, leaden grey colour as the day grew brighter.

Watching the slight movement on the ships, he was all the time listening to his own heart.

"It is true," it was murmuring. "It is true."

"Yes," said the Stranger, "we cannot go back to our day-work. ⟨Look, I am a temple. In the centre⟩ ⌜Only the strong spurting of life can rouse us. If you drink spirit, trivial liquids won't quench you."⌝ ⟨there is the fissure, and⟩ ⟨the ⟨⌜life-voice speaking hoarsely⌝⟩ earth-voice roaring down in the dark⟩⟨:⟩ ⟨all around are the rooms. But in most of my rooms they are buying and selling trash, in some they are haggling, in some fighting, here ⟨?⟩ praying vulgarly. My God, I am crowded out of myself. I have seen too much, and heard too much. There is no place but the cavern of the Life's heart ⟨⌜dark stairs⌝⟩ ⟨⌜the blackness full of sound⌝⟩ the dark incoherence. ⟨How much of myself is left to me. I am like the owner of a crowded ⟨?⟩ ⟨?⟩ alone and ⟨?⟩ without a room. We let ourselves out to the public⟩. She has left me, I tell you, and I cannot live where the old crowd is haggling and cursing. I creep ⟨⌜wander⌝⟩ back to the dark cave.⟩ ⌜He was silent for some time.⌝

"Now she has left me," he quietly resumed, "I wince at the sight of a face, at the sound of a voice. I seem scathed clean off from the rest of life."

He looked at Siegmund, who was gazing out over the sea with a dreadful face.

"Thou and I" said the stranger, "we go the same way. I see you look at the windows of the ⟨grand⟩ blue ⟨house⟩ ⌜hall⌝ of today, pulling back the blue curtains, peering into the ⟨cold, wild⟩ dark. It is no good, brother, there is no more for me and thee in this blue feast-chamber. My part lies outside. I am ⟨satisfied⟩ ⌜replete⌝ with this feast of life. I must go home, ⟨into the dark.⟩ ⌜outside, to digest it."⌝ The stranger ⟨too⟩ ⌜also⌝ gazed ⟨wildly⟩ ⌜fixedly⌝ over the sea.

"I can ⟨split⟩ ⌜open⌝ the blue heavens with looking" he said, "and see into the ⟨black⟩ ⌜outside,⌝ beyond. I can pull open the blue doors of day, and let myself out into the freedom,—soon."

Siegmund at length found himself saying, hoarsely:

"It is ⟨dreadful⟩ ⌜wrong⌝ to talk so. What have you been doing?"

"And thou and I, and I and thou?" ⟨mocked⟩ ⌜smiled⌝ the other. He looked at his ⌜own⌝ hands which lay on the stone.

"I shall soon have done with them," he said softly. "I shall soon have done with them. Poor things! Yet I love them."

His hands were very white and fragile, showing the blue veins. He looked at them pityingly.

"What have they done amiss?" he said. Siegmund, fascinated, ⟨sprea⟩ looked down also at his hands, lying carelessly curving on the sea-wall. Siegmund's hands were small, for a man of his stature, and fair, ⟨but⟩ ⌜and⌝ now ⌜that⌝ they were ⟨warm⟩ ⌜ripe⌝ ⟨ruddy⟩ with the sun and the sea, they looked full of ⟨life and strength and vigour⟩ ⌜security, of reposing vigour.⌝ Siegmund could not detach himself from them. He loved them, and was glad of them. Instinctively he closed his fists over his thumbs, hiding his thumbs

"Ah," cried the stranger, "I am ⟨so⟩ sorry. Ah, I am ⟨so⟩ sorry for you. You are ⟨so⟩ beautiful and full of life. I would not tempt you to ⟨death⟩ ⌜it⌝. Ah no! Yet she loves you and does it. ⟨Ah,⟩ It is awful!"

Siegmund looked at him with the awe-stricken eyes of a condemned thing. The stranger laughed suddenly.

"Fools, fools!" he cried. "⟨Fools⟩ ⌜Asses⌝! It is all nonsense,—for you. Remember, all nonsense. Your neck is so thick with compressed life. It is a stem so tense with life that ⟨the stem is clothed in⟩ ⟨petalled in spendour, magnificent as a blossom.⟩ ⌜it is indomitable, and fleshed and coloured like blossom, a stately thing.⌝ A magnificent thing—you cannot break it. You remember."

He suddenly abandoned his extravagant manner, and smiled.

"I'm afraid I *was very* drunk" he said "worse than usual. Alas, ⟨and⟩ alack, you look serious. Pardon me, it is time I should go. They will be frowning over the coffee cups. You must wear a hat, it will be very hot. It is very hot—", he pulled open his fine flannel shirt—"very hot already. I feel the sun among my hair."

Dashing the long hair on his forehead into some sort of order, he bowed, and smiling in his ⟨old⟩ brilliant fashion, walked lightly, leisurely towards the village. Siegmund watched him go. Then he sighed deeply, as one does when a bout of pain dies away, and he ⟨went⟩ ⌜proceeded⌝ to find Sieglinde.

Edward Garnett's note on this chapter was:

Pages 170–82
Something is wanted to carry off this passage with the Stranger, ie.,—
You must intersect his talk with little realistic touches to make him very *actual*. He must not spring quite out of the blue & disappear into it again. He's too much a *deus ex machina*, for your purposes. Make him seem in talk more ordinary & natural & slip in the pregnant things at moments.

(The late David Garnett completed a partial transcription at the request of the editor, 21 June 1977. Cf. *Letters*, i. 353n.)

Appendix 5

FROM *THE SURREY COMET*, FOR WEDNESDAY, 11 AUGUST 1909

Violinist's Tragic End
Member of Covent Garden Orchestra Terminates His Life

Dr. Michael H. Taylor, the Coroner, held an inquest at the Council Offices yesterday morning concerning the death of Herbert Baldwin Macartney, aged 39, of 49, Alric-avenue, New Malden, a professor of music and a violinist in the Covent Garden Orchestra.

From the evidence it appeared that Mrs. Macartney took some shaving water up to her husband at nine o'clock on Saturday morning, when he seemed in his usual spirits. Returning to his bedroom some two hours later, however, she was unable to effect an entrance. She at once summoned assistance, and Joseph Humphreys, of Merton-road, Wandsworth, endeavoured to force the door, but without success. With the help of other men he procured a ladder and entered by the window, when he saw Macartney with a three foot strap round his neck hanging from a hook on the back of the bedroom door. He promptly cut down the body, and Dr. Davison, who was immediately sent for, pronounced life extinct. So far as was known the deceased had no worries, and no reason could be assigned for his act.

A verdict of suicide during temporary insanity was returned.

Appendix 6

WAGNER AND *THE TRESPASSER*

There are numerous references to Wagner's operas in *The Trespasser*. Early in the novel, Siegmund – the name is Wagnerian and he is an orchestral first-violin-player as well as Helena's teacher – is shown leaving the Opera House at Covent Garden on the last night of the season (i.e. at the very end of July). During the season of 1909, Wagner's four-part cycle *Der Ring des Nibelungen* was played at Covent Garden, conducted by Hans Richter. Helen Corke saw at least two parts of this performance, and her teacher and lover H. B. Macartney (Siegmund's counterpart) played in the orchestra. (She alludes to this in *Neutral Ground* and in *In Our Infancy*.)

Most of the allusions in *The Trespasser* are to *Tristan und Isolde* and to the *Ring*. The relevance of *Tristan*, a story of tragic love, is that one partner is married (Isolde, to King Mark of Cornwall) and both die. The opera is pervaded with longing, at first sexual: this is transformed into a longing for death as a release from the limitations of life. Debussy's opera *Pelléas et Mélisande*, referred to on p. 52, has a similar Celtic setting, medieval romantic origin and tragic outcome.

Der Ring des Nibelungen (*The Ring of the Nibelung*) has a dramatic prelude, *Das Rheingold* (*Rhine-gold*); followed by a trilogy: *Die Walküre* (*The Valkyrie*); *Siegfried*; *Götterdämmerung* (*Twilight of the Gods*). The four parts are meant to be played on successive nights. They are bound together by the progressive unfolding of a plot which extends over at least two human generations, and by a musical structure in which constantly recurring themes or motives (representing characters, emotional themes, even stage-properties) are intertwined and transformed in Wagner's music.

The two non-human protagonists are Wotan, leader of the gods and guarantor of treaties, who lives above earth in Walhalla; and Alberich, the leader of the Nibelungs, dwarfs who live below earth in Nibelheim. In *Rheingold*, Alberich steals the Rhine-gold from the protection of the Rhine-maidens, and takes it down to Nibelheim, where part of the hoard is forged into a magic helm, the Tarnhelm, and into a Ring. Whoever owns this Ring has universal power, but must renounce love, and thus Alberich enslaves the Nibelungs. Wotan has just had the giants Fafner and Fasolt build the gods' new home, Walhalla. He has promised them as payment the hand of the goddess Freia, but when the time comes to pay, repents his bargain. Descending to Nibelheim, he and the fire-god Loge trick Alberich into his power, and extort the gold, helm and Ring from him, and Wotan offers these to the giants. In despair Alberich curses the Ring. Immediately Fafner strikes Fasolt dead, and goes off with the treasures into a distant forest, where he is transformed into a dragon, and guards the hoard. Whoever can get the Ring from him inherits both its power and Alberich's curse. Since Alberich has forsworn love, he has little to lose, but Wotan, fearful of the Ring's power but bound by honour from repossessing it, cannot let Alberich win back the Ring, and dominion of the universe.

At the opening of *Walküre*, years have passed. Since Wotan cannot win the Ring directly, he has fathered a human champion. Under the name of Wälse, Wotan became the father of twins, a boy Siegmund and a girl Sieglinde (the Wälsungen or Volsungs). Separated as children, they are reunited as strangers at the beginning of the opera, after Sieglinde has become the unwilling wife of Hunding. Siegmund takes shelter in Hunding's house, falls in love with Sieglinde, and they consummate their love, expressed by the Spring music at the end of Act I. News of this reaches Wotan's wife Fricka, who as goddess of matrimony and the hearth, is outraged and demands that Wotan allow Hunding to kill Siegmund. He is heartbroken, but agrees. He sends his Valkyrie daughter Brünnhilde to tell Siegmund that he must die. Brünnhilde, seeing into Wotan's mind (she is known as Wishmaiden), senses his grief and his love for Siegmund. Meeting Siegmund, she feels love for him; dissuades him from killing Sieglinde and himself by telling him that Sieglinde is to bear his child, who will be a great hero; and promises that she will help Siegmund in the fight. Wotan, however, intervenes, shatters Siegmund's sword with his spear, and lets Siegmund be killed. Brünnhilde hastens Sieglinde off to safety. In the last Act, the Valkyries assemble to the music of the Valkyrie Ride and await Brünnhilde, but do not dare to shield her from Wotan's wrath. He insists that for her defiance she must become mortal and marry the first mortal man who finds her in the sleep-trance which Wotan will induce. She persuades him that she divined his anguish and was trying to carry out his deeper will and persuades him also to surround her with fire while she is in the trance so that only the bravest man in the world will dare to wake her. He does so, and the Fire Music creates the musical equivalent of this magic.

In *Siegfried*, another generation has passed. Sieglinde has died in childbirth and her son Siegfried, raised by Alberich's brother, is now nearing manhood. He succeeds in re-forging from its shattered fragments the sword of his father and kills the dragon Fafner. The Forest Bird tells Siegfried to take only the Tarnhelm and the Ring (Siegfried does not know their true significance), and the Forest Bird's music conducts him to Brünnhilde's rock. Wotan formally attempts to bar his path as a final test of the hero's independence; Siegfried shatters Wotan's spear with the sword. He enters the circle of fire, wakes Brünnhilde, and they pledge their love.

In *Götterdämmerung*, Wotan's and Alberich's long conflict comes to an end. Siegfried departs from Brünnhilde to pursue further adventure. As the heroic Siegfried is to Wotan, so is the crafty Hagen to Alberich. Hagen, a son of Alberich, practices a complicated deception on Siegfried, using a magic potion to make Siegfried forget Brünnhilde and win her for Hagen's half-brother Gunther, and finally kills Siegfried treacherously. Hagen is unable to recapture the Ring, since Brünnhilde takes it from Siegfried's corpse, and rides her horse into his funeral pyre in a loving self-immolation. The Rhine overflows its banks, sweeping Hagen away, and the Rhine-maidens recover their gold. In the last scene, Walhalla is in flames, fulfilling the curse.

The deeper preoccupations of the drama are with greed, power, violence, and deception (forms of self-hood) set against love, courage, and the ability of the favoured individual to become a heroic self; also the need to accept death, and to give oneself in love (both being forms of self-transcendence).

Some things in *The Trespasser* are more deeply Wagnerian than the allusions, which are merely the exchange of references between cultured persons. Siegmund's remark on pp. 98–9 shows a real sense of Wagner's method: 'You seem to have knit all things in a piece for me. Things are not separate: they are all in a symphony. They go moving on and on. You are the motive, in everything.' Some of the structural symbolism is also Wagnerian: for instance the cluster of images (the equivalent of musical motives) which associates wings, birds, bees, flowers, pollen, the 'flowers of passion', and flight out to sea, and which culminates in the thematic and tonal transformation on p. 169 where 'the great burning bees' in one paragraph generate, two paragraphs later, the sequence ending with the tragic premonition 'Siegmund went on slowly, like a slow bullet winging into the heart of life.' This kind of associated imagery is most developed in the early pages of *The Rainbow*, which are in that respect the most Wagnerian in Lawrence.